SARAH MacLEAN

P9-BBP-979

No Good Duke Goes Unpunished

Goes Unpunished

THE THIRD RULE OF SCOUNDRELS

AVON

An Imprint of HarperCollinsPublishers

AVON BOOKS
An Imprint of HarperCollins*Publishers*
10 East 53rd Street
New York, New York 10022-5299

First Avon Books mass market printing: December 2013

For Eric, my own gentle giant,
for taking such good care of me.

In loving memory of
Helen, Lady Lowe.

No Good
Duke
Goes Unpunished

Temple

Whitefawn Abbey, Devonshire
November 1819

*H*e woke with a splitting head and a hard cock.

The situation was not uncommon. He had, after all, woken each day for more than half a decade with one of the items in question, and on more mornings than he could count with both.

William Harrow, Marquess of Chapin and heir to the dukedom of Lamont, was wealthy, titled, privileged and handsome—and a young man blessed with those traits rarely wanted for anything relating to wine or women.

So it was that on this morning, he did not fret. Knowing (as skilled drinkers do) that the splitting head would dissipate by midday, he moved to cure the other affliction and, without opening his eyes, reached for the female no doubt nearby.

Except, she wasn't.

Instead of a handful of warm, willing flesh, William came up with a handful of unsatisfying pillow.

He opened his eyes, the bright light of the Devonshire sun assaulting his senses and emphasizing the thundering in his head.

He cursed, draped one forearm over his closed eyes, sunlight burning red behind the lids, and took a deep breath.

Daylight was the fastest way to ruin a morning.

Likely, it was for the best that the woman from the previous evening had disappeared, though the memory of lovely lush breasts, a mane of auburn curls, and a mouth made for sin did bring with it a wave of regret.

She had been gorgeous.

And in bed—

In bed she'd been—

He stilled.

He couldn't remember.

Surely he hadn't had that much drink. Had he? She'd been long and full of curves, made just the way he liked his women, a match for the height and breadth that was too often his curse when it came to them. He did not like feeling like he might crush a girl.

And she'd had a smile that made him think of innocence and sin all at once. She'd refused to tell him her name . . . refused to hear his . . .

Utter perfection.

And her eyes—he'd never seen eyes like hers, one the blue of the summer sea, and one just on the edge of green. He'd spent too long looking at those eyes, fascinated by them, wide and welcoming.

They'd crept through the kitchens and up the servants' stairs, she'd poured him a scotch . . .

And that was all he remembered.

Good Lord. He had to stop drinking.

Just as soon as today was over. He would need drink to survive his father's wedding day—the day William gained his fourth stepmother. Younger than all the others. Younger than him.

And very very rich.

Not that he'd met her, this paragon of brideliness. He'd meet her at the ceremony and not before, just as he'd done the other three. And then, once the familial coffers had been once again filled, he would leave. Back to Oxford, having done his duty and played the role of doting son. Back to the glorious, libidinal life that belonged to heirs to dukedoms, filled with drink and dice and women and not a worry in the world.

Back to the life he adored.

But tonight, he would honor his father and greet his new mother and pretend that he cared for the sake of propriety. And perhaps, after he was done playing the role of heir, he'd seek out the playful young thing from the gardens and do his best to recall the events of the night before.

Thank Heaven for country estates and well-attended nuptials. There wasn't a female in creation who could resist the sexual lure of a wedding, and because of that, William had a great affinity for holy matrimony.

How lucky that his father had such a knack for it.

He grinned and stretched across the bed, throwing one arm wide over the cool linen sheets.

Cold linen sheets.

Cold *wet* linen sheets.

What in hell?

His eyes flew open.

It was only then that he realized it wasn't his room.

It wasn't his bed.

And the red wash across the bedsheets, dampening his fingers with its sticky residue, was not his blood.

Before he could speak, or move, or understand, the door to the strange bedchamber opened and a maid appeared, fresh-faced and eager.

There were a dozen different things that could have gone through his mind at that moment . . . a hundred of them. And yet, in the fleeting seconds between the young maid's entrance and her notice of him, William thought of only one thing—that he was about to ruin the poor girl's life.

He knew, without doubt, that she would never again casually open a door, or spread sheets across a bed, or bask in the rare, bright sunlight of a Devonshire winter morning without remembering this moment.

A moment he could not change.

He did not speak when she noticed him, nor when she froze in place, nor when she went deathly pale and her brown eyes—funny that he noticed their color—went wide with first recognition and then horror.

Nor did he speak when she opened her mouth and screamed. No doubt he would have done the same, had he been in her position.

It was only when she was through with that first, ear-shattering shriek—the one that brought footmen and maids and wedding guests and his father running—that he spoke, taking the quiet moment before the coming storm to ask, "Where am I?"

The maid simply stared, dumbstruck.

He made to move from the bed, the sheets falling to his waist, stopping short as he realized his clothes were nowhere in sight.

He was naked. In a bed that was not his own.

And he was covered in blood.

He met the maid's horrified gaze again, and when he spoke, the words came out young and full of something he would later identify as fear. "Whose bed is this?"

Remarkably, she found her answer without stuttering. "Miss Lowe."

Miss Mara Lowe, daughter of a wealthy financier, with a dowry large enough to catch a duke.

Miss Mara Lowe, soon-to-be the Duchess of Lamont.

His future stepmother.

Chapter 1

The Fallen Angel
London
Twelve Years Later

There is beauty in the moment when flesh meets bone.

It is born of the violent crunch of knuckles against jaw, and the deep thud of fist against abdomen, and the hollow grunt that echoes from the chest of a man in the split second before his defeat.

Those who revel in such beauty, fight.

Some fight for pleasure. For the moment when an opponent collapses to the floor in a cloud of sawdust, without strength or breath or honor.

Some fight for glory. For the moment when a champion looms over his beaten and broken adversary, slick with sweat and dust and blood.

And some fight for power. Underscored by the strain of sinew and the ache of soon-to-be bruises that whisper as victory comes with the promise of spoils.

But the Duke of Lamont, known throughout London's darkest corners as Temple, fought for peace.

He fought for the moment when he was nothing but

muscle and bone, movement and force, sleight and feint. For the way brutality blocked the world beyond, silencing the thunder of the crowd and the memories of his mind, and left him with only breath and might.

He fought because, for twelve years, it was in the ring alone that he knew the truth of himself and of the world.

Violence was pure. All else, tainted.

And that knowledge made him the best there was.

Undefeated throughout London—throughout Europe, many wagered—it was Temple who stood in the ring each night, wounds rarely scarred over before they threatened to bleed again, knuckles wrapped in long strips of linen. There, in the ring, he faced his next opponent—a different man each night, each one believing Temple could be bested.

Each one believing himself the man to reduce the great, immovable Temple to a mass of heavy flesh on the floor of the largest room of London's most exclusive gaming hell.

The draw of The Fallen Angel was powerful, built upon tens of thousands of pounds wagered each evening, on the promise of vice and sin that called to Mayfair at sunset, on the men of title and wealth and unparalleled worth who stood shoulder to shoulder and learned of their weakness from the rattle of ivory and the whisper of baize and the spin of mahogany.

And when they had lost everything in the glittering, glorious rooms above, their last resort was the room that lurked below—the ring. The underworld over which Temple reigned.

The Angel's founders had created a single path of redemption for these men. There was a way those who lost their fortune to the casino could regain it.

Fight Temple.

Win.

And all was forgiven.

It had never happened, of course. For twelve years, Temple had fought, first in dark alleys filled with darker characters for survival, and then in lower clubs, for money and power and influence.

All the things he'd been promised.

All the things he'd been born to.

All the things he had lost in one, unremembered night.

The thought crept into the rhythm of the fight and for a barely-there moment, his body weighed heavy on his feet, and his opponent—half Temple's size and a third of his strength—landed a blow, forceful and lucky, at the perfect angle to jar the teeth and bring stars to the eyes.

Temple danced backward, propelled by the unexpected cross, pain and shock banishing thought as he met the triumphant gaze of his unnamed opponent. *Not unnamed.* Of course he was named. But Temple rarely spoke the names. The men were merely a means to his end.

Just as he was a means to theirs.

One second—less—and he had regained his balance, already feinting left, then right, knowing his reach was half a foot longer than that of his foe, sensing the ache in his opponent's muscles, understanding the way the younger, angrier man fell victim to fatigue and emotion.

This one had much to fight for: forty thousand pounds and an estate in Essex; a farm in Wales that bred the best racehorses in Britain; and a half-dozen paintings from a Dutch master for whom Temple had never cared. A young daughter's dowry. A younger son's education. All of it lost at the tables above. All of it on the line below.

Temple met his opponent's gaze, seeing the desperation there. The hate. Hatred for the club that had proven to be his downfall, for the men who ran it, and for Temple most of all—the centurion who guarded the hoard thieved from the pockets of fine, upstanding gentlemen.

That line of thinking was how the losers slept at night.

As though it were the Angel's fault that loose purse strings and unlucky dice were a disastrous combination.

As though it were Temple's fault.

But it was the hate that always lost them. A useless emotion born of fear and hope and desire. They did not know the trick of it—the truth of it.

That those who fought for something were bound to lose. It was time to put this one out of his misery.

The cacophony of calls from the edges of the ring rose to a fever pitch as Temple attacked, sending his opponent scurrying across the sawdust-covered floor.

Where he had once toyed with the other man, his fists now delivered unsympathetic, unwavering blows, connecting in a barrage of hits. Cheek. Jaw. Torso.

The other man reached the ropes marking the edge of the ring, tripping backward into them as Temple continued his assault, taking pity on this man who had hoped he might win. Had hoped he might beat Temple. Might beat the Angel.

The final blow stole the strength from his opponent, and Temple watched him collapse in a heap at his feet, the din of the crowd deafening and laced with bloodlust.

He waited, breath coming harsh, for his opponent to move. To rise to his feet for a second bout. For another chance.

The man remained still, arms wrapped about his head.

Smart.

Smarter than most of the others.

Temple turned, meeting the eyes of the oddsmaker at the side of the ring. Lifted his chin in a silent question.

The older man's gaze flickered over the heap at Temple's feet, barely settling before moving on. He raised a gnarled finger and pointed to the red flag at the far corner of the ring. Temple's flag.

The crowd roared.

Temple turned to face the enormous mirror that stretched along one side of the room, meeting his own black gaze for a long moment, nodding once before turning his back to the reflection and climbing between the ropes.

Pushing through the throng of men who paid good money

to watch the fight, he ignored the reach of the grinning, cheering multitudes, their fingers clamoring for a touch of the sweat-dampened skin turned black with ink that encircled his arms —something they could brag about for years to come.

They'd touched a killer and lived to tell the tale.

The ritual had made him angry at the beginning, then proud as time marched.

Now, it left him bored.

He threw open the heavy steel door that lead to his private rooms, allowing it to swing shut behind him, already unraveling one long strip of linen from his aching knuckles. He did not look back when the door slammed closed, knowing none on the floor of the fight would dare follow him into his dark, underground sanctum. Not without invitation.

The room was dark and quiet, insulated from the public space beyond, where he knew from past experience that men were rushing to claim their winnings, a handful helping the loser up, calling for a surgeon to wrap broken ribs and assess bruises.

He tossed the length of linen to the floor, reaching in the darkness for a nearby lamp and lighting it without faltering. Light spread through the room, revealing a low oak table, bare save a neat stack of papers and an ornately carved ebony box. He began to unravel the bandage from the other fist, gaze settling on the papers, now unnecessary.

Never necessary.

Adding the second strip of fabric to the first, Temple crossed the near-empty room, reaching for a leather strap affixed to the ceiling, allowing his weight to settle, flexing the muscles of his arms and shoulders and back. He could not help the long breath that came with the deep stretch, punctuated by a quiet knock on a second door at the dark end of the room.

"Come," he said, not turning to look as the door opened and closed.

"Another falls."

"They always do," Temple completed the stretch and faced Chase, the founder of The Fallen Angel, who crossed the room and sat in a low wooden chair nearby.

"It was a good fight."

"Was it?" They all seemed the same these days.

"It's remarkable that they continue to imagine they might beat you," Chase said, leaning back, long legs extending wide across the bare floor. "You'd think by now, they'd have given up."

Temple moved to pour a glass of water from a carafe nearby. "It's difficult to turn from the promise of retribution. Even if it's the barest promise." As one who had never had a chance at retribution, Temple knew that better than anyone.

"You broke three of Montlake's ribs."

Temple drank deep, a rivulet of water spilling down his chin. He swiped the back of his hand across his face and said, "Ribs heal."

Chase nodded once, shifting in the chair. "Your Spartan lifestyle is not the most comfortable, you know."

Temple set the glass down. "No one asked you to linger. You've velour and stuffing somewhere above, no doubt."

Chase smiled, brushing a speck of lint from one trouser leg and placing a piece of paper on the table, next to the stack already there. The list of challenges for the next night and the one after. A never-ending list of men who wished to fight for their fortunes.

Temple exhaled, long and low. He didn't want to think on the next fight. All he wanted was hot water and a soft bed. He yanked on a nearby bellpull, requesting his bath be drawn.

Temple's gaze flickered to the paper, close enough to see that there were a half-dozen names scrawled upon it, too far to read the names themselves. He met his friend's knowing gaze.

"Lowe challenges you again."

He should have expected the words—Christopher Lowe

had challenged him twelve times in as many days—and yet they came like a blow. "No." The same answer he'd given eleven times. "And you should stop bringing him to me."

"Why? Shouldn't the boy have his chance like all the others?"

Temple met Chase's gaze. "You're a bloodthirsty bastard."

Chase laughed. "Much to my family's dismay, not a bastard."

"Bloodthirsty, though."

"I simply enjoy an impassioned fight." Chase shrugged. "He's lost thousands."

"I don't care if he's lost the crown jewels. I won't fight him."

"Temple—"

"When we made this deal . . . when I agreed to come in on the Angel, we agreed that the fights were mine. Didn't we?"

Chase hesitated, seeing where the conversation was headed.

Temple repeated himself. "Didn't we?"

"Yes."

"I won't fight Lowe." Temple paused, then added, "He's not even a member."

"He's a member of Knight's. Now afforded the same rights as any of the Angel's members."

Knight's, the newest holding of The Fallen Angel, a lower club that carried the pleasure and debt of four hundred less-than-savory characters. Anger flared. "Goddammit . . . if not for Cross and his idiot decisions—"

"He had his reasons," Chase said.

"Lord deliver us from men in love."

"Hear hear," Chase agreed. "But we've a second hell to run, nonetheless, and that hell carries Lowe's debt. And he's due a fight if he asks for it."

"How has the boy lost thousands?" Temple asked, hating

the frustration that edged into his tone. "Everything his father touched turned to gold."

It was why Lowe's sister had been such a welcome bride.

He hated the thought. The memories that came with it.

Chase lifted one shoulder in a shrug. "Luck turns quickly."

The truth they all lived by.

Temple swore. "I'm not fighting him. Cut him loose."

Chase met his eyes. "There's no proof you killed her."

Temple's gaze did not waver. "There's no proof I didn't."

"I'd wager everything I have that you didn't."

"But not because you know it's true."

Temple didn't even know it.

"I know you."

No one knew him. Not really. "Well, Lowe doesn't. I won't fight him. And I won't have this conversation again. If you want to give the boy a fight, you fight him."

He waited for Chase's next words. A new attack.

It didn't come.

"Well, London would like that." The founder of the Angel stood, lifting the list of potential fights along with the stack of papers that had been on the table since before the fight. "Shall I return these to the books?"

Temple shook his head, extending one hand for them. "I shall do it."

It was part of the ritual.

"Why pull the files in the first place?" Chase asked.

Temple looked to the papers, where Montlake's debt to the Angel was accounted in clear, concise script: one hundred pounds here, one thousand there, a dozen acres. A hundred. A house, a horse, a carriage.

A life.

He lifted one shoulder, enjoying the sting of the muscle there. "He might have won."

One of Chase's blond brows rose. "He might have done."

But he hadn't.

Temple returned the record to the scarred oak table.

"They lay everything on the fight. It seems the least I can do to acknowledge the magnitude of their loss."

"And yet you still win."

It was true. But he understood what it was to lose everything. To have one's entire life changed in an instant because of a choice that should not have been made. An action that should not have been taken.

There was a difference, of course.

The men who came to scratch in the ring beyond remembered making the choice. Taking the action.

Temple didn't.

Not that it mattered.

A bell on the wall above the door rang, announcing that his bath was drawn, pulling him back to the present.

"I did not say they do not deserve to lose."

Chase laughed, the sound loud in the quiet room. "So very sure of yourself. Someday, you may not win so handily."

Temple reached for a towel, draping the fine Turkish cotton around his neck.

"Wicked promises," he said as he headed for the adjourning bathing chamber, dismissing Chase, the fight, and the wounds he'd inflicted. "Wicked, wonderful promises."

The streets east of Temple Bar came alive at night, filled with the worst of London—thieves and prostitutes and cutthroats set free from their daytime hiding places, released into the wild darkness. Thriving in it.

They reveled in the way corners rose from shadows, carving welcome blackness from the city, not half a mile from its most stately homes and wealthiest inhabitants, marking territory where proper nobs would not tread, too afraid to face the truth of the city—that it was more than they knew.

Or perhaps it was exactly what they knew.

It was everything that Temple knew.

Everything he was, everything he had become, everything he would ever be, this place, riddled with drunks and whores—the perfect place for a man to fade away. Unseen.

Of course, they did see him. They had for years, since the moment, twelve years earlier, when he'd arrived young and stinking of fear and fury, with nothing but his fists to recommend him to this brave new world.

The whispers had followed him through filth and sin, marking time. At first, he pretended not to hear the word, but as the years passed, he had embraced it—and the epithet turned honorific.

Killer.

It kept them far from him, even as they watched. *The Killer Duke.* He felt the curiosity in their gazes—why would an aristocratic nob, born on the right side of the blanket with a diamond-crusted spoon in his mouth, have any reason to kill?

What devastating, dark secret did the rich and privileged hide so well behind their silks and jewels and coin?

Temple gave the darkest souls in London hope.

The chance to believe that their lives, dank and layered in soot and grime, might not be so very different from those that seemed so far above. So unattainable.

If the Killer Duke could fall, he heard in their furtive gazes, *so, too, might we rise.*

And in that flickering hope was the danger. He turned a corner, leaving the lights and sound of Long Acre, cloaking himself in the darkened streets where he had spent most of his adult life.

His steps quieted with years of instinct, knowing that it was this walk—the last hundred yards to his town house—where those who lurked found their courage.

Because of this, it was no surprise he was being followed.

It had happened before—men desperate enough to take

him on, to wield knives and clubs in the hope that a single, well-placed blow would level him long enough to relieve him of his purse.

And if it laid him flat forever, well then, so be it. It was the way of the streets, after all.

He'd faced them before. He'd fought them before, spilling blood and teeth here on the cobblestones of Newgate with a ferocity that was missing in the ring of The Fallen Angel.

He'd fought them, and won. Dozens. Scores.

And still, there was always some new, desperate sinner who followed, mistaking the fine wool of Temple's coat for weakness.

He slowed, fixed on the steps behind him, different than usual. Missing the weight of drink and poor judgment. Fast and focused and nearly on top of him before he noticed what it was that set these footsteps apart.

He should have noticed earlier. Should have understood immediately why there was something so uncommon about this particular pursuer. So unsettling. He should have sensed it, if for no other reason than because of what this follower was *not*.

Because, in all the years that he had been shadowed down these darkened alleyways—in all the years he'd lifted his fists to a stranger—his attacker had never been female.

He waited for her to close the distance.

There was a hesitation in her step as she came closer, and he marked time with his stride, long and languorous, knowing that he could turn and eliminate this particular threat at any moment.

But it wasn't every day that he was surprised.

And the chit behind him was nothing if not surprising.

She was close enough to hear her breath, fast and shallow—the telltale sign of energy and fear. As though she were new at this. As though she were the victim.

And perhaps she was.

She was a yard from him. A foot. Six inches before he turned, reaching for and catching her by the wrists, pulling her close—the realization that she was unarmed coming on a wave of warmth and lemon scent.

She wasn't wearing gloves.

He barely had time to register the fact before she gasped, going utterly still for a split second before first tugging at her wrists and, once discovering them caught in his strong grip, struggling in earnest.

She was taller than most, and stronger than he expected. She didn't cry or call out, instead using all her breath, all her strength, to fuel her attempt to extricate herself, which made her smarter than most of the men he'd met in the ring.

She was no match for him, however, and so he held her. Tight and firm, until she gave up.

He rather regretted that she gave up.

But she did, realizing the futility of her actions after a long moment . . . hesitating briefly before she turned her face up to his and said, "Release me."

There was something in the words, a quiet, unexpected honesty that almost made him do it. Almost made him let her go, to run off into the night.

Almost.

But it had been a long time since he'd been so intrigued by an opponent.

Pulling her closer, he easily transferred both her wrists into one of his hands as he used the other to check her cloak for weapons.

His hand closed on the hilt of a knife, hidden deep in the lining of the cloak. He extracted it. "No, I don't think I will."

"That's mine," she said, reaching for the weapon, cursing as he held it out of her reach.

"I don't care for late-night meetings with armed attackers."

"I'm not armed."

He raised a brow.

She exhaled harshly. "I mean, I am armed, of course. It's

the dead of night and anyone with the sense of a trout would be. But I have no intention of stabbing you."

"And I'm simply to take your word for it?"

Her words came straight and true. "If I wanted to stab you, you'd have been stabbed."

He cursed the darkness and its secrets, wanting to see her face. "What are you after?" He asked softly, sliding the knife into his boot, "My pockets? You should have picked a smaller mark." Though he wasn't exactly sorry that she'd chosen him. He liked it.

Even more when she answered.

"I'm after you."

The response was quick enough to be true, and to shock the hell out of him.

Wariness flared. "You're not a lightskirt."

The words were not a question. It was clear the woman wasn't a whore—in the way she stiffened in response to his statement, keeping space between them.

She wasn't comfortable with a man's touch.

With his touch.

She redoubled her efforts to free herself. "Is that all people want from you? Your purse or your—" She stopped, and Temple resisted the urge to laugh. She most certainly was not a prostitute.

"The two options are usually enough for women." He stared into her dark face, wishing for a street lamp. For a shadow of light from a nearby window. "All right, darling, if not my purse or my . . ." He trailed off, enjoying the way her breath caught before he finished. She was curious. " . . . prowess, what then?"

She took a deep breath, its weight falling between them, as though what she were about to say would change her world. Would change his. He waited, barely noticing that his breath held, as well.

"I'm here to challenge you."

He let her go and turned away, irritation and frustration

and not a small amount of disappointment flaring. She hadn't come for him as a man. She'd come for him as a means to an end. Just as they always did.

Her boots clattered on the cobblestones as she ran after him. "Wait."

He did not wait.

"Your Grace—" The title cut through the darkness. Stung. *She wouldn't get anywhere with such good manners.* "Hold a moment. Please."

It might have been the softness in the word. It might have been the word itself—one the Killer Duke did not often hear—that stopped him. Turned him back. "I don't fight women. I don't care who your lover is. Tell him to find his manhood and come after me himself."

"He doesn't know I'm here."

"Perhaps you should have told him. Then he might have stopped you from making the rash and reckless decision to stand in the dead of night in the middle of a dark alley with a man widely believed to be one of the most dangerous in Britain."

"I don't believe that."

Something flared deep in him at the words. At the truth in them. And for the briefest of moments, he considered reaching for her again. Taking her to his town house.

It had been a long time since a woman had intrigued him.

Sanity returned. "You should believe it."

"It's nonsense. It has been since the beginning."

His gaze narrowed on her. "Go home and find yourself a man who cares enough to save you from yourself."

"My brother lost a great deal of money," she said, her words clear in the darkness, tinged at the same time with proper education and an East London edge. Not that he cared about her accent. *Or about her.*

"I don't fight women." There was comfort in the repetition. In the reminder that he had never hurt a woman. *An-*

other woman. "And your brother seems smarter than most. I also don't lose to men."

"I wish to reclaim the money, nonetheless."

"I want a number of things that I shan't have," he tossed back at her.

"I know. That's why I'm here. To give them to you." Something echoed in the words. Strength. Truth. He did not reply, but curiosity had him waiting for her next words. Words that came like a blow. "I am here to propose a trade."

"So you are a lightskirt, after all?"

He meant to insult her. Failed. She gave a little half laugh in the darkness, the breathy sound more intriguing than he'd like to admit. "Not that kind of trade. And besides, you don't want me half as much as you want what I can give you."

The words were a challenge, and he itched to accept it. For there was something in the stupid, brave woman's words that called to him. That made him consider making whatever idiot trade she was offering.

He focused on her, taking a step toward her, her scent coming warm and welcome. In a moment, he'd caught her in his arms, pressed her chest to his. "I confess, I've always liked the combination of beauty and boldness." He whispered into her ear, loving the way her breath caught in her throat. "Perhaps we can make an arrangement after all."

"My body is not on the table."

It was a pity. She was brazen as hell, and one night in her bed might be worth whatever she was after. "Then what makes you think I'm interested in dealing with you?"

She hesitated. A second. Less. But he heard it. "Because you want what I offer."

"I'm rich as Croesus, love. So if you don't offer your willing participation in my bed, there's nothing you have that I can't get on my own."

He turned back to the house, going several steps before she called out, "Even absolution?"

He froze.

Absolution.

How many times had the word whispered through his mind? How many times had he tested it, low and quiet on his tongue as he lay in the darkness, guilt and anger his only bedmates?

Absolution.

Something rushed through him, cold and furious, and it took him a moment to understand it. Warning. *She was dangerous.*

He should walk away.

And yet . . .

He moved to capture her, using the speed for which he was renowned, one strong hand clasping her arm. He ignored her sharp intake of breath and pulled her along the street to a patch of lamplight at the door of his town house.

He lifted one gloved hand to her face, turning her into the light, taking her in—smooth skin gone ruddy in the evening's frigid air, jaw set firm and defiant. Her eyes wide and clear, filled with honesty.

One blue. One green.

Too strange to be common. Too memorable.

She tried to pull her chin away. His grip tightened, making movement impossible. His question came quick and harsh in the night. "Who is your brother?"

She swallowed. He felt the movement in his hand. In his whole body. An eternity passed while he waited for her reply. "Christopher Lowe."

The name singed him, and he released her instantly, stepping back from the heat that threatened, thickening his blood and setting his ears to roaring.

Absolution.

He shook his head slowly, unable to stop himself from speaking, "You are . . ." He trailed off and she closed her eyes, unable to meet his gaze. No. He wasn't having that. "Look at me."

She straightened, shoulders back, spine stiff. And she met his gaze without shame. Without remorse.

Christ.

"Say it." Not a request.

"I am Mara Lowe."

It couldn't be true.

"You're dead."

She shook her head, auburn gleaming red in the light. "I am alive."

Everything in him stilled. Everything that had simmered for so many years. Everything that he had resisted and loathed and feared. It all went quiet.

Until it roared like Hell itself.

He turned to unlock the door to his flat, needing something to keep him from his anger. The iron locks moved beneath his strength, clicking and sliding, punctuating his harsh breath.

"Your Grace?"

The question brought him back to the world. *Your Grace.* The title to which he had been born. The title he had ignored for years. His, once more. Bestowed by the one who had stripped him of it.

His Grace, the Duke of Lamont.

He opened the door wide and turned back to face her, this woman who had changed his life. Who had ruined his life.

"Mara Lowe." The name came out harsh and mangled and coated in history.

She nodded.

He laughed, a single, harsh syllable in the darkness. It was all he could do. Her brow furrowed in confusion. He gave her a quick, mocking bow. "My apologies. You see, it is not every day a killer meets a past kill."

She raised her chin. "You didn't kill me."

The words were soft and strong and filled with a courage he might have admired. A courage he should have hated.

He hadn't killed her. Emotion came, hard and angry. Relief. Fury. Confusion. A dozen others.

Dear God.

What in hell had happened?

He stepped aside, waving toward the dark hallway beyond the threshold. "In." Again, not a request.

She hesitated, eyes wide, and for a moment, he thought she would run.

But she didn't.

Stupid girl. She should have run.

Her skirts brushed against his boots as she moved past him, the touch reminding him that she was flesh and blood.

And alive.

Alive, and his.

$\mathcal{A}$s the door closed, clicking locks punctuating the quiet darkness of his home, it occurred to Mara that this could well be the biggest mistake she'd made in her life.

Which was saying something, considering the fact that two weeks after her sixteenth birthday, she'd absconded from her planned wedding to a duke, leaving his son to face false accusations of her murder.

His son, who was no doubt considering turning those false accusations into truth.

His son, who had every right to unleash his fury.

His son, with whom she stood now in an unsettlingly narrow hallway. Alone. In the dead of night. Mara's heart raced in the confined space, every inch of her screaming to flee.

But she couldn't. Her brother had made it impossible. Fate had turned. Desperation had brought her here, and it was time she faced her past.

It was time she faced *him*.

Steeling herself, she turned to do just that, trying to ignore the way his enormous form—taller and broader than any man she'd ever known—loomed in the darkness, blocking her exit.

He was already moving past her, leading the way up a flight of stairs.

She hesitated, casting a look back at the door. She could disappear again. Exile Mara Lowe once more. She had lost herself once before; she could do it again.

She could run.

And lose everything she had. Everything she was. Everything for which she had worked so hard.

"You wouldn't go ten yards without my catching you," he said.

There was that, as well.

She looked up at him, watching her from above, his face cast in light for the first time that evening. Twelve years had changed him, and not in the ordinary way—from a boy of eighteen to a man of thirty. Soft, perfect skin had given way to weathered angles and dark stubble.

More than that, his eyes held no hint of the laughter they'd held that night, a lifetime ago. They remained black as midnight, but now they held its secrets.

Of course he would catch her if she ran. That was why she was here, wasn't it? To be caught. To reveal herself.

Mara Lowe.

It had been more than a decade since she'd said the name aloud. She'd been Margaret MacIntyre since the moment she'd left that night. But now, she was Mara again, the only way to save the one thing that mattered to her. The thing that gave her purpose.

She had no choice but to be Mara.

The thought propelled her upstairs, into a room that was part-library, part-study, and all male. As he lit the candles throughout, a golden glow spread over furniture large and leathered in heavy dark colors.

He was already crouching to light a fire in the hearth when she entered. It was so incongruous—the great duke setting a fire—that she couldn't help herself. "You don't have servants?"

He stood, brushing his hands on his massive thighs. "A woman comes in the mornings to clean."

"But no others?"

"No."

"Why not?"

"No one wants to sleep in the same house as the Killer Duke." There was no anger in the words. No sadness. Just truth.

He moved to pour himself a scotch, but did not offer her one. Nor did he offer her a seat when he folded himself into a large leather chair. He took a long pull of amber liquid and crossed ankle over knee, letting the glass dangle from his grip as he watched her, black eyes taking her in, watching, seeing everything.

She folded her hands to control their trembling, and met his gaze. Two could play at this. Twelve years away from money and power and the aristocracy made for a strong will.

A will they shared.

The thought whispered through her on a thread of guilt. She'd chosen this life. Chosen to change everything. He hadn't. He'd been a casualty of a child's stupid, silly plan.

I am sorry.

It was true, after all. She'd never meant for that charming young man—all muscle and grace and wide, smiling mouth—to become an unwitting victim in her escape.

Not that she'd tried to save him.

She ignored the thought. It was too late for apologies. She'd made her bed; now she would lie in it.

He drank again, lids shuttering his gaze, as though she could miss the way he stared at her. As though she didn't feel it right to her toes.

It was a battle. He would not speak first, which left it to her to begin the conversation.

A losing move.

She would not lose to him.

So she waited, trying not to fidget. Trying not jump from

her skin with every crack of the logs in the fireplace. Trying not to go mad under the weight of the silence.

Apparently, he was not interested in losing, either.

She narrowed her gaze on his.

She waited until she could wait no longer, and then told him the truth. "I don't like being here any more than you like having me."

The words turned him to stone for a moment, and she bit her tongue, afraid to speak. Afraid to make things worse.

He laughed again—the laugh she'd heard earlier, outside—devoid of humor, a graveled expulsion that sounded more like pain than pleasure. "Amazing. Until this moment, I actually had allowed for the possibility that you have been a victim of fate as well."

"Aren't we all victims of fate?"

And she had been. She did not pretend that she had not been a willing participant in everything that had happened all those years ago . . . but had she known how it would change her . . . what it would do to her . . .

She stopped the lie from completing.

She would have done it anyway. She didn't have a choice then. Just as she had no choice tonight.

There were moments that changed one's life. And paths that came without a fork in the road.

"You are alive and well, Miss Lowe."

The man was a duke, powerful and wealthy, with all of London at his feet if he wanted it. She lifted her chin at the accusation in his tone. "As are you, *Your Grace.*"

His eyes went dark. "That is debatable." He leaned back in his chair. "So it appears that fate was not my attacker, after all. You were."

When he'd caught her outside, before he'd known why she was there and who she was, there had been warmth in his voice—a hint of heaviness that she'd been drawn to, even as she'd known better.

That warmth was gone now, replaced with cold calm—a

calm by which she was not fooled. A calm she would wager shielded a terrible storm.

"I didn't attack you."

Fact, even if it was not entirely truth.

He did not release her gaze. "A liar through and through, I see."

She lifted her chin. "I never lied."

"No? You made the world believe you were dead."

"The world believed what it wished."

His black gaze narrowed. "You disappeared, and left it to draw its own conclusions."

His free hand—the one that did not grip his scotch in an approximation of casualness—betrayed his ire, fingers twitching with barely contained energy. She noticed the movement, recognizing it from the boys she'd met on the streets. There was always something that betrayed their frustration. Their anger. Their plans.

But this was no boy.

She was not a fool—twelve years had taught her a hundred lessons in safety and self-preservation, and for a moment, regret gave way to nerves and she considered fleeing again—running from this man and this place and this choice she'd made.

The choice that would both save the life she had built and tear it down.

The choice that would force her to face her past, and place her future in this man's hands.

She watched those fingers move.

I never meant for you to be hurt. She wanted to say it, but he wouldn't believe her. She knew that. This was not about his forgiveness or his understanding. This was about her future. And the fact that he held its key.

"I disappeared, yes. And I cannot erase that. But I am here now."

"And we get to it, finally. Why?"

So many reasons.

She resisted the thought. There was only one reason. Only one that mattered.

"Money." It was true. And also false.

His brows rose in surprise. "I confess I would not have expected such honesty."

She lifted one shoulder in a little shrug. "I find that lies overcomplicate."

He exhaled on a long breath. "You are here to plead your brother's case."

She ignored the flood of anger that came with the words. "I am."

"He is in debt to his eyeballs."

With her money.

"I'm told you can change that."

"Can is not will."

She took a breath, threw herself into the fray. "I know he can't beat you. I know the fight with the great Temple is a phantom. That you always win. Which, I assume, is why you haven't accepted one of his dozen challenges. Frankly, I'm rather happy you haven't. You've given me room to negotiate."

It was hard to believe his dark eyes could grow darker. "You are in contact with him."

She stilled, considering the miscalculated reveal of information.

He gave her no time. "How long have you been in contact with him?"

She hesitated a second too long. Less. Enough for him to shoot from his chair and stalk her across the room, pressing her back, far and fast enough to send her tripping over her skirts.

One massive arm shot out. Caught her, the corded strength like steel across her back. Pulled her to him; she was caged against him. "For how long?" He paused, but before she could answer, he added, "You don't have to tell me. I can smell the guilt on you."

She put her hands to his chest, feeling the wall of iron muscle there. Pushed. The effort was futile. He would not move until he was ready.

"You and your idiot brother concocted an idiot plan, and you disappeared." He was so close. Too close. "Maybe not idiot. Maybe genius. After all, everyone thought you were dead. *I thought you were dead.*" There was fury in the words, fury and something else. Something she could not help but wish to assuage.

"That was never the plan."

He ignored the words. "But here you are, twelve years later, flesh and blood. Hale and healthy." The words were soft, a whisper of sound at her ear. "I should make good on our past. On my reputation."

She heard the anger in his words. Felt it in his touch. Later, she would marvel at her own courage when she looked up at him and said, "Perhaps you should. But you won't."

He released her, so quickly that she stumbled back as he turned away, pacing the length of the room, reminding her of a tiger she'd seen once in a traveling show, caged and frustrated. It occurred to her that she would gladly trade the wild beast for the Duke of Lamont in that moment.

Untamed, himself.

When he finally turned back, he said, "I wouldn't be so certain. Twelve years marked as a killer change a man."

She shook her head, holding his black gaze. "You are not a killer."

"You're the only one who knew that."

The words were quiet and rife with emotion. Mara recognized fury and shock and surprise, but it was the accusation that unsettled her. It wasn't possible that he'd thought himself her killer.

It wasn't possible that he'd believed the gossip. The speculation.

Was it?

She should say something. But what? What did one say to the man falsely accused of one's murder?

"Would it help if I apologized?"

He narrowed his gaze on her. "Do you feel remorse?"

She would not change it. Not for the world. "I am sorry that you were caught in the fray."

"Do you regret your actions?"

She met his eyes. "Do you wish the truth? Or a platitude?"

"You could not imagine the things I wish."

She could, no doubt. "I understand that you are angry."

The words seemed to call to him, and he came toward her, glass still in hand, stalking her backward, across the too-small room. "You *understand*, do you?"

It had been the wrong thing to say. She skirted around an ottoman, holding her hands up, as though she could stop him, searching for the right thing.

He did not wait for her to find it. "You *understand* what it is to have lost everything?"

Yes.

"You *understand* what it is to have lost my name?"

She did, rather. But she knew better than to say it.

He pressed on. "To have lost my title, my land, my *life*?"

"But you didn't lose all that . . . you're still a duke. The Duke of Lamont," she said, the words—things she'd told herself for years—coming quick and defensive. "The land is still yours. The money. You've tripled the holdings of the dukedom."

His eyes went wide. "How do you know that?"

"I pay attention."

"Why?"

"Why have you never returned to the estate?"

"What good would it have done if I returned?"

"You might have been reminded that you haven't lost so very much." The words were out before she could stop them. Before she realized how inciting they were. She scurried backward, putting a high-backed chair between them and peeking around it. "I did not mean—"

"Of course you did." He started around the chair toward her.

She moved counter to him, keeping the furniture between them. Attempted to calm the beast. "You are angry."

He shook his head. "Angry does not even begin to describe the depths of my emotion."

She nodded, skipping backward across the room once more. "Fair enough. Furious."

He advanced. "That's closer."

"Irate."

"That, too."

She looked behind her, saw the sideboard looming. This wasn't a very large room, after all. "Livid."

"And that."

She felt the hard oak at her back. *Trapped again.* "I can repair it," she said, desperate to regain the upper hand. "What's broken." He stopped, and for a moment, she had his full attention. "If I am not dead, you are not"—*a killer*— "what they say you are." He did not reply, and she rushed to fill the silence. "That's why I'm here. I shall come forward. Show myself to Society. I shall prove you're not what they say you are."

He set his glass on the sideboard. "You shall."

She released a breath she had not known she was holding. *He was not as unforgiving as she had imagined he might be.* She nodded. "Yes, I will. I will tell everyone—"

"You shall tell them the truth."

She hesitated at the words, hating them, the way they threatened. And still she nodded. "I shall tell them the truth." It would be the most difficult thing she'd ever done, but she would do it.

She hadn't a choice.

It would ruin her, but it might be enough to save what was important.

She had one chance to negotiate with Temple. She had to do it correctly. "On one condition."

He laughed. A great, booming guffaw of laughter. Her brow furrowed at the noise. She did not like the sound, especially not when it ended with a wicked, humorless smile. "You think to barter with me?" He was close enough to touch. "You think tonight has put me in a negotiating frame of mind?"

"I disappeared once before. I can do it again." The threat did not endear her to him.

"I will find you." The words were so serious, so honest, that she did not doubt him.

Still, she soldiered on. "Perhaps, but I've hidden for twelve years, and I've become quite good at it. And even if you did find me, the aristocracy shan't simply take your word for it that I am alive. You need me as a willing participant in this play."

His gaze narrowed, and a muscle in his jaw twitched. When he spoke, the words came like ice. "I assure you, I will never need you."

She ignored him. Forged ahead. "I shall tell the truth. Come forward with proof of my birth. And you shall forgive my brother's debt."

There was a moment of silence as the words fell between them, and for those fleeting seconds, Mara thought she might have succeeded in negotiating with him.

"No."

Panic flared. He couldn't refuse. She lifted her chin. "I think it's a fair trade."

"A fair trade for *destroying my life*?"

Irritation flared. He was one of the wealthiest men in London. In Britain, for heaven's sake. With women tossing themselves into his arms and men desperate to gain his confidence. He retained his title, his entail, and now had an entire empire to his name. What did he know of ruined lives?

"And how many lives have you destroyed?" she asked,

knowing she shouldn't, but unable to keep herself from it. "You are no saint, my lord."

"Whatever I've done—" he started, then stopped, changing tack with another huff of disbelief. "Enough. You are as much an idiot now as you were when you were sixteen if you think you hold a position to negotiate the terms of our agreement."

She had thought that at the start, of course, but one look into this man's cold, angry gaze made her see her miscalculation. This man did not want absolution.

He wanted vengeance.

And she was the path by which he would get it.

"Don't you see, Mara," He leaned in and whispered, "You're mine, now."

The words unsettled, but she refused to show him. *He wasn't a killer.* She knew that better than anyone.

He might not have killed you . . . but you haven't any idea what he's done since.

Nonsense. He wasn't a killer. He was simply angry. Which she'd expected, hadn't she? Hadn't she prepared for it? Hadn't she considered her options before donning her cloak and heading out into the streets to find him?

She'd been alone for twelve years. She'd learned to take care of herself. She'd learned to be strong.

He moved away from her then, heading for one chair near the fireplace. "You might as well sit. You're not going anywhere."

Unease threaded through her at the words. "What does that mean?"

"It means that you turned up outside my door, Miss Lowe. And I have no intention of letting you escape again."

Her heart pounded. "I'm to be your prisoner, then?"

He did not reply, but his earlier words echoed through her. *You're mine, now.*

Dammit. She'd made a dreadful miscalculation.

And he left her little choice.

Ignoring the way he waved at the other seat by the hearth, she headed for the decanter on the far end of the sideboard, pouring first one, then a second glass, carefully measuring the liquid.

She turned to face him, noting one dark brow raised in accusation.

"I am allowed a drink, am I not? Or do you plan to take that along with your pound of flesh?"

He seemed to think about his response before saying, "You are welcome to it."

She crossed the room and offered him the second glass, hoping he would not see the shaking in her hand. "Thank you."

"You think politeness will win you points?"

She sat down on the edge of the chair across from him. "I think it cannot hurt." He drank, and she exhaled, staring down at the liquid, marking time before she said, "I did not want to do this."

"I don't imagine you did," he said, wryly. "I imagine you've quite enjoyed twelve years of freedom."

That wasn't what she'd meant, but she knew better than to correct him. "And if I told you I haven't always enjoyed it? That it hasn't always been easy?"

"I would counsel against telling me those things. I find that I've lost my sympathetic ear."

She narrowed her gaze on him. "You are a difficult man."

He drank again. "A symptom of twelve years of solitude."

"I didn't mean for it to happen the way it did," she said, realizing even as she spoke the words that they were revealing more than she'd been willing to reveal. "We did not recognize you."

He stilled. "We?"

She did not reply.

"*We?*" He leaned forward. "Your brother. I should have fought him when he asked. He deserves a trouncing. He was . . ." He hesitated. She held her breath. "He helped you run. He helped you . . ." He lifted a hand to his head. " . . . *drug me*."

His black eyes went wide with shock and realization, and she shot up from her chair, heart pounding.

He followed, coming to his full height—more than six feet, tall and broad and bigger than any man she'd ever known. When they were younger, she'd marveled at his size. She'd been intrigued by it.

Drawn to it.

He interrupted her thoughts. "You drugged me!"

She put the chair between them. "We were children," she defended herself.

What's your excuse now?

He hadn't given her any choice.

Liar.

"Goddammit!" he said, his glass falling from his hand as he lunged toward her, missing his mark, catching himself on the edge of the chair. "You did it . . . again . . ."

And he collapsed to the floor.

It was one thing to drug a man once . . . but twice did seem overmuch. Even in one lifetime. She wasn't a monster, after all.

Not that he would believe that when he woke.

Mara stood over the Duke of Lamont, now felled like a great oak in his own study, and considered her options.

He hadn't given her any choice.

Perhaps if she kept telling herself that, she'd believe it. And she'd stop feeling guilty about the whole thing.

He'd threatened to keep her prisoner, like some monster.

Which of them was the monster?

Good Lord, he was enormous.

And intimidating, somehow, despite being unconscious.

And handsome, though not in a classical way.

He was all size and force, even motionless. Her gaze

tracked the length of him, the long arms and legs in perfectly tailored clothes, the cords of his neck peeking out from above the uncravatted collar of his shirt, the stretch of bronze to his strong jaw and dimpled chin, and the scars.

Even with the scars, the angles of his face betrayed his aristocratic lineage, all sharp edges and long slopes—the kind that set women to swooning.

Mara couldn't entirely blame them for swooning.

She'd nearly swooned herself, once.

Not nearly. *Had.*

When he was young, he'd been quick to smile, baring straight white teeth and an expression that promised more than pleasantry. That promised pleasure. His size, combined with that ease, had been so calm, so unpracticed that she'd thought him anything but the aristocracy. A stable boy. Or a footman. Or perhaps a member of the gentry, invited by her father to the enormous wedding that would make his daughter a duchess.

He'd looked like someone who did not have to worry about appearances.

It hadn't occurred to her that the heir to one of the most powerful dukedoms in the country would be the most carefree gentleman for miles. Of course, it should have. She should have known the moment that they came together in that cold garden and he smiled at her as though she were the only woman in Britain and he the only man, that he was an aristocrat.

But she hadn't.

And she certainly hadn't imagined that he was the Marquess of Chapin. The heir to the dukedom to which she would soon become duchess. Her future stepson.

The man sprawled across mahogany and carpet didn't look anything stepson-like.

But she would not think on that.

She crouched low to check his breathing, taking no small amount of relief in the way his wide chest rose and fell beneath his jacket in even strokes. Her heart pounded, no doubt in fear—after all, if he were to wake, he would not be happy.

She gave a little huff of laughter at the thought.

Happy was not the word.

He would not be *human*.

And then, with the giddiness of panic coursing through her, she did something she never would have imagined doing. Or, rather, she would have imagined doing, but never would have found the courage to do.

She touched him.

Her hand was moving before she could stop it. Before she really even knew what she was about. But then her fingers were on his skin—smooth and warm and alive. And ever so tempting.

Her fingers traced the angles of his face, finding the smooth ridges of the inch-long white scar along the bone at the base of his left eye, then down the barely-there bumps and angles of his once-perfect nose, her chest tightening as she considered the battles that would have produced the breaks. The pain of them.

The life he'd lived to wear them.

The life she'd given him.

"What happened to you?" The question came out on a whisper.

He did not answer, and her touch slid to his final scar, at the curve of his lower lip.

She knew she shouldn't . . . that it wouldn't do . . . but then her fingers were on that thin white line, barely there against rich skin, edging into the soft swell of his lip. And then she was touching his mouth, tracing the dips and curves of it, marveling at its softness.

Remembering the way it had felt on hers.

Wishing for—

No.

Her hand came away from him as though she'd been burned, and she turned her attention to the rest of him, to the way one arm spread haphazardly across the carpet, the victim of laudanum. He looked uncomfortable, and so she reached across him, intending to straighten that arm, to lay it flat against his side. But once his hand was in hers, she couldn't help but consider it, the spray of black hair that dusted the back of it, the way the veins tracked like rivers across its landscape, the way the knuckles rose and dipped, scarred and calloused from years of fighting. Bruised with experience.

"Why do you do this to yourself?" She ran her thumb across those knuckles, unable to resist, unable to remain aloof in the feel of him.

In the memory of him—young and charming and handsome, with the world at his feet—tempting her like nothing else.

Nothing else, but freedom.

She shivered in the cool room, her gaze moving to the fire, where the flames he'd stoked had died away to a quiet ember. She stood and moved to add another log to the hearth, stirring the coals to raise the fire. Once golden flames licked and danced again, she returned to him, staring down at him arms akimbo, and took a moment to speak to him, finding the act much easier with his accusing eyes closed. "If you hadn't threatened me, we would not be in this position. If you'd simply agreed to my trade, you'd be conscious. And I'd not feel so guilty."

He did not reply.

"Yes, I left you holding the guilt for my death."

And still nothing.

"But I swear I did not mean it to go the way I did. The whole thing got away from me."

Yet still she'd run.

"If you knew why I did it—"

His chest rose in a long, even breath.

"Why I returned—"

And fell.

If he knew, he'd still be furious. She sighed. "Well. Here we are. And I am tired of running."

No answer.

"I shan't run now."

It seemed important to say it. Perhaps because there was a part of her—a very sane and intelligent part of her—that wished to run. That wished to leave him here on his cold, hard floor, and escape as she had so many years ago.

But there was another part of her—not so sane, and not so intelligent—that knew that it was time for her penance. And that if she played her cards right, she could get what she wanted in the bargain.

"Assuming you negotiate."

She turned to the sideboard, where the day's paper sat, unread. She wondered if he were the kind of man who read his news each day. If he were the kind of man who cared about the world.

Guilt flared, and she pushed it away.

She tore the sheet of newsprint in half, then searched the drawers in the room until she found what she was looking for—a pot of ink and a quill. She scrawled a note, haphazardly waving the wet ink in the air as she returned to him, still as a corpse.

Extracting a hairpin, she crouched beside him again. "No blood this time," she whispered to him. "I hope you'll notice that."

Still, he slept.

She pinned the note to his chest, reached into his boot to extract her knife, and made to leave.

Except she couldn't.

At the door, she turned back, noting the chill in the room. She couldn't leave him like this. He'd catch a death of cold. On a chair in the corner, there was a green and black tartan. It was the least she could do.

She had drugged the man, after all.

She was across the room and had the blanket in her hands

before she could change her mind. She spread it across him, tucking it around his body carefully, trying not to notice the size of him. The way he exuded warmth and the tempting scent of clove and thyme. The memory of him. The now of him.

Failing.

"I'm sorry," she whispered.

And then she left.

Chapter 3

$\mathscr{H}$e dreamed of the ballroom at Whitefawn Abbey, gleaming sun-bright in the shade of a thousand candles and the sheen of silks and satins in a myriad of color.

The room belied the darkness that lurked beyond the enormous windows overlooking the massive gardens of the Devonshire estate—the country seat of the Duke of Lamont.

His estate.

He descended the wide marble stairs to the ballroom floor, where a crush of bodies writhed in time to the orchestra situated behind a wall of greenery at the far end of the room. The heat of the revelers overwhelmed him as he made his way through the throngs, pressing against him, pulsing with laughter and sighs, hands reaching for him, touching, grasping. Wide smiles and unintelligible words beckoned him deeper into the mass of people—welcoming him into its center.

Home.

There was a glass in his hand; he lifted it to his lips, the cool stream of champagne quenching the thirst he hadn't noticed before, but was now nearly unbearable. He lowered the glass, letting it fall into nothingness as a beautiful woman turned and stepped into his arms.

"Your Grace." The title echoed through him, coming on a wave of pleasure.

They danced.

The steps came from distant memory, a slow, spinning eternity of long-forgotten skill. The woman in his arms was all warmth, tall enough to make him a proper match, and curved enough to fit his long arms.

The music swelled, and still they danced, turning again and again, the sea of faces in the ballroom fading into blackness—the walls of the room falling away as he was distracted by a sudden, heavy weight on his sleeve. He turned his attention to his forearm, wrapped in black wool, pristine but for a sixpence-sized white spot.

Wax, fallen from the chandeliers overhead.

As he watched, the spot liquefied, spreading across his coat sleeve in a thread of molten honey. The woman in his arms reached for the liquid—her long, delicate fingers stroking along the fabric, her touch spreading fire as it crept toward the spot, hot wax coating her fingertips before she turned them up to his gaze.

She had beautiful hands.

Beautiful skin.

She wore no gloves.

He followed the line of her long arm from wrist to shoulder, taking in her piecemeal perfection—the curves and valleys of her collarbone; the long rise of her neck; her angled jaw; her wide, welcoming mouth; long, equine nose; and eyes like none he'd ever seen. One blue, one green.

Her lips curved around the words he'd craved and feared for so long. "Your Grace."

And, like that, she was in focus.

Mara Lowe.

He woke on the floor of his library, coming to his feet in a mad rush, a foul curse echoing in the blue fog of breaking dawn.

A green and black tartan fell to his feet as he rose, and

the fact that the woman had covered him with a blanket after drugging him in the dead of night was no kind of comfort. He imagined her standing over him at his most vulnerable moment, and wanted to roar his anger.

She had drugged him and left.

Again.

On the heels of that thought came another.

Dear God. She was alive.

He hadn't killed her.

Relief burst full and high in his lungs, warring with frustration and ire.

He wasn't a killer.

He ran one hand down his face to ease the tightness of the emotion, and noticed that she had not simply left him.

She'd also left a note, scrawled across yesterday's news, and pinned to his chest with a simple hairpin, as though he were a package to be delivered by post.

He tore the missive from its mooring, knowing that whatever she had to say would do little to assuage his anger.

> *I had hoped it would not come to this, but I will not*
> *be intimidated, and I will not be strong-armed.*

He resisted the urge to crumple the note and throw it into the fire. She thought *she* was the one being strong-armed? When it was *he* who had been knocked out on the floor of his own study?

> *The offer is a trade, and nothing less.*
> *When you are in a negotiating frame of mind, I*
> *welcome your visit for a discussion of equals.*

That would be impossible. He was not nearly mad enough to be her equal.

> *You will find me at No. 9 Cursitor Street.*

She'd left her address. Mistake. She should have run. Not that he wouldn't have caught her; he would have spent the rest of his life chasing her if she'd run.

He deserved his retribution, after all. And she would give it to him.

Who was this stupid, brave woman?

Mara Lowe. Alive. Found.

Strong as steel.

The thought came, another fast on its heels, and he reached inside his boot, knowing what he would find.

The harpy had stolen her knife.

*W*ithin the hour, he was washed and on his way to No. 9 Cursitor Street, uncertain of what to expect. It was possible the woman had run, after all, and as he made his way deeper and deeper into the streets of Holborn, he wondered if she had done just that and left him with directions to her personal cutthroats to finish the job she'd begun the prior evening.

The neighborhood was less than pleasant, even at seven in the morning. Drunks were nestled in doorways of unsavory taverns, empty bottles fallen haphazardly to their sides as they lolled in their early-morning stupors. A haggard prostitute stumbled into the street from an alleyway beyond, eyes bloodshot and heavy as she plowed into him.

Her eyes met his, and he recognized the faraway look in them. "Wot's a fancy bloke like yerself doin' 'ere?"

Chasing ghosts.

Like an imbecile.

The prostitute's touch was everywhere, and he caught her as she searched his coat for his purse.

"No luck today, darling," he said, extracting the empty hand.

She did not hesitate to lean in, and he steeled himself against her sour breath. "'Ow 'bout a bit o' business, then? I've never 'ad one yer size."

"Thank you," he replied, lifting her and setting her to the side. "But I'm afraid I've an appointment."

She grinned, two teeth missing. "Tell me, luv. Are you big all over?"

Another man would have ignored the question, but Temple had lived a long time on these streets, and he was comfortable with whores. For years, they'd been the only women willing to keep him company—luckily, he'd never had to settle for ones quite so . . . well used.

Fate had dealt the woman an unfortunate circumstance, a truth that Temple understood better than most. She did not deserve scorn for the way she managed.

He winked. "I've never had a complaint."

She cackled. "Any time you like, luv. A right bargain, I am."

He tipped his hat. "I shall remember that." And he was off, down Cursitor, counting the doors until he reached number nine.

The building was out of place—cleaner than all the others on the row, with flower boxes in the windows, each boasting a mass of mums in bright colors—and as he stood outside, staring up at the flagstones, he knew that he'd found the place. And that she hadn't run.

But why live here, on a filth-ridden street in Holborn?

He raised the knocker and let it fall with a firm rap.

"I see I wouldn't be the first to sample the wares." He turned back to the street, where the prostitute stood watching him. She came closer, gaze suddenly knowing. "I know you."

He looked away.

"Yer the Killer Duke." He returned his attention to the door, frustration coursing through him. It never went away, that cold thread of anger mixed with something worse. Something far more devastating. "Not that I care, luv. A girl like me can't be too choosy."

But he heard the change in her voice. The edge. Wariness

and knowledge and a tinge of equality. They both lived in the darkness, after all, didn't they?

He ignored her, but she continued. "You've a boy for MacIntyre?"

He looked to the door again, then back at the woman in the street. "A boy?"

She raised a brow. "Y'ain't the first y'know. Won't be the last. It's the way of it. The way of *men*. Girls ought to be careful these days. Especially around the likes of you."

The woman hadn't met Mara Lowe, evidently.

The door opened, ending the woman's sermon and revealing a young lady with a cherubic face in the house beyond. She couldn't have been older than sixteen, peering up at him with wide, surprised eyes.

He tipped his hat. "Good morning. I'm here for Mara."

The girl's brow furrowed. "Mrs. MacIntyre, you mean?"

He should have known she wouldn't be here. Should have known she'd lied to him. Had the woman ever told a truth in her life? "I don't—"

He couldn't finish the sentence, however, as hell chose that precise moment to break loose inside the house.

A cacophony of shouting erupted from a room beyond his view, and a half-dozen small figures came tearing through the foyer, chased by a handful of slightly larger figures, one of which was carrying—was that a table leg?

Three of the smaller creatures seemed to sense their impending demise and did what any intelligent being would do in such a scenario—ran for the exit. They made a tactical error, however, in that they did not count on either Temple or the young woman to be in the vicinity, and so instead of a straight shot into the street, they found themselves captured like flies in a wide web of skirt.

The trio cried out in frustration. The maid at the door cried out in what Temple could only imagine was terror, and not improperly placed. And the leg-brandishing creature cried out in conquest, leaping onto a small table in the entryway, raising his club high above his head and launching himself into the fray.

For one fleeting moment, Temple admired both the child's courage and his form in battle.

The girl at the door stood no chance. She toppled like a felled poplar, and the boys scurried from their cambric trap, tumbling across the floor, kicking and screeching and wrestling.

And it was only when squeals began to emanate from the pile that Temple realized he could not in good conscience back away from the door and let the insanity ensue without him.

If these children escaped, they would wreak havoc on London.

He was the only one qualified to contain them. Obviously.

Without asking permission, he stepped over the threshold and entered the house, the door closing behind him with a great thud even as he helped the maid to her feet. Once he had confirmed that all her extremities were in working order, he turned to the more unsettling matter at hand . . . the writhing pile of boys at the center of the foyer.

And then he did what he did best.

He entered the fight.

He pulled boys one by one out of the pile and set them on their feet, removing wooden swords and bags of rocks and other makeshift weapons from hands and pockets before setting them free, placing each of them on the ground with a firm "That's enough," before going back to extract the next.

He had taken the last two boys in hand—the one with the table leg and another who was quite small—and lifted them clear off the floor when he saw it, small and pink and unmoving.

He leaned in, still holding the two boys.

"Aww . . ." said the boy with the table leg, seeming not to mind that his feet were dangling two feet above the floor. "She'll get away."

Was that a—

The piglet sprang to life with an ear-splitting squeal, running for the nearest room and startling Temple, who leapt back. "Jesus Christ!"

And, for the first time since he'd knocked on the door, there was silence inside No. 9 Cursitor Street.

He turned to face the boys, each of whom was staring up at him wide-eyed.

"What is it?"

None of them replied, instead all looking to their leader, who still held his weapon, but luckily seemed disinclined to use it. "You took the Lord's name in vain," he said, accusation and something close to admiration in his tone.

"Your pig startled me."

The boy shook his head. "Mrs. MacIntyre doesn't like cursing."

From what Temple had seen, Mrs. MacIntyre might do well to worry less about the boys' language and more about their lives, but he refrained from saying as much.

"Well then," he said, "let's not tell her it happened."

"Too late," said the little one in his other hand, and Temple turned to look at the boy, who was pointing to something behind him.

"I am afraid I already heard it."

He turned to the voice, soft and feminine. And familiar.

He set the boys down.

She hadn't run. "Mrs. MacIntyre, I presume?"

Mara did not reply, instead turning to the boys. "What have I said about chasing Lavender?"

"We weren't chasing her!" several boys cried at the same time.

"She was our booty!" another said.

"Stolen from *our* treasure!" said the leader of the pack. He looked to Mara. "We were *rescuing* her."

Temple's brow furrowed. "The pig's name is Lavender?"

She did not look at him, instead letting her attention

move from one boy to the next with an expression he found distinctly familiar—an expression he'd seen a million times on the face of his childhood governess. Disappointment.

"Daniel? What did I say?" she asked, staring down the leader of the once-merry band. "What is the rule?"

The boy looked away. "Lavender is not treasure."

She snapped her attention to the boy on the other side of Temple. "And what else? Matthew?"

"Don't chase Lavender."

"Precisely. Even if—? George?"

George shuffled his feet. "Even if she starts it."

Mara nodded. "Good. Now that we've all remembered the rules regarding Lavender, please tidy yourselves and put away your weaponry. It's time for breakfast."

A ripple of hesitation passed over the boys, each one of the dozen or so faces peering up at Temple in frank assessment.

"Young men," Mara said, gaining their attention. "I believe I spoke in proper English, did I not?"

Daniel stepped forward, a small, sharp chin jutting in Temple's direction. "Who's he?"

"No one for you to worry about," Mara assured him.

The boys seemed skeptical. *Smart boys.*

Matthew tilted his head, considering Temple. "He's very big."

"Strong, too," another pointed out.

Daniel nodded, and Temple noticed that the boy's gaze tracked the scar high on his cheek. "Is he 'ere to take us? For work?"

Years of practice kept Temple from revealing his surprise at the question, a split second before understanding rocketed through him. The building was an orphanage. He supposed he should have seen that earlier, but orphanages tended to conjure visions of miserable boys in long lines for bowls of steaming grey mush. Not battalions of screaming warriors chasing after pigs.

"Of course not. No one is taking you."

Daniel turned his attention to her. "Who is he, then?"

Temple raised a brow, wondering just how she'd reply to that. It wasn't as though she could tell the truth.

She met Temple's gaze, firm and fierce. "He's here to exact his revenge."

A dozen little mouths gaped. Temple resisted the urge to join them. Daniel spoke again. "Revenge for what?"

"A lie I told."

Christ. She was fearless.

"Lying is a sin," little George pointed out.

Mara smiled a little, secret smile. "Indeed it is. And if you do it, men like this will come and punish you."

Like that, she'd turned him into a villain again. Temple scowled as a roomful of round, wide eyes turned on him. He spoke then. "So you see, boys . . . I've business with Mrs. MacIntyre."

"She didn't mean to lie," Daniel defended her.

Temple was certain that Mrs. MacIntyre had absolutely meant to lie, but when he looked to the boy, he couldn't resist saying, "Nonetheless, she did."

"She must've had a good reason. Didn't you?" A sea of young faces looked to Mara.

Something sparkled in her gaze. Humor? She found this situation amusing? "I did indeed, Henry, which is why I fully intend to make a deal with our guest."

Over his rotting corpse. There would be no deals. "Perhaps we should discuss the reason, *Mrs. MacIntyre*."

She tilted her head, refusing to cower. "Perhaps," she said, sounding as though she meant the absolute opposite.

It seemed to be enough for most of the boys, but Daniel's gaze narrowed. "We should stay. Just to be safe," and, for a moment, Temple saw something eerily familiar in the boy.

Mistrust.

Suspicion.

Strength.

"That's very kind of you, Daniel," Mara said, moving to usher the boys through a door on one side of the foyer, "but I assure you, I shall be quite fine."

And she would be. Temple had no doubt.

Neither did most of the boys, it seemed, who went, as though there had been no pig stealing or chasing or sparring or vaulting through the air or anything else—all except Daniel, who didn't seem sure, but allowed himself to be filed from the room, looking over his shoulder the whole way, assessing Temple with serious dark eyes.

It had been a long time since someone had so fearlessly faced him.

The boy was loyal to Mara.

Temple was almost impressed, until he remembered the woman in question was a demon and deserved no such loyalty.

When she closed the door firmly behind the pack of boys, he rocked back on one heel. "Mrs. *MacIntyre*?"

At the pointed question, she darted her attention to the wide-eyed maid, still frozen in place at the door. "That will be all, Alice. Please tell Cook that the boys are ready for breakfast. And send tea to the receiving room for our guest."

Temple raised a brow. "Even if I were a man who drank tea, I know better than to ingest anything you offer me. Ever again." He looked quickly to Alice. "No offense, Alice."

Mara's cheeks went red. Good. She should be embarrassed. She could have killed him with her reckless behavior.

"Thank you, Alice." The girl couldn't have been happier to leave the room.

When she did, Temple spoke. "Mrs. MacIntyre?"

She met him head on. "Yes."

"What happened to Mr. MacIntyre?"

"He was a soldier," she said simply, "killed in action."

He raised a brow. "Where?"

She narrowed her gaze. "Most people are not rude enough to ask."

"I lack breeding."

She scowled. "The Battle of Nsamankow, if you must know."

"Well done. Obscure enough that no one could trace him." He looked around the foyer. "And respectable enough to land you here."

She changed the subject. "I didn't expect you so soon."

"Not enough arsenic in the scotch?"

"It wasn't arsenic," she snapped before lowering her voice. "It was laudanum."

"So you admit you drugged me."

She hesitated. "Yes."

"And, to confirm, it was not the first time?" When she did not reply, he added, "The first time you drugged me and ran, that is."

She exhaled a little huff of irritation before coming forward and taking his arm, ushering him toward the room into which the pig had fled. Her touch was firm and somehow warm even through the wool of his jacket, and he had a fleeting memory of his dream—of her fingers trailing through the drop of wax on his sleeve.

She was unsettling.

No doubt because she was a danger to his life. Both literally and figuratively.

She shut the door, closing them into a clean, unassuming receiving room. A small iron stove stood in the far corner of the space, a fire burning happily inside, warming the piglet who had narrowly escaped certain death only minutes earlier and now appeared to be asleep. On a cushion.

The woman had a pig on a cushion. Named Lavender.

If he hadn't spent his last several conscious hours in a state of surprise, he would have thought the animal strange. Instead, he turned to face the pig's owner, who was pressed against the door of the room.

"I did not exactly *run*," she qualified. "I left you my address. I practically—no. I *definitely* invited you to come after me."

He raised a brow. "How magnanimous of you."

"If you hadn't been so angry—" she began.

He couldn't help but interrupt her. "You think that leaving me unconscious on the floor of my library assuaged my anger?"

"I covered you with a blanket," she defended herself.

"Silly me. Of course, that resolves everything."

She sighed, her strange, compelling gaze meeting his. "I did not mean for it to go the way it did."

"And yet you packed an excess of laudanum for the journey to my home."

"Well, you're a bit larger than most men—I had to be prepared with an excess dosage. And you'd taken my knife."

He raised a brow. "Your sharp tongue will not endear you to me."

She mirrored his expression. "A pity, as I was doing such a good job of it beforehand."

A laugh threatened, and he quashed it. He would not be amused by her.

She was toxic. Toxic was not amusing.

She pressed on. "I do not deny that I deserve a modicum of your anger, but I will not be strong-armed."

"That's the second time you've used that word with me. Need I remind you that for the duration of our acquaintance only one of us has drugged the other? Twice?"

A red wash appeared on her cheeks. Guilt? Impossible. "Nevertheless, it seems an apt description of how you might behave with me, Your Grace."

He wished she'd stop calling him that. He hated the honorific—the way it scraped up his spine, reminding him of all the years he'd longed for it. The years he couldn't have it, even though it was his by right.

Even though he deserved it.

Of course, he hadn't known that.

He hadn't killed her.

The realization remained a shock.

He hadn't known. All those years—he'd lived with the idea that he might have been a killer. All those years.

She'd stolen them from him.

A wave of anger washed through him, hot and uncomfortable. Vengeance had never been his nourishment, and now, even as he could not resist it, he tasted the bitterness of it on his tongue.

He snapped his attention to her. "What happened?"

Her eyes went wide. "I beg your pardon?"

"Twelve years ago, at Whitefawn. On the eve of your wedding. What happened?"

She hesitated. "You don't remember?"

"I was quite drugged. So, no, in fact, I don't remember."

Not for lack of trying. He'd played the evening over and over in his head, hundreds of times, thousands. He remembered scotch. He remembered wanting a woman. Reaching for one. He couldn't picture a face, but he remembered strange eyes and auburn curls and pretty curves and laughter that was half innocence, half sin.

And those eyes. No one could forget those eyes. "I remember you were with me."

She nodded, and pink scored her cheeks again.

He'd known it. It was one of the things he'd never doubted. He'd been young and full of liquor and had never met a woman he couldn't seduce. Of course he'd been with her.

And, suddenly, he wanted to know everything. He moved closer, noting the way she stiffened, pressing back against the door. "And before you set me up—before you faked your death and ran like a coward—we were alone?"

She swallowed, and he couldn't help but watch the muscles of her throat, the way the muscles there betrayed her nerves. Her guilt. "Yes."

She looked down at her skirts. Smoothed them. He noticed she wasn't wearing gloves—same as the prior evening. As in his dream. But now, in the light of day, he saw the marks of work on them: blunt, clean nails; sun-worn skin; and a ghost of a scar on her left hand, just pale enough to have been long healed.

He did not like that scar.

And he did not like that he'd noticed it.

"For how long?"

"Not long."

He exhaled a humorless laugh at that. "Long enough."

Her gaze flew to his, wide and open and filled with . . . something. "Long enough for what?"

"Long enough for you to incapacitate me."

She exhaled, and he knew she'd hidden something from him. He considered her for a long moment, wishing he were in the ring. There, he saw his opponents' vulnerability, open and raw. There, he knew where to strike.

Here, in this strange building, in this strange battle with this strange woman, things were not so easy.

"Tell me one thing. Did you know who I was?" For some reason, it mattered.

Her eyes met his, and there was truth in them, for once. "No."

Of course she hadn't. So what had she done? What had happened in that pretty yellow bedchamber all those years ago?

Dammit.

He understood combat enough to know that she wouldn't tell him. And he understood it enough to know that if he showed his interest, she held the power.

And he'd be damned if he gave her any more power.

Today was his. He changed tack.

"You shouldn't have returned. But since you did, your mistake is my reward. And the world will know the truth about us both."

*M*ara was never so grateful in her life as she was the moment he shifted the conversation away from that long-ago night, and back to the matter at hand. She could handle him here. Now. Angry.

But the moment the present clouded over with past, she lost her nerve, uncertain of how to proceed with this enormous brute of a man and the years that had passed since the last time she'd seen him.

She resisted the thought and returned her attention to the matter at hand. "Then you are ready to negotiate?" Pretending not to be overwhelmed by him, she returned to her desk. Sat. "I shall draft the letter to the *News* today, assuming you are ready to clear the debts in question."

He laughed. "Surely, you did not think it would be so easy."

"I would not say easy." It would not be easy. She'd written the letter a hundred times in her head. A dozen on paper. For years. And it never got easier. "I would say quick, however. Surely that is of interest."

He raised a brow. "I've waited twelve years for this. Neither ease nor quickness is paramount."

She asked the question despite knowing the answer. "Then what is?"

"Retribution."

She huffed a little laugh to cover the way the words unnerved her. "What do you plan to do? Parade me through the streets? Tarred and feathered?"

"The image is not entirely unpleasant." He smiled then, and she imagined he'd smiled that particular smile a hundred times in his club. In his ring. "I do plan to parade you through London. But not tarred and feathered."

Her brows rose. "What, then?"

"Painted. And primped."

She shook her head. "They won't have me."

"Not like the wealthy heiress you once were, no."

They'd barely accepted her then. She'd been a threat to everything they were. Everything they had. The pretty young daughter of a wealthy working man. She might have been rich enough, but she'd never been good enough for them.

"They won't have me in their company."

"They shall do what I say. You see, I am a duke. And, if I remember correctly, while killer dukes are not favored by the doyennes of the *ton*, those of us who have not committed murder tend to be well received." He leaned closer. "Ladies like the idea of dukes." The words were more breath than sound, and Mara resisted the urge to touch the exposed skin of her neck, to at once rub them away and to keep them there. "And you are mine to do with as I please."

Her brows knit together at the words. At the way they spread through her, hot and threatening. "And what is that, precisely?"

"Precisely, whatever I desire."

She stiffened. "I shan't be your mistress."

"First, you are in no position to make such demands. And second, I don't recall offering to have you."

She went hot with embarrassment. "Then what?"

He shrugged, and she hated him in that moment. "I don't trust you anywhere near my sleeping form . . . but they needn't know that."

The words stung. "Mistress in name only?"

He came closer, close enough to feel the heat of him. "Twelve years of lying to my detriment has no doubt made you a convincing actress. It's time to use all that practice to lie for my benefit. As I please."

She straightened her shoulders and tilted her face up to meet his gaze. He was so close—close enough that at another time, in another place, as another woman, she might come up on her toes and press her lips to his.

Where had that thought come from?

She wanted nothing to do with kissing this man.

He was not for kissing. Not anymore.

She pursed her lips. "So you wish to ruin me."

"You ruined my life," he said, all casualness. "I think it only fair, don't you?"

She had been ruined for twelve years—from the moment she'd bloodied the sheets and ran from that room.

She had been ruined before then.

But she'd hidden it well, and she had a houseful of boys to care for. Perhaps her ruin was his due. Perhaps it was hers as well. But she'd be damned if he'd ruin MacIntyre's and the safe haven she'd built for these boys.

"So I will have to leave. Start over."

"You've done it before," he said.

As had he.

Vengeance was a pretty thing, wasn't it?

She straightened her shoulders. "I accept." For a half second, his eyes went wide, and she took pleasure in his shock. Evidently, he'd underestimated her strength and her purpose. "But I've a condition of my own."

Tell him.

The thought came from nowhere.

Tell him Christopher's debt included all the orphanage's funds.

She met his gaze. Cold. Unyielding. Uncaring. Like the eyes of the boys' fathers.

Tell him that what he does threatens the boys.

"I see no reason why I should allow for any of your conditions," he said.

"Because you haven't a choice. I disappeared once. I can do it again."

He watched her for a long moment, the threat hanging between them, his gaze going dark with irritation. With something worse. Something closer to hate. And perhaps he should hate her. She'd crafted him with the skill of a master sculptor, not from marble, but from flesh and blood and fury. "If you ran, I would find you. And I would take no prisoners."

The promise was thick with anger and truth.

He would stop at nothing to exact his vengeance. She was at risk, and everything she loved.

But she would not put the boys at risk.

She threw herself into the fray, already considering her next steps . . . how she would protect the boys, the house, and its legacy if he made good on his promise. She straightened her shoulders, and entered the fray. "If you treat me like a whore, you pay me like one."

The words stung him. She could see it, the blow there and then gone, as though they were in the ring where he reigned. When he did not retaliate, she threw her next punch. "I shall do whatever you ask. However you ask it. I shall play your silly game until you decide to reveal me to the world. Until you decide to send me packing. And when you do, I shall go."

"For your brother's debt."

"For whatever I wish."

One side of his mouth kicked up in a fleeting half smile, and for a moment Mara thought that in another place, in another time, as another woman, she might have enjoyed making him smile.

But right now, she hated it.

"He's not worth you."

"He's not your concern."

"Why? Some kind of sisterly love?" His eyes blackened, and she let him believe it. Anything to keep him from the orphanage. "His is a face badly in need of a fist."

Retribution.

"And yet you will not fight him," she said, feeling angrier than she would have imagined. "Are you afraid to give him a chance?"

He raised a brow, but did not rise to the bait. "I've never been bested."

She smiled. "Did I not best you last night?"

He stilled at the words, then looked up. She saw shock in

his black eyes, in the way they widened just barely for just a moment. She resisted the urge to grin her triumph. "You gloat over drugging me?"

She shook her head. "I gloat over *felling* you. That is the goal, is it not? You owe me the money."

"In the *ring*, Miss Lowe. That is where it counts."

She did smile then, knowing it would annoy him. *Hoping* it would annoy him. "Semantics. You're embarrassed to admit I beat you handily."

"With the help of enough narcotics to take down an ox."

"Nonsense. A horse, maybe. But not an ox. And you are embarrassed. I work with boys, Your Grace. Need I remind you that I know one who is embarrassed when I see one?"

His gaze grew dark and serious again, and he leaned in, closer to her. Close enough for him to tower over her, more than six feet of muscle and bone, power and might, scars and sinew. He smelled of clove and thyme.

Not that she noticed.

And then he whispered, so close to her ear that she felt the words more than heard them as they sent a chill down her spine. "I am no boy."

That much was true.

She opened her mouth to reply, but no words came.

It was his turn to smile. "If you wish to fell me, Miss Lowe, I encourage you to meet me in the ring."

"You will have to pay me for it."

"And if I don't agree? What then? You haven't any choice."

Truth.

"I also haven't anything to lose."

Lie.

"Nonsense," he said. "There's always something else to lose. I assure you. I would find it."

He had her in his trap. She couldn't run. Not without making sure the boys were safe. Not without securing the money that Kit had lost.

She met Temple's black gaze, even as he seemed to read her thoughts. "You could run," he whispered, "but I would find you. And you wouldn't like what happened then."

Damn him.

He wasn't going to agree.

She wanted to scream. Nearly did, until he said, "You won't be the first woman I have paid to do my bidding . . ."

A vision flashed—arms and legs tangled in crisp white sheets, dark hair and black eyes, and more muscle than one man should have.

" . . . but I assure you, Miss Lowe, you will be the last."

The words fell between them, and it took her a moment to refocus her thoughts on them. To realize that he'd agreed. That the orphanage would be saved.

Its price, her ruin. Her life. Her future.

But it would be saved.

Relief was fleeting, interrupted by his low promise. "We begin tonight."

Chapter 4

"*And* who is able to tell me what happened to Napoleon after Waterloo?"

A sea of hands shot up inside the small, well-appointed schoolroom of the MacIntyre Home for Boys. Daniel did not wait to be called upon. "He died!"

Mara chose to ignore the positive glee oozing from the young man as he pronounced the emperor dead. "He did, indeed, die. But I'm looking for the bit before that."

Daniel thought for a moment and then offered, "He ran weeping and wailing from Wellington . . . and died!"

Mara shook her head. "Not quite. Matthew?"

"He rode his horse into a French ditch . . . and died!"

Her lips twitched. "Unfortunately, not." She chose one of the hands straining for the ceiling. "Charles?"

Charles considered the options, then chose, "He shot himself in the foot, it turned green and fell off, and *then* he died?"

Mara did smile then. "You know, gentlemen, I am not certain that I am a very effective teacher."

The hands lowered and a collective grumble went through the room, knowing that they would be required to learn an extra hour of history that day. The boys were saved, however, when a knock sounded, and Alice was silhouetted in the door to the boys' schoolroom. "Pardon me, Mrs. MacIntyre."

Mara lowered the book she held. "Yes?"

"There is . . ." Alice opened her mouth, closed it, then opened it again. "That is . . . someone is here to see you."

Temple.

He was back.

She glanced at the clock in the corner of the room. He'd said *tonight*. As it was still *today*, she could only assume that he was a blackguard and a cheat. And she intended to tell him such.

Just as soon as her heart ceased its racing.

The air seemed to leave the room as she looked over the sea of little faces around her and realized that she was not ready to tell the world the truth. She was not ready to be Mara Lowe again.

She wanted to remain Mrs. MacIntyre, born nowhere, come from nothing, now governess and caretaker to a motley group of boys. Mrs. MacIntyre had purpose. Mrs. MacIntyre had meaning. Mrs. MacIntyre had life.

Mara had nothing.

Nothing but truth.

She forced her legs to move, to carry her through the collection of boys to meet Alice. To face the man who had returned to the house, no doubt with a plan in place to change both their lives. Once at the door, she turned back to her students.

"If I . . ."

No. She cleared her throat. Tried again.

"*When* I return, I expect to hear what happened to Napoleon."

Their collective groan sounded as she pulled the door shut with a snap.

Alice seemed to know better than to say anything on the walk through the dark, narrow hallways. Mara appreciated the young maid's intuition—she was not certain that she would be able to carry on a conversation with her heart pounding and thoughts racing.

He was there. Below. Judge and jury and executioner, all in one.

She descended the stairs slowly, knowing that she would never escape her past, and that she could not avoid her future.

The door to the little study where they'd spoken earlier that morning was ajar, and it occurred to Mara that the two-inch gap between door and jamb was a curious thing— eliciting excitement or dread depending upon the situation.

She ignored the fact that somehow, in this moment, it elicited both.

He was not even a little bit exciting; he was entirely dreadful.

She took a deep breath, willing her heart to cease pounding, and released Alice from duty with a halfhearted smile— the most she could manage under the circumstances—before pushing the door open to face the man inside the room.

"You saw him."

She stepped inside and closed the door firmly. "What are you doing here?"

Her brother came toward her. "What are you doing approaching that man?"

"I asked first," she said, meeting him at the center of the room in two short strides. "We agreed you'd never come here. You should have sent a note." It was the way they'd met for the past twelve years. Never in this building, and never anywhere that she might be recognized.

"We also agreed we'd never tell that man that you were alive and living right under his nose."

"He has a name, Kit."

"Not one he uses."

"He has one he uses, as well." *Temple.* It wasn't hard to think of him that way. Big as one, and as unmoving.

Had he always been unmoving? She hadn't known him

when they were young, but his reputation had preceded him—and no one had ever called him cold. A rake, a rogue, a scoundrel, certainly. But never cold. Never angry.

She'd done that to him.

Kit ran a hand through already disheveled brown locks, and Mara recognized the weariness in him. Two years younger, her brother had been filled with life as a child, eager for excitement, and ready with a plan.

And then she'd run, ruining Temple and leaving Kit to pick up the pieces of their unbearably foolish evening. And he'd changed. They'd traded secret letters for years, until she'd resurfaced, hidden in plain sight, Mrs. MacIntyre, widowed proprietress of the MacIntyre Home for Boys.

But he'd been different. Colder. Harsher.

Never speaking of the life she'd left him to. Of the man she'd left him with.

And then he'd gone and lost all her money.

She noted the hunch of his shoulders and the hollows in his cheeks and the scuff on his normally pristine black boots, and she recognized that he at least understood their predicament. *Her* predicament. She let out a little sigh. "Kit . . ."

"I wish you wouldn't call me that," he snapped. "I'm not a boy anymore."

"I know." It was all she could think to say.

"You shouldn't have gone to see him. Do you know what they call him?"

She raised her brows. "They call him that because of me."

"It doesn't mean he hasn't come to deserve it. I don't want you near him again."

Too late.

"You don't want?" she said, suddenly irrevocably irritated. "You haven't a choice. The man holds all our money and all the cards. And I've done what I can to save the home."

Kit scowled. "It's always the home. Always the boys."

Of course it was. They were the important part. They were what she'd done right. They were her good.

But it wasn't worth fighting Kit. "How did you even know he was here?"

He narrowed his gaze on her. "Do you think I am an idiot? I pay the whore in the street good money to look out for you."

"To look out for me? Or to keep track of me?"

"She saw the Killer Duke. Sent word to me."

Anger flared at the idea that her brother would spy on her. "I don't need protection."

"Of course you do. You always have."

She bit back the retort—that she'd faced more demons than he had, for years. Alone. And returned to the matter at hand. "Kit—" She stopped. Reframed. "Christopher, I went to him because we needed it. You . . ." She hesitated, not knowing quite how to say the words. Spreading her hands wide, she tried again. "You lost *everything*."

Christopher pushed his fingers through his hair once more, the move violent and unsettling. "You think I don't *know that*? Christ, Mara!" His tone was raised, and she was instantly, keenly aware of where they were—of the name he'd used. She looked to the door, confirming it was closed.

He did not care. "Of course I know it! I lost everything he left me."

Everything of hers as well. Scraped together and stupidly entrusted to his keeping. But all that was nothing compared to the funds that had been set aside to run the orphanage. Every cent the men had left with their sons.

He'd told her his bank would protect the funds. Grow them, perhaps. But she was a woman and without proof of her marriage or her husband's death, and so her brother had made the deposits.

Her brother, who couldn't stop gaming.

Anger flared, even as she wished it wouldn't. Even as she wished she were sixteen again, able to comfort her younger, gentler, sweeter brother, without hating the man he'd become. Without judging his transgressions.

"You don't know what it was like to live in his shadow," he said.

Their father. The man who had unwittingly set them all on this path. Rich as Croesus and never satisfied. He'd always wanted more. Always better. He'd wanted a son smarter and bolder and braver and cleverer.

He'd wanted a duchess for a daughter.

And he'd received neither.

Kit laughed, bitterly. "He's no doubt watching from his perch in Hell, devastatingly disappointed."

She shook her head. "He doesn't own us any longer."

Her brother's gaze met hers. "Of course he does. Without him, none of this would have happened. You wouldn't have run. I wouldn't have gamed. I wouldn't have lost." He raised a long arm, pointed in the direction of the street. "You wouldn't live among waifs and whores—" He stopped. Took a breath. "Why did you go to him?"

"He holds our debt."

Kit's gaze narrowed. "What did he say?"

She hesitated. He wouldn't like it.

"What did you agree to?" he pressed. She heard the irritation in his tone. The frustration.

"What do you think I agreed to?"

"You sold yourself."

If only it had been so simple. "I told him I would show myself. Return him to society."

He considered the words, and for a moment, she thought he might protest. But she had forgotten that desperate men turned mercenary. "And I get my money back?"

She heard the pronouns. Hated them. "It's not only your money."

He scoffed. "What was yours was minimal."

"What was the orphanage's was enough to run the place for a year. Maybe longer."

"I've a great deal to worry about, Mara. I'm not about to worry over your whelps, too."

"They're children! They rely upon me for everything!"

He sighed, clearly through with her. "Did you get my money back or not?"

It did not matter to him that she would lose everything. This life she'd built. This place that had kept her safe. Given her purpose. He didn't care, as long as his money was returned.

And so she did what she was so good at.

She lied.

"Not."

Fury crossed his handsome face. "You made a deal with the devil and you get nothing in return? What good are you? What good was this?" His lips twisted in irritation as he paced the room. "You've ruined everything!"

Her gaze narrowed on her brother. "I did what had to be done. He isn't going to fight you, Kit. Now, at least, he will leave you alone."

Kit turned and tossed a chair out of the way, the furniture crashing against the wall and splintering into a dozen pieces. Mara stilled.

The anger was familiar.

In all senses of the word.

She stepped behind her desk, pressing her knuckles to the desktop, hiding the shaking of her hands.

She was losing control of the situation.

Perhaps she deserved it. Perhaps this was what happened to women who tried to take fate into their own hands. She'd done just that, changed her future. Changed her life. Lived it for twelve years.

But now it was time to let Kit live his. "This is the deal we struck. Your only chance at honor is my agreeing to admit what I did. I brought the man to my room. I drugged him. I bloodied the damn sheets." She shook her head. "*I* ran. It is *I* who require forgiveness. *I* who can give him retribution. And he knows it."

"And what of me?"

"He is not interested in you."

Christopher went to the window and looked out on the cold November afternoon. He was quiet for a long moment before whispering, "He should be. He doesn't know what I could do."

The sun sinking into the western sky turned his brown locks gold, and Mara recalled a long-ago afternoon at their childhood home in Bristol, Kit laughing and running along the edge of a little pond near their house, pulling a new toy boat behind him.

He'd tripped on a tree root and fallen, releasing the string attached to the boat to catch himself, and the high wind had carried the boat out to the middle of the pond, where it promptly capsized and sank.

They'd been beaten for their transgressions, then sent to bed without supper—Kit, because he hadn't seen fit to rescue the boat, which had cost their father money, and Mara, because she'd had the gall to remind their father that neither of his children was able to swim.

It was not the first time Kit had been unlucky, nor was it the first time she had tried to protect him from their father's scorn.

It was also not the last.

But today, she was not protecting him. Today, she was protecting something much more important. And she did not trust him to be a part of her plan. "You remain free of this."

"And if I don't?"

She opened the door to the room with a quick snap, indicating that she was done with the conversation. "You haven't a choice."

He turned to face her, and for a moment the light played tricks with her. For a moment, he looked like their father. "You in the hands of the Killer Duke? He and his club have taken everything I own. I'm supposed to simply allow it? What of my money?"

Not what of *you*. Not what of *my sister*.

The omission should not have surprised her, and yet it did. But she held back her surprise and lifted her chin. "Money isn't everything."

"Oh, Mara," he said, sounding older and wiser than she'd ever heard him. "Of course it is."

The lesson of their father, burned into them.

He met her gaze. "I am not free of this. And now, neither are you."

Truth at last.

*H*ours later, Lavender on a cushion at her feet, Mara was attempting to focus on her work when Lydia Baker stepped into her small office and said, "I'm tired of pretending as though I have not noticed."

Mara attempted surprise, turning wide eyes on her closest friend. "I beg your pardon?"

"Do not pretend to misunderstand me," Lydia said, seating herself in a small wooden chair on the opposite side of Mara's escritoire, and patted her lap to get Lavender's attention. The piglet raised her head, considered the human, and decided to remain on her pillow. "That pig doesn't like me."

Mara grasped at the change in topic. "That pig spent half the morning running from a dozen maniacal boys."

"Better than a farmer with an axe." Lydia narrowed her gaze on the beast.

Lavender sighed.

Mara laughed.

Lydia returned her attention to Mara. "For seven years, we've worked side by side, and I've never once asked you about your past."

Mara sat back in her chair. "A fact for which I am ever grateful."

Lydia raised a blond brow and waved one deceivingly delicate hand in the air. "If it had only been the man who visited this afternoon, I might have ignored it. But combined with this *morning's* visitor, I'm through with not asking. Dukes change everything."

No doubt *that* was the understatement of the century.

Lydia leaned forward, tapping the edge of the letter in her hand on the desk with perfect rhythm. "I may work at an orphanage, Margaret, but I am not completely unaware of the world beyond the door. The enormous man who arrived at the crack of dawn was the Duke of Lamont." She paused, then qualified, "The *Killer* Duke of Lamont."

Lord, she was coming to hate that moniker.

"He's not a killer." The words were out before Mara could stop them—before she could realize that they were a tacit admission that she knew the man in question.

She pressed her lips together in a thin line as Lydia's eyes went wide with interest. "Isn't he?"

Mara considered her next words carefully. She settled on "No."

Lydia waited for Mara to continue for a long moment, her blond curls wild and unruly, barely contained by the two dozen pins shoved into the nest. When Mara said nothing more, her first employee and the closest thing she could call a friend sat back in her own chair, crossed her legs, rested her hands in her lap, and said, "He wasn't here to deliver a child."

It was not unheard of for men of the aristocracy to arrive toting their illegitimate sons. "No."

Lydia nodded. "He was not here to *retrieve* one."

Mara set her pen into its holder. "No."

"And he was not here to make a generous, exorbitantly summed donation to the orphanage."

One side of Mara's mouth kicked up. "No."

Lydia cocked her head. "Do you think you might convince him to do so?"

Mara laughed. "He is not in a generous spirit when I am near, sadly."

"Ah. So he was not here for anything relating to the orphanage."

"No."

"Which means he was here because of your second visitor of the day."

Alarm shot through Mara as she met her friend's eyes. "I don't understand."

"Liar," Lydia replied. "Your second caller was Mr. Christopher Lowe. Very wealthy, as I understand it, having inherited a glorious fortune from his dead father."

Mara pressed her lips into a thin line. "Not wealthy anymore."

Lydia cocked her head. "No. I hear he's lost everything to the man who killed *his sister*."

"He didn't kill—" Mara stopped. *Lydia knew.*

"Mmm." Lydia brushed a speck of lint from her skirt. "You seem very sure of that."

"I am."

Lydia nodded. "How long have you known the Duke of Lamont?"

There it was—the question that would change everything. The question that would bring her out of hiding and reveal her to the world.

She was going to have to start telling the truth at some point. She should consider it a gift of sorts that she could begin with Lydia. Except telling her closest friend, who had trusted her for seven long years, that she had been lying all that time was about the most difficult thing she'd ever done.

Mara took a breath. Let it out. "Twelve years."

Lydia nodded slowly. "Since he killed Lowe's sister?"

Since he supposedly killed me.

It should have been easy to say it. Lydia knew more about Mara than anyone in the world. She knew about Mara's life, her work, her thoughts, her plans. She had come to work for Mara as a young, untried governess to a motley group of boys, sent from a large estate in Yorkshire—the one where Mara had herself hidden all those years ago.

Lydia lowered her voice, her tone gentle. Accepting. Filled with friendship. "We all have secrets, Margaret."

"That's not my name," Mara whispered.

"Of course it isn't," Lydia said, and the simple words proved to be Mara's undoing. Tears sprang to her eyes and Lydia smiled, leaning forward. "You no more grew up on a farm in Shropshire than Lavender will."

Mara huffed a little laugh in the direction of the pig, who snorted in her sleep. "A farm in Shropshire would quite suit her."

Lydia grinned. "Nonsense. She is a spoiled little porker who sleeps on a stuffed pillow and is fed from the table. She would care for neither the weather, nor the slop." Her eyes grew large and filled with sympathy. "If not Shropshire, then where?"

Mara looked to the desk where she'd worked for seven years, every day hoping that these questions would never come. She spoke to the papers there. "Bristol."

Lydia nodded. "You don't sound like you were raised on the Bristol docks."

A vision of the enormous house where she'd spent her youth flashed. Her father used to say that he could buy Britain if he'd wanted to, and he'd built a house to prove that fact to the rest of the world. The house had been gilded and painted, filled with oils and marbles that made the Elgins look minuscule. He'd been particularly fond of portraits, filling every inch of wall with the faces of strangers. *Someday, I'll replace them with my own family*, he used to say every time he hung a new one.

The house had been exorbitant at best, outrageous at worst.

And it had been the only thing he'd loved.

"I wasn't."

"And the duke?" Lydia knew. No doubt.

"I . . ." Mara paused, chose her next words carefully. "I met him. Once."

Not false, and yet somehow not true. *Met* wasn't precisely the word she would use to describe her interactions with him. The hour had been late, the night dark, the situation desperate. And she'd taken advantage of him. Briefly.

Long enough.

"On the eve of your wedding."

She had dreaded this moment for twelve years—had feared that it would destroy her. And yet, as she stood on the precipice of admitting the truth for the first time in twelve years—of being honest with her friend and, somehow, with the universe, she did not hesitate. "Yes."

Lydia nodded. "He didn't kill you."

"No."

Lydia waited.

Mara shook her head, rubbing her forearm absently. "I never meant for it to look so . . . dire." She'd meant to bloody her sheets. To make it look like she'd been ruined. Like she'd run off with a man. He was to have escaped before anyone saw what had happened. But there'd been too much laudanum. And too much blood.

There was a long moment while Lydia considered the words. She turned the envelope in her hand over and over, and Mara could not help but watch the small ecru rectangle flip again and again. "I can't remember your name."

"Mara."

"Mara." Lydia repeated, testing the name. "*Mara.*"

Mara nodded, pleasure coursing through her at the sound of her name on someone's lips. Pleasure and not a little bit of fear.

No going back now.

Finally, Lydia smiled, bright and honest. "It's *very* nice to meet you."

Mara caught her breath at the words, at the way they

flooded her with relief. "When he gets his way, I shall be found out."

Lydia met her gaze evenly, knowing what the words meant. Knowing that Mara would be run out of London. That the orphanage would lose everything if she were linked to it. Knowing that she would have to leave. "And will he get his way?"

Retribution.

The man would not stop until he did so. But she had plans as well. This life she'd built might be over, but she would not leave without ensuring the boys' security. "Not without my getting a way of my own as well."

Lydia's lips kicked up in a wry smile. "Just as I expected."

"I understand if you want away from here. If you want to leave."

Lydia shook her head. "I don't wish to leave."

Mara smiled. "Good. As this place will need you when I am gone."

Lydia nodded. "I will be here."

The clock in the hallway beyond chimed, as if marking the moment's importance. The sound shook them from the moment. "Now that that's done," Lydia said, extending the envelopes she held to Mara, "perhaps you'd like to tell me why you are receiving missives from a gaming hell?"

Mara's eyes went wide as she took the offered envelope, and turned it over in her hands. On the front, in deep black, close-to-illegible scrawl, was her name and direction. On the back, a stunning silver seal, marked with a delicate female angel, lithe and lovely with wings that spanned the wax.

The seal was unfamiliar.

Mara brought it closer, for inspection.

Lydia spoke. "The seal is from The Fallen Angel."

Mara looked up, heart suddenly pounding. "The duke's club."

Blue eyes lit with excitement. "The most exclusive

gaming hell in London, where half of the aristocracy wagers an obscene fortune each night." Lydia lowered her voice. "I hear that the members need only ask for what they want—however extravagant or lascivious or impossible to acquire—and the club provides."

Mara rolled her eyes. "If it's impossible to acquire, how does the club acquire it?"

Lydia shrugged. "I imagine they are quite powerful men."

A memory flashed of Temple's broad shoulders and broken nose, of the way he commanded her into his home. Of the way he negotiated the terms of their agreement.

"I imagine so," she said, sliding a finger under the silver wax and opening the letter.

Two words were scrawled across the paper—two words, surrounded by an enormous amount of wasted space. It would never occur to her to use paper so extravagantly. Apparently, economy was not at the forefront of Temple's mind—except, perhaps, for economy of language.

Nine o'clock.

That was it. No signature, not that she required one. It had been a dozen years since someone had exhibited such imperious control over her.

"I do not think I like this duke of yours very much." Lydia was leaning across the desk, neck craned to see the note.

"As he is not my duke, I have little problem with that."

"You intend to go?"

She had made an arrangement. This was her punishment. Her penance.

Her only chance.

Ignoring the question, she set the paper aside, her gaze falling to the second envelope. "That's much less interesting," Lydia said.

It was a bill, Mara knew without opening it. "How much?"

"Two pounds, sixteen. For coal."

More than they had in the coffers. And if November was any indication of what was to come, the winter would only get colder. Anger and frustration and panic threatened, but Mara swallowed back the emotion.

She would regain control.

She reached for the duke's terse note, turning the paper over and going for her pen, dipping the nib carefully in ink before she replied.

£10.

She returned the note to its envelope, heart in her throat, full of power. He might dictate the terms, but she dictated the price. And ten pounds would keep the boys of MacIntyre House warm for a year.

She crossed out her name on the envelope and wrote in his before handing it back to Lydia.

"We'll discuss the bill tomorrow."

Chapter 5

A dressmaker. He'd brought her to a dressmaker.

In the dead of night, as though it was a crime to buy new gowns.

Of course, in the dead of night, creeping through the back door to one of Bond Street's most legendary modistes, it did feel a bit criminal. As criminal as the shiver of pleasure that threaded through her as she brushed past him into the sewing room of the shop, unable to avoid contact with him—big as an ox.

Not that she noticed.

Nor did she notice that he was far too agile for his size, leaping up and down from carriages, opening doors—holding them for her entry with quiet smoothness—as though he were a ballet dancer and not a boxer.

As though grace had been imparted to him in the womb.

But she refused to notice all that, even when her heart pounded as the door closed behind him, his bulk crowding her further into the room, its half-dozen lanterns doing little more than cast shadows around the space.

"Why are we here?"

"You needn't whisper. Hebert knows we are coming."

She cut him a look. "Does she know why?"

He did not meet her eyes, instead heading through the shop, weaving in and out of the empty seamstress stations. "I would imagine she thinks I want to dress a woman and I'd like to keep the situation secret."

She followed. "Do you do this often?"

He stopped, and she nearly ran into the back of him before he looked over his shoulder at her. "I've little reason to keep women secret."

A vision flashed, young, handsome Temple full of bold smiles and even bolder touches, tempting her with broad shoulders and black eyes. He needn't keep them secret. No doubt, women fell over themselves to assume the role. She cast the thought aside. "I don't imagine you do."

"Thanks in large part to you," he said, and pushed through a heavy curtain into the dressing room, leaving her to follow.

She should have expected the reminder that his life had been something else before it was this. He'd been the son and heir to one of the wealthiest, most revered dukedoms in Britain. And now he might still have the wealth, but he spent it in shadows. He had lost the reverence.

Because of her.

She swallowed back the twinge of guilt she felt at the thought, and instead hovered at the exit. "When do I receive my funds?"

"When our agreement is fulfilled."

"How am I to know that you will keep your word?"

He considered her for a long moment, and she had the keen sense that she should not have questioned his honor. "You shall have to trust me."

She scowled. "I've never met an aristocratic male worthy of trust." She'd met them desperate and angry and abusive and lascivious and filled with disgust. But never honorable.

"Then you should be grateful that I am rarely considered aristocratic," he replied, and turned away from her, the conversation complete.

She followed him into the dressing room of Madame Hebert's, where the proprietress was already waiting, as though she had nothing better to do in all the world than stand here and wait for the Duke of Lamont to arrive.

His words, still echoing in her ears, proved true inside the salon. She wasn't here for the Duke of Lamont. She was here for one of the powerful owners of London's most legendary gaming hell.

"Temple," Madame Hebert welcomed him, coming forward to rise up on her toes and deposit kisses on both of his cheeks. "You great, handsome beast. Were it anyone else, I would have denied the request." She smiled, the pleasure in the expression matching the tenor of her rich French accent. "But I cannot resist you."

Mara resisted the urge to wrinkle her nose as a chuckle rumbled from Temple's chest. "You cannot resist Chase."

Hebert laughed, the sound like fine crystal. "Well, a businesswoman must know where—as you English say— her bread is buttered." Mara bit her tongue rather than ask if Temple hadn't sent a fair number of customers in the dressmaker's direction himself. She did not care to know.

And then Mara couldn't speak, because the modiste's dark gaze flickered to her, eyes going wide. "This one is beautiful."

No one had ever described her as such. Well, perhaps someone once . . . a lifetime ago . . . but no one since that night she'd run.

Another thing that had changed.

The dressmaker was wrong. Mara was twenty-eight, with work-hewn hands and more lines around her eyes than she'd like to admit. She wasn't painted or primped or pretty like the women she'd seen at The Fallen Angel that night, nor was she petite the way ladies in style were, or soft-spoken the way they should be.

And she certainly wasn't gorgeous.

She opened her mouth, ready to refute the label, but

Temple was already speaking, chasing the compliment away with his lack of acknowledgment. "She needs dressing."

Mara shook her head. "I don't need dressing."

The Frenchwoman was already moving to light a series of candles surrounding a small platform at the center of the dressing room, as though Mara hadn't spoken. "Remove your cloak, please." The dressmaker cast a quick look in Temple's direction. "An entire trousseau?"

"A half-dozen gowns. Another six day dresses."

"I don't—" Mara began before Madame Hebert cut her off.

"That won't see her through two weeks."

"She won't need more than two weeks' worth."

Mara's gaze narrowed. "*She* is still present, is she not? In this room?"

The dressmaker's brows rose in surprise. "*Oui*, Miss—"

Temple spoke. "You don't need to know her name yet."

Yet. That single, small word that held so much meaning. Someday, the dressmaker would know her name and her history. But not tonight, and not tomorrow, as she draped and crafted the gowns that would be Mara's ruin.

Hebert had finished lighting the candles, each new flame adding to the lovely golden pool into which Mara could only guess she was supposed to enter. Reaching into a deep pocket, the dressmaker extracted a measure and turned to Mara. "Miss. The coat. It must go."

Mara did not move.

"Take it off," Temple said, the words menacing in the darkness as he removed his own greatcoat and relaxed onto a nearby settee, placing one ankle on the opposite knee and draping the massive grey cloak across his lap. His face was cast in the room's shadows.

Mara laughed, a short, humorless sound. "I suppose you think it is that simple? You command and women simply jump to do your bidding?"

"When it comes to the removal of ladies' clothing, it

often works that way, yes." The words oozed from him, and Mara wanted to stomp her foot.

Instead, she took a deep breath and attempted to regain control. She extracted a little black book and a pencil from the deep pocket of her skirts and said, "How much does disrobing typically cost you?"

He looked as though he'd swallowed a great big insect. She would have laughed, if she weren't so infuriated. Once he collected himself he said, "Fewer than ten pounds."

She smiled. "Oh, was I unclear? That was the starting price of the evening."

She opened the book, pretending to consider the blank page there. "I should think that dress fittings are another . . . five, shall we say?"

He barked his laughter. "You're getting a selection of the most coveted gowns in London and I'm to pay you for it?"

"One cannot eat dresses, Your Grace," she pointed out, using her very best governess voice.

It worked. "One pound."

She smiled. "Four."

"Two."

"Three and ten."

"*Two* and ten."

"Two and sixteen."

"You are a professional fleecer."

She smiled and turned to her book, light with excitement. She'd expected no more than two. "Two and sixteen it is." The coal bill was paid.

"Go on then," he said. "Off with the coat."

She returned the book to her pocket. "You are a prince among men, truly." She removed her coat, marching it over to where he sat and draping it over the arm of the settee. "Shall I dispense with my dress as well?"

"Yes." The answer came from the dressmaker, feet behind them, and Mara could have sworn she saw surprise flash through Temple's gaze before it turned to humor.

She stuck one of her fingers out to hover around the tip of his nose. "Don't you dare laugh."

One black brow rose. "And if I did?"

"If I'm to measure you, miss, I need you wearing as little as possible. Perhaps if it were summer and the dress were cotton, but now . . ." She did not have to finish. It was late November and bitterly cold already. And Mara was wearing both a wool chemise and a wool dress.

She placed her hands on her hips, facing Temple. "Turn around."

He shook his head. "No."

"I did not give you permission to humiliate me."

"Nevertheless, I purchased it," he said, easing back onto the settee. "Relax. Hebert has impeccable taste. Let her drape you in silks and satins, and let me pay for it."

"You think three pounds makes me malleable?"

"I do not pretend to think you shall ever be malleable. But I expect you to honor our arrangement. Your word." He paused. "And think—when all is said and done, you'll have a dozen new frocks."

"A gentleman would allow me my modesty."

"I have been labeled a scoundrel more often than not."

It was her turn to raise a brow. "I do believe that over the course of our acquaintance, I shall call you much, much worse."

He did laugh then. A warm, rich promise in the dim light. A sound she should not have liked so much. "No doubt." His voice lowered. "Surely you're strong enough to suffer my presence while you're in your underclothes. You've a chaperone, even."

The man was infuriating. Utterly, completely infuriating. And she wanted to hit him. No. That was too easy. She wanted to addle him. To best him in this battle of wits . . . in this game of words that he no doubt won any time he played. Because it wasn't enough that Temple was strong in the ring. He had to be strong out of the ring as well—not agile simply with bones and sinew, but with thought and word.

She'd spent a lifetime under men's control. When she was a child, her father had made it impossible for her to live as she liked, dictating her every deed with his army of spying servants and cloying nannies and treasonous governesses. He'd been ready to sell her off to a man three times her age who would have no doubt been just as domineering, and so she'd run.

But even when she'd run, even as she'd found a life in the wilds of Yorkshire and then in the sullied streets of London, she'd never escaped the specter of those men. She'd never been able to shake off their control—and they did control her, even as they didn't know it. They overpowered her with fear—fear of being discovered and forced back into that life she'd so desperately wanted to escape. Fear of losing herself. Fear of losing everything for which she had worked.

Everything for which she had fought.

Everything she had risked.

And now, even as she promised herself she would get what it was she wanted, she could not escape the feeling that this man was another in a long line of men who wielded power like a weapon. Yes, he wished retribution, and perhaps it was his due. And yes, she might have agreed to his demands and turned herself over to him, and yes, she would honor her word and their agreement, but she would have to face herself when all was said and done.

And she would be damned if she would fear him, too.

He was smug, and self-important, and she badly wished to give him a dressing-down.

Even if it meant she would be the one dressing down.

Perhaps she shouldn't have said the words. Perhaps she should have held them back. Perhaps, if she hadn't been so very irritated with him, she would have. Perhaps if she had known what would come once he heard the words . . . she would have held her tongue.

But it didn't matter. Because instead of not saying them, she turned away, marched back to that golden pool of light, and took her place on the platform there before facing him once more, and allowing the modiste access to the buttons and fastenings on her dress.

She stared, unblinking, into the darkness, where she imagined a look of arrogant triumph spread across his face, and said them anyway.

"I suppose it shouldn't matter. After all, it is not the first time you've seen my underclothes."

Everything froze. She couldn't have said what he thought she'd said. She couldn't have *meant* what he thought she meant.

Except she clearly did, for the smug look on her face, the dancing sparkle in her knowing gaze, as though she had been waiting a lifetime to set him on his heels.

And perhaps she had.

He snapped forward in his seat, both feet firmly on the ground, the residual glow from the candles casting him in light. "What did you say?"

She raised a brow, and he knew she was mocking him. "Is there a problem with your hearing, Your Grace?"

She was the most disastrous, damaging, difficult woman he'd ever know. She made him want to upturn the dainty, velvet furniture in this utterly feminine place, and tear the clothes from his back in irritation.

He was about to stand and intimidate her into repeating herself—into explaining herself—when the fastenings of her dress came loose, and the frock fell to her feet in a remarkable, fluid swoosh, leaving her standing there in her pale wool chemise, unadorned corset, and little else.

And then he couldn't move at all.

Goddammit.

The Frenchwoman circled Mara, considering her for a

long moment while Temple attempted to find his speech.

Hebert found hers first. "She will require lingerie as well."

Temple disagreed. Mara did not require undergarments at all. In fact, he'd prefer she never wore another stitch of unmentionables again.

Or anything else, for that matter.

Good Lord.

She was perfect.

She was also lying.

For if he had seen her in her underclothes—in anything close to the things she wore now—he would remember.

He would remember the slope of her breasts, the spray of freckles across them, the way they curved in pretty, plump rounds topped with . . . he couldn't see, but he knew that her nipples were very likely as gloriously well-formed as the rest of her breasts.

He would remember those breasts.

Wouldn't he?

It is not the first time you've seen me in my underclothes.

He closed his eyes against the frustration that flared—the recollection that would not come. There had been a woman, one he'd thought was more muse than memory. More piece-meal than not.

Wide smile. Strange, intoxicating eyes.

"Is it red?"

The modiste's words were like gunfire in the dark, quiet room. They startled Mara as well. "I beg your pardon?"

"Your hair," Hebert replied. "Candlelight plays tricks on the eye. But it is red, no?"

Mara shook her head. "It's brown."

A silken waterfall of auburn curls.

"It's auburn," Temple said.

"You do not seem the kind of man to notice the differ-ence," she said, refusing to look at him, her eyes instead tracking the slender Frenchwoman now kneeling at her feet.

"I notice more than you could imagine."

That hair had flickered in his memory for twelve years. There had been countless points when he'd decided it wasn't real. In his darkest moments, he'd thought he'd fabricated it. Her. Something good to remember of that night.

But she'd been real.

He'd known Mara was the key to that night. That she remembered more than he did. That she was his only chance at piecing together his fall. But it had never occurred to him that she'd been with him for longer than it took to destroy him.

Perhaps she hadn't. Perhaps it was a lie. Perhaps she'd drugged him and left him to distract the world while she ran from God knew what to God knew where, and those teasing words were her latest attempt at torture.

It wasn't a lie.

He knew that as well as he knew anything.

But somehow, knowing the truth made everything worse. Because she hadn't left him with no memory of the night.

She'd left him with no memory of her.

He had to pull himself together. To regain the upper hand. He forced himself to lean back against the settee, refusing to allow her to see that she'd riled him. "For example, I notice that you never wear gloves."

As if on strings, her hands came together, clasping tight. "When one works for a living . . . one can't."

But she hadn't been required to work. She could have been a duchess.

He wanted answers. Itched for them.

"All the governesses I've ever known have worn them." He tracked the movement of her hands, knowing that they were well-hewn, the skin rough in places, the knuckles red with cold. They were hands that knew work.

He knew, because his hands looked the same.

As though she could hear his thoughts, she unclasped the hands in question, holding them straight and still at her sides. "I am not an ordinary governess."

No doubt. "I never imagined you an ordinary anything."

Madame Hebert stood then, excusing herself and leaving them alone in the room. For long moments, Mara stood silent before saying, "I feel a bit like a sacrificial offering up here."

He could see why. The platform was cast in a warm golden glow, the rest of the room in utter darkness. In her awkward, pale underclothes, she could have easily played the part of the unsuspecting virgin, about to be tossed into a volcano.

Virgin.

The word gave him pause.

Had they—

The question dissolved into a vision of her spread across crisp linen sheets, long, lithe limbs spread wide, perfect and nude. His mouth went dry at the thought, at the image of her splayed open to him, then watered as he considered where he would start with her . . . the long column of her neck, the slope of her breasts, the swell of her belly, the secrets nestled between what he knew would be long, perfect thighs.

He would start there.

He stood, coming toward her, unable to keep himself from it, as though reeled in on a long, sturdy fishing line. She wrapped her arms about her midsection as he approached, and he noticed the gooseflesh on them.

He could warm her.

"Are you cold?" he asked.

"Yes," she said, smartly, "I'm half naked."

It was a lie. She wasn't cold. She was nervous. "I don't think so."

She cut him a look. "Why don't you take off your clothes and see how you feel?"

The words were out before she had a chance to think on them. Before she—or he, if he were honest—realized what they might evoke. Curiosity. Frustration. More. He stopped just short of the pool of light where she stood, unable to hide her face. "Have I done that before?" he asked, the words coming harsher than he intended. Filled with more meaning than he expected.

She looked down at her feet. He followed the gaze, taking in her stockinged toes. When she did not answer, he pressed further. "I woke naked that morning. Naked and covered in someone else's blood. A damn lot of it," he said, though the blood didn't seem to matter so very much. He stepped into the light. "Not your blood."

She shook her head, finally looking up at him. "Not mine."

"Whose?"

"Pig's blood."

"Why?"

"I didn't mean—"

Dammit. He didn't want apologies. He wanted the truth. "Enough. Where were my clothes?"

She shook her head again. "I don't know. I gave them to—"

"To your brother, no doubt. But why?"

"We—I—" She hesitated. "I thought that if you were naked, it would postpone your looking for me. It would give me more time to get away."

"Is that it?" He was horrified to discover that the explanation disappointed him. What had he been expecting? That she'd confess a deep, abiding attraction to him?

Perhaps.

No. Goddammit. She was trouble.

He didn't know what he wanted from this woman any longer. "I was naked, Mara. I remember your hair, down. Your body above me." She blushed in the candlelight, and then he knew precisely what he wanted. He stepped up, crowding her on the little round platform, but somehow—by the grace of something far more divine than either of them deserved—not touching her. "Did we—"

"*Excusez moi*, Your Grace."

He did not hesitate, did not move. Did not look back. "A moment, Hebert."

The Frenchwoman knew better than to linger.

He snaked an arm around Mara's waist, hating himself for the weakness in the movement. He pulled her close, her breasts pressed tight against his chest, as their torsos met. Their thighs.

She gasped, but there was no fear in the sound.

Dear God, she wasn't afraid of him. When was the last time he'd held a woman who did not fear him?

The last time he'd held her.

"Did we, Mara?" He spoke in a low whisper at her ear, his lips close enough to brush the soft curve of it, the warm skin. He couldn't resist taking that lobe in his mouth, worrying it with his teeth until she shivered with pleasure.

Not fear.

"Did we fuck?"

She stiffened at the word, hot and wicked at the sensitive skin of her neck, and a thread of guilt shot through him even as he refused to acknowledge it. Even as he refused to feel regret insulting her.

Not that he needed to.

The woman fought her own battles. She turned her own head then, and matched him measure for measure, pressing her soft lips to his ear, kissing once, twice, softly, before biting the lobe and sending a river of desire through him. Good Lord, he wanted this woman like he'd never wanted anything in his life. Even as he knew she was poison.

Even as she proved it, lifting her lips from him, making him desperate for their return, and saying, "If I tell you, will you forgive the debt?"

She was the most skilled opponent he'd ever faced.

Because in that moment, he actually considered doing it. Forgiving it all and letting her run. And perhaps he would have, if she could have restored his memory.

But she'd taken that, too.

"Oh, Mara," he said, releasing her in a slow slide, fury and something startlingly close to disappointment threading through him. He harnessed one and ignored the other. "Nothing you could say will make me forgive."

He spun off the little platform, calling for Hebert as he retreated into the darkness.

The modiste entered again, a pile of satin and lace in her hands, and approached Mara. "*Mademoiselle, s'il vous plaît*," she said, indicating that Mara should put the dress on. Mara hesitated, but Temple saw the way she eyed the frock as though she hadn't eaten for days and there, in the French-woman's hands, was food.

Once she was headfirst inside it, her arms swimming through fabric to find egress, he caught his breath and his sanity and looked to the dressmaker. "I don't want her in another's clothes. I want everything made. By you."

Madame Hebert gave Temple a quick look. "Of course. The dress is for style. You indicated a desire to approve the collection."

Mara gave a yelp of disagreement at that, her head finally poking out into the light. "It is not enough that you humiliate me by remaining in attendance as I am fitted? You must choose the gown as well?"

Hebert was already adjusting the fall of the gown and fastening it up the back, affording Temple a view of Mara in the mauve concoction, slightly too tight in the bodice and slightly too loose in the waist, but a gown nonetheless.

He'd never put much credence into the idea that frocks could make a woman more beautiful. Women were women; if they were attractive, they were attractive no matter what they wore. And if they weren't, well . . . fabric was not magic.

And yet this gown seemed to be magic with its beautiful lines and the way it shimmered in the candlelight and the way the color offset her pretty pale skin and played with the reds in her hair and the blues and greens in her eyes.

Hell. He sounded like a damn woman.

The point was, this was the Mara he'd never known—the one he'd not had a chance to formally meet. The one who had been raised wealthy as sin, with all of London at her feet. The one who had been set to be Duchess of Lamont.

And damned if she didn't look remarkably like a duchess in that dress.

Too much like a duchess.

Too much like a lady.

Too much like something Temple wanted to reach out and—

No.

"The bodice should be cut lower."

"*Mais non*, Your Grace," the dressmaker protested. "The bodice is perfect. Look at the way it reveals without revealing."

She was right, of course. The bodice was the most perfect part of the dress, cut beautifully, just low enough to tantalize without being too obvious. He'd noticed it the moment Mara had put it on—the way it displayed those pretty, freckled breasts to their very best advantage. The way it made him want to catalog every one of those little blemishes.

It was perfect.

But he didn't want perfect.

He wanted ruinous.

"Lower."

The dressmaker looked at Mara, then, and Temple willed her to protest. To fight the demand. To insist the cut of the dress be left as is.

Then he would have felt better about his decision.

It was as though she knew that, of course. Knew that he wished her to fight. Because instead, she stood straight, her head bowed in obedience he knew held no honesty, and said nothing.

Leaving him feeling twenty times the ass.

"How long?" he barked the question at the modiste.

"Three days."

He nodded. Three days would work well. "She requires a mask, as well."

"Why? Isn't the goal to unmask me?" Mara answered for the dressmaker, her tone betraying her pique at being left out of the conversation. "Why hide me?"

He met her eyes then. She was a poplar, and he was a storm. She would not break. Admiration flared, and he hid it. She'd ruined him. She'd stolen from him.

"You are hidden until I choose to reveal you."

She stiffened. "Fair enough." She paused for a moment as the dressmaker unfastened the dress, and he gritted his teeth as it came loose, grateful that she caught it to her chest before revealing herself to him once more. "Tell me, Your Grace, am I to undress forever in your presence now?"

The room was hot and cloying, and he itched for a fight. And he didn't think he could bear seeing her in her under-clothes again.

He inclined his head. "I shall give you privacy, with pleasure." He headed for the front of the shop, stopping before he pushed through the curtains to add, "But when I return, you had best be prepared to tell me the truth about that night. I shan't let you out of my sight until you do. It is not negotiable."

He did not wait for her answer before entering the storefront, with its walls filled with bolts of fabric and frippery. He took a deep breath in the dimly lit space, running his hand along the edge of a long glass case, waiting for an acknowledgment that he could return.

That she was once more clothed.

That Pandora's box was once more closed.

He reached into a basket at the top of the case, and he extracted a long, dark feather, worrying it with his fingers, wondering at its softness. He wondered what it would look like in her hair. Against her skin.

In her fingers against his.

He dropped the feather as though it had burned him, and

spun back toward the dressing room to find Madame Hebert standing in the entryway. "Green," she said.

He didn't care what color she wore. He didn't plan to give her enough attention to notice.

And still he said, "I want the mauve as well. The one she tried."

Years of practice kept Madame Hebert from showing her thoughts. "The lady should be in green more than anything else."

For a moment he wondered at that, imagining Mara in green. In satins and lace and lingerie—in finely spun chemises and boned corsets and clocked silk stockings that went all the way to the floor.

He would pay good money to see her legs.

Perhaps he had seen them.

With that, frustration flared once more. He was irritated by the idea of her keeping secrets from him. Secrets that were as much his as they were hers.

"Put her in whatever color you like. I care not." He moved to push past the Frenchwoman. "But send the mauve, too."

"Temple," The name on Hebert's lips stopped him, and when he turned back, one hand on the curtains, she said, "I've dressed dozens of your women."

"The Angel's women." For some reason, the qualifier felt necessary.

She did not argue. "This one is not like the others."

It was a colossal understatement. "She is not."

"Clothes," the Frenchwoman continued. "They have a power that is undeniable. They can change everything."

It was rubbish, but he was not in the mood to argue with a modiste on her field of expertise, so he allowed her to finish.

"Be certain you wish for what you ask."

Just what he needed. A cryptic French dressmaker.

He pushed through the curtains, his gaze flying to the platform where Mara had stood in that beautiful gown, proud and tall.

The now-empty platform.
The now-empty room.
Shit.
She had finally run.

Chapter 6

Three minutes. Perhaps fewer.

She had that long to hide before he would be after her.

And if he caught her, the evening would take a turn.

Not that it hadn't already done just that.

Mara pulled her cloak tight around her, thanking Lydia for convincing her to purchase a warm winter coat for her excursions with the boys, and tore down the alleyway behind the dress shop, desperate to find a nook in which to hide herself well and wait him out. She'd escaped while his driver wasn't looking, the universe on her side for once.

Now, to hide.

The closer to the shop, the better.

Temple would think she'd have run. He'd be calculating the time she'd had and the distance she could have made, and he'd be checking that radius. She simply needed to sit quietly and wait for Temple to pass her.

He'd never expect her to stay close.

She'd learned well how to hide in the last twelve years. Indeed, she'd learned to hide in the first twelve hours after she'd run. But she didn't have a mail coach with a well-paid driver and a legion of people willing to help her now. Now she was in Mayfair in the dead of night. And she was on the wrong side of one of London's most powerful men.

If he caught her, she believed he would force her to tell the truth.

But the truth about that night—about her life—was her only power. And she would be damned if he'd get it from her so easily.

That wasn't why she'd run, though. She'd run because she worried she might not be able to resist him as well as she'd once thought.

Her heart began to pound.

Thank goodness for Mayfair's strange architecture. She was quickly lost in a maze of mews and tiny alleyways before long, and she tucked herself behind a large pile of God knew what, trying not to inhale too strongly for the stench.

Even the aristocracy made garbage.

In her experience, the aristocracy made more garbage than most. And the things they made that were halfway decent were those they attempted to toss out anyway.

One man's meat was another's poison, after all.

Footsteps.

Heavy, masculine footsteps.

She pressed her forehead to her knees, willing herself smaller, holding herself utterly still, refusing to move or even breathe. Waiting for him to pass.

When the footsteps faded away, she leapt to her feet, knowing now was the most important time. She had to run. Far and fast. In the opposite direction.

It wouldn't work. They were impossibly intertwined, now.

It would work for tonight. And with distance, she could think. Regroup. Strategize. Wage war.

She took a deep, stabilizing breath and tore out of the alleyway, getting not five feet before slamming straight into a wall of man.

Temple.

Except it wasn't. She knew because, of all the things

he made her feel—fury and frustration and irritation—he never made her feel fear.

Not like the man who held her now with his heavy, painful grip and his foul stench. And his "Well, well, wot 'ave we 'ere?"

She stilled, a rabbit caught in a trap, as he tossed her to his companion, who held her in an iron grasp as the first man gave her a long assessment from head to toe and back again. When he was finished, his appraisal turned to a leer, and his lips spread wide into a rotted-toothed grin. "Ain't we the luckiest men in London tonight? A girl just landin' in our laps?"

Her captor leaned in close, speaking in her ear, the words a horrifying threat on a wave of sour breath. "That's where ye'll be in a bit."

The words unstuck her, and she began to struggle, kicking and squirming until her captor caught her close and the stink of him—drink and sweat and days of unwashed clothing—overwhelmed her. He leaned in and whispered at her ear. "We don't like it when women get uppity."

"Well," she said, "that is a bit of a problem, as I am feeling quite uppity."

He pushed her back into the alley, up against the stone wall, hard enough to expel the air from her lungs. Fear and panic flared, and she squirmed beneath his hand, no longer desperate to scream.

She couldn't get enough air into her lungs.

She couldn't breathe.

She knew that he hadn't done enough to kill her. That he'd simply knocked the wind from her. But it was enough to terrify her.

The terror turned to anger.

Tears sprang to her eyes, and she struggled more, willing to do anything to free herself from his hand. She squirmed and pushed, and still he held her, his free hand tearing her coat apart, sending buttons flying before he grasped at her skirts, pulling them up, letting the frigid air curl around her ankles, her calves, her knees.

"Hold 'er," the first man said, reaching for the fall of his trousers as breath returned, miraculously, and her fear turned from death to something else. Something worse.

She clawed at her captor, hands punching and hitting at his arms, but she was no match for him. She changed tack, feeling for the knife in the lining of her cloak, trying to stay calm. Trying to focus.

She found it as she felt the other man's hands grab harshly at the skin above her knee, and she closed her eyes, unable to shake the vision of his filthy hand on her skin there. Slid the knife from its mooring.

But her captor saw it before she could use it. Caught her.

Was too strong for her.

He wrenched it from her hands and pressed it to her throat. "Silly girl. Weapons like this are too dangerous for the likes of you."

Fear gave way to horror.

And then he was gone, her blade clattering to the cobblestones, the loss of his weight accompanied by a deafening roar that should have increased her fear, but instead brought relief like none she'd ever known.

Temple.

She was free, her captor releasing her the moment the duke arrived, at first attempting to rescue his friend, but now standing back, unable to tear his gaze from the fight. She scurried backward, clutching her knees to her chest, and watched as well.

Temple pummeled her attacker, now pressed against the wall just as she had been, and no doubt feeling a fear similar to hers as England's winningest bare-knuckle boxer used every ounce of his skill and force to mete out justice.

But this was not a professional fighter who fought with rules and regulations, somehow finding a space for sport in the fight.

This Temple was out for blood. The movements were precise and economical, no doubt the product of years of training and practice, but every blow carried the heavy weight of his anger, hitting again and again until it was the momentum of his fists that kept her attacker upright, and nothing else.

He was stronger than gravity.

The second man in the alleyway seemed to have a similar realization, and decided that rescuing his friend was far less important than rescuing himself. He pushed past Temple, headed for escape.

But luck was not on the man's side.

Temple dropped his current foe into an unconscious heap at his feet and reached out to catch the second man by the neck, pulling him off balance and throwing him to the ground. Mara saw the glint of silver in the villain's hand. Her knife. He'd found it in the darkness.

"Blade!" she called out. She came to a crouch, ready to enter the fight. To protect him as he'd protected her. Before she could, however, Temple took a knee next to the man and resumed his battle. As though weaponry could not hurt him. As though he were immune to threat.

The knife flew through the air, finding its mark before Temple knocked it away, sending it skittering across the cobblestones, coming to a stop mere inches from her boots. She lifted it, held it tight in her hands, and did not stop watching Temple.

This time, he spoke, his blows punctuating the words that came through clenched teeth. "You. Will. Never. Hurt. Another. Woman."

The man whimpered.

Temple leaned in close. "What did you say?"

The man whimpered again.

Temple lifted him from the ground by the lapels, then dropped him, allowing his head to fall back on the cobblestones. "I cannot hear you."

The man shook his head, eyes closed. "I—I won't."

Temple landed another blow, then leaned in. "Won't what?"

"Hurt another."

"Another what?"

"Another woman."

Temple leaned back on his haunches then, his massive thighs firm and wide, his breath coming hard and fast. "Get up."

The man did as he was told, scrambling to his feet.

"Take your bastard friend with you if you wish him to live."

The man did as he was told, pulling Mara's groaning attacker to his feet and beating a path from the alleyway with as much haste as possible.

She watched them go, and it took her several long moments before she looked to Temple, who was staring at her from his place, several feet away, still as stone.

Once he met her eyes, everything changed. He swore once, under his breath, and came toward her, on his hands and knees, slowly. "Mara?"

The sound of her name on his lips, soft and graveled, unlocked her, and she began to tremble there in the darkness, on that grimy London street. He was by her side in seconds, reaching out, his hand hesitating in the space between them, hovering scant inches from her. Less. Not touching her. Not wanting to scare her, she imagined. Not wanting to impose.

The movement was so gentle, so kind, that it was hard to believe that he was anything but a friend.

You came, she wished to say. *Thank you.*

She couldn't find any of the words. And she did not have to, because he was swearing softly and pulling her into his enormous embrace.

And she felt safe for the first time in years.

Perhaps ever.

She leaned into him, reveling in his warmth, his strength, his size. His arms came around her, pulling her tight against him, and his head bowed over hers, his whole body encircling her, protecting her.

"You're safe now," he whispered to the top of her head. "You're safe." He rocked her back and forth. "They shan't be back." His lips grazed her temple as he spoke to her.

She believed him.

She believed the way he spoke with care, the way his hands, instruments of her attackers' retribution, now stroked softly along her back and down her legs, tucking her skirts carefully around her, spreading warmth through the parts of her that had gone cold with fear.

"You bested them. There were two. And you are one."

"I told you, I do not lose." There was lightness in the tone, one she could tell he did not entirely feel.

She smiled at the words, nonetheless. "Such arrogance."

"Not arrogance. Truth."

She didn't know what to say to that, so she decided on: "You are not wearing a coat."

He hesitated at that, barely, then said, "There wasn't time. I had to find you."

And he had.

"Thank you," she said, the words strange and strangled and unfamiliar.

He pulled her closer. "Don't thank me," he whispered. "I was quite angry."

She smiled into his topcoat. "I imagine you were."

"I might still be angry, but you'll have to wait until I am through being terrified."

Her head snapped up, and she cursed the darkness in the alleyway, wishing that she could see his eyes. "Terrified?"

He turned away from her. "It doesn't matter. You're safe now."

And she was. Because he was here.

Remarkably.

"How did you—"

He gave her a little smile. "I also told you I would find you if you ran."

She shook her head, tears threatening. He'd passed. She'd heard him.

And still, he had found her.

He brushed her hair back from his face. "I doubled back."

"If you hadn't—"

He shook his head and pressed her tight against him again. "I did," he said firmly.

And he had. She was safe.

"Thank you," she said to his chest, one hand falling to his arm, causing him to stiffen and hiss in pain.

She sat up immediately, her hand dropping to his thigh. "Your arm."

He shook his head. "It's nothing."

"It's not nothing." There was a deep slice in the fabric of his topcoat, and she pulled at the fabric to find a similar cut in the lawn shirt beneath, and in his skin.

"He hurt you." The buttons of his coat had burst in the fight, no doubt scattered somewhere on the dark cobblestones, and she pulled one lapel aside. "Take it off," she said, as she started to unravel his cravat, to get at the collar of his shirt. "You need treatment."

He caught her hand in his. "It's fine."

"It's not," she protested, guilt threading through her. "I shouldn't have run."

He stilled, his gaze finding hers. "What?"

"If I hadn't run . . ." She'd hurt him.

As ever.

"No." She ignored him, pulling her hands free, working at his cravat once more.

He stopped her again, one hand coming up to catch her cheek, his hands warm and sure. "Don't say it. Don't think it. This wasn't your fault."

She met his black gaze. "You're hurt."

One side of his mouth kicked up. "I was itching for a fight."

She shook her head. "That wasn't what this was."

"I wouldn't be so certain," he teased before growing serious. "Those men were beasts. And you—" He stopped, but not before the words reminded them both of who he was.

Of who they were, together.

But now, it was her turn to care for him. "We must get you inside," she said, standing, reaching down to help him up.

He ignored her hand, coming to his feet in a single, smooth motion. Once at his full height, he paused for a moment, and she imagined that he was weak from the pain of the wound. She moved to tuck herself under his good arm.

"Lean on me."

He barked a laugh in the darkness. "No."

"Why not?"

"Aside from the possibility of my crushing you?"

She smiled. "I am stronger than I seem."

He looked down at her. "I think that is first truth you've told me."

The words sent a thread of something indefinable through her. Something exciting and unsettling and half a dozen other things. "I shall take that as a compliment."

"You should."

No. She did not wish to like him.

Too late.

"Then why not lean on me?"

"I don't require help."

She peered up at him and saw something in the set of his jaw, in the firm line of his lips. Something familiar.

How many times had she said such a thing to those who offered her aid? She'd spent so much time alone, she immediately resisted the idea that someone might offer help without expecting some form of payment.

Or, worse, making themselves a part of her life.

"I see," she said, softly.

There was a long moment as the words fell between them before he said quietly, "Sometimes, I think you do see me."

He took her hand, and she stilled at the touch. He looked down at her. "Do I have to pay for this, as well?"

The words were a reminder of their deal, of how they were at odds. But the touch felt nothing like odds. The slide of his warm, rough skin against her own felt like pleasure. Pleasure she did not wish to acknowledge, but that she could not deny.

"No," she said, a cold wind sending a shiver through her. "No charge for this."

He did not reply, as they returned to the carriage. They found a quiet camaraderie in the darkness—something that would no doubt be chased away by daylight, when they would remember their past and their present. And the future, so clearly cast in stone.

And so she did not speak.

Not as they emerged from the alley, turning back toward his coach, nor when the driver leapt down from his box and came to assist them, nor when they were closed into the quiet, dark space, too confined not to touch—knees brushing against knees—and too proud to acknowledge the touch.

She did not speak when they arrived at his town house, and he leapt down to the cold, dark London street and said, "Come inside."

There was no need for words as she followed him.

"The history of our acquaintance is rather too stained with violence, Your Grace," Mara said when they were inside the library where she'd first revealed herself and her reason for reappearing. Where she'd drugged him for the second time.

He stripped off his topcoat to reveal his bloodstained

shirt. "And whose fault is that?" he asked, the words gentler than she would have imagined they might be.

Gentle.

It was strange that the word seemed to so suddenly define this man who was known to much of London as a brutal force, all unyielding muscle and indestructible bone.

But with her, he was somehow hard angles and soft touch.

He hissed his discomfort as he peeled the shirt from his arm, shucking it over his head and across the room, revealing the clean, straight wound above a wide swath of darkened skin—black with a swirling, geometric design. Mara's gaze flew to that cuff. To its twin on the opposite arm. Ink. She'd seen it before, but never on someone like him.

Never on an aristocrat.

He'd fetched himself hot water and linens with a skill that suggested that it was not the first time he'd returned to this empty house and mended himself, and he sat in the chair by the fire he'd stoked when they'd entered the room, dropping cloth into the steaming water.

His movement unstuck her, and Mara went to him where he stood by the fire.

"Sit," she said softly, dipping a length of linen into the water as he folded into one of the chairs by the hearth. She wrung the scalding liquid from the cloth before setting to the task of cleaning his wound.

He allowed it, which should have surprised her. Should have surprised them both.

He was quiet for long minutes, and she forced herself to look only at his wound, at the straight slash of torn flesh that served as a reminder of the gruesome violence she might have suffered. From which he had rescued her.

Her mind raced, obsessed with not touching him anywhere but there, on the spot just above the wide, black swath of skin—as though the darkness inside him had seeped to the surface in beautiful patterns, so wicked and incongruous with his past. With the duke he should have been.

The darkness she'd had a hand in making.

She tried not to breathe too heavily, even as the tang of him—clove and thyme mixed with something unidentifiable and yet thoroughly Temple—teased at her senses, daring her to breathe him in.

Instead, she focused on healing him with soft strokes, cleaning his arm of dried blood and stemming the flow of fresh. She watched the linen cloth move from his skin to the now pink-tinged bowl and back again, refusing to look elsewhere.

Refusing to catalog the other scars that littered his torso. The wicked hills and valleys of his chest. The dark whorls of hair that made her fingers itch to touch him in another, much more dangerous way.

"You needn't tend to me," he said, the words soft in the quiet, dark room.

"Of course I must," she replied, not looking up at him. Knowing he was looking down at her. "If not for me—"

His hand captured hers, pressing it against his now clean chest, and she could feel the spring of his chest hair against her wrist. "Mara," he said, the name coming foreign, as though it was another's.

This man, this place was not for her.

She twisted her hand in his grip, and he released her, letting her return to her ministrations as though he'd never had her in his grasp to begin with. "Tend to me then."

"It needs stitching," she said.

His brows rose. "You've knowledge of wounds needing stitching?"

She'd stitched dozens of wounds in her life. More than she could count. Too many when she was still a child. But she said none of those things. "I do. And this one needs it."

"I suppose it will cost me?"

The words were a surprise. The reminder of their agreement. For a moment, she'd allowed herself to pretend they were different people. In a different place.

Silly girl.

Nothing had changed that night. He was still out for vengeance and she was still out for money. And the longer they both remembered it, the better.

She took a breath, steeled herself. "I shall give you a bargain."

One black brow rose. "Name your price."

"Two pounds." She disliked the words on her lips.

Something flashed in his eyes. Boredom? No. It was gone before she could take the time to identify it, and he was already opening a small compartment in the table at his elbow and removed a needle and thread. "Stitch it, then."

It occurred to her that only a man who was regularly wounded would have a needle and thread at arm's length. Her gaze skittered over his chest, tracking a score of scars in various stages of healing. More.

How much pain had he suffered over the last twelve years?

She ignored the question, instead moving to the sideboard and pouring two fingers of whiskey in a glass. When she returned to him, he shook his head. "I won't drink that."

She cut him a look. "I did not drug it."

He inclined his head. "Nevertheless, I prefer to be sure."

"It wasn't for you, anyway," she said, dropping the needle into the glass before cutting a long piece of thread.

"That's a waste of good whiskey."

"It will make the stitches less painful."

"Bollocks."

She lifted one shoulder and said, "The woman who taught me to sew a wound learned it from men in battle. Seems reasonable."

"Men in battle no doubt wanted the bottle nearby."

She ignored the words and threaded the needle carefully,

before returning her attention to his wound. "It shall hurt."

"Despite the addition of my excellent scotch?"

She inserted the needle. "You tell me."

He hissed at the sting. "Dammit."

She raised a brow at him. "Shall I pour you a drink now?"

"No. I'd rather have your weapon visible."

Her lips twitched. She would not be amused. She would not like him. He was foe, not friend.

She completed the stitching quickly and with experienced precision. As she snipped the final length of string, he reached into the drawer once more and extracted a pot of liniment from within. She opened it to a waft of thyme and clove—familiar. "This is why you smell as you do."

He raised a wry brow. "You've noticed my scent?"

Her cheeks warmed at the words, to her great dismay. "It's impossible to miss," she defended. Still, she brought the pot to her nose, inhaling, the scent sending a tight thread of awareness through her. She dipped a finger in the pot and spread it across the enflamed skin around his wound, taking care not to hurt him before folding a piece of clean linen carefully and securing it with a long strip of the cloth.

Once finished, she cleared her throat, said the first thing that came to her. "You shall have a wicked scar."

"Neither the first, nor the last," he said.

"But the one for which I am responsible," she replied. He chuckled at that, and she couldn't help but look up, meeting his black gaze. "You think it is amusing?"

He shrugged one shoulder. "I think it is interesting that you claim the one scar that has nothing to do with you."

Her eyes went wide. "But the others do?"

He tilted his head, watching her carefully. "Each one, earned in a fight. Bouts I would not have fought were I not . . ." He hesitated, and she wondered how he would finish the sentence.

Were I not ruined.

Were I not destroyed.

Were I not disowned.

" . . . Temple," he finished simply.

Temple. The name he had assumed only after she'd run. After he'd been exorcised from family and Society and God knew what else. The name that had no bearing on the life he'd had. The one where he'd been William Harrow, Marquess of Chapin. Heir to the dukedom of Lamont.

All-powerful.

Until she'd stripped him of that power.

She looked at him then, cataloging his scars. The map of white and pink lines that ended in week-old bruises, the hallmarks of his profession.

Except it was not a profession.

He was wealthy and titled and with or without her death on his head, he was not required to fight. And still he did.

Temple. The fighter.

She'd made him. Perhaps that was why it seemed so right to tend to him now.

Who had tended to him the other times?

Because she could not allow herself to ask that, she asked instead, "Why Temple?"

He inhaled at the question, the hand of his good arm flexing into a fist, then back. "What do you mean?"

"Why choose that name?"

One side of his mouth kicked up. "I'm built like one."

It was a flippant, practiced answer. Years of telling truth from lies told her it was the latter, but she did not press him to say more. Instead, her gaze tracked down one massive arm to the place where the wide black band of ink stood stark against his skin.

"And the ink?"

"Tattoos."

Her hand moved of its own volition, fingers inching toward him before she realized that she was overstepping her bounds. She stopped a hairsbreadth from him.

"Go ahead," he said, his voice low.

She looked up to him, but his gaze was on the band. On her fingers. "I shouldn't," she said, and the words unstuck her. She snatched her hand back.

"You want to." He flexed his arm, the muscle making the ink shift as though it breathed. "It will not hurt."

The room was not warm—the fire was new and it was winter outside the walls of the home—but still his arm was burning with heat. She ran her fingertips across the elaborate markings, all curving lines and dark space, amazed by the smoothness of his skin. "How?" she asked.

"A small needle and a large pot of ink," he said.

"Who did it?" she met his black gaze.

His flickered away, back to where her fingers slid across smooth skin. Comfortable now. "One of the girls in the club."

Her fingers stilled. "She is very skilled."

He shifted beneath her touch. "She is. And thankfully has a steady hand."

Is she your lover? Mara wanted to ask. Except she didn't want the answer. Didn't want to want it.

She didn't want to think of a beautiful woman leaning over him with her keen sense of artistry and her wicked needle. Did not want to think of what happened later, after the needle had pricked his skin a thousand times. More. "Did it hurt?"

"No more than a fight on any given night."

Pain was his currency, after all. She didn't care for that thought, either.

"It's my turn," he said, and she returned her attention to him as he qualified. "To ask questions."

The words broke the spell between them, and she let her hand fall away from his arm. "What kind of questions?" As though she didn't know.

As though she hadn't known for years that there would come a point when she had to answer them.

She wished he would put on a shirt.

No, she didn't.

Except, if he was to press her into telling him about that night, ages ago, when she'd made a dozen life-altering mistakes, perhaps it would be best if he were fully clothed. If he were not so close. If he were not so suddenly compelling.

It was not sudden.

"How is it that you know so much about tending wounds?"

It was not the question she expected, and so she was blindsided by the images that came in response. Blood and screams. Knives and piles of red-stained linens. Her mother's last gasp of breath and Kit's tears and her father's cold, brutal face, revealing nothing. Not emotion. Not guilt.

Certainly not remorse.

She looked down at her hands, the fingers now twisted together, a confusing tangle of cold skin, and she considered her words, finally settling on: "Twelve years has afforded me much opportunity to tend any number of wounds."

He did not reply, and the silence stretched for an eternity before he slipped a finger beneath her chin and urged her to meet his serious black gaze. "The truth, now."

She tried to ignore the way the simple touch shattered her concentration. "You think you know me well enough to see when I am lying?"

He did not speak for a long while, the tips of his fingers stroking across her cheek to her temple, then around the curve of her ear, reminding her of the way he'd whispered and kissed at that place in the dressmaker's shop. She caught her breath as those wicked fingers slid down the column of her neck, resting on the place where her pulse threatened to thunder from beneath her skin.

And through it all, she kept her gaze on his, refusing to be the first to look away. Refusing to let him win, even when he closed in on her, tilting her face up and to the side, until her lips were parting at the promise of the caress he threatened.

The caress she found she wanted more than anything.

He almost gave it to her, his lips stroking once, twice, featherlight, across hers, until every inch of her ached for the touch to come firmer. To deliver on the whisper of a promise.

She sighed against his lips, and a dark, wicked sound rolled in his throat, sending a thrill through her. Had he growled? How scandalous. How wonderful.

But he didn't kiss her properly. Instead, he spoke, wretched man. "I have spent a lifetime watching men lie, Mara. Gentlemen and scoundrels. I've become a tremendous judge of truth."

She swallowed, feeling his fingers at her throat. "And I suppose you never lie?"

He watched her for a long moment. "I lie all the time. I'm the worst kind of scoundrel."

Now, as she hovered on the edge of the caress with which he teased, she believed it. He was a scoundrel. Worse.

But it did not stop her from wondering what it would be like to tell him the truth. To unload it like a bricklayer into a perfect little pile right at his feet. All of it.

And if she did? If she told him everything—all she'd done, and why? If she laid herself bare and let him judge her for her good deeds as well as her sins?

"Tell me the truth." The words were a caress. A temptation. "Who have you healed, Mara?" and the echo of patience in them—as though he would wait an eternity for the answer—was enough to make her ache to tell him.

Nothing you could say would make me forgive.

His words from earlier echoed through her, a threat and a promise. A warning not to give herself over to him.

He wanted his retribution, and she was the means to that end.

She'd best remember that.

Truth was a strange, ethereal thing—so few ever used it, and it was so often only noticeable in the lies one told.

"No one of consequence," she said, "I am simply good with a needle, as well."

"I would pay you for the truth," he said, and even as the words came gentle, like a caress, they stung, harsh and unpleasant. This was the game they played.

She shook her head. "It's not for sale."

He was not through. She could see it in his gaze. And so she did the only thing she could think to distract him. She came up on her toes, and kissed him.

$\mathcal{I}$f he'd been asked to wager everything he owned on what would happen in that room that evening, he might have laid it on his kissing her.

He'd wanted to kiss her from the moment he'd taken her in his arms in that alleyway.

From before that.

From the moment she'd wrecked him with the hint that there might have been something more between them that night twelve years earlier.

From before that.

There was always an edge after a handy trouncing, one that did not go away until an opponent landed a strong, sure blow. The theory held true if the opponent was a woman, and the blow one of pleasure.

So he'd ignored the desire, sure it was no more than a need to ease post-fight tension. He'd experienced the edge enough to know that it would wane.

Except it hadn't. It had roared through him as her hands had stroked down his arm in that dark alley, even as she'd worried his wound and sent pain coursing through him. And it had nearly consumed him as they rode to his town house—so much that he hadn't been able to stop himself from asking her to join him inside.

The request had been salt in the wound, for he'd known that if she came, he would only desire her more. Her long legs and her pretty face and that hair that he itched to release from its moorings on a sea of auburn silk. And all that was nothing compared to the way her strength moved him. The way her sharp retorts and her smart words set him on edge. The way she made a strong, worthy opponent.

The desire had come to a head as she'd stitched his wound and kept her secrets. And when he'd finally touched her, it had coursed through him, undeniable and dangerous.

So, yes. He'd have wagered on kissing her.

But he wouldn't have laid a penny on her kissing him. He would have miswagered, for it seemed that Mara Lowe was full of secrets, and willing to do anything to keep them from him.

Even kiss the Killer Duke.

And Christ, did she kiss him—her strong, soft hand tilting him down to her even as she lifted to meet him, capturing his lips with hers. Stealing his breath with the soft, tentative, devastating caress. Teasing him with the way her lips brushed across his, testing the waters. Questioning.

He willed himself still, refusing to touch her, to take control. Terrified that if he put his giant, brutal hands on her, he would scare her away. That she would run again. And then her mouth opened beneath his, unschooled and still so perfect, and the tip of her tongue edged along his bottom lip, a smooth, slick caress.

A man could only take so much.

His control snapped.

He caught her into his arms, a groan escaping from him, the sound low and likely terrifying for her, but he couldn't stop it. He couldn't stop any part of it, not as he took hold of her, as he tilted his head and lifted her to him, and found the perfect angle at which he could kiss her like she was meant to be kissed.

Like he'd dreamed of kissing her.

Claiming her.

And damned if she didn't claim him in return. Her hands wrapped around his neck, her fingers sinking into his hair, and he settled into her mouth, stroking deep until she sighed her pleasure, the sound rushing through him, straight to the core of him, where he'd been heavy and hard for what seemed like days—any time he was around her.

He worried her lower lip with his teeth, loving the way she shivered in his arms, letting his hands find their way into her hair, scattering pins and setting loose a tide of curls. He traced the silken strands with his touch once, twice, until he couldn't bear not to look any longer. He pulled back, loving the way she followed him, the way she resisted their separation. "Temple," she sighed, an edge of irritation in the name.

"Wait," he whispered. "Let me look at you."

She was the most beautiful thing he'd ever seen. His gaze devoured her, her dark hair spread wild around her shoulders, gleaming hints of red in the candlelight, her strange, gorgeous eyes filled with frustration and desire. Her lips swollen from his kiss—

He took those lips again, unable to resist them. Kissed her deep and thoroughly, memorizing the sound of her sighs, the spice of her, the feel of her against him, like nothing he'd ever felt before—

Except . . .

His head snapped up, and her eyes blinked open. "You really ought to stop stopping," she said with a smile.

He shook his head. "At the dressmaker's," he began, hating the way her gaze cleared of sensuality at the words. "What you said . . ."

It is not the first time you've seen my underclothes.

"We've done this before," he said.

Her eyes flickered to his arm, to his tattoo. "Yes."

No. It couldn't be the truth. He would remember this—

the way her mouth felt right against hers. The way she felt right in his arms.

He kissed her again, this time a test. An experiment. He would remember her. Surely he would remember the taste of her. The sounds she made. The way she somehow drove the caress and gave herself up to it.

He would remember her.

He released her mouth, directing his kiss down the column of her neck, to the hollow of her collarbone, dipping his tongue into the indentation there, tasting her. Savoring the sigh that escaped from her lips as he slid his hands to the front tie of her bodice and released the tension there, sliding his hand into the fabric to caress the straining tip of one breast.

To bare it to the firelight.

Dear God. He would remember her.

He met her gaze, glassy with desire. "We've done this before."

She hesitated, and the pause sent a thread of frustration through him. He wouldn't let her avoid him. He wouldn't let her lie. Not about this.

Suddenly, somehow, this seemed far more important than all the rest. He lowered the layers of fabric, watching as dark dress and pale chemise gave way to even paler skin. To perfect skin, tipped with straining flesh turned the color of honey gold in the firelight.

His mouth watered, and he lowered his lips to that place where she strained for him.

Where, somehow, he strained for her.

It took all his strength to pause there, a breath from her skin, and whisper, "We've done this before."

"William." She gasped his name in the firelight.

His real name.

He froze. As did she.

"What did you call me?"

She hesitated. "I—"

No one had called him that for a decade. For longer. Few had called him that before—but he'd always liked his women to do so. He'd liked the way the familiarity of the name brought them closer. Made them more accommodating. It had been an easy way to make them love his naïve, idiot self.

"Say it." The command was not to be refused.

"William," she said, beautiful eyes filled with fire, the curve of the syllables on her warm lips making him at once furious and filled with longing.

Christ.

This had happened.

He would remember her.

Except he couldn't. Because she'd made certain he wouldn't. She'd stolen that night from him. This moment from him.

He released her as though she'd burned him, and perhaps she had. Perhaps the not remembering that night was the most serious of her infractions, now that he knew just what it was he could not remember.

He stood, the blood rushing through him at the movement, making his head light and his frustration acute. This woman was too much for him. He turned from her, moving away, wanting to leave her and still feeling her pull. He paced one end of the room once, twice before turning back to her.

"What else happened that night?"

She remained quiet.

Goddammit. What had happened? Had he lain her bare? Had he kissed her in a half-dozen forbidden places? Had she reciprocated? Had they enjoyed each other on that last, final night before he had woken as the Killer Duke—never to touch another woman without seeing trepidation in her gaze?

Or had Mara simply used him?

Anger flooded him like a fever. "We kissed. I saw you in your underclothes. Did we—?"

She stiffened at the question, waiting for him to finish it with the cold, crass word he'd offered in the dressmaker's salon. The wait was as much of a blow as the word, however. She did not respond. And he hated that he couldn't leave the silence almost as much as he hated the sound of his wrecked voice when he added, "Did we?"

I've never met an aristocrat worthy of trusting.

Christ. Had he hurt her?

He couldn't remember it—if she'd been a virgin, he would have hurt her. He wouldn't have been careful enough not to. He ran a hand through his hair. He'd never been with a virgin.

Had he?

And what if—he froze. The orphanage. The boys.

What if one of them was his?

His heart began to race.

No. It was impossible. She wouldn't have left like that. She wouldn't have taken his child. *Would she?*

She restored her bodice and stood, calm and collected, as though they were discussing the weather. Or Parliament. Refusing to be insulted.

He came at her, stopping inches from her, resisting the urge to shake her. "You owe me the truth."

For a moment, something was there in her gaze. For a moment, she considered it. *He saw her consider it.* And then, she stopped. And he saw her mind racing. Conniving. Planning.

When she spoke, she did not cow. She was not afraid. "We negotiated the terms of our agreement, Your Grace. You get your vengeance, and I get my money. If you would like the truth, I am happy to discuss its cost."

He'd never met anyone like her. And damned if he didn't admire the hell out of her even as he wanted to tie her up and scream his questions until she answered. "It seems you are no stranger to scoundrels after all."

"You would be surprised by what twelve years alone can do to a person," she said, those stunning, unusual eyes filled with fire.

They stood toe to toe, and Temple felt more equal to this woman than to anyone he'd ever known. Perhaps because they'd both sinned so greatly. Perhaps because trust was not a thing in which either of them had faith.

"I would not be surprised at all," he replied.

She took a step back. "Then you are willing to discuss additional terms?"

For a moment, he almost agreed. He almost turned over the entire debt, houses, horses, all of it. She almost won.

Because he wanted the memories of that night more than he had ever wanted anything in his life. More than his name. More than his title. More than all his wins and money and everything else.

But she could not give him his memory any more than she could give him his lost years.

All she could give him was the truth.

And he would get it.

There was a man outside the orphanage.

She should have expected it, of course, from the moment she left him at his town house the night before, sent home in a cold carriage that yawned huge and empty with his absence. Should have predicted that he would have her followed the moment she tossed caution into the wind and offered him the truth about the night she'd left him—for a price. Of course he would watch her. She was more valuable to him now than ever before.

The past was the most valuable commodity of them all.

The carriage had waited as she'd entered the house and stood sentry as she'd climbed the stairs and pulled back the bedcovers. She'd fallen asleep with the lanterns of the conveyance swaying in the wind, casting shadows across the ceiling of her little room, upsetting her sanctuary.

Snow had come overnight, its light dusting marking the first day of December, and when she looked out her bedchamber window into the grey light of dawn, she was surprised to find the carriage was gone, its tracks covered by the white down, and it had been replaced by an enormous man, bundled in a heavy wool coat, hat low over his brow, scarf wrapped high on his cheeks, leaving only a swath of dark skin and watchful eyes.

He would catch his death out there.

She told herself she shouldn't be surprised, as he had no doubt been sent to stand watch by Temple, out of a lack of trust that she would remain in London and take the punishment he planned to mete out.

She told herself she shouldn't care, as she washed and dressed and mentally prepared her lessons for the day ahead, swearing to keep Temple from her mind. The memory of their constant sparring. The memory of his kiss.

The kiss was thoroughly out of her mind.

She spent the entire descent from the upper rooms of the home to the ground floor putting it out of her mind.

Lydia met her in the foyer, a stack of envelopes in her hands and a furrow between her brows. "We've a problem."

"I shall send him away," Mara said, already heading for the door.

Lydia blinked. "Whatever it is you think I am referring to, not that kind of problem." She lifted the stack of papers, and Mara's heart sank. It seemed Temple's sentry was the smallest of their worries today.

She waved Lydia into her office and sat behind the desk. Lydia sat, too. "Not one problem. More like one large problem made up of many small ones." Mara waited, knowing what was to come. "We've lost our credit."

It was to be expected. They hadn't paid their debts in months. There wasn't any money for it. "With whom?"

Lydia began to sift through the bills. "The tailor. The bookshop. The cobbler. The haberdasher. The dairy. The butcher—"

"Good Lord, did they all attend some kind of citywide meeting and decide to uniformly come collecting?"

"It would seem so. But that is not the worst of it."

"The boys shan't be able to eat and that's not the worst of it?"

Mara shivered and moved to the fire, opening the coal bin to discover it empty. She closed it.

Lydia held up a single envelope. "*That's* the worst of it."

Mara looked to the bin. Coal.

Again.

London winters were long and cold and wet, and the orphanage would require coal to keep the boys healthy. Hell. To keep the boys *alive*. "Two pounds, sixteen." Lydia nodded, and Mara said what anyone would say in such a situation. "Damn."

Lydia did not flinch. "My thoughts, precisely."

Damn bills.

Damn bill collectors.

Damn her father for sending her into hiding.

Damn her brother for losing everything.

And damn Temple and his gaming hell for taking it.

"We've a houseful of boys bred from the richest men in England." Lydia said, "Is there no one who can help us?"

"No one who would not expect our lists in return." The lists of bloodlines, two dozen names that would scandalize London and in the process ruin the boys. Not to mention the reputation of the orphanage, which was of the utmost importance.

"What of the fathers themselves?"

Men who came in the dead of night to pass off their unwanted offspring. Men who made unthinkable threats to keep their identities secret. Men who Mara never wanted to see again. Who would not want to see her ever again. "They've washed their hands of the boys." She shook her head. "I won't go to them."

There was a long pause. "And the duke?"

Mara did not pretend to misunderstand. The Duke of Lamont. Rich as Croesus and doubly powerful. And rightfully furious with Mara. "What of him?"

Lydia hesitated, and Mara knew her friend was searching for the right words. As though she hadn't thought them herself. "If you told him the truth—that your brother's funds were not his to gamble . . ."

Nothing you could say would make me forgive.

The words echoed, their dark promise sending a chill through her. He'd been so angry with her last night. And she'd brought it upon herself—telling him half tales, tempting him with partial truths, and then asking him to pay for his memories.

She sat.

No. The duke would not help. She was alone in this. The boys were her charges. Her responsibility.

It was she who must care for them.

She stood and moved to a nearby bookcase, extracting a fat volume. She held the book in her hands, her breath coming hard and fast, every inch of her resisting what she was about to do. The book was her safety. Her future. Her promise to herself that she would never go poor or hungry again. That she would never have to rely on the aid of others.

It was her protection, cobbled together with twelve years of work and saving.

Everything that would keep her from the streets.

Everything she'd planned to use once Temple ruined her.

But the boys were more important.

She set the book on the desk and opened it, revealing a

large hollow space, filled with a cloth sack that jingled when she lifted it.

Lydia gasped. "Where did that come from?"

From years of work. Of saving. Of a shilling here and sixpence there.

Twelve pounds, four shillings, ten pence.

All she had.

Mara ignored the question, extracting coins. "Pay the coal, the dairy, and the butcher. Take your salary. And Alice's. And Cook's. And do what you can to put off the others—until the eldest require new shoes and clothes."

Lydia considered the money, shook her head. "Even with that—"

She did not have to finish the sentence. The money wouldn't be enough to carry them through winter. It would barely get them into the New Year.

There was only one way.

More time with the Duke of Lamont.

She stood, and headed for the foyer, now filled with boys. They were all at the two front windows of the house, teetering on chair arms and clinging to windowpanes, eyes riveted on the man across the street.

Lavender sat several feet away, watching them, and Mara lifted her to safety before the piglet could be crushed by a falling boy.

"He's been there for an hour, at least!" Henry said.

"He doesn't seem cold at all!"

"Impossible! It's snowing!" Henry replied, as though the rest of them hadn't eyes.

"He's nearly as big as the man who came for Mrs. Mac-Intyre," Daniel said, amazement in his tone.

He nearly was, but Temple was bigger.

"Aye! That one was big as a house!"

Bigger, and no doubt stronger. And handsomer. She stilled at the thought. She had no interest in his handsomeness. None whatsoever. She hadn't even noticed it. Just as she hadn't noticed the way his kisses made her weak.

He was infuriating. And impossible. And controlling in the very worst way.

And more handsome than the man across the street.

Not that she noticed.

"Do you think he's here for one of us?"

The trepidation in little George's voice brought her back to the matter at hand. "Gentlemen."

The boys started, releasing curtains and unbalancing each other until their strangely crafted structure toppled, leaving half a dozen boys in a heap on the floor. Mara resisted the urge to laugh at the boys' antics as they scurried to their feet, straightening sleeves and pushing hair from their eyes.

Daniel spoke first. "Mrs. MacIntyre! You are back!"

She forced a smile. "Of course I am."

"You were not at supper last evening. We thought you'd left," Henry said.

"For good," George added.

Mara's heart constricted at the words. Though they played at being fearless, the boys at the MacIntyre Home were terrified of being left. It was a vestige of being marked as orphans, no doubt, and Mara spent much of her time convincing them that she would not leave them. Indeed—that they would be the ones to leave her, eventually.

Except it was a lie now.

She would leave them. She would write her letter to the newspapers, and show her face to London, and then she would have no choice but to leave them. It was how she would protect them. How she would keep their lives on track. How she would ensure that funds continued into the orphanage, and they were never marked by her scandal.

Deep sadness coursed through her, and she crouched low, Lavender struggling for freedom, and pressed a kiss to George's blond head before smiling at Henry. "Never."

The boys believed her lies.

"Where did you go, then?" Daniel asked, always one to get to the heart of the matter.

She hesitated, turning over the answer in her mind. She couldn't, after all, tell the boys that she'd been traipsing about London in the dead of night being fitted for clothes worthy of a prostitute and chased by villains. *And kissed by them.* "I had a bit of . . . business . . . to tend to."

Henry turned back to the window. "There are *two* men out there now! And with a great black carriage, too! Cor! We could all fit into it! With room to spare!"

The pronouncement drew the attention of the rest of the boys, and—despite her attempt to resist—of Mara. She knew before she looked out the window, through a web of young, spindly limbs, who would be in the snowy street beyond.

Of course it was he.

Without thinking, she headed for the door of the orphanage, tearing it open and heading straight for the carriage. Temple's back was to her as he and his man-at-arms were deep in conversation, but Mara had taken no more than a half-dozen steps before he turned to look over his shoulder at her. "Get back inside. You'll catch your death."

She would catch *her* death? She held her head high, not wavering. "What are you doing here?"

He looked back to his companion, saying something that made the other man smirk, then turned to face her. "This is a busy street, Mrs. MacIntyre," he said. "I could have any number of reasons to be here." He took a step toward her. "Now do as I tell you and get inside. Now."

"I am quite warm," she said, her gaze narrowing. "Unless you're searching for a woman to warm your bed, Your Grace, you really couldn't have any number of reasons to be here. And in your condition, I would think that effort would prove futile."

He raised a brow. "Do you?"

"I stitched your arm closed not twelve hours ago."

He shrugged one shoulder. "I am quite well today. Well enough to carry you inside and stuff you into a cloak."

She hesitated at the image that wrought, the way he simply oozed strength beneath his greatcoat, which made him look even wider and more unsettlingly large than ordinary.

He did look well. Wickedly, powerfully well.

She resisted the urge to identify the emotion that coursed through her at the look of him. Instead, she said, "You should not be cavorting about London with a fresh wound. It shall tear open."

He tilted his head. "Is that concern you exhibit?"

"No," she said quickly, the word coming on instinct.

"I think it is."

"Perhaps the wound has addled your brain." She huffed her irritation. "I simply don't want to have to repeat my work."

"Why not? You could fleece me out of another two pounds. I checked that price, by the way. Robbery. A surgeon would do it for a shilling, three."

"A pity you didn't have a surgeon nearby, then. I charged what the market would bear. And it shall cost you double if you tear it open and require me to do it again."

He ignored the words. "If you won't go inside for yourself, perhaps you will for the pig. She will catch a chill."

She looked down at Lavender, asleep in the crook of her arm. "Yes, she looks quite uncomfortable."

His gaze slid past her, over her shoulder, making her feel slight and small, even as she herself stood a half a head taller than most men she knew. "Good morning, gentlemen."

She turned at the words to find the wide-eyed residents of the MacIntyre Home for Boys collected in the open door, edging out onto the snowy steps leading up to the orphanage. "Boys," she said, putting on her very best governess voice. "Go inside and find your breakfast."

The boys did not move.

"Is every male of the species utterly infuriating?" she muttered.

"It would seem so," Temple replied.

"The question was rhetorical," she snapped.

"I see you making eyes at the carriage, boys. Have at it if you like."

The words unlocked the children, who tumbled down the stairs as though a tide were pushing them toward the great black conveyance. Temple nodded to the coachman, who climbed down from his perch and opened the door, lowering the steps to allow the boys access to the interior of the coach.

Mara was distracted by the exclamations of excitement and amazement and glee that came from the dozen or so boys who were now clamoring about the carriage. She turned to Temple. "You didn't have to do that."

She did not want him to be kind to them. She did not want them trusting him—not when he held the keys to their full bellies and warm beds.

He gave a little shrug, watching the boys intently. "I'm happy to. They don't get much chance to ride in carriages, I'm guessing."

"They don't. They don't see much beyond Holborn, I'm afraid."

"I understand."

Except he didn't. Not really. He'd grown up in one of the wealthiest families in England, heir to one of the largest dukedoms in Britain. He'd had the world at his fingertips—clubs and schools and culture and politics—and a half-dozen carriages. More.

But still, she heard the truth in the words as he watched the boys explore. He did understand what it was to be alone. To be limited by circumstances beyond one's control.

She let out a long breath. There, at least, they were similar.

"Your Grace—"

"Temple," he corrected her. "No one else uses the title."

"But they will," she said, recalling their deal. Her debt. "Soon."

Something lit in his black gaze. "Yes. They will."

The words came threaded with pleasure and something more. Something colder. More frightening. Something that reminded her of the promise he'd made the night they had agreed on their arrangement. When he'd told her that she would be the last woman he paid for companionship.

And perhaps it was the cold or lack of sleep, but her question was out before she knew it. "What then?"

She wished she could take it back when he turned surprised eyes on her. Wished she hadn't shown him just how interested she was in his world.

He waited a long moment, and she thought perhaps he would not answer. But he did, in his own, quiet way. With the truth. As ever. "Then it will be different."

His attention returned to the boys, and he pointed to Daniel. "How old is he?"

She followed his attention to the dark-haired boy leading the pack that now clamored over the carriage. "Eleven," she said.

Temple's serious gaze found hers. "How long has he been with you?"

She watched the boy. "From the beginning."

Black eyes turned blacker. "Tell me," he said, and she heard the bitterness in his voice. "Did you always have plans to hold that night over my head? Did you come back knowing you'd use it to get your brother's money? Did you sew me up knowing it would soften me? Did you kiss me for it? Was this your grand plan the moment he lost it all?"

Cacophonous laughter saved her from answering—gave her a moment to collect herself at the thought that he might believe such things of her. At the instant desire to defend herself. To tell him everything.

Nothing you could say would make me forgive.

She looked away as the words echoed through her, to the

coach, where nearly a score of boys were attempting to fit themselves.

"Sixteen!" someone called out, as Henry headed into the crush, hands first, Daniel pushing him from behind.

Mara moved to stop them.

Temple stayed her movement with a hand. "Leave them. They deserve some play."

She turned back to him. "They shall ruin your upholstery."

"It can be repaired."

Of course it could. He was rich beyond measure. She returned to the conversation. "I didn't plan it."

He looked up into the grey sky, his breath coming in little clouds. "And yet you offer a trade instead of the truth."

She hadn't a choice.

But he didn't see that.

A frigid wind ripped down Cursitor Street and she turned to brace herself from it, her wool walking dress no match for the cold. Lavender woke, giving a little snuffle of protest before Temple captured Mara in his strong grip, moving her to one side, shielding her with his enormous body.

She resisted the urge to lean into him. How was he so warm?

He cursed softly and said, "Your pig is getting cold."

He had released her once she was shielded from the wind, his free hand stealing between them. Mara watched long fingers stroke down Lavender's little, soft cheek and felt the piglet snuggle into the caress.

For a fleeting moment, she wondered how those fingers would feel on her own cheek. And then she realized she was vaguely jealous of a pig.

Which was unacceptable.

She pulled herself straight, looking up into his face, forcing herself not to notice the way his lips twisted in wry amusement at the piglet's abandon. "How long will you have me watched?"

He was watching the boys again. "Until I am through with you."

The words were cold and unwelcoming. And they made her retort easier. "And my trade?"

He stopped stroking Lavender, and returned his cool attention to Mara. "I believe I can extract the information in another way."

A shiver coursed through her. Trepidation. Fear. Something else that she did not wish to acknowledge.

"No doubt you do. But I am stronger than you think."

"You are precisely as strong as I think."

The promise in the words seemed echoed in the cold wind that whipped her skirts against her legs. "And until then, I am the lucky recipient of your watchful eye."

One side of his mouth kicked up in a humorless smile. "It is good that you see the silver lining in this cloud."

"More like the lightning storm." She took a deep breath. "And what is the watch worth to you?"

"Nothing."

"That was not the agreement."

"No, the agreement was that I pay you for your time. This is my time. And my men's."

"Watching us, like villains."

"Does it make you feel better, putting me in the role of the villain? Does it help to absolve you of your sins?" The words were soft and unsettling and far too astute.

Mara looked away. "I simply prefer that you and your men not scare the children."

Temple cut a look at the carriage. "I see that we are threats on that account."

She followed his gaze, noting that the boys were through with their earlier game and had now set about conquering the huge conveyance. There were seven or eight standing on the roof of the coach, and others scaling the sides with the help of his dark sentry and the coachman.

He and his men had come here, into her life and won over her charges with nothing but a handsome carriage and a few kind words. He'd changed her life in mere days—threatening everything she held dear.

Stripping her of every inch of her control.

She wouldn't have it.

She clutched Lavender to her chest and extracted the little black book from her pocket. "You've had enough of my time today, Your Grace," she said, opening it. "Shall we call it a crown?"

His brows rose. "I did not ask you to join me."

She smiled falsely, "But join you, I did. Aren't you lucky?"

"Oh, yes," he replied, rocking back on his heels. "I have ever been lucky in your presence."

She scowled. "A crown it is," she marked the fee in her book, then turned to the carriage. "Boys!" she called. "It's time to go in."

They didn't hear her. It was as though she did not exist.

"Lads," he said, and they stopped, frozen in their play. "Enough for today."

The boys descended as though they'd been waiting for those precise words. Of course they did. Of course they listened to him.

She wanted to scream.

Instead she headed for the house, making it halfway across the street before she realized he was on her heels, as though his escort was perfectly ordinary. She stopped. As did he.

"You are not invited in."

His lips twitched. "The truth will out, Mara."

She scowled at him. "Not today."

His brows rose. "Tomorrow, then."

"That depends."

"On?"

"On whether you intend to bring your purse."

He chuckled at that, the laughter there, then gone, and she hated herself for enjoying the sound.

"I require you in the evening," he said quietly. "I imagine it's another ten pounds for the privilege?"

The words unsettled, the discussion of money somehow powerful on her lips and insulting on his. But she refused to acknowledge the way it made her feel. "That's a fair start."

He watched her for a long moment, something equally disquiet in his countenance.

Something she ignored.

Chapter 8

When Mara entered her office the following morning, it was to discover that Lydia was a traitor.

Lydia was perched on the edge of a small chair on one side of Mara's desk, in casual conversation with the Duke of Lamont, as though it was perfectly ordinary for a man of his size and ilk to loiter in an orphanage, and equally ordinary for a governess to keep him company. Lydia was tittering, fairly hanging on every one of his words, when Mara shut the door behind her with a snap.

Temple stood, and Mara ignored the warmth that spread through her. It was December. And bitterly cold, as the coal delivery had not yet arrived. This man was not warming. She redirected her attention to Lydia. "We're allowing just anyone in these days?"

Lydia had worked alongside Mara for long enough not to be cowed. "The duke indicated that you had an appointment."

"We don't." She rounded her desk and sat. "You may leave, Your Grace. I am quite busy."

He did not leave. Instead, he returned to his chair and overflowed the delicate piece of furniture. "Perhaps you don't remember. We agreed that I would return today."

"We agreed you would return *this evening*."

"Miss Baker invited me in."

"He was outside when I woke," Lydia explained. "It's bitterly cold, and I thought he might like tea."

Temple had clearly addled the other woman's brain.

"He does not want tea."

"Tea sounds lovely." There was perhaps no word stranger on this enormous man's lips than *lovely*.

"You don't drink tea," Mara pointed out.

"I'm thinking of starting."

Lydia stood. "I shall ring for it."

"No need, Miss Baker, I can't drink it."

Lydia looked crestfallen. "Why not?"

Mara answered for him. "Because he's afraid I'll poison him."

"Oh," the other woman said. "Yes, I can imagine that is a worry." She leaned toward Temple. "I would not poison you, Your Grace."

He grinned. "I believe you."

Mara huffed her disapproval, glaring at Lydia. "This is a betrayal."

Lydia seemed to be enjoying herself entirely too much. "It's only fair, considering we are putting him to work today."

"I beg your pardon?" Mara could not help her exclamation. Nor the way she shot to her feet.

Temple stood, as well.

"He's offered to help with the boys."

Mara sat. "He cannot."

Temple sat.

She looked to him. "What are you doing?"

He shrugged. "A gentleman does not sit when a lady stands," he said, simply.

"So you're a gentleman now? Yesterday you were a self-professed scoundrel."

"Perhaps I am turning over a new leaf." One side of his mouth rose in a small smile. "Like tea."

A smile that brought attention to his lips.

Those infuriating lips about which she had no intention of thinking.

Dear God. She'd kissed him.

No. She wouldn't think on it.

She scowled at him. "I highly doubt that."

He was infuriating. She stood again.

As did he, patient as ever.

She sat, knowing she was being obstinate, but not much caring.

He remained standing.

"Shouldn't you sit, as a gentleman?" she snapped.

"The standing-sitting rule does not hold true in reverse. I think it might be best if I remain standing while you—frustrate."

Mara narrowed her gaze on him. "I assure you, Your Grace, if you wait for me to cease *frustrating*, you may never sit again."

Lydia's blue eyes gleamed with unreleased laughter.

Mara glared at her. "If you laugh, I shall set Lavender loose in your bedchamber in the dead of night. You shall awake to pig noises."

The threat worked. Lydia sobered. "It is simply that the gentleman offered, and it occurs to me that the boys could benefit from a man's tutelage."

Mara's gaze went wide. "You must be joking."

"Not at all," Lydia said. "There are things the boys should learn for which we are—not ideal."

"Nonsense. We are excellent teachers."

Lydia cleared her throat and passed a small piece of paper across the desk to Mara. "I confiscated this from Daniel's reader yesterday evening."

Mara unfolded the paper to discover a line drawing of— "What is . . ." She turned the paper and tilted her head. Temple leaned over the desk, his head now dangerously close to her own—and turned the page once more. At which point everything became clear.

She folded the paper with military efficiency, heat spreading furiously across her face. "He's a child!"

Lydia inclined her head. "Apparently, boys of eleven are rather curious."

"Well, it is entirely inappropriate for *him* to address their curiosity." She waved a hand in Temple's direction, refusing to look at him. *Unable* to look at him. "Not that he isn't well qualified to serve as an expert, I imagine."

"I shall take that as a compliment," he said, far too close to her.

She turned in her chair to look up at him. "It was not meant as one. I was merely pointing out your libidinous ways."

His brows rose. "Libidinous."

"Roguish. Rakish. Scallawaginous. Scoundrelly."

"I'm certain that some of those words are not words."

"Now you're angling for a position as governess?"

"If the boys are learning words like *scallawaginous*, it might not be the worst idea."

Mara turned to Lydia. "He is leaving."

"Mara," Lydia said. "He's ideal. He's a duke, and, I imagine, was trained as a gentleman."

"He's a fighter for heaven's sake. He owns a gaming hell. He's no kind of tutor for young, impressionable men who must be models of gentlemanliness."

"I was quite skilled in the gentlemanly arts, once."

Mara cut him a look. "You, sirrah, could have fooled me."

The words were out before she could stop them—knowing instantly that she'd reminded him of the night that had caused all this difficulty, that had set them on the path to this moment, where he appeared destined to overtake every aspect of her life.

His gaze darkened. "I might remind you that I was the one who was fooled that evening, *Mrs. MacIntrye*." The emphasis on the false name had her pressing her lips together as he addressed Lydia. "I am free for the day and happy to tutor your young charges in any aspect of gentlemanliness required."

The entire situation was out of control.

She did not want him here. Close. Anywhere near her. The man was plotting her demise. She didn't want him near her boys or her friend or her life.

She didn't want him. Full stop.

It did not matter that she'd spent much of the night tossing and turning in her little bed, thinking on the kiss they'd shared. And the way he'd handled the boys, clamoring in and out of his coach yesterday.

It did not matter that when she forgot about their past, she rather liked him in the present. None of it mattered. Not when he held her future and the future of this orphanage in his hands.

"Has it escaped both of your attentions that I am the mistress of this orphanage? And that I have no intention of allowing this man to stay for the day?"

"Nonsense," Lydia said. "You wouldn't limit the boys' access to a duke."

"Not exactly the most in-demand duke of the *ton*." The words were out before she knew they'd formed. Temple stiffened. Lydia's mouth opened, then closed. Then opened again. And Mara felt like an ass. "I did not mean—"

His gaze found hers, guarded. "Of course not."

"I know better than any that—"

He did not speak. She turned to Lydia, hoping for help, and the governess simply shook her head, wide-eyed. And guilt spread through Mara, hot and unpleasant. She had to repair the damage. She returned her attention to Temple. "You are schooled in the courtly arts?"

He met her gaze for a long moment before executing a perfect bow, and looking more ducal than Mara had ever seen him. "I am."

A truce.

"And appropriate conversation with ladies?" Lydia was grateful for the détente, her gaze flickering to the paper in Mara's hand. "We may need a bit of that."

"I have had few complaints."

He was an excellent conversationalist. Mara had no doubt.

Lydia continued. "And sport? I think sport has been neglected from the boys' education for far too long."

Mara huffed at that. "The man is built like a Greek god. I think sport is the one thing he can teach them."

The words rattled around the room, shocking everyone. Lydia's eyes went wide. Temple went still.

Mara's mouth dropped open.

She hadn't said it.

A Greek god?

It was his fault. He'd scrambled her thoughts. And he was interjecting himself into every aspect of her life—every bit for which she'd worked so hard and fought so long. Surely that was what had made her say it.

A Greek god??

She closed her eyes and willed him to lose the power of speech. Immediately and irreversibly. "Obviously, I didn't mean—"

"Well. Thank you."

In the entire history of time, had willing ever worked?

She straightened. Soldiered on. "I would not take it as a compliment. The Greek gods were a strange bunch. Always turning into animals and abducting virgins."

Dear God. Could she not keep her mouth shut?

"It's not such a terrible fate, that," he said.

Lydia snickered.

Mara glared at her. "You just asked him to teach the boys to be gentlemen."

Lydia turned enormous eyes on Temple. "Your Grace, you do realize you cannot speak to the boys in such . . . innuendo."

"Of course," he said. "But you do realize that your employer started it."

Mara wanted to tread upon his foot. But seeing as he was a great giant of a man, she doubted he would feel it at all.

"Well then. It's settled," Lydia said, as though it were. Which it seemed to be, despite Mara being against the entire thing. "You shall spend the morning with the boys, and they will no doubt learn a great deal." She turned to Mara, immense meaning in her eyes as she finished, casually, "And perhaps once you have spent the day with the boys, you and Mrs. MacIntyre can discuss a charitable donation to our very good work."

Lydia was nothing if not shrewd. Where Mara looked at Temple and saw a dangerous foe, Lydia saw a wealthy potential ally. A man who could pay all their bills.

Temple raised a brow. "Your business acumen rivals that of your employer."

Lydia smiled. "I shall take that as a compliment."

She shouldn't, of course.

Temple would not simply decide to give to the orphanage. He, too, was shrewd. And their best chance of paying their bills was for Mara to continue on her path. A thread of unease slid through her at the mercenary thought. She ignored it.

This was about the orphanage and the boys' safety.

Her means would justify that end.

Lydia stood then. "Well. This is a treat. It's not every day a duke gives up his title to take on work."

"I hear it happens quite often in novels," Temple said.

"This is not exactly a novel," Mara said. In a novel, she'd be a perfect, beautiful maid with an unblemished past to match her complexion. And he'd be a handsome, brooding duke.

Well, the last bit was rather like real life, she supposed.

"Really?" he teased, "I confess, the events of the last week have been strange enough to convince me otherwise."

Lydia laughed. "Indeed."

Mara pointed at her. "Do not come to like him."

The laugh turned into a grin. "That might prove difficult."

Temple bowed.

They were flirting now, and it occurred to Mara that if this were a novel, she would not be the heroine. Lydia might be. The kind, pretty, blond governess, with bright laughs and big eyes, just the thing to turn the brooding duke around.

Mara scowled. It was not a novel.

"Lydia, prepare the boys for a special lesson with His Grace," she said, meeting Temple's eyes. "You remain here."

Curiosity flooded Lydia's expression, but she knew better than to linger, leaving immediately to collect her charges. Once the door closed behind her, she came around the desk to face him. "You needn't do this."

"It's kind of you to think of my comfort."

"I did not mean to imply that I was doing that."

His mouth twisted in a wry smile. "I shall infer it nonetheless."

He was distracting. She could smell the clove and thyme on him—the salve she'd spread on his wound while he'd waited patiently, her fingers sliding over his warm, smooth skin.

And from there, it was a quick leap to the memory of his lips on hers.

She couldn't believe she'd kissed him.

Could believe even less that he'd kissed her in return.

And she would not think on the fact that she'd liked it.

Or that *like* seemed not at all a strong enough word for how the caress had made her feel.

He was smirking now, as though he knew the thoughts that were running through her mind.

She cleared her throat. Straightened her shoulders. "The boys do not have much time with gentlemen. They will be interested in you."

He nodded. "That makes sense."

"Don't . . ." She hesitated, searching for the right words. "Don't make them like you."

His brows rose.

"It will only make it harder when you leave and never return. Don't let them grow attached to you." Suddenly, the possibility of becoming attached to him did not seem so unrealistic.

There was a thick hesitation before he said, "It's just a morning, Mara."

She nodded, ignoring the way the words twisted in the air between them. "I'll have your word on that."

He exhaled on a little huff. Humor? Frustration? "As a gentleman? Or a scoundrel?"

"As both."

He nodded. "My word, as both."

She opened the door, turned back to him, trying not to notice how handsome he was. How tempting. "I hope at least one of them sticks."

He left, and she closed the door behind him. After several moments of wanting to follow him, she turned the lock, and returned to her desk.

*O*ne hour.

That was how long it took for her curiosity to get the better of her, and for her to go hunting for him.

She found Lydia standing sentry in the main hall of the orphanage.

"Where are they?" Mara asked.

Lydia tipped her head in the direction of the firmly shut door to the dining room. "He has been with them for three-quarters of an hour."

"Doing what?"

"I haven't any idea."

She approached her friend, lowered her voice to a whisper. "I cannot believe you asked him this."

Lydia shrugged. "He seems a decent man."

He was. "You don't know that."

Lydia's blue gaze turned knowing. "I know indecent men. And you yourself said he did not do what the world thinks he did." She paused, then added, "And he's rich enough to save us all."

If only he knew they were in danger.

Nothing you could say will make me forgive.

Nothing she could say would make him help.

Lydia was still talking. " . . . but they seem to be enjoying it."

Laughter and excited chatter streamed from the dining room, returning Mara to the present. She knocked and opened the door, the laughter noise immediately subsiding.

Temple looked up from his place at the head of the table and immediately stood when she entered. The boys followed suit. "Ah," he said, "Mrs. MacIntyre. We were just finishing our discussion."

She looked from one boy to the next, each more tight-lipped than his neighbor, appearing as though they'd been instructed in a series of mysterious arts. When her gaze fell on Temple once more, she said, "I trust all is well?"

He nodded, circumspect. "I believe it was a success."

She left them again, vowing to leave them alone.

That vow lasted a full two hours, until she could no longer stop herself from leaving her office to ostensibly check on the status of luncheon, which happened to take her through the main foyer of the orphanage, where she was unable to miss the line of serious, attentive boys snaking along its edge, each one watching Temple, who stood in the middle of the room, Lavender in hand, Daniel and George with him.

She hesitated at the foot of the stairs, immediately backing away from the space to watch.

"He made me angry," George was saying, simply. It was

not the first time he and Daniel had gone head to head. It would not be the last.

Temple nodded, his attention focused on the boy. "And so?"

"And so I hit him."

Shock flooded Mara. Physical aggression was not allowed inside MacIntyre's. Obviously, allowing a bare-knuckle boxer into the orphanage was a horrible idea. She started into the foyer when Temple said, "Why?"

She stopped at the strange question, one she would not have though to ask. One George had trouble answering. He shrugged, looking down at his shuffling feet.

"A gentleman looks into the eyes of those with whom he is speaking."

George looked up at Temple. "Because I wanted to make him angry, too."

Temple nodded. "You wanted revenge."

If the building had collapsed in that moment, Mara could not have stopped watching.

"Yes," George said.

"And Daniel, did he have it?"

The other boy did not hesitate, pulling himself up straight. "No."

Temple wanted to smile at the bravado; Mara could see it. Instead, he turned to face the other boy. "Truly? Because you seemed to grow quite angry once you were hit."

"Of course I did!" Daniel said, as though Temple were mad. "He hit me! I was defending myself!"

Temple nodded, "Which is your right. But do you feel better now that you hit back?"

Daniel scowled. "No."

Temple turned to George. "And do you feel avenged for whatever slight Daniel inflicted?"

George considered the question, his head tilted as he looked at Daniel for a long moment before he realized the truth. "No."

Temple nodded. "Why not?"

"Because I am still angry."

"Precisely. And what else?"

"And now Daniel is angry as well."

"Exactly. And Lavender?"

The boys looked to Lavender.

"We didn't see her!" Daniel said.

"She came from nowhere!" George cried.

"And she was nearly caught in your fray. Which could have been painful for her. Perhaps worse." The boys were horrified. "Let that be the lesson. I am not telling you not to fight. I am simply telling you that when you do, you should do it for the right reasons."

"Revenge isn't the right reason?"

He went quiet for a long moment, and Mara held her breath, waiting for his answer. Knowing that he was thinking of something bigger than whatever had started the sparring match between the two boys. "In my experience," he said, finally, "it does not always proceed as expected."

What did that mean?

Another pause, and he added, "And sometimes it ends with a piglet in danger." The boys smiled, George reaching out to pat Lavender's little pink head as Temple moved on. "Now, more importantly, I would imagine your fists hurt no small amount."

George shook out his hand. "How did you know that?"

Temple held out his own hand, the size of one of the boys' heads. He made a fist. "You tucked your thumb inside." He opened his hand and closed it again. "If you leave it on the outside, the blow hurts less."

"Would you teach us how to fight?"

He did smile then, one side of his mouth turning up. Lord, he was handsome. And from here, tucked behind the stairs, she could look her fill. No one ever need know.

"I would be happy to."

She should stop him before she had a battalion of well-trained pugilists on hand. And she might have, if he hadn't turned to look at her, his gaze finding hers quick and true, sending her heart straight into her throat.

"Mrs. MacIntyre," he said, "why don't you join us?"

*S*he'd been watching him for an age, quiet and still in the corner. If she were another woman, perhaps he wouldn't have noticed.

But she was Mara Lowe, and he'd resigned himself to the realization that he would always notice her. That he was consumed with awareness of her, even as he wished he wasn't. Even as he mistrusted her, and doubted her, and raged at her.

Even as he stood in her place of business and willed her to tell him the truth.

And so, when her young charges gave him an opportunity to bring her closer, he used it, enjoying the look of surprise on her face when she realized she'd been seen.

She came forward, doing her best to seem as though she hadn't been eavesdropping. "Good afternoon, gentlemen!"

They faced her like little toy soldiers, each executing a perfect little bow. "Good afternoon, Mrs. MacIntyre," they intoned as one.

She came up short. "My goodness! What a fine greeting."

She loved the boys; that much was clear. A vision flashed. Mara, smiling down at a row of boys on the wide green grounds of Whitefawn Abbey. A row of dark-haired, dark-eyed boys, each happier than the next. His boys.

His Mara.

He shook his head and returned his attention to the situation at hand. "Mrs. MacIntyre, the boys are asking for a lesson in fighting, and I thought perhaps you would like to help."

Her gaze went wide. "I wouldn't know how to begin."

The woman carried a knife on her person. Temple was

willing to wager everything he had that she knew precisely where to begin. "All the more reason for you to learn."

The boys, who had remained quiet up until that point, began to protest. "She can't learn; she's a girl!" one called out.

"Right," another chimed in, "girls learn things like dancing. And sewing."

The idea of Mara Lowe sewing anything but a knife wound was fairly laughable.

"She can learn," George said, "but she doesn't need to. Girls don't have to fight."

He did not like the memory that came quick and powerful, of Mara trapped on a Mayfair street by two animals stronger than her by half. He wanted her safe. Protected. And he could give her the tools to keep herself that way. "First, gentlemen don't refer to ladies as girls," Temple pointed out. "Second, you will all be learning to dance soon enough, I would think." That bit drew a chorus of groans from his pupils. "And third, everyone should be prepared to protect him or herself." He turned to Mara, extending his hand, "Mrs. MacIntyre?"

She hesitated, considering his hand for a long moment before making her decision, approaching, sliding her fingers into his. Once again, she was not wearing gloves, and in that moment, he wished that he wasn't wearing them, either.

Perhaps this had not been a good idea. He'd meant to unsettle her, to draw her out.

He had not expected to be the one unsettled.

But this was the way of things with Mara Lowe.

He turned her to face the boys, and wrapped his hand around hers, moving her fingers into position, until she made a perfect fist. He spoke as he did so, attempting to ignore her nearness. "Try to keep all the muscles loose when you make your fist. It's not the tightness of it that hurts your opponent, but the force. The tighter your fist, the more the blow will hurt you."

The boys were nodding, watching, making their own fists, arms flailing about. Not so Mara. She held her fists like a fighter—close to her face, as though someone might come at her at any moment. She met his gaze, focused on him. Warming him.

He turned back to the boys. "Remember that, lads. The angrier you are, the more likely you are to lose."

Daniel paused in his shadowboxing, his brow furrowed with confusion. "If you aren't to fight when you're angry, why then?"

An excellent question. "Defense."

"If someone hits you first," one of the other boys said.

"But why would they hit you first?" George countered. "Unless they're angry, and breaking the rules?"

"Perhaps they've bad manners," Daniel suggested, and everyone laughed.

"Or they've poor training," Temple added with a smile.

"Or you're hurting someone they care for," Henry said. "I would hit someone if they hurt Lavender."

The boys nodded as one.

"Protection." Temple's knuckles still ached from the night of Mara's attack. He looked to her, grateful for her safety. "That's the very best reason to fight."

Her cheeks pinkened, and he found he enjoyed the view. "Or perhaps they've made a mistake," she said.

What did that mean?

Something was there, in those strange, beautiful eyes. Regret?

Was it possible?

"What next, Your Grace?" The boys recaptured his attention.

He made his own fists, holding them high at his face. "You protect your head always. Even when taking your punch." He moved his left leg forward. "Your left arm and leg should lead. Knees bent."

The boys moved into position, and he went down their

line, adjusting a shoulder here, a fist there. Reminding them to keep knees bent and stay fluid on their feet. And when he was through with the last of the boys, he turned to Mara, who stood, fists up, waiting for him.

As though they were in constant battle.

Which they were.

He came toward her. "It's more difficult with ladies," he said softly, "as I cannot see your legs." What he wouldn't give to see her legs. He moved behind her, settling his hands to her shoulders. "May I?"

She nodded. "You may."

There were two dozen watchful boys with them, all playing chaperone. Nothing about touching her should feel clandestine, and yet the contact sizzled through him.

He rocked her back and forth on her feet, one knee sliding forward to test the length of her stride, the slide of fabric against his trouser leg enough to make his mouth dry. He was close enough to hear her quick intake of breath, to smell her—the light scent of lemons even now, in December, when only the wealthiest of Londoners had them.

If she were his, he'd fill the house with lemon trees.

If she were his?

What nonsense. She was tall and lithe and beautiful, and he would want any woman of her ilk if she were this close.

Lie.

He stepped away. "Keep your fists high and your head down. Remember that a man fights from his shoulders."

"And what of a woman?" she asked. "Do they fight from somewhere else?"

He looked to her, finding her gaze light with humor. Was she teasing him? The idea was strange and incongruous with their past, but no—those blue-green eyes were fairly twinkling. She *was* teasing him.

"In my experience, women fight dirty."

She smiled, then. "Nonsense. We simply fight from the heart."

He believed that about her. Without question. This was a woman who fought for what she wanted, and for those in whom she believed. She would fight for these boys, and—it seemed—for her brother, despite his being thoroughly despicable.

But she fought with purpose. And there was honor in that.

He wondered what it would be like to have her fight for him.

It would be like nothing else.

He pushed the thought from his mind and returned his attention to the boys, even as he couldn't stop himself from touching her. He adjusted her head, making it seem utterly professional, even as each touch rocketed through him. "Keep your heads tilted forward." Had her hair always been so soft?

"Don't hold your chin up, or you'll risk being clocked here . . ." He brushed his knuckles beneath her chin, where soft skin tempted him like a pile of sweets. "And here." His fisted fingers slid down the long column of her neck, to where her pulse pounded strong and firm beneath his touch.

She inhaled sharply, and he knew she felt it, too.

The pleasure.

The want.

Who was this woman? What were they doing to each other?

With difficulty, he pulled away from her. Raised his voice. Spoke to the boys. "The blow doesn't come from your arm. It comes from your body. From your legs. Your arms are simply the messenger." He threw a punch into the air, and the boys gasped.

"Cor! That was fast!"

"You must be the strongest man in the world?"

"Now all of you take a turn."

The boys were thrilled to punch at the air, bouncing back and forth on their newly light feet. He watched them for a long while, gaze lingering on the eldest—Daniel. The dark-haired, serious boy was focused on his jabs, eager for Temple's approval, and there was something familiar there. Something Temple recognized as like him.

Dark hair. Dark eyes. Eleven years old.

The boy had blue eyes, but otherwise, he had Temple's coloring.

Eyes the blue of Mara's.

She'd said the boy had been with her forever. He took that to mean since birth. Since she'd given birth to him?

Was the child his son?

And if he was, why had she hidden from him for so long? Didn't she know he would have taken them in? Protected them? He would have married her. Immediately.

They would have been a family.

The thought held more power than he could have imagined, packed with images of breakfasts and dinners and happy occasions filled with laughter and more. And Daniel wasn't alone. He had brothers and sisters, all dark-haired with eyes the color of summer. Greens and blues. And they were happy.

Happiness was a strange, fleeting thing.

But in that moment, his mysterious, missing family had it.

The sound of the boys' boxing returned his attention to the present. He would get his answers from Mara Lowe. But now was not the time. "You look very good, gentlemen."

He and Mara stood side by side for long minutes, watching their charges, before she said, quietly, "No wonder you are undefeated."

He lifted one shoulder. Let it fall. "This is what I do. It is who I am." It was the only thing he'd done well for twelve years.

"I don't think so, you know."

He turned to her, easily meeting her gaze, enjoying the way she looked at him. The way she focused on him. Wishing they were alone. Wanting to say a dozen things. To ask them. Settling on: "You try it."

She raised her fists, shadowboxed weakly in the air between them.

He shook his head. "No." He tapped his chest. "Me."

Her eyes went wide. "You want me to hit you?"

He nodded. "It's the only way to know if you're doing it correctly."

It was her turn to shake her head. "No." She lowered her fists. "No."

"Why not?"

She lowered her eyes, and he wondered at the spray of freckles across her cheeks. How had he not noticed them before? He attempted humor. "Surely, you like the idea of doing a bit of damage to me."

She was quiet for a long moment, and his hand itched to reach out and tilt her face to his. Instead, he settled on whispering, "Mrs. MacIntyre?"

She shook her head, but did not look to him when she said, "I don't wish to hurt you."

Of all the words she could have spoken, those were the most shocking. They were a lie. They had to be. After all, they were enemies—brought together for mutual benefit. Revenge in exchange for money. Of course she wanted to hurt him.

Why keep so much from him, then?

Her lie should have made him angry.

But somehow, it came on a wave of something akin to hope.

He didn't like that, either. "Look at me."

She did. And he saw truth there.

If she didn't wish to hurt him, what were they doing? What game did they play?

He stepped toward her, grasped her fist, and pulled it toward him until it settled, featherlight, at his chest, just left of center. She tried to pull it back, but he wouldn't let her, and instead, she ended the false blow the only way she could, stepping closer, opening her palm, and spreading it wide and flat over his chest.

She shook her head. "No," she repeated.

The touch was scandalous in that room, in full view of all those boys, but he didn't care. Didn't think of anything but the warmth of her hand. The softness of her touch. The honesty in it.

When was the last time a woman had touched him with such honesty?

She was destroying him.

He nearly pulled her into his arms and kissed her until she told him everything. The truth about that night twelve years ago and what it led to and how they'd come to be here. Now. About where they were. And where they were headed.

He lowered his head, she was inches away. Less.

She cleared her throat. "Your Grace, I'm sure you will not mind if I send the boys to tidy themselves. It is nearly time for luncheon."

He released her like she was aflame. Dear God. He'd nearly— In front of two dozen children. "Not at all, we are finished for the day, I think."

She turned to the boys. "I expect you all to remember the duke's lesson. Gentlemen do not start fights."

"We only finish them!" George announced, and the boys were off instantly, dispersed in their separate ways, except little Henry, who headed straight for Lavender, at Temple's feet.

Grateful for the distraction, Temple scooped up the pig. "I'm afraid not. Lavender remains with me."

Henry pursed his lips at that. "We're not allowed to lay claim to her," he pointed out. "Mrs. MacIntyre does not like it."

Temple met Mara's gaze over Henry's little blond head. "Well, Mrs. MacIntyre is welcome to scold me, then."

Henry seemed fine with that plan, and hurried off in the direction of luncheon. Temple straightened, and faced Mara, who looked as flustered as he felt.

"He's right, you know. The rule is, no using Lavender as booty."

"Whose rule?"

"Mine," Mara said, reaching for the piglet.

Temple stepped backward, out of reach. "Well, by my rules, I rescued her. And she is therefore mine."

"Ah. The rules of scoundrels."

"You seem to have no trouble playing by them when you see fit," he pointed out.

She smiled. "I am quite aboveboard where Lavender is concerned."

He stepped closer then, and his voice lowered. "You are the worst kind of scoundrel, then."

She raised a brow. "How so?"

"You assume the mantle only when you require it. You lack conviction."

He was very close now, looming over her. "Are you attempting to intimidate me into agreeing with you?"

"Is it working?"

She swallowed, and he resisted the urge to stroke the column of her neck. "No."

"Men cower at the mere mention of my name, you know."

She laughed. "The look of you now, cradling a piglet, might ease their fear."

He looked down at the sleeping Lavender and couldn't hold in his soft chuckle. Mara stilled at the sound, then cleared her throat. Temple found her gaze. She was aware of him. As aware of him as he was of her.

"Did you mean what you said about vengeance not being worth the trouble?"

He raised a brow. "I did not say that."

"You said it rarely proceeded as expected."

"Which is true," he said, "but that does not mean that it does not end as such." He had to believe it.

She looked straight ahead, her gaze settling at the indentation in his chin. "Where does this revenge end?"

I don't know.

He would not admit that. Instead, he said, "It cnds with

me a duke once more. With what I was promised as a child. With the life I was bred for. With a wife." He ignored the thought of strange eyes. "A child." And dark hair. "A legacy."

She did look at him then. "And for me?"

He thought for a long moment. Imagined them different. He a different man, she a different woman. Imagined they'd met under different circumstances. There was much to recommend her—she was brave and strong and deeply loyal to her boys. To this life she had built.

She was not his concern.

He wished that was not becoming so difficult to believe.

His free hand came to her face, tilted it up to meet him. Told her the truth. "I don't know. I shouldn't have come here today."

"Why did you?"

"Because I wanted to see you in your element. I wanted to meet your boys."

"To what end?"

He did not have an answer to that. He shouldn't want to know her better. To understand her. But he couldn't help himself. Perhaps because they were forever linked. Perhaps because she'd made him, in a way. Perhaps because he wished to understand her.

But he hadn't expected to begin to like her.

And he definitely hadn't expected to want her so much.

Knowing he couldn't say any of that to her, he chose another path—distraction—and he closed the distance between them and kissed her.

She leaned into the kiss, her lips a barely there promise, light and sweet enough for her to wonder if it could be called a kiss at all. It was more of a tease. A temptation that rolled in, surprising him with its power. With the way he wanted it. The way she wanted it. She sighed against him, and it was precisely that for which he was waiting.

She offered him entry; he took it.

The moment her lips parted, he captured them, deepening the caress, his hand sliding from her cheek to her neck and finally down her back to wrap around her waist and pull her close. Her sigh became his satisfaction, a deep, primitive growl that surprised him. She tested his control again and again.

And he enjoyed it.

Then his tongue was stroking across her lower lip and her hands were in his hair and she pressed against him, as though there were nothing in the world she wanted more than to be close to him. As though she weren't afraid of him.

He gathered her closer, wanting to bask in her fearlessness, wanting to block out everything that had been and would be and live only in this moment. With this woman who seemed to want the same.

That's when Lavender protested.

The piglet offered an outraged squeal and began to squirm quite desperately in her place between them, wishing to be either released or restored to her prior state of naptime abandon.

Mara and Temple tore apart from each other, her hand at her throat, his keeping Lavender from leaping to her death. He set the piglet down, and she scurried off, leaving them alone in the foyer, out of breath, staring at each other as though they did not know whether to run from the house or back into each others' arms.

He wasn't leaving that house.

Instead, he came at her once more, beside her in two long strides, lifting her in his arms—loving the weight of her there, the way his muscles bunched and tightened. The way they served a new, infinitely more valuable purpose. He took her mouth again, hard and fast, and tasted a frustration there—one he recognized because it mirrored his own.

Christ. He couldn't stay.

He released her as quickly as he'd captured her, leaving her unsteady on her feet, capturing her face in his hand, staring deep into her eyes and saying, "You are trouble," before punctuating the statement with a firm, final kiss and stepping away from her.

Her hand flew to her lips, and he watched the movement with desperation, loving the way those pretty fingers pressed against swollen flesh. Wishing they were anyone but them. Anywhere but here.

If wishes were horses.

He turned to leave. Knowing he had to. Not trusting himself to stay.

She called after him. "Will you join us for luncheon?"

"No, thank you," he said, at sea. "My morning is complete." Too complete. He should not have touched her. She was his ruin. His revenge.

Why couldn't he remember that?

"You look hungry."

He nearly laughed. He'd never been so hungry in his life. "I am fine."

"Are you still afraid I might poison you?"

He inclined his head, the excuse welcome. "A man cannot be too careful."

She smiled. He enjoyed that smile. Too much.

He had to stop this.

And so he said the one thing that he knew would do just that. "Mara."

She met his gaze, trying not to notice how handsome he was. How tempting. "Yes?"

"That night. Did we make love?"

Her eyes went wide. He'd shocked her. She'd been expecting a dozen things, but not that. Not the reminder of their past. Of their deal.

She recovered quickly—quick enough for him to admire her. "Have you decided to forgive my brother's debt?"

Like that, they were on solid ground once more. Thankfully. "No."

"Then I am afraid I cannot remember."

"Well." He turned for the door, fetching his greatcoat

from its hook nearby. "I certainly understand that predicament."

His hand was on the handle of the door when she said, "Another two pounds, either way."

He looked back, a thread of ice spreading through him. "For what?"

She stood tall and proud in the foyer. "For the kiss."

He hadn't been thinking of their deal when he'd kissed her, and he'd wager everything he had that she hadn't been thinking of it, either. The discussion of funds made the moment base and unpleasant, and he hated that she'd returned them to this place.

"Two pounds sounds fine." She needn't know that he'd pay two hundred for another moment like that. Two thousand. "I shall see you tonight." He opened the door and added, "Wear what arrives from Hebert today."

Chapter 9

"*Y*ou shouldn't fight him."

Temple did not look up from lacing his boots. "It's a bit late for that, don't you think? Half the club is already ringside."

The Marquess of Bourne, Temple's oldest friend and co-owner of The Fallen Angel, leaned against the wall to one side of the door to the boxing ring, watching as Temple prepared for the fight. "That's not what I mean and you know it. Tonight, you are welcome to fight all you like—though if I were a betting man, I'd have twenty quid on Drake falling in the first minute." He pointed to the low table at the center of the room. "You shouldn't accept the challenge from Lowe."

Temple looked to the list of names there. *Christopher Lowe* at the top, as it had been for weeks. Calling him. Tempting him. Daring him to accept. Evidently, Mara had not told her brother that she'd arranged a deal with the Killer Duke, and that she was earning back their money. Either that, or Lowe wanted to free his sister from ruin—but Temple couldn't imagine his sister's reputation had anything to do with the young man's plans.

Damned if he didn't want that fight more than anything. Lowe deserved a sound trouncing.

"It would be the fight of the year," Temple said. "The Angel would make sinful amounts of money."

"I don't care if the King and his royal guard sat ringside, with the crown jewels on the match. You shouldn't fight him."

Temple stretched against the leather strap hanging from the ceiling of his office, letting his weight loosen his shoulders, preparing him for what was to come. In a half an hour, he would enter the ring and fight, and every man in the audience would fight with him. Some would fight on his side, seeing themselves in the fallen duke who, despite shame and ruin and loathing, could be king here. But most would fight as his opponent, David to Temple's Goliath. They, too, knew what it was to lose to the Angel. And even as they paid their dues and basked in the glow of the tables above, a small part of them ached for the club's ruin.

"It is the game," he said, pretending not to care about the words. "It is what they come for. It is what we agree to give them."

"Bollocks," Bourne said. "We agree to take the bastards' money and give them a fight to watch. We don't agree to put ourselves on show. And that's what you would be doing." He came off the wall toward Temple, lifting Lowe's file from the table. "It would not be a fight. It would be a hanging. They would think that Lowe is finally getting a chance at retribution for his sister's death. If you're even considering fighting him, at least wait until the bitch is revealed. Then the world will be for you."

Temple's jaw set at the description, unwelcome. "I don't care who they are for."

"What a lie that is." Bourne huffed a humorless laugh and ran a hand through his hair. "I know better than anyone how you want them to think of you."

When Temple did not reply, Bourne continued. "I looked at Lowe's file today. He's lost everything that wasn't attached to him by birth, and a fair amount of money that he'd earned, somehow. I'm surprised Chase hasn't sent Bruno for the clothes from his back. Houses, horses, carriages, businesses. A fucking silver tea set. What the hell do we need with that?"

Temple smirked, working another long strip around his free hand. "Some people like tea."

Bourne raised a brow and threw the file to the table. "Christopher Lowe is the unluckiest man in Britain, and he either doesn't see it or doesn't care. Either way, his dead father is rolling in his grave, willing to make a deal with the devil or worse to rise up and kill the stupid boy himself."

"You take issue with a man losing everything at the tables? There's an irony."

Bourne's eyes glittered with irritation. "I might have lost it all, but I earned it back. Tenfold. More."

"Vengeance worked well for you."

Bourne scowled. "I spent a decade dreaming of retribution, convincing myself that there was nothing in the world that would satisfy me more than destroying the man who robbed me of my inheritance."

Temple raised a brow. "And you did just that."

The other man's voice grew soft and serious. "And I nearly lost the only thing that mattered."

Temple groaned, and reached for the leather strap that hung from the ceiling of the room, using it to lean into a stretch. "If the men in the room beyond knew how you and Cross go soft every time you speak of your wives, the Angel would lose all power."

"As we speak, my wife is warm and waiting. The men in the room beyond can hang." He paused, then added, "Vengeance was my goal, Temple. Never yours."

Temple met his friend's gaze. "Goals change."

"No doubt. But be prepared. Retribution is angry and cold. It makes a man a bastard. I should know."

"I'm already a bastard," Temple said.

One side of Bourne's mouth twisted in a wry smile. "You're a pussy cat."

"You think so? Tell me that in the ring."

Bourne ignored the threat. "It won't end as you think it will."

It would end precisely as Temple thought it would. Mara might have been the mastermind of his ruin, but her brother had played his part—weeping and wailing and feigning accusation and making all the world, Temple included, believe that he'd been dreadfully wronged.

Memory flared, Temple on the street five years earlier, in broad daylight, all of London giving him a wide berth. No one wished to cross the Killer Duke. No one wished to incite his anger. Christopher Lowe had exited a pub with his debauched friends, pouring out onto the road into Temple, so rarely touched in anything but violence or fear that he started at the contact.

Lowe had looked up at him, drunk and slurring his words, and blustered for the crowd's approval, "My sister's killer in the daylight. What a surprise."

The crowd of idiot drunks had laughed, and Temple had gone cold, believing Lowe's anger. Believing himself worthy of it.

Believing himself a killer.

He looked to Bourne. "She might have stolen twelve years, but he kept them from me."

"And both of them should suffer. God knows he deserves a thrashing, and yes, you'll feel as though you've exacted your revenge, and you'll trot the lady out through London as the second half of your master plan, and she'll be shamed, and you'll be welcomed with open arms and chased by marriage-making mamas. But you'll still be angry."

Revenge does not always proceed as expected.

The lesson he'd taught her boys.

The one he knew was true. He knew that this moment could not be undone. That it would forever mark him. That it would forever change him.

Bourne sat in a low, leather chair. "I'm simply saying you've everything you want. Money, power, a title that is growing dusty from lack of use, but yours nonetheless. And let's not forget Whitefawn. You may not be there, but the place has made you a fortune in its own right—you've been a better master to it than your father ever was. You could take it all. Return to Society. Find yourself a wallflower. Wallflowers love scoundrels."

Bourne was right. Temple could take it all back. Funds and a sullied title were more than most men had. Someone would have him.

But anger was a cunning mistress.

"I don't want a wallflower."

"What then?"

He wanted someone with passion. With pride.

Temple met his friend's eyes. "I want my name."

"Lowe can't give it to you. Losing to you in the ring only makes him a martyr." Temple was quiet for a long moment before he nodded once. He wanted the conversation done. Bourne added, "And the girl?"

A vision of Mara came, auburn hair wild, those strange, compelling eyes flashing. Never wearing gloves. Why did he notice that?

Why did he care?

He didn't.

"We've a score to settle."

"No doubt."

"She drugged me."

Bourne raised a brow. "A long time ago."

Temple shook his head. "The night she revealed herself to me."

A moment passed while Bourne registered the words. Temple gritted his teeth, knowing what was to come. Wishing he hadn't said anything.

Bourne burst out laughing. "No!"

Temple rocked up on his toes, bouncing once, twice,

swinging at the air. Pretending not to be infuriated by the truth. "Yes."

The laugh turned booming. "Oh, wait until the others hear this. The great, immovable Temple—drugged by a governess. Where?"

"The town house." Where she'd kissed him. Where he'd nearly taken more.

Bourne crowed, "In his own home!"

Goddammit.

Temple scowled. "Get out."

Bourne crossed his arms over his chest. "Oh, no. I'm not through enjoying this."

A sharp rap sounded on the door, and the two men looked to the clock. It was too early for the fight to begin. Temple called out, "Come."

The door opened, revealing Asriel, Temple's man and the second in command of security at the Angel. He did not acknowledge Bourne, instead looking straight to Temple. "The lady you invited."

Mara.

The thrill that coursed through him at the thought of her name grated.

"Bring her in." He waited for Asriel to leave, then returned his attention to Bourne. "I thought you were leaving."

Bourne sat in a nearby chair, extending his legs and crossing them at the ankles. "I believe I'll stay to watch this," he said, all humor. "After all, I wouldn't like the woman to try to kill you again. You might require protection."

"If you aren't careful, you shall be the one requiring protection."

The door opened before Bourne could retort, and Mara stepped over the threshold into his sanctum. She was wearing an enormous black cloak, the hood pulled up and low over her brow, but he recognized her nonetheless.

She was tall and beautifully made—all soft curves and pretty flesh—a woman to whom he would be naturally drawn if she weren't the devil incarnate. And that mouth . . . wide and wicked and made for sin. He shouldn't have tasted it. All it had done was make him starved for more.

She pushed the hood of her cloak back, revealing herself, her wide eyes immediately meeting his. He registered the nervousness in them—the uncertainty—and hated it as they moved to where Bourne sat, several feet away.

And suddenly, whether because of the excitement of the fight to come or something much more dangerous, Temple wanted to hit Bourne. Hard.

It had to be the coming fight, because it couldn't possibly be Mara. He didn't care who she looked at. Who looked at her. Indeed, his whole plan rested on all of London looking at her.

Bourne did not stand—a deliberate show of disrespect that set Temple on edge. "I am—"

"I know who you are," she interrupted, not using Bourne's title or the honorific he was due. A matching show of disrespect. "All of London knows who you are." She turned to Temple. "What is this? You ask me to come here and watch while you brutalize some poor man?"

The words did not sit well. She was back, strong as steel, but he stood his ground, knowing she used bravado to cover her discomfort. He knew the tactic well. Had used it many times. "And here I was, hoping you would give me a token to wear into battle."

Her gaze narrowed. "I ought to have your sabre tampered with."

Temple raised a brow. "Sabre tampering, is that how they refer to it at the MacIntyre Home for Boys?"

Bourne snickered, and Mara cut him a look. "You are a marquess, are you not?"

"I am."

"Tell me, do you ever act like it? I only ask because it does not seem that your friend cares much for behaving like a duke. I thought the immaturity was perhaps catching. Like influenza."

Admiration flashed in Bourne's gaze. He turned to Temple. "Charming."

"And she's armed with laudanum."

Bourne nodded. "I shan't drink anything she gives me, then."

"And a knife," she added, dryly.

He raised a brow. "And keep a vigilant watch."

"It's an intelligent plan," Temple offered.

Mara gave a little huff of displeasure, one Temple imagined she often repeated with her young charges. "You are about to pummel a man to bits, and you stand here and make *jokes*?"

"It's interesting that she takes the moral high ground, don't you think?" Bourne said from his chair.

Mara turned on the marquess. "I wish you would leave, my lord."

One of Bourne's brows rose. "I would be careful with that tone, darling."

Mara's eyes flashed with anger. "I imagine you'd like me to apologize?"

Bourne stood, straightening the lines of his perfect coat. And nodded in Temple's direction. "Apologize to him. He's not as forgiving as I am." He extracted his pocket watch and checked the time before turning to Temple. "Ten minutes. Is there anything you need before the fight?"

Temple did not speak. Nor did he move his gaze from Mara.

"Until after, then."

Temple nodded. "Until after."

The marquess left, closing the door behind him. Mara looked to Temple. "He did not wish you good luck."

"We do not say good luck." He moved to the table at the center of the room, and opened the mahogany box there and extracted a coil of wax.

"Why not?"

He pulled off two large clumps and set them on the table,

pretending that he wasn't utterly aware of her standing in the too-dark corner of the room. He wanted to see her.

He shouldn't.

"*Good luck* is bad luck."

"That's ridiculous."

"That's fighting at the Angel."

She did not say anything to that, instead crossing her arms across her chest. "Why am I here?"

He lifted a long, clean strip of linen from the wooden table at the center of the room, then laid one end across his palm and began to wrap the strip around his hand, being careful to keep it from twisting or folding. The nightly ritual was not designed merely to protect muscle and bone, though there was no doubt that in the heat of a battle, broken fingers were not unheard of.

Instead, the easy movement reminded him of the rhythm of the sport, of the way men had stood for centuries in this moment, minutes from battle, calming their mind and heart and nerves.

But there was nothing calm about his nerves with Mara Lowe in the room. He looked to her, enjoying the way her gaze locked on the movement. "Come."

She met his eyes. "Why?"

He nodded to his hand. "How much to wrap it for me?"

She watched the movement. "Twenty pounds."

He shook his head. "Try again."

"Five."

He wanted her close, despite the fact that he shouldn't want any such thing. And he could afford it. "Done."

She approached, removing her cloak to reveal the mauve dress Madame Hebert had promised him. She was beautiful in it, with skin like porcelain. His heart pounded as she came closer, pausing an arm's length from him and extracting that little black book that she carried everywhere. "Five," she repeated, marking the amount in her register. "And ten for the evening. As always."

Reminding him that she had her own reasons for being here.

She returned the book to its place and reached for his hand. No gloves. Again. Skin against skin, this time. Heat against heat.

He was paying for it.

Perhaps if he remembered that, it would help him forget her. The feel of her. The smell of her, lemons in winter. The taste of her.

She resumed his ritual, careful to wrap the linen about his wrist and around his thumb, keeping the long strips flat and firm against his skin. "You're very good at that," he said, his voice unfamiliar even to him. She did that to him. She made him feel unfamiliar.

"I have wrapped broken bones. I assume it's a similar principle."

Again, a little snippet of Mara, of where she'd been. Of who she'd been. Enough to make him want to ask a dozen questions she wouldn't answer. So he settled on: "It is."

Her fingers were soft and sure on his hands, making him ache for them in other places. Her head bowed over her handiwork, and he stared down at the top of her head, into auburn curls that he itched to touch. He wondered what her hair would look like spread in wide waves across his pillow. Across the floor of this room. Across his bare chest. Across hers.

His gaze moved to her shoulders, to the way they rose and fell with each breath, as though she labored far more intensely than she did.

He recognized that breath. Experienced it himself.

She wanted him.

She tucked the end of the linen gently into the rest of the wrap, and he tested the binds, impressed.

Another thing she did expertly.

He turned away from her, lifted the other length of linen. Passed it to her and held out his free hand. Watched her repeat her ministrations in silence, muscles aching as he tensed beneath her touch, desperate for more of it. Desperate to touch her in return.

Christ, he needed another stretch.

That wasn't all he needed.

But it was all he was getting. He extracted a mask from a nearby drawer. "Put that on."

She hesitated. "Why?"

"You will have your first moment before London tonight."

She froze, and he did not like the way it made him feel. "Masked?"

"I don't want you seen yet."

I don't want it to be over.

"Tonight," she repeated.

"After the fight."

"If you don't lose, you mean."

"Even if I lose, Mara."

"If you aren't brutalized and left for dead. That's the goal, isn't it?"

It wasn't, but he didn't correct her. "All right; if I don't lose." He inclined his head. "But I won't lose."

"What is your plan?" she asked.

"You'll see The Fallen Angel. Many women would kill for the opportunity."

She lifted her chin, proudly. "Not I."

"You'll enjoy it."

"I doubt it."

Her obstinacy made him smile, and to hide it, he pulled his shirt off, yanking it over his shoulders, baring his chest to her. She immediately looked away, playing the prim and proper miss perfectly.

He laughed. "I am not naked," he replied, smoothing the waist of his trousers and pretending to inspect a long-healed scar on one of his arms while watching her. "You have seen it before, have you not?"

She looked to him, then snapped her attention back to the wall. "That was different. You were wounded!"

His eyes darkened. "Before that," he said, knowing he had her when her cheeks went red. He would give his entire fortune to know what had happened that night. But he would not simply hand her what she wanted. On principle.

And therein lay the challenge with her.

Between them. Exhilarating even as it made him mad.

"Do you not manage a home for boys?"

She exhaled in a little frustrated puff and stared at the ceiling. "It is not the same."

"It is precisely the same."

"They are aged three through eleven!" she insisted.

He smirked. "So, they are smaller."

She lifted her hands wide in the universal signal for frustration. She was quiet for a long moment, before she said, "I did not thank you for giving them time today."

A thread of pleasure went through him at the words— something akin to pride. He ignored it. "You needn't thank me."

"Nevertheless." She looked down at the floor, her shoulders straight. "They enjoyed their time with you immensely."

The small acknowledgment was an enormous concession in the battle they waged. He could not resist moving toward her, walking her backward, across the floor of his rooms. He knew it would unsettle her, but he couldn't seem to care. When he was a foot or so from her, he lowered his voice. "And what of you? Did you enjoy it?"

Her cheeks flamed. "No."

He smiled at the instant lie. "Not even the bit where I kissed you?"

"Certainly not."

He came closer, pushing her back, drawn to the heat of her. Finally catching her in his arms, loving the way she gasped at his touch, loving the way the silk of her dress, warm from her body, brushed against his bare chest. He slid his hand down her arm, finding her hand, lifting it to the strap that hung from the ceiling above her.

She knew precisely what to do, grasping the leather strip as he repeated the movement with the other hand until she stood long and lush, arms extended overhead, like a sacrifice. Like a gift.

She could release it at any time. Deny him the moment. But she didn't, instead staring up at him, daring him with her beautiful gaze to come closer. To touch her more. To tempt her.

He took the dare, cupping her cheek in his hand, spreading his thumb across the high arc of it. Loving the softness of the skin there even as he told himself he did not notice it. "No?"

"No," she exhaled, and the sound of her breath turned him hard as a rock.

He looked down at her, her dress cut scandalously low, her breasts straining at the fabric because of her position, and he at once praised and cursed Hebert for doing his bidding.

Mara Lowe was the most tempting thing he'd ever seen.

But strangely, it wasn't her face or her body or the perfect breasts that rose and fell in an unsettled rhythm that convinced him of the fact. It was the way she faced him head-on. It was the way she refused to cow to him. The way she refused to fear him. The way she met him partway.

The way she saw him.

He was no killer, and she was the only person in the world who had always believed it. The only person who had ever known it to be true.

He lifted her chin, exposing the long column of her neck, and pressed a long, lingering kiss to the pulse beneath her chin, then to its mate at the place where neck met shoulder. "Are you sure you didn't enjoy it?"

The words teased at her warm skin, and she shook her head in a broken movement, swaying against the strap, holding tight to combat the way the caress impacted her. "Quite," she replied, the breath shuddering out of her, as he moved on, kissing the slope of her breast, once, twice, a third time—until he reached the edge of her dress, and slid a single finger between silk and skin, barely able to tell the two apart, until he reached the pebbled flesh that ached for him.

For which he ached.

He pulled the silk down, and spoke to her. "Even now?"

One hand fell from its mooring, coming to rest on his shoulders. Her bare skin against his. He could feel the want in them. "Even now."

It was a taunt. A challenge.

One he did not refuse. He set his lips to her breast, loving the little cry that escaped her as he worried that sacred skin, sucking low and soft until the cry became a moan in the dark room. He could not stop himself from pulling her closer, lifting her from her feet, wrapping her legs about his waist, worshipping her there in that room that rarely knew pleasure and too often knew pain.

And then she'd released the strap altogether, her weight in his arms and her fingers in his hair, holding him tight against her, encouraging his caress, begging him for more, urging him to give her everything he could.

He was hard and aching, loving the way she directed him. The way she took her pleasure with abandon. He wanted to give her everything for which she asked.

He pressed her to the wall of the room, his hands everywhere, pulling them up, higher and higher, his fingertips sliding against stocking and then glorious smooth skin, tracking the curve of her thigh up . . . up until he could feel the heat of her. Wicked, promising warmth guarded by perfect, soft curls. A promise he could not wait to uncover. To explore.

He paused there, lifting his lips to find her eyes.

She gasped. "Yes."

He'd never in his life heard such a glorious word. Never received such coveted permission.

"Say it again," he said. To be certain.

"Yes." The word coursed through him, her fingers tight in his hair.

He would give anything for a night with this woman.

But had he already done so?

The icy thought tore him from her, placing distance between them. Hating her all over again even as he felt nothing near hate. Nothing so cold. "Tell me," he shoved his fingers through his hair, trying to erase the memory of hers. "Did we do this? Were we—"

Lovers.

For a moment, he thought she would answer him. He thought he saw it there. Sympathy. Worse. Pity.

Fuck.

He didn't want her pity. She'd stolen that night from him, and she refused to give it back.

And then the emotion was gone from her gaze, and he knew what she was about to say.

He raised his voice before she could speak. "Tell me!"

"You know the cost of that information."

Vaguely, it occurred to him in that in another place, at another time, he would find this woman perfect in every way. There was something strong and firm and fearless about her.

The same something that had drugged him on their first meeting. And their second. The same something that had sent her fleeing into the darkness the prior evening.

The same something that had set him up to be a murderer twelve years ago.

The same something that would no doubt attempt to thwart him again.

But it was this place. This time.

And he had never been so infuriated in his whole life. "I will give you this, Mrs. MacIntyre, if the orphanage fails, you've a tremendous career as a whore."

She stilled like a doe on the hunt for a half second, before she moved, her hand flying fast and true and landing with remarkable precision on his cheek, stinging with her anger and his shame.

He didn't dodge or duck or feint. He took the slap as his due, feeling a dozen times an ass. He shouldn't have said it. He'd never said anything so insulting to a woman before. The apology was nearly on his lips when a bell rang above the door leading to the ring. She lowered her hand, the only sign of the blow the slight increase in her breath and the way her words shook in her throat. "What is that?"

What were they doing?

He turned away, refusing to touch the place where a furious red mark no doubt blossomed. "My opponent is ready. We shall continue this after the bout."

She inhaled, and he hated the way the soft sound filled the room almost as much as he hated the way she said, "I hope he wins."

He returned to the table, lifting the wax, molding it into two long strips. "I'm sure you do. But he won't." He inserted first one strip, then the second, into his mouth, and he did not hide the way he molded the wax along the edge of his teeth, daring her to look away.

She watched the coarse movements for a long moment before firing her own parting shot. "*Good luck*, Your Grace."

Chapter 10

The unmitigated gall.

The unmitigated *ass*.

He'd called her a whore.

With the insidious arrogance that came of being a wealthy, unencumbered man. A *duke*. He'd suggested that the idea that she provide him the information he required for a price made her a trollop.

If she'd been a man, the word wouldn't have occurred to him. If she'd been a man, he never would have said it.

If you treat me like a whore, you pay me like one.

So, she'd used the word first. This was different. He'd turned her inside out with his touch. He'd tempted her. He'd made her like him.

And then he'd called her a whore.

He deserved an immense setting down. The great, unbeatable Temple deserved to be beaten. By her.

Seething, a masked Mara followed the guard to whom she'd been assigned through a winding, curving passageway that kept her from view of the club's members. She was too angry to care where they were going or what came next— too lost in her mental evisceration of Temple.

Until her guide waved her into a new space and closed

the door behind her, leaving her alone in a sea of people. *Of women.* Surprise coursed through her. Women did not belong in a men's club. In a casino.

Her gaze threaded through the room, across the collection of chattering women. Recognizing several. A marchioness. Two countesses. An Italian duchess known for her scandals.

Surprise warred with curiosity as Mara considered the rest of the women—all of whom were dressed in stunning silks and satins, some masked, most chattering as though they were at a ladies' tea.

These weren't simply women. They were aristocrats.

And it was only once she'd recovered from that discovery that she noticed what she should have noticed the moment she'd been shepherded into the room, like a lamb to slaughter.

One entire length of the long, narrow, extraordinarily dark room was a window—a great shaded window that looked out on a roomful of men, all dressed for evening, clustered in a horseshoe of a crowd, at once not moving and in constant motion—shouting and laughing and enjoying themselves, vibrating with energy like leaves on a thriving oak in the heat of summer. The throngs of men surrounded a great empty space, blocked by rope and covered in sawdust, of which the women were afforded a perfect, unobstructed view.

The ring.

Mara moved closer to the glass, unable to stop herself from reaching out to touch it, amazed by the way the room glowed.

Thankfully, it occurred to her just in time that the men would see her if she came too close to the window. She stopped, pulling her hand back, even as she could not understand why not one of the men beyond seemed at all interested in the window or the ladies inside the small, dark room.

Were they so used to women watching the fights that they weren't scandalized by the women's presence? That they didn't yearn to control them? To keep them at bay? What kind of place was this?

What kind of perfect, wondrous place?

"They won't see you," said a lady nearby, drawing Mara's attention to her serious blue gaze, large and unsettling behind thick spectacles. "It's not a window. It's a mirror."

"A mirror." There was nothing mirrorlike about this window.

Mara's confusion must have shown, as the woman continued, "We can see them . . . but they only see themselves."

As if on cue, a gentleman crossed in front of the ring, close enough to the window to touch, before pausing for a moment and turning to face Mara. She leaned forward as he did the same on the other side, lifting his chin to fluff his cravat.

She waved a hand in front of his long, pale face.

He bared his teeth.

She dropped her hand.

He lifted one gloved finger, scrubbing it back and forth over the crooked, tea-and-tobacco-stained grimace before turning and walking away.

A collection of women nearby laughed uproariously. "Well. No doubt Lord Houndswell would be terribly embarrassed to know we have all witnessed the remains of his dinner." The woman smiled at Mara. "Do you believe it now?"

Mara grinned. "This must provide you hours of entertainment."

"When there isn't a fight to do the job," another woman replied. "Look! Drake's entered the ring."

The chatter inside the room dimmed as the women turned their attention to the young man climbing through the ropes into the sawdust-covered space where two others waited— the Marquess of Bourne and another pure aristocrat, pale and unnerved.

The crowd at the far end of the ring parted to reveal a large steel door, and the air in the room seemed to change, to grow thick with anticipation.

"Any minute now," a feminine sigh came from several yards away, and the entire room—on both sides of the window—seemed to still, waiting.

They were waiting for Temple.

And Mara found that she, too, was waiting.

Even though she hated him.

And then he was there, filling the doorway as though it were cut to his size, broad and tall and big as a house, bare from the waist up, wearing only those scandalous tattoos and buckskin breeches fitted to his massive thighs, and the long linen strips she'd wrapped along the hills and valleys of his knuckles and around the muscles of his thumb and wrist, as she tried not to notice his hands. Tried not to remember how they felt on her skin. Tried to remember that he was a weapon.

And when he'd kissed her, she'd remembered the truth of all of it. He was a weapon, spreading desire through her body, like bullets. Wounding her with want.

"He's the biggest, most beautiful brute of a man," another woman sighed, and Mara went still, forcing herself not to look. Not to care that there was admiration and something more in the tone—something like experience.

"Too bad he's never shown interest in you, Harriet," another said, calling forth a symphony of laughter from the rest.

Forcing herself not to care that the experience in the lady's words was a lie.

And then he was moving toward them, and it might have been her mind playing tricks, but it seemed like he was looking right at her, as though the magic window were a mirror for everyone in the room but him.

As though he knew himself well enough to never have to see his reflection ever again.

He was through the ropes then, and Bourne—now dwarfed by Temple—moved to Mr. Drake, saying words that Mara couldn't hear. Drake lifted his arms wide and the marquess smoothed his palms down his sides, patting the fabric of his breeches in a clinical, if rather shocking movement.

Mara could not keep quiet. "What are they doing?"

A lady came to her side. "Checking for weapons. The fighters are allowed a second to make sure that the bout is a fair one."

"Temple would never cheat," Mara said, the words drawing the attention of the women around her before she could hold them back. Heat flooded her cheeks as she looked from one to the next, finally settling on the woman who had spoken, uncommonly tall and blond, brown eyes glittering near gold in the reflection of the brightly lit ring.

"No," the lady said. "He wouldn't."

There. There was the experience that Mara had misheard earlier. This woman knew him.

She was beautiful enough for it.

They were no doubt beautiful together, matched only in height—with everything else perfectly contrasted to each other. She imagined this woman's long arms wrapped around his neck, her long fingers threaded through his dark hair. His massive hands at her waist. Possessing her. Loving her.

And she hated him all over again, but now for another, more confusing reason.

A long whistle sounded from the other end of the room, "What I wouldn't give to be Drake's second right now!"

Mara's attention returned to the ring, where the well-dressed aristocrat approached Temple, awkwardly indicating that he, too, should raise his arms. He did, the muscles of his chest and abdomen rippling with the movement, and Mara's mouth went dry at the image he made, waiting for the man to check his person for weapons, smirk on his lips, as though he had the devil himself on his side, and therefore had no need of trickery.

She imagined his arms high above his head, caught in the scandalous strap that hung from his ceiling, where she'd held herself still, the cool leather biting into her palms, a contrast with his heat. With his touch. With his kiss.

But she hated him.

"Go on, man! Touch him!"

"Take him in hand!"

"Make sure to check all the nooks and crannies!"

The ladies were competing for bawdiest encouragement now, laughing and crying out as the aristocrat in the ring checked the Duke of Lamont with a speed born of fear or embarrassment or both.

"Not so quickly!"

"Or so soft!"

"I'd bet my fortune that Temple likes a firm hand!"

"Don't you mean your husband's fortune?" came the retort, and the redhead at the window turned to the room, a wide grin on her pretty face.

"What the earl doesn't know shan't hurt him. Look at the size of him!"

"Ten quid says he's that big all over."

"No one will take that bet, Flora," someone replied, laughter seeping into the tone. "Not one of us wants you to be wrong."

"I'd risk a night with the Killer Duke to find out!"

The laughter fairly shook the room, nearly all of the women taking immense pleasure from the words—from their own additions to the lewd suggestions. Mara looked down the room, at the long row of silks and satins and perfect coifs and maquillage, and the way the women fairly salivated at Temple, remembering his moniker but not the truth of it—that he was a duke. That he deserved their respect.

And that, even if he weren't a duke . . . he wasn't an animal.

As they were treating him.

As her actions had made them treat him.

The realization came on a wave of regret, and the keen knowledge that if she could go back in time . . . if she could change everything, she would have found another way to escape that life. A way that would have freed her from the chains of a cruel father and a cold husband, and still saved this man from such wicked, unpleasant shame.

But she couldn't.

This was their life. Their dance. Their battle.

Blessedly, the seconds completed their inspections, leaving Temple to run a line in the sawdust at the center of the ring with his boot. Even that movement, which should have been harsh and unmeasured, was graceful.

"The scratch line," her new companion explained. "The men face off on either side of the line. As many rounds as necessary until one falls and does not rise."

"Bets are closed, ladies," the dark-skinned man who had escorted her to this room spoke for the first time, reminding Mara that they were in a gaming hell—that even this moment was worth money to The Fallen Angel.

Temple waited, unmoving, for Drake to approach.

The narration continued. "Temple always allows the opponent to take the first hold."

"Why?" she asked, hating the breathlessness in the word. She'd been dragged here, against her will, to watch this expression of utter brutality.

So why did she suddenly care so much for the answer?

"He is undefeated," the woman said, simply. "He likes to give his opponents a fair chance."

Fairness. Something he'd never had. He was a good man. Even if no one saw it. Even if she didn't wish to believe it.

She looked to his bare feet, the wide black bands on his massive arms, the myriad of scars on his chest and cheek and the new fresh one on his arm, still bearing the stitches from her hand.

She couldn't find his dark gaze, couldn't bring herself to see him as a whole and face the things that she'd done to him, to put him here, in this ring, watched by half of London. Wagered on. Marveled at, like a bottled creature in a cabinet of curiosities.

She looked away, turning to Drake, who was easier to watch. He took a deep breath and steeled himself for battle.

The fight began, brutal and unforgiving.

Drake came at Temple with undeniable force, and Temple deflected it, bending backward and using the momentum of the smaller man's blow to bring him off balance and land a powerful punch to Drake's side.

The hit was hard and precise, and Drake stumbled away, catching himself on the ropes of the ring before coming around to face Temple again.

The massive duke stood at the scratch line, barely breathing heavily. He waited.

"Aww, 'twon't be a good fight tonight, girls," one of the ladies said. "Drake's going to drop like a stone."

"They always do," another said.

"If only there were an opponent who would keep him in the ring," sighed a third, and Mara wished all these women would simply stop talking.

Drake came at him again, arms outstretched, like a small child angling for an embrace. He never had a chance. Temple moved like lightning, swatting away the long arms and delivering a wicked blow to Drake's jaw and another to his torso immediately after.

Drake fell to his knees, and Temple immediately stepped back.

Mara's gaze flew to his face, registering none of the triumph or pride that one might have expected. There was no emotion there—nothing that revealed his feelings about the bout.

He waited, patient as Job as Drake pressed his hands to the sawdust-covered floor, and the room around her went quiet.

"Is he going to get up again?"

She watched the fallen man breathe deeply, his chest heaving once, twice, before he raised his hand in the universal sign for *enough*.

"Awww," one of the ladies sighed in disappointment. "A forfeit."

"Come on, Drake! Fight like a man!"

The women around her whined and whinged, as though they'd lost a favorite toy. She turned to the woman who had become her tacit guide for the evening. "What now?"

Temple stepped forward as the woman spoke, reaching toward his opponent. "A forfeit is an immediate loss."

Drake accepted Temple's help, coming to his feet unsteadily. The aged oddsmaker at one side of the ring pointed a finger to a red flag at one corner of the space, and the crowd on both sides of the window erupted into shouts and jeers.

"And Temple wins," the woman explained to Mara, "but not the way they like."

"A win is a win, is it not?"

One brown brow rose in amusement. "Tell that to the men who just lost hours of entertainment in thirty seconds." She returned her attention to the ring, as men throughout the room protested, waving scraps of paper in the air. "Those men have placed enormous bets on the fights—never against Temple, but on the number of rounds and the punches thrown . . . even the way Drake fell." The lady paused. "They don't care for short bouts."

"Anna," the man in the corner called out, and the lady turned to him.

He nodded once, and she returned her attention to Mara. "I am sorry. I'm afraid I have work to do." Mara's brow furrowed, and the lady tilted her head. "Unhappy patrons require . . . appeasing."

And Mara understood. The woman was a prostitute. A highly paid one if Mara had to make a guess. "Of course."

The woman tipped her head. "My lady."

"Oh, I'm not . . ."

Anna smiled. "Those of us who are not must stick together."

And then she was gone, leaving Mara with the aftermath of the fight and the keen knowledge that she deserved no kind of honorific considering the consequences of her long-ago actions.

Temple seemed not to care about the way the men screamed and fought around him, desperate for a way to regain their bets. Instead, he turned to face the mirror, black eyes scanning its breadth.

"Here it is!" a lady called from nearby.

He nodded once, sending titters and sighs through the room, leaving Mara breathless with the knowledge that with the bout now over, he was coming for her.

And with that knowledge came the memory of their last conversation. Of the words he'd used. Of the blow she'd dealt.

Of the bed she had made for them, where they were enemies. Where she did all she could to regain her funds, and he did all he could to exact his revenge.

Her anger returned.

"Poor Temple!" someone called. "He didn't get his fight!"

"I should like to give him a fight," another lady retorted, and the innuendo set the rest of the room tittering.

I don't fight women.

How many times had he said it that first night?

But what if one were to challenge him anyway? In the open? What if a women were to offer to fight him for the money that was rightfully hers?

What if she were to back him into that corner where his red flag flew with cocksure arrogance?

Would he forfeit?

Could she win?

Her heart pounded in her chest. *She could.* This moment, this place was her answer. The Marquess of Bourne had climbed into the ring with him, and the two were in discussion.

Mara's thoughts raced.

It could be that easy.

A reed-thin bespectacled man materialized at her side. "Temple requests that you meet him in his rooms. I am to take you there."

Excellent. "I have every intention of meeting the duke."

She intended to set him down. To prove him wrong. To prove herself stronger and smarter and more powerful than he thought her. To make him regret his words. To make him rescind them.

His kisses had distracted her too well. His strange, unexpected kindness had upended her keen awareness of this war they waged. But then he'd called her a whore. And she was reminded of his purpose. Of hers.

He wanted retribution; she wanted the orphanage safe.

And she would get what she wanted.

Tonight.

Her commitment redoubled, she and her guide emerged from the quiet passageway into a crush of bodies beyond, and Mara was grateful for her mask, the way it focused her view—men moving in and out of frame—the wheres and whyfors of their journey made irrelevant by her limited view.

The mask turned the entire evening into a performance of some kind—the men moving across a stage just for her, dressing for a larger, more important scene. For the main player.

Temple.

She let the man guide her back to Temple's rooms, where he deposited her in the dimly lit space and closed the door behind her, throwing the lock without hesitation.

But Mara was already moving across the room, already heading for the steel door she'd watched from the other side of the ring. Knowing where it led.

She yanked it open, her plan clear in her mind—as clear

as the plan twelve years earlier that had set her on this course. That had led her to here. To this moment. To this man.

She ignored the men on either side of the aisle that marked the clear path to the ring, grateful for her mask in those fifty short feet even as her gaze tracked no one but the enormous man still in the ring, his back to her as he reached for grasping, congratulatory hands.

The poor thing had no knowledge of what was to come.

She was so focused on Temple, she did not see the Marquess of Bourne before he stepped into her path, catching her by the arms. "I don't think so."

She met his eyes. "I won't be stopped."

"I don't think you'd like to test me."

She laughed at the words. "Tell me, Lord Bourne," she said, considering her options. "Do you really think that you have any place in this? My entire life has led to this moment."

"I will not let you ruin his retribution," he said. "If you ask me, you deserve every ounce of it, for the devastation you've wrought."

Perhaps it was the implication that he understood the long thread of past that stretched between Mara and Temple. Or perhaps it was the ridiculous entitlement in the words, as though the Marquess of Bourne could stop the globe from spinning on its axis if he wished. Or perhaps it was the smug look on his face.

She would never know.

But Mara did not hesitate, using all the strength and skill and lessons she'd learned from twelve years living on her own with no one to care for her, and from the man beyond, who'd refreshed them.

Bourne didn't see the punch coming.

The smug aristocrat reeled back, a sound of shock and surprise coming on a flood of red from his nose, but Mara did not have time to marvel at her accomplishments.

She was ringside and through the ropes in seconds, and

the moment she stood there, in the uneven sawdust, the room began to quiet. The men clamoring to claim their bets and call for a second bout turned to face her, like layers of onion peeling off for stew.

It took him a moment to hear the silence. To realize it was directed at him. At the ring.

A thread of uncertainty began at the back of her neck, starting its slow, curling journey down her spine. She willed it away.

This was her choice.

This was her next step.

She met his black eyes even as he started toward her, and she saw the surprise there. The irritation. The frustration. And something more. Something she could not identify before it was locked away in that unforgiving gaze.

She took a deep breath and spoke, letting her voice run loud and clear in the enormous room. "I, too, have a debt with The Fallen Angel, Duke."

One black brow rose, but he did not speak.

"So tell me. Will you accept my challenge?"

Chapter 11

If he'd been offered ten thousand pounds to guess who would step into his ring next, he would not have imagined it would be she.

But when the room quieted and he turned from a collection of men on the other side of the ropes to see what had distracted them, he *knew* it would be she. Even as he was sure it couldn't possibly be.

There she was, standing tall and proud and strong at the center of the ring, Drake's blood splattered at her feet, as though she were in a tea shop. Or a haberdashery. As though it was perfectly ordinary for a masked woman to enter a boxing ring, in the middle of a men's club.

She was barking mad.

And then she spoke, issuing her challenge in her calm, clear way, as though she were perfectly within her rights to do so. As though the entire club wouldn't explode with the scandal.

Which it did, in a cacophony of harrumphs and guffaws and affronted grunts that quickly devolved into a chattering masculine din. Under cover of noise, Temple collected himself and approached her, his opponent in every way, and yet not his opponent at all.

He raised a brow.

She did not move, and he wished the mask gone so he could read her expression.

It could be gone. Instantly, if he willed it.

He could call her bluff, unmask her in front of the lion's share of the most powerful men in London, and resume the life that had been frozen in time for twelve years.

And the one that had been frozen in time for less than a week.

But then he would not see how far she would go.

He tilted his head and spoke so only she could hear. "A bold move."

She matched his movement, her lips curving gently. Teasing him. Tempting him. "Whores must be bold, I'm told."

And with that, he understood. She was furious.

As well she should be. He'd called her a whore. Guilt threaded through him, somehow discernable from frustration and fascination.

She did not let him find the right reply. Which was best, as he wasn't sure he could. Instead, she added, "As should an opening gambit, don't you think?"

Guilt was chased away by the words. By the challenge in them. By the excitement that thrummed through him every time they faced each other. This was more powerful than any bout he'd ever had. "You think I will allow you to win?"

The curve became a smile. "I think you haven't a choice."

"You've miscalculated."

"How so?"

He had her. "My ring, my rules." He raised a hand to the room, and the collection of men—two hundred, perhaps more—went quiet. Her eyes went wide behind the mask at the way he controlled the space and its inhabitants.

"Gentlemen!" he called to the room at large. "It seems tonight's entertainment is not complete." He stepped closer to her, and the soft scent of lemons curled around him—clean where this place was filthy. Light where it was dark. She did not belong here. And somehow, she did.

Perhaps it was simply that he did not wish her to leave, even as he knew she should.

She was close enough to touch, and he pulled her close to him, sliding one leg between hers, loving the way her silk skirts clung to his trousers. Loving the feel of her in his arm, firm and right. Hating it, too, the way she seemed to consume his thoughts when she was near him. The way she distracted him from his goal.

Retribution.

He pulled her close, and she gasped, her bare hands coming up to rest on his bare chest, her touch cool and smooth against his sweat-dampened skin. He lowered his voice for her ears only. "You have made your bed."

She stilled at the words, as though they meant something to her, for a half second. Maybe less. "Then by all means, Your Grace, it is time I lie in it."

The words surprised him, the thread of daring and conflict and something more in them. He wondered if the imagery that clattered through his mind echoed in hers—both of them in bed. Naked. Entwined.

Glorious.

Equal.

He turned to the crowd, hating the hungry gazes fixed upon her even as he knew they were necessary. "Shall I check her for weapons?"

A roar of approval came from the assembly of men, and he reached for her skirts, knowing the knife she carried so religiously would not be far. She gasped as his hands slid over her torso and hip, recognized the sound as one of pleasure. He met her gaze. "I never thought you an exhibitionist."

She pursed her lips. "I would not begin to do so now."

"Hmm," he let the sound ooze over her. "Your actions tonight suggest otherwise." In the pocket of her skirts, his fingers found the book that cataloged their story in pounds and shillings and pence.

She felt the touch and met his gaze. "Be careful, Your Grace, lest tonight cost you more than you think."

He couldn't help his smile as he found the hilt of her knife. Ubiquitous. "Hebert made you a pocket?"

She narrowed her gaze on him through the mask. "I thought I'd made it clear that I am quite skilled with a needle."

He couldn't stop the laugh that came then. The woman was remarkable. She'd received a dress that cost more than her salary for a year, and immediately installed a pocket to keep her weapon close.

He removed the knife and held it high above their heads. "The lady is equipped with steel."

In more ways than one.

The men roared their own laughter as Temple tossed the knife across the ring, ignoring the way it slid through the sawdust. Too focused on her.

"A woman cannot be too careful, Your Grace." It was her turn to raise her voice. To play to the crowd. To win their laughter. She smiled at him, bright and brilliant, and he wished they were anywhere but here. "But what of my challenge? Are we not evenly matched now that you've taken my blade?"

The crowd erupted in guffaws and a chorus of *oh-ho*s, and Temple realized what she was doing. "Not in the ring, my love. But perhaps we can find another place to . . . discuss it."

The men chortled, and she stiffened in his arms, her words carrying across the room. "I don't think so. You hold a debt of mine. I am here to win it back. 'Tis the way of the Angel, is it not?"

Oooh, sang the crowd.

He shook his head slowly, playing to the crowd even as

he spoke to her, quiet and serious. "I don't fight women." Remembering the first time he'd said it to her. The man he was then. Unsure of himself. Uncertain of his actions. No longer.

She curled one of the hands on his chest into a fist. "And tell me, Your Grace, have any of them ever challenged you here? In the ring?"

"She's got a point, Temple!" someone in the assembly cried out.

"I'll give you a hundred pounds to let me accept the challenge for you, Temple!"

"A hundred only? I've got five for a chit like that! I'd wager she's glorious in the sheets!"

He released her and turned toward the words to find Oliver Densmore, the biggest ass in London, hanging on the ropes, tongue fairly hanging out of his mouth.

Temple resisted the urge to kick the man's teeth in.

"Well, Your Grace?" Mara distracted him. "Have you ever had a challenge from one of my sex?"

The word *sex* rioted through him like a blow, and he was suddenly certain that she was the most skilled opponent he'd ever faced in this ring. "No."

She turned in a slow circle to show her masked face to the room, finally stopping and facing the mirror where the women no doubt tittered and gossiped and wondered about her.

She met his gaze in the mirror and smiled, the expression wide and welcome, and for the first time since they'd met on that dark London street, he wondered what it would be like for that smile to be commonplace in his life. To know it well. "Ah," she said, the words carrying through the room. "So you forfeit."

He hesitated, not liking the thread of unease that came with the words. "No."

She turned to the oddsmaker, whose wide eyes were

in danger of escaping his head. "Is that not the way of the bouts, sirrah? The fight happens, or the fighter forfeits?"

The older man opened his mouth and closed it, looking to Temple for guidance. *Smart man.*

Temple crossed his arms over his chest and saved the poor git. "There are other ways to fight. Other ways for me to win."

She turned then, looking over her shoulder, those lips curved and calm and defiant. And unbearably tempting. "Other ways for *me* to win, you mean."

The crowd went wild. They adored her, this mysterious woman who seemed to have Temple and the rest of the world wrapped about her finger.

And somehow, in that moment, he did, too.

He was beside her in an instant, collecting her in his arms, pulling her tight to him, and taking her lips. Claiming her in front of God and London. Tasting her sweetness. Her spice. The roar of those assembled faded away as he consumed her, the kiss too rough, too searing, until he realized that she was matching it with her own passion. Her own fervor.

She'd felt it, too.

She wanted him just as he wanted her.

What a disaster. One he would worry about later.

He kissed her again and again, his hands coming to cup her face and hold her still as he claimed her with lips and tongue and teeth until the whole world had disappeared and there was nothing but her. And him. And this moment. And the way they matched.

The way she saw him.

The way he saw her.

But they weren't alone, of course. And he was close to ravishing her in front of all of London.

Christ. He was kissing her in front of *all of London.*

He was ruining her.

He stopped, lifting his mouth from hers, loving the way

she followed his lips, loving the way she ached for him as
he ached for her.

No.

She was ruined. As though she were the whore he'd
called her. The whore he'd meant them to think her. Except
now the plan seemed flawed.

Christ. What had he done?

It had been the goal, had it not? Retribution? But somehow, it was all wrong. The plan hadn't included desire. Or
passion. Or emotion.

What had she done to him?

She lifted one auburn brow. "Well, Your Grace? Do you
fight? Or forfeit?"

"Neither."

He did not wait for her to reply, instead lifting her into
his arms, grateful that her mask was still affixed to her face,
and carrying her from the ring, the cheers of all of London
in his ears.

It would have been an excellent plan, if not for the man
blocking his path.

Christopher Lowe.

ℋeart pounding, Mara was caught up in Temple's
arms, too distracted by the strength of him and the excitement of their verbal bout and the euphoria of her unsettling
him to realize that he'd stopped. She didn't notice until he
set her down, her body sliding along his until her feet found
the sawdust-covered floor.

"Lowe," he said, low and dark, and she spun toward the
word. He was revealing her now? She supposed it was a
good move. The checkmate of their game.

But disappointment came, nonetheless.

Until she realized he wasn't looking at her. He was looking past her, over her right shoulder, into the eyes of her

brother, who stood several feet away, on the edge of the ring, frustration and something worse in his gaze. Something unsettling. Something incalculable.

"You think you have won? You think you can take everything of mine . . ." He paused. "And my sister?"

The room went silent, every man present leaning forward to hear the conversation.

She stepped toward her brother, knowing that he was furious. Eager to calm him. To keep him from Temple. From ruining her plans. From ruining what she was building.

The good and the bad.

Temple stopped her with a hand on her arm, immediately placing himself between her and her brother. Kit was already shaking his head, coming forward, driven by stupidity, his voice loud and angry. "All of London thinks you a winner. A hero. But the Killer Duke is nothing more than a coward." He looked to Mara, and she saw the loathing there, her father's as much as Kit's. "A coward and a whoremonger."

The gasp that rippled through the room was Mara's as much as any others'. The words were a blow, dealt from the one man who should have been concerned for her reputation. Temple would have to fight him now. He wouldn't have a choice, and Kit knew it. One did not call a man a coward and not receive a fight. She stepped toward him, wanting to stop it. Wishing she could hurt him herself.

Temple's arm came across her chest. He turned to her. Spoke softly, for her ears only. "No. This is my fight."

There was anger in his gaze, too. But it was different, somehow.

It was for her.

Who was this man?

Kit did not see the anger, too blinded by his own bluster. "You won't fight the one man who has an honest reason for it." He lifted his fists. "But now I am here, and you can't ignore me. You'll fight me."

The words unlocked the men assembled. They moved in

a wave of humanity, bombarding the bookmakers around the room, each eager to place their bets.

"It's the Fight of the Century!" someone called out.

"Two hundred on Temple for an immediate win!" Another cried, "A single round—repeated!"

"Fifty says Temple breaks three of Lowe's ribs!" A deep voice called.

"I've seventy-five on the Killer Duke earning his moniker again!"

London had been waiting for this fight for a decade. For longer. The Killer Duke versus the brother of his kill. The ultimate David and Goliath.

Kit's words from their meeting days earlier echoed through her. *I am not free of this. And now, neither are you.* He would ruin everything. Lose it all, again. And destroy everything she'd worked for in the process. Temple would get his vengeance; she would get nothing.

The thought should have brought resignation. Should have brought devastation. Should have come on the urge to flee. But instead, it brought sadness, for hadn't there been a time, a moment, when she'd had a taste of what it would be to win it all? The money, the orphanage . . . the man?

She pushed the thought away.

He was not for winning. Certainly not by her.

She didn't deserve him.

Now, after this, he would be rid of her.

Temple turned to her, pushing her back to the ropes. "Temple," she said quietly, not knowing how she would finish.

This wasn't my plan.

I didn't know he was here.

Win.

He didn't look at her. It was as though she didn't exist. And in that moment, nothing else mattered. All she wanted was for him to see her. All she wanted was to go back. To the dressmaker. To the night on the street outside his home. To twelve years earlier.

All she wanted was to change it.

"Temple," she said, again, wishing his name said all of it.

He ignored her, lifting her over the ropes and passing her down to the Marquess of Bourne standing on the other side. Bourne caught her and held her, keeping her safe from the throngs around them. "He should kill you for setting him up."

Dear God. They couldn't possibly think she'd planned this.

He couldn't possibly.

Except, it was precisely what she would have thought, if the situation was reversed.

And she and Temple were two sides to the same coin.

She would tell him everything once he'd won. All of it. From the beginning. She would tell him that the money belonged to the orphanage. That she fought for the boys, and nothing else. That she did not wish him ill.

That she wished him to win.

But for now, she had no choice but to watch the bout. Temple faced Kit—faced her—and she saw that this was nothing like the fight with Drake. There was emotion in his eyes this time. Anger. Fury.

More.

He dragged his foot through the sawdust in a powerful, undeniable beginning.

Or perhaps it was an end.

The fight began, and even now, Temple followed his own rules. Allowing Kit the first move. Her brother grabbed at Temple with vicious intensity, landing a blow to the eye.

She hadn't expected the sound of flesh on bone, the way fists fell with hollow thuds. The way knuckles slapped against bone. The sound turned her stomach as she watched Temple take first one hit, then another, then a third. And then, as though he'd been counting the blows, offering them for free before forcing her brother to pay for them, he came at Kit the way she'd always heard he fought.

His fists landed like thunder, pummeling Kit's abdomen and sides, until her brother turned from the assault, taking a moment to find his breath. To find his strength. And went at Temple again.

Perhaps he was named because he was built like stone, impenetrable. Unbeatable. As though the world could come to an end, and Temple alone would survive. His fists rained down upon her brother. Jabbing and crossing and cutting until Kit fell away, coming to rest on the ropes mere inches from her, one eye nearly shut from the blows.

She might hate him at times. He might no longer be the boy she'd known—the one she'd left—but he was still her brother. And she did not wish him dead. She pled with him. "Kit! Stop this! He'll kill you!"

He met her gaze, and she expected to see pain or regret or surprise there . . . but instead, she saw something unexpected. Hatred. "You chose him."

She shook her head, instinctively. "No." It wasn't true. Was it? She'd chosen the boys. She'd chosen their safety.

And then . . . somehow, she'd chosen Temple.

The thought shocked her. Dear God. Had she chosen him?

Would he allow it? Her gaze flickered to him, coming at them. Coming to fetch Kit. Temple's eyes found hers instead. Cold. Hard.

Betrayed.

She hated that look. Couldn't face it. Turned back to her brother, who smiled, the way he always had when they were children and he was about to do something that they would enjoy, but that would no doubt earn him a beating from their father.

And then he reached for the floor of the ring.

For her knife.

She saw the gleam of silver before anyone else.

Mara gasped and screamed out, "No!"

But it was too late. He went at Temple without finesse—with sheer, unmitigated force.

Her gaze flew to Temple, who was not watching Kit.

He was watching her.

Dear God.

"He'll kill you!" The same words, now with a different meaning. "No!" She was a madwoman, breaking free of Bourne's grasp and pushing toward the ring, grasping at the ropes, trying to get to Temple.

Trying to save him.

The words were lost in the roar of the crowd, in the way they seethed and barked and howled like dogs on the hunt for blood.

Kit gave it to them.

The knife landed hard and deep in Temple's chest, blood blooming from it like a perverse blossom.

She froze at the sight, halfway into the ring as someone caught her by the waist, pulling her back with wicked strength. She didn't notice her scream until it was out and earsplitting.

And, for the first time since he'd taken to the ring twelve years earlier, the Killer Duke fell.

She couldn't stop watching, unable to tear her gaze from the awkward angle of his legs and the river of blood pouring from him, spreading dark and ominous over the sawdust on the floor. A tall, ginger-haired man was in the ring then, on his knees at Temple's side, stripping off his coat, barking orders, bending over to inspect the wound.

And then Mara couldn't see at all, her view blocked by the dozen men already in the ring, trying to get to him. Each eager to be the first to make the call.

"He's dead!"

"No," she whispered, refusing to believe it.

What had she done?

Temple was too strong, too big, *too alive* for it to be true. She struggled against the arms holding her in an iron grip, desperate to be free. Desperate to get to him. To prove the words wrong. "No. It can't be true."

The arms around her tight almost to the point of pain. Bourne's voice was a vicious promise at her ear. "You shall pay dearly if it is."

Chapter 12

The men of The Fallen Angel stood watch over their fallen comrade.

It had taken three men to carry Temple from the ring—Bourne; Asriel; and Cross, the club's financier—and the trio was winded when they barreled through the great steel door into Temple's private rooms—the place he had crafted for quiet and peace.

They'd cleared the large, low table, and lay him on it before lighting every candle in the room. Without needing to be asked, Asriel left in search of hot water, linen, and a surgeon, though there was no promise that a surgeon could help. There was no promise that anyone but God himself could help. And to the owners of The Fallen Angel, God had rarely taken kindly.

Cross moved with quick, economical precision to investigate the wound. "Stay awake, you heavy bastard. You're too big to fall."

Temple struggled. "I shouldn't be here," he said, his thoughts clouded and his tongue heavy. "I've a fight." Cross angled one of Temple's arms outward to test the location of the knife and Temple bowed off the pallet at the pain, fighting the movement.

"You've had a fight," Justin, the club's majordomo, said quietly from a few feet away. "You've had two."

Temple shook his head, the movement loose, like a broken doll, a sign of delirium. "No. He's run the dice too far this time. Too long. There are too many of them."

Bourne came to hold him down, swearing harshly. "That was a long time ago, Temple. Years. We don't run dice on the streets anymore."

The door to the room opened, and neither man looked toward the sound. This room was as secure as if the King himself were here, clinging to life. If someone were entering, it was because they had access to the darkest secrets of the club.

"Justin, get back to the floor." Chase had arrived. "We do not stop the fleecing of the aristocracy simply because Temple's suffered a flesh wound."

Bourne cut Chase a wicked look. "It took you long enough to get here."

"I was the only one who remembered that we have a club to run. Where will Temple be if we bankrupt ourselves while he convalesces?"

Cross did not look up from the knife. "This is more than a flesh wound."

Temple struggled against his partners' hold. "I have to get to the fight! Bourne can't beat them!"

"We beat them together," Bourne said quietly, his face pale with frustration and worry. "We fought them together."

Temple's eyes shot open and he met Bourne's gaze. "We will lose."

Bourne shook his head. "Not with the devil on our side. Chase came."

"I saved your ass then," Chase said, leaning in, something catching in the words—something the founder of the Angel would never dream of admitting to. "I saved it then, just as we shall save it now."

Temple shook his head. "I have to fight . . ." The words faded away, and he went limp on the pallet.

Bourne turned instantly to Cross, his voice gravel. "Is he—"

Cross shook his head. "No. Passed out." He inspected the place where the knife was buried deep in Temple's chest, thick and deep halfway between shoulder and breast. "It might not be fatal."

The words lacked conviction.

"As none of us are doctors," Bourne said, "you'll forgive me if I am not comforted by your diagnosis."

"It might be muscle. Nerve."

"Pull it out."

Cross shook his head. "We don't know what that would do. We don't know if it would—" He stopped, and the words rang in the room despite his not saying them. *Kill him faster.*

Chase swore, low and furious.

"Justin?" Cross called and the pit boss pushed his spectacles high on his nose, waiting for the order. "Summon the surgeon. And my wife." The Countess of Harlow's knowledge of human anatomy was impressive, and she was the closest they had to a doctor if the surgeon weren't nearby.

Chase spoke low and dark. "And get me everything there is to know about Christopher Lowe."

Bourne looked to Chase. "I presume he's gone?"

"Lost in the fray tonight."

Bourne swore, harsh and wicked. "How?"

"Security was so concerned about Temple, they forgot that their job was to protect the exits. I shall have all their heads. Every damn one."

"They care for him," Cross said.

A golden brow rose. "Interesting, that. Considering they could have captured his killer if they weren't all wailing like banshees. They shall answer to me for behaving like children who lost their sweets."

"You're a cold bastard," Cross said.

Chase ignored the words, instead turning to Bourne. "What happened to you?"

A bruise was blossoming on Bourne's face, coloring his right eye socket black. Bourne scowled. "I would prefer not to discuss it."

Chase did not seem to mind. "Where's the girl?"

"Locked in Prometheus, where she belongs."

Chase nodded. "Good. Let her think on what she's done."

"What do you plan to do with her?"

The founder of the Angel stood over Temple, watching his shallow breath, the barely-there rise and fall of his massive chest, the way his normally brown skin had gone sallow under the threat of death. "I shall kill her myself if he dies. With pleasure."

"Lowe thought she'd betrayed him," Bourne said.

"She tricked us all." Chase did not look up. "I did not think she had it in her."

Cross raised a brow. "She faked her death and blamed him for it."

The door opened again, and Philippa, Lady Harlow entered, out of breath, spectacles askew, Asriel on her heels with hot water and linens.

Pippa ignored everyone in the room, heading straight for Cross, touching her husband's shoulder in a fleeting expression of comfort. After Cross lifted her hand and pressed a kiss to her knuckles, she turned her attention to Temple, running her fingers along his shoulder and down the skin to the place where the hilt of Lowe's knife protruded, perverse and unnatural.

She pressed at the flesh and Temple groaned.

"You hurt him," Chase said, warning in the words.

Pippa did not look back. "That he can feel pain—that he can protest it—is a good thing. It indicates consciousness." She turned to her husband. "The surgeon left once the first fight was complete. They've sent several men to search for him, but we mustn't wait. You must pull it out. Straight and true. We must treat this wound before—"

She stopped. No one in the room needed hear the rest.

"And if it's somehow keeping him from bleeding out?" Chase asked.

"If that's the case," Pippa said, her tone turning gentle, "then we prolong the inevitable."

"Lady Harlow, while I am certain that you are exceedingly competent in all areas of science," Chase said, "you will forgive me for questioning your skill as a doctor."

Pippa paused, looking to Cross. Waiting.

"In light of the current circumstance, I shall ignore the tone you've taken with my wife," Cross said. "We cannot wait for the surgeon. It could be hours."

Chase swore, the reveal of emotion from one so stoic harsh and unsettling for the rest in the room.

"He won't die," Bourne said, the words half vow, half prayer. "He's Temple. Stronger than all of us. Haler. Christ. He's big as an ox. Unbeatable."

Except, he had been beaten.

"Bring me the girl," Chase said.

Cross was simple and direct. "No."

Bourne was more colorful. "Over my rotting corpse does that bitch gain access to this room."

Chase did not rise to the anger. "She will see what she's done to him."

"I would prefer she *experience* what she's done to him."

Chase looked to Asriel. "Bring me the girl."

Asriel did not hesitate again. Chase's will was done.

"You watch her. She's as likely as her brother was to take a knife to any one of us." Bourne lifted his hand to his eye. "And she's got a surprising right cross."

Pippa looked to him. Her wide eyes blinked once behind her spectacles and Bourne resisted the urge to fidget. "She hit you."

"I wasn't expecting it."

Cross couldn't resist. "I don't imagine you were."

He returned his attention to Temple's wide expanse, watching as Pippa cleaned around the knife, her task Sisyphean—blood blossoming anew with every swipe.

After long moments, she said, without looking up, "You can't plan to reveal yourself to her."

Chase looked to her. "I hadn't thought about it."

"She can't know who you are," Cross agreed with his wife. "She's not to be trusted."

Pippa brought a clean cloth to Temple's brow as they all watched, wiping away the sweat and sawdust that clung to him from the ring.

Bourne spoke, "If she knew . . ."

The words trailed off, completion unnecessary.

If Mara—if anyone aside from a trusted few—knew Chase's true identity, the Angel would be in peril.

And the Angel's peril belonged to them all.

There was a gruesome painting of Prometheus on the wall of Mara's prison cell. A torture scene.

The hero lay prone, chained on his back to a rock, his face a portrait of agony as Zeus, in the form of a wicked black eagle, tore at his flesh. Punishing him for insolence. For stealing fire from the gods. For thinking he could beat them.

It was a terrifying piece, enormous and threatening, no doubt designed to make those who defied the Angel aware of the consequences of their actions and amenable to confession.

A vision flashed, Temple collapsed on the floor of the ring, the life spilling from him as she screamed.

Kit had stabbed him. With her knife.

Fire from the gods.

The door opened and she turned, her words out before she could stop them. "The duke. He lives?"

Temple's second, the man who had stood sentry outside the orphanage, tall and broad with skin dark as midnight, did not reply, instead silently indicating that she should walk ahead of him into the dark hallway with a seriousness that suggested it would be a mistake to push him for an answer or to ignore his instructions.

He'd clearly been trained by Temple.

Heart pounding, she did as she was bid, and as she passed him, he did speak, his voice low and gruff. "Try nothing."

She wanted to tell him she wouldn't. That she hated what had happened. That, had she known it would come to pass, she would have done everything in her power to stop it. That even at her most angry, she'd never intended to hurt Temple. But she knew the words would be futile and their meaning mistaken for lie or worse. And so, instead, she held herself straight and tall and made her way past him into the dimly lit hallway.

The corridor was lined with men and women in a variety of uniforms—from livery to lady of the evening—each face pale with shadow and concern. Each gaze hot with loathing.

She longed for the mask that had been taken from her after the fight.

They watched her with angry eyes as she made her way through the already unsettling passageways designed to overpower with their size and curvature—designed to make it exceedingly clear to all who passed who held the power. Designed to dissuade Prometheus from thinking he might fare well in his quest.

"I hope you're taking 'er to Chase," one of the women said, blond and beautiful and filled with vitriol. "I hope 'e plans to deal with 'er."

A murmur of agreement rolled through the too-small space at the suggestion, and a man nearby added, "She deserves everything Temple got."

"She deserves more," a wicked shout came from behind her, and Mara crossed her arms tightly, moving more quickly, desperate to get away from them. From their hate.

And then her escort opened a door and she threw herself from the hallway into the chamber, pulling up short as she realized where she was.

Wishing she had remained in the corridor beyond.

She was in Temple's rooms, where she'd watched him strip his shirt earlier in the evening. Where they'd sparred. Where he'd kissed her on lips and more, giving her a taste of a vast amount of pleasure to which he had access. Where she'd tried to stand firm and tried not to notice his muscles and sinew and bone. His warmth. His vitality.

Vitality that was gone now. A woman and two men leaned low over him, candlelight wrapping him in its warm glow, highlighting the paleness of his skin, still as death. She closed her eyes against the words, wishing she hadn't thought them. Willing the word *death* away.

She stepped toward him, a knot in her throat. "My God," she said, her chest heavy with fear and sorrow, unable to stop herself from reaching for him before her guide placed a strong hand on her arm and stopped her forward momentum.

The Marquess of Bourne turned at the sound of her voice, and she noted the bruise blossoming at the inner corner of his eye, feeling the related sting in her right hand. He pointed at her. "You don't come near him."

There was hatred in the words, and a different woman might not have replied. But she could not bear another moment of not knowing. "Is he dead?"

"You'd like that, wouldn't you?"

"No," she said, the truth coming on a flood of relief, knowing that the quiet word would mean nothing in this room, but wanting to say it nonetheless. Wanting to remind herself that she'd never intended to hurt Temple. Never. Not since the beginning. And certainly not now. "No."

He raised a brow. "I don't believe you."

She met his gaze. "I didn't expect you would."

"Enough, Bourne." The woman at the table looked up and Mara recognized the blond, bespectacled woman from the mysterious room where they'd watched the fight earlier. "We can't wait any longer. We must extract the knife."

It had been an hour . . . longer.

Mara could not keep quiet. "Straight and true, as it went in."

"She would know how it went in, as she fairly put it there herself," Bourne said. "Look upon your work, you fucking harpy."

As though Mara couldn't see it. As though she hadn't seen her brother plunge it deep into Temple's chest.

As though she didn't will it away.

She met Bourne's hating, hazel gaze. "I did not do this."

"Of course you did." This, from the other aristocrat in the room—tall and ginger-haired. When she looked to him, he added, "You did this the moment you set him up for a murder he didn't commit. Twelve years end here. With this."

"It was a . . ." Mara trailed off, shaking her head. They did not understand. Few did.

It was a mistake.

She did not say it, because they neither cared to hear her story, nor deserved to. Temple was another tale. Temple deserved the truth.

If he lived, she'd give it to him. All of it.

She would lay herself at his feet and give him his chance at retribution. At vengeance. And she'd give him the truth.

If only he would live.

She moved toward his still form, and was stayed once more by the strong grip of his man-at-arms. She looked to the pile of linen near Temple's head on the low table.

"You must remove it swiftly, and immediately apply pressure," she said, deliberately avoiding the gazes of the men in the room, looking only to the surprised eyes of the countess. "You'll need more linen than that." Her gaze flickered to the knife. "The wound is deep."

"You're a doctoress, now?" The words oozed lazy con-descension.

She steeled herself and met the marquess's eyes. "I've ex-tracted knives before."

"From whom?"

She looked back to Temple. "From whomever."

The countess was through waiting. "Asriel, you will have to release Miss Lowe. We shall require your strength to keep him down."

"He is unconscious," Bourne said.

"If we're lucky, he shan't be when we do this. It will hurt. A great deal, I imagine." Mara closed her eyes at the words, willing them to be true. Willing him to wake. Willing him not to be dead. She watched the men move to hold Temple down—three of them to keep his massive body still—and she tried not to notice the way his skin had gone sallow, life seeping from him on a river of blood.

So much life.

Her throat closed at the thought.

What had she done to this man? What had he done to deserve her in his life? If he lived . . . She bargained again. If he lived, she'd give him everything he wanted and leave him to his happiness.

To some beautiful woman and their beautiful children on his beautiful estate.

She'd give him back everything she took.

If only he would live.

It was the closest she'd come to a bargain with God in a decade. In longer.

The countess looked from one man to the next, then to Mara. "You've done this before?"

Mara nodded, thinking of another knife. Another time. More pale skin. "I have."

"You should do it."

Mara did not hesitate, moving toward him. Wanting to touch him. Bourne stopped her. "If you hurt him, I kill you."

She nodded. "It seems reasonable."

She would do everything she could to save him. She wanted him alive. She wanted to give him everything for which he asked. All the truth.

Perhaps he would forgive her.

Perhaps they could begin anew.

And if not, at least she could give him all she had. All he deserved.

Bourne released her and she moved to the stack of linens, folding them into a haphazard bandage and bringing the bucket of steaming water closer. When the earl and the marquess cut her vicious looks, she stared back, refusing to be cowed. Bollocks to them.

She handed the stack of linens to the countess before hiking up her skirts to kneel on the table next to Temple's head, placing firm hands on the knife's bloody hilt. "On my count." The room stood still. She looked down at Temple, his face pale. "Don't you dare die," she whispered. "I've things to tell you."

He did not move, and she ignored the ache in her chest at his stillness.

"One . . ." she counted. "Two . . ." she did not wait for three, instead yanking the knife from his chest, straight and true.

He screamed his pain, bowing from the table, and Mara nearly wept with relief at the sound as the countess leaned over him, flooding the wound with scalding water, to clear away the blood and hopefully, hopefully show a less deadly incision.

Hope was a fool's emotion.

Temple's scream renewed itself, the searing liquid burning his skin and bringing forth a new river of blood. Refusing to flinch at the sound, Mara grabbed a stack of linen, covering the wound and leaning all her weight into the cloth, willing the tide to stem even as it soaked through the fabric. Even as he bled.

Even as he died at her hands.

"You won't die," she whispered. Over and over. "You won't die."

She had to stop the bleeding.

The words were all she could think as she rose above him, pressing as hard as she could, trying to ignore the way he bucked beneath the force, attempting to throw them all off. Even now, she was shocked by the size of him. By his strength. By his will as he roared his anger and pain and his eyes shot open, black as midnight and filled with its demons.

He looked right at her and swore, dark and unhesitating, the muscles in his neck straining.

"You hurt him." The Marquess of Bourne gave voice to Temple's look. "You take pleasure in it."

"I don't," she whispered, only to him, to her great duke. "I never wanted you hurt." She pressed harder on the shoulder, feeling vaguely grateful that the tall, redheaded gentleman across from her was strong enough to hold Temple's arm down, as she had no doubt that he would like nothing more than to strike her. "I want you well."

Temple resisted her touch, and she changed tack. "Stop straining," she said, loudly. As firm as the pressure she exerted. "The more you fight, the more you'll bleed, and you can't spare it."

He did not look away from her, and his teeth remained clenched, but he stopped fighting.

Hopefully by choice.

The linens were soaked through, as she'd expected. He was bleeding profusely, and she would need more padding to soak it all up.

She turned to the countess. "My lady . . . would you . . ."

The bespectacled woman responded without hesitation, knowing what Mara wanted without articulation. She took hold of the bandage as Mara reached for the bloody knife on the table.

"No—" The redheaded gentleman saw her movement first.

Bourne instantly released Temple. "Put it down."

She did not hide her irritation. "You think I'll slit his throat with all of you here? You think I'm so hateful I've gone mad?"

"I think I'd rather not risk it," Bourne said, but Mara was already turning away, lifting her skirts quickly—even as the marquess came at her—and cutting away a layer of beautiful mauve underskirt. Bourne pulled up short, and Mara would have enjoyed the look of shock on his face if she weren't so busy thrusting the hilt of the knife in his direction. "Make yourself useful. We'll likely need your shirts, as well."

Later, she would marvel at the speed with which the men responded to her demand, shrugging out of their coats and pulling their shirts over their heads, but in the moment, she added, "His is somewhere in this room, as well. Find it."

And then she was nudging the countess out of the way and pressing her petticoats to Temple's bare chest, hating the way his roars had turned to quiet, inarticulate protest at the feel of her firm touch. Hating that she couldn't keep the life from seeping out of him.

"You made me ruin my new dress," she said, meeting his gaze, trying to keep him awake. Alert. "You shall owe me another."

He did not respond, his eyelids growing heavy. She registered the waning fight there. *No.* She said the only words she could think to say.

"Don't you dare die."

His black eyes rolled back beneath their lids, long dark lashes coming to rest on pale cheeks.

And Mara was alone once more, her only companion the ache in her chest. She closed her eyes and willed back the sting of tears.

"If he dies, you shall follow him into Hell."

It was a moment before she realized that it was not the marquess—the man who had quickly become her nemesis—

speaking. It was the other man, the ginger-haired, circumspect aristocrat with the lean face and the square jaw. She met his gaze, noting the way his grey eyes shone with barely contained emotion. And she knew without doubt that the threat in the words was true.

They would kill her if Temple died. They would not think twice of it.

And perhaps she would deserve it.

But he did not.

And so she would keep him alive if it took every ounce of her being.

She took a deep breath and exchanged her skirts for the man's shirt. "Then he shall not die."

He did not die that night.

Instead, he fell into an unsettling sleep, which continued when the surgeon arrived, instantly fussing over the wound.

"You should have waited for me to return before extracting the knife," he said, inspecting the wound, deliberately not looking to the women in the room.

"You did not come," Bourne said, anger in his tone, and Mara was happy to see it directed to one who so rightly deserved it. "We were to do nothing?"

"I have other business," the doctor replied without remorse, lifting the linen from Temple's shoulder and inspecting the now dry wound. "Nothing would have been better. You could have caused more damage. Certainly putting him in a woman's hands was a questionable decision."

The Countess of Harlow raised a brow at the words, looking to the redheaded aristocrat whom Mara had discovered was her husband, but said nothing, obviously not wishing to scare the elusive doctor away now that he had arrived.

Mara did not feel the same way. She'd seen too many doctors arrive, magic potions and tools in hand, and leave having done nothing but make the situation worse. Temple had never been luckier than when the doctor had been delayed eight hours. "I prefer a female doctor to none at all."

The surgeon looked to her then. "*You* are no doctor."

She'd faced stronger and worthier adversaries than this little surgeon. Including the unconscious man on the table. "I might say the same of you, for all the evidence I have seen of your medical acumen this evening."

The Countess of Harlow blinked large eyes behind her thick spectacles, her lips tilting upward at one corner. When Mara met her gaze, the other woman looked away, but not before Mara caught the admiration there.

An ally, perhaps, in a roomful of enemies.

The surgeon had turned away, and was already speaking to the Earl of Harlow. "He should be bloodlet."

Mara winced, a vision coming, fast and unsettling, leeches dotting flesh, each one fat with her mother's blood. "No."

No one looked to her. No one seemed to hear her.

"Is it necessary?" The earl did not seem convinced.

The doctor looked to the wound. "Yes."

"No!" she repeated, louder this time. Bloodletting killed. And it would take Temple's life as sure as it had taken her mother's.

The doctor continued. "And who knows what else the woman did to him. What might need to be reversed. Bloodletting is the answer."

"Bloodletting is not the answer," Mara said, placing herself at Temple's side, between him and the surgeon, who was now extracting a large square box from his bag. No one listened.

No one but the Countess of Harlow.

"I am not certain that this is the right course of treatment, either," she said, all seriousness, coming to stand next to Mara.

"You are not a doctor, either, my lady."

"We may not be doctors, sirrah, but we were the best he had, were we not?"

The surgeon pursed his lips. "I will not stand for being spoken to in such a way. And by—" He waved a hand at them.

Cross stepped forward, ready to do battle for his wife. "By whom, precisely?"

The doctor noticed his misstep. "Of course I don't mean Lady Harlow, my lord. I mean"—he waved at Mara—"*this woman.*"

He said *woman* like it was a filthy word.

Mara might have cared if Temple's life were not hanging in the balance. She ignored the insult. "Have you blooded him before?"

There was a pause, and she thought the surgeon might not answer her until the countess stood her ground and added, "It's an excellent question."

The doctor hesitated, until Cross prompted, "Doctor?"

"No. He's never required it."

Mara looked to Temple, still as death on the table. Of course he hadn't. The man was unbeatable. He'd doubtfully required any treatment at all. Until now.

Until he'd nearly died.

She looked to the countess. "My lady?" she asked, letting her feelings on the matter sound in the words. Show on her face. *Don't allow this.*

Please, let him live.

The countess nodded once and turned to her husband. "We should wait. He is healthy and strong. I would rather he be given the opportunity to mend on his own than lose additional blood."

Mara released the breath she had not known she was holding, hot emotion burning at her eyes.

"Women cannot possibly understand the basics of this kind of medicine. Their minds—" He waved a hand in the air. "They are not equipped for such knowledge."

"I beg your pardon." Countess Harlow was obviously displeased.

Mara could not waste energy on taking offense. Not when Temple's life was in the balance. She stood her ground. "Even women can understand that blood does not typically leave the body. I see no reason to believe we do not require all we have."

It was an uncommon theory. And unpopular. But most people hadn't seen their mothers die, paler and sicker by the minute, covered in leeches and cut with blades. She'd seen proof that bloodletting was never the answer.

The surgeon sighed, no doubt realizing he was going to have to deal with the women in the room. He spoke as though to a child, and Mara noted the earl's jaw set in irritation. "We must offset the balance. What he has lost in the shoulder, we must take from the leg."

"That is utter idiocy." Mara turned to the countess—her only ally. "If a roof leaks, one does not bore a second hole in the ceiling."

The doctor had had enough. He puffed up and turned to Bourne. "I won't be schooled on my field of expertise by women. They leave, or I do."

"Then you should leave, and we shall find another surgeon," the countess said.

"Pippa," Cross said, the words soft but firm, and Mara could hear the edge in them. He did not wish his friend to die.

If only he would realize that Mara did not wish it, either.

"Give him the night," she begged. "Twelve hours to present a fever—an infection of any kind—and then let your barber at him."

The doctor's eyes went wide at the insulting words, and Mara would have laughed if she weren't so desperate to keep the man and his cruel contraption from Temple. "I wouldn't treat him now if you tripled my fee."

Mara hated the man then, so similar he was to the myriad

of London doctors who had poked and prodded and pronounced her mother untreatable. They'd left her to die, even as Mara had begged her father to push them. To find someone who would treat her with something other than leeches and laudanum.

Even as he'd ignored her and left her without control.

Bourne spoke, the irony not lost upon her that the marquess was attempting to calm the surgeon's temper. "Doctor. Please. Twelve hours is not so very long."

"Twelve hours could kill him. If he dies, it's on your females' hands."

"My hands," Mara said, meeting the marquess's eyes, noticing the ring around the right one, now shiny and black, which would not endear her to him. She was amazed he did not look away. "His blood is on my hands. Let me clean it off."

It was the closest she would come to begging him.

Close enough.

She would never know why, but Bourne looked to Cross, then back to her. "Twelve hours."

Relief coursed through her, and she was tempted to apologize to the supercilious marquess. Almost.

"I shan't be back," the doctor said, acid in his tone.

She was already wringing hot water from a clean cloth. "We shan't need you."

The door closed behind him, and the marquess extracted a watch from his pocket. "Twelve hours begins now." He looked to Cross. "Chase shall have our heads for letting him leave."

The words did not make sense to Mara, but she was too focused on Temple to care to understand, instead speaking to the countess. "We must do what we can to stave off a fever."

Pippa nodded once and moved away, heading for the door to call for more cloths and fresh water.

Mara looked down at Temple's still face, taking in the

dark slash of brows, the crooked line of his once-patrician nose, the scars at his brow and lip, the cut from the earlier fight that evening that now ran black across one cheek, and regret bloomed, tight and high in her chest.

She'd done all this to him, she thought, pressing the linen to his brow, hating his stillness.

Now she would save him.

Chapter 13

They lied, those who told stories of death and filled them with choirs of angels and a sense of utter, irresistible peace.

There were no angels. There was no peace.

At least, not for Temple.

There was nothing that tempted him toward bright, comforting light, nothing that gave him solace as pain burned through him, threatening his thought and breath.

And the heat. It burned like fire through his chest and down his arm, shooting into his hand as though they'd set the limb aflame. He couldn't fight it—they held him down and forced him to take it. As though they enjoyed it.

It was the heat that made him realize he was on the edge of Hell.

His angels did not come from above; they came from below, and they tempted him to join them. His angels were the fallen ones. And they did not speak in melodic hymns.

Instead, they swore and cursed and willed him to them with temptation and threat. Promising him everything he'd loved in life—women and fine scotch and good food and better sport. They promised him he'd reign again if only he joined them. Their voices were myriad—rough cockney accents, and deep aristocratic ones, and women. The women whispered to him, promising him immense pleasure if only he'd follow them.

By God, he was tempted.

And then there was she.

The one who seemed to whisper most harshly. The one who bordered on berating him. The one who spoke the words that called to him more than any of the other pretty promises.

Words like *revenge*. And *power*. And *strength*.

And duke.

Of course, he hadn't been a duke in a very long time.

Not since he'd killed his father's bride.

Something tickled at the edge of his consciousness at that, something that ebbed and flowed as he heard the others whispering around him, calling to him. *It's only a matter of time.*

He can't hear us. He can't fight it.

He's lost too much . . .

And he had. He'd lost his name and his family and his history and his life. He'd lost the world into which he'd been born . . . the world he'd enjoyed so damn much.

But every time he was tempted by the darkness, he heard her.

He will fight. He will live.

Her voice wasn't kind or angelic. It was strong as steel, and it made prettier promises than any of the others. It would not be ignored.

Bollocks to them.

You're stronger than any of them by half.

Your work isn't done. Your life isn't over.

But it was, wasn't it? Hadn't it been over for years? Hadn't it been over since the day he'd woken in that bloody bed, his father's fiancée dead at his hands?

He'd killed her.

He'd killed her with his giant fists and his unnatural

strength and God knew what else. He'd murdered her, even as he'd murdered everything his life could have possibly been. He'd killed her, and now he was here, dying—finally, finally getting what he deserved.

It was said that at death, one's life flashed before one's eyes. Temple had always liked the idea of that, not to remember his childhood on the great estate in Devonshire, but to remember that night. The one that had changed everything.

Somewhere, in the dark recesses of his mind, he'd always thought that this moment, when he hovered on death, he'd be shown that night. The night that had sealed his fate. The night that had promised him entry into Hell.

But even now, he couldn't remember it, and he wanted to roar his frustration. "Why?"

He didn't hear his whisper echo in the room.

All he heard was his angry fallen angel taunting him with wicked lies, even as he slipped into delirium.

Because you will live, Temple.

You will live, and I will tell you everything.

She was there, the girl from that night—the pretty, laughing girl dancing away from him in the gardens, and rising over him on crisp linen sheets, all silken hair and smooth skin and eyes that haunted him.

She was there, with the line of boys, dark-haired with eyes like jewels.

She was there, her touch cool in the darkness, her promises tempting him away from the light. Back to her.

Back to life.

She was saving him.

*H*ours passed and he did not wake, even as he grew more fitful in his sleep—straining against the treatment every time they flushed the wound with hot water.

Mara was shuttled to and from the room, allowed near

him only when it was time to clean the wound or change its dressing. Each time she entered, there were new people keeping vigil. Bourne and Cross and Pippa remained constant, joined once the last gamer left by the men who worked the tables of the Angel, dealers and croupiers, and followed by the women who worked the floor of the club—a steady stream of weeping maids and worried companions and who knew what else.

The blonde called Anna, whom Mara had met in the strange windowed room, arrived, her work complete, and Mara watched from the corner of her eye as the prostitute kept quiet vigil over Temple for long minutes, her fingers stroking the tattooed skin of his arms, tracing the cords of his muscles, holding one strong hand as she whispered in his ear.

It occurred that she might be Temple's paramour, what with the way she'd spoken of him in the dark, mirrored room. With the way all the women had panted and leered over him, he no doubt had a string of women. And this one was beautiful enough to be the general of his petticoated army.

Long, slender fingers trailed over smooth skin, perfectly filed nails worrying the hair of his arms in a gesture that could not be misread. This woman knew Temple. Cared for him. Was comfortable touching him as he lay still and naked in the dark.

Mara looked away, hating her. Hating herself for the hot jealousy that coursed through her. For not telling him everything when she had the chance. For not trusting him.

For tormenting him, when he had done nothing to deserve it.

She kept her head down as she cared for him, flushing and cleaning and packing his wound, mopping his brow, and feeling for his blessedly strong, steady heartbeat. Someone had covered him with a blanket and placed a pillow beneath his head—a concession to comfort even as they feared moving him from the table, as though the scarred oak had some kind of life-giving property.

Mara grew more and more concerned as day gave way to dusk in the world beyond the casino, and he remained still. Bourne threatened to call another doctor but during one of her exiles, the elusive Chase apparently sided with Pippa and gave them the night to bring Temple back to consciousness.

Chase was gone before Mara returned to the room for another round of wound cleaning and dressing, but his words were gospel to the others.

When she was near Temple, she spoke to him, desperate to wake him, to bring him back to consciousness. Desperate for him to open his eyes and see.

Sometimes, I think you do see me.

Words whispered in the darkness on a London street.

She hadn't seen him then. Not really. But now she did. And now she wanted him to see her. She needed it. She needed to explain everything to him. She needed to make him see the truth.

Her truth.

But he did not wake except to struggle and fret when they washed the wound with near-boiling water, the discomfort enough to rouse him into some new layer of consciousness, where he seemed unable to do anything but ask, over and over, "Why?"

She answered him quietly, not wanting the others to hear what she said—what she promised—answers, and truth and even vengeance, hoping that something she said would bring him back from wherever it was his mind had gone, before the others decided that she and the countess were mad and sent for the cruel man who called himself a doctor.

The countess had become her one ally, seeming to understand after several hours of ministrations that Mara shared her goal.

All their goals.

More.

The door to the room opened, and two women entered, one plain and proper, clearly a lady, and the other large and aproned, carrying a teapot. The lady's gaze found Bourne's across the room, and she flew to him, landing in his strong embrace. He crushed her to him and pressed his face to the crook of her neck as she wrapped her arms about his head, threading her fingers into his dark locks and whispering to him.

Mara was torn between gaping at the display—so incongruous with the man with whom she had interacted—and looking away from the deeply emotional moment.

When he finally pulled away, his unpleasant personality returned. "What the hell are you doing here?"

The lady did not seem to register the tone. "You should have summoned me yourself. I should not have to receive word from Pippa." She paused, her fingers coming to his cheek. "What happened to your eye?"

"Nothing." He looked away, and so did Mara, her gaze falling to Pippa, standing at Temple's other side, watching her.

"It's not nothing, Michael."

"It's fine." He caught her hand and pressed a kiss to her fingertips.

"Who hit you?"

The countess's lips twitched. Mara willed her to stay quiet. Luck was not on her side. "Miss Lowe hit him."

The plain woman pulled herself up to her full height and looked to Pippa. "Who is Miss Lowe?"

Pippa pointed at Mara, who wished she could disappear. "She is."

The other woman faced her, gaze tracking her bloodied dress and haphazard hair and no doubt haggard face before landing on Mara's right hand, which had dealt the blow.

One blond brow rose. "I suppose he deserved it?"

Shock had her meeting the lady's eyes. "He did, rather."

The lady nodded. "It happens." She turned back to Bourne.

"I most certainly did not deserve it."

She raised a brow. "Have you apologized?"

"Apologized!" he sputtered. "She hit me. On her way to kill Temple."

Mara opened her mouth to protest, but the woman did not give her a chance to finish her sentence. "Miss Lowe, have you plans to kill Temple?"

It was the first time anyone had thought to ask the question. Mara told the truth. "No."

The woman nodded, and returned her attention to Bourne. "Then my husband no doubt deserved it."

Bourne's gaze narrowed as Mara registered the meaning of the words. This woman was the Marchioness of Bourne, and willing to stand up to the horrible man without hesitation. Surely she should be sainted.

"You should not be here," Bourne grumbled.

"Why not? I'm a member and married to one of the owners of the club."

"This is no place for a woman in your condition."

"Oh, for heaven's sake. I am increasing, Michael, not infirm. Pippa is here." The marchioness indicated the countess, who was, indeed, with child.

"It is not my fault that Cross does not love his wife the way I love mine."

Cross raised a brow at the words before looking seriously to Pippa. "I love you a great deal."

"I know," Pippa said, and Mara wondered at the simplicity in the words. The countess's perfect understanding that she was loved.

She imagined what it would be like to be loved with such certainty. Her gaze flickered to the man on the table. To his strong jaw and long arms, and the hand that lay flat against the wood, palm curved and empty. She wondered what it would be like to slide her hand into that space. To fill it.

To love and be loved.

Mara returned her attention to the Marchioness of Bourne, whose attention remained fixed on her husband. "Michael," she said softly, "Temple is as much mine as any of yours."

The woman turned to face Temple's still form, and worry etched her brow as she reached for him, her fingers grazing his good shoulder before pushing dark hair from his brow. Bourne came to stand with his wife, pulling her tight against his side, anger and pain etched on his handsome face.

"Good God," she whispered, leaning into her husband's embrace.

"He will live." The words were harsh, torn from Bourne's throat, equal parts will and worry.

Something tightened in Mara's chest as she watched the tableau. This man—whose life she'd toyed with—she hadn't ruined him. He had dozens who cared for him, friends who would go to any lengths to save him.

How long had it been since someone had worried for her? How long since she'd dreamed of it?

How long since she'd deserved it?

She did not like the answer that threatened.

She turned to the woman with the teapot. "Is that the tepid tea?"

The woman nodded, her own gaze glassy as she watched Temple. "*Oui.* I brewed it myself."

"Thank you, Didier," Pippa said as Mara took the pot and poured the brown liquid into a tumbler she pulled from a nearby decanter of scotch.

"I hope there's some magic in that brew. Lord knows he could use it," said the marchioness.

"Willow bark," the countess replied. "It's said to fight fever."

"Which he does not seem to have, would that it would remain as such," Mara added, looking to Cross. "Help me lift his head. We must try to get him to drink."

Cross came forward, and he and Asriel lifted Temple's limp body to a seated position. Mara righted his lolling head, tipping the liquid into his mouth by the teaspoonful. "You've got to drink if you're going to heal," she said firmly after several unsuccessful attempts.

Trying again, she lost another batch of liquid down his chin and chest, along with her patience. He would drink if she had to force the tea down his throat. She tipped the liquid in. "Swallow, damn you."

His eyes flipped open, alert and bright, and he sputtered against the flow of tea, a lukewarm spray covering her face and neck as she squeaked her surprise and his partners swore their disbelief.

Temple coughed, his black gaze finding hers as he pushed the glass away. "Christ," he said, the words harsh in his throat. "Haven't you tried to kill me enough?"

The words elicited a low, reverent curse from Bourne and a wide grin from Cross. Relief came quick and nearly overwhelming to Mara . . . and she closed her eyes against tears and laughter for a moment, collecting herself before moving to bring the glass to his lips once more.

He shook his head, holding her hand at bay. "Who made that swill?" He looked to the woman who'd brought the pot in. "Didier?"

The Frenchwoman came forward, tears of relief in her eyes. "*Oui*, Temple. *Je l'ai fait.*" She nodded again. Found her English. "Yes. I made it."

He looked to Mara, wariness in his gaze. "And you didn't touch it?"

She shook her head, finding her tongue. "Only to pour it."

He pushed the glass to her. "Drink."

Her brows furrowed. "I don't—"

"You drink it first."

Understanding dawned, and then she did laugh, the sound light and foreign and remarkably welcome. As welcome as his black gaze, free of hallucination.

Something lit in those handsome eyes, and he pushed the glass toward her again. "Drink it, Mara."

Her name was beautiful on his lips.

"What on—" the Marchioness of Bourne stepped forward, stayed by Bourne. She turned on her husband. "It's preposterous."

"It's Temple's choice."

He didn't trust her.

He was conscious enough to mistrust her.

She lifted the glass to her mouth and tossed the liquid back before opening her mouth and sticking her tongue out wide at him. "I am not in the market to poison you today."

He watched her carefully. "Good."

She ignored the pleasure that coursed through her at the word, turning instead to refill the glass. "That is not to say that you do not drive a woman to consider it."

His hand met hers, guiding the tea to his lips. "Another day, then."

She wanted to smile. Wanted to say a dozen different things. Things he wouldn't hear. Things he wouldn't believe.

Things she couldn't say.

So she settled on: "Drink, you great ox."

And he did, the whole glass. When she began to move away, he clasped her hand in an unyielding grip, his skin somehow warm despite his shocking loss of blood. Her gaze flew to his.

"You made me a promise."

She stiffened at the words. "I did. I said I would return to Society. Prove you not a killer."

"I'm not talking about that promise."

She looked to him. "What then?"

"You promised me answers. You promised me truth."

Her blood roared in her ears. She had not imagined that he could hear her as she'd nursed him. As she'd whispered to him, fear and hope warring for control of her words. "You remember."

"My memory is a rare thing when it comes to you, I know." He drank again. "But you will tell me the truth about that night. You will keep your promises."

Promises for vengeance. For truth. As long as he lived.

And here he was, alive.

She nodded. "I shall honor them."

"I know," he said.

And then he slept.

Three mornings later, Temple sank into the brutally hot water in the great brass bathtub that had been custom built for his post-fight ablutions at The Fallen Angel.

He hissed at the pain that shot down his left arm when he lifted it, careful to keep his bandaged wound from the bath, not wanting to give the as yet unhealed injury any reason to return him to fever or infirmary. He rolled his shoulder tentatively, grimacing as he leaned back into the curved brass, resting his head on the lip of the bath.

He let out a long sigh, and closed his eyes, letting the steam and the heat engulf him, taking his thoughts with them.

Most of his thoughts.

Thoughts that did not include *her*, with her pretty, soft hair and her strange, irresistible eyes and her strength beyond measure. Thoughts that did not make him question just why she had done what she'd done so many years ago. What she had done that night in the ring. Whether she'd aided her brother in his quest. Whether she'd passed him the knife that had ended up in Temple's breast.

Thoughts that did not make him remember the kindness with which she had washed his wound the morning he'd regained consciousness. The way she'd served him tea. The way she'd healed him. Thoughts that did not have him wondering what it would be like to have that kindness again. More frequently.

Or worse, what that kindness meant.

He swore harshly in the quiet, steam-filled room.

He did not want her kindness. He wanted her remorse. Her repentance. Did he not?

He moved his arm carefully, disliking the twinge of pain that came with the motion. Disliking the way his arm seemed to be trapped in sand when he used it. Disliking the fear that came with thoughts of the limitation.

The feeling would come back. The strength, too.

It had to.

A memory flashed, fresh from the evening of the fight— Mara at the edge of the ring, meeting his gaze, terror in her large eyes. *He'll kill you!* She'd called out to him. Warned him, but he'd been so damn transfixed by the worry in her gaze—by the thought that she might care for him—that he hadn't understood the words until the knife was in his chest.

Until later.

Until he'd danced in and out of consciousness and her voice had whispered promises in his ear.

You will live.

You will live, and I will tell you everything.

He had lived.

And she would tell him the truth about that night and her decision to run. She would tell him why she'd chosen him. Why she'd punished him.

Why she'd stolen his life. And how she would give it back to him.

"Do you know what you're about?"

He did not show his surprise at the intrusion, even as his heart beat slightly faster at the realization that someone had entered the room without his notice.

"I don't doubt you're going to tell me," he said, opening

his eyes to find Chase at the end of the bathtub. "How long have you been watching me bathe?"

"Long enough for London's female half to become quite jealous." Chase dropped onto a nearby stool and leaned forward, legs spread wide, elbows on knees. "How is the arm?"

"Painful," Temple said, fisting the hand of the bad arm and attempting a slow uppercut into the air. "Stiff."

He left out other words. *Numb. Weak. Useless.*

"It hasn't been a week; give it time," Chase said. "You should be abed."

Temple shifted in the water, wincing at the way the movement sent a pain through him. "I do not require a keeper."

"Nonetheless, every night you are out of the ring is a night we lose money."

"I should have known that you weren't concerned about my well-being."

They both knew it wasn't true, and that Chase would raze London if it would help Temple's recovery. But they pretended nonetheless. "I'm concerned about your well-being as it relates to my profit margin."

Temple laughed. "Ever the businessman."

They were quiet for a long moment before Chase spoke again. "We have to discuss the girl."

Temple did not pretend not to understand. "Which girl?"

Chase ignored the stupid question. "She has requested to return to her post."

He hadn't seen her in days—had wanted to recover before he saw her again. He'd wanted his strength back before they did battle again. Before he faced her.

But he did not want her far from him. He refused to consider the reason why.

"And the brother?"

Chase let out a long breath and looked away. "Still missing."

"He can't stay that way forever. He hasn't any money."

"It's possible the girl funded the plan." Chase ran a hand

through blond locks. "After all, she's something of an expert at hiding in plain sight."

It wasn't possible. She was too concerned about money. "She didn't help him."

"You don't know that."

Except he did. He had played the fight over again and again. "I saw her at the fight. I saw her try to stop him." He paused, her whispered promises in his mind. "She saved me. She healed me."

"She had little choice." Chase was ever skeptical.

Temple shook his head. She hadn't tried to kill him. He couldn't believe it. He wouldn't.

Chase's brows rose. "You champion the girl?"

"No." *Liar.* "I simply want to be clear that her punishment is not her brother's."

"And how shall her punishment be meted out?"

"I need West." Duncan West, one of the wealthiest members of the club and the owner of half a dozen London papers.

Chase nodded and stood, understanding Temple's plan without having to be told more. "Easy enough."

So it began.

Did he want it this way? He'd been so sure. He'd imagined it night after night, this moment where he revealed her to London and took his justice. He imagined her ruined. With no choice but to leave again. To start over. To know what it was that she had done to him.

But now . . . "It will be on my terms, Chase."

Brown eyes went wide with feigned innocence. "Who else's?"

"I know how you like to meddle."

"Nonsense." Chase straightened one sleeve, brushing a speck of lint from the cuff. "I merely remind you that women are excellent actresses, Temple. Yours is no different." Temple resisted the thread of pleasure that coiled through him at the possessive. "She was scandalizing London and causing the biggest distraction the Angel had ever seen minutes before her brother stabbed you. The whole situation stinks of collusion."

"Then why didn't she run, too? Why did she stay?" The questions had rattled through him for days, since he'd woken from stabbing-induced sleep to find her at his bedside looking grateful. Pleased to see him alive.

Beautiful.

His.

No. Not his. Never his.

"Bourne wasn't about to let her go," Chase replied. "The point is, she's not to be trusted. Your wound isn't healed, and you're half the man you were a week ago. Allow her to leave. Asriel will watch her."

Temple stiffened at the words, disliking their truth. Disliking his weakness. Disliking the way the idea of anyone watching Mara unsettled him. She was his responsibility. His path to truth. "I can't risk him losing her."

Chase cut him a disbelieving look. "Asriel has never lost a thing in his life." When Temple did not reply, the founder of The Fallen Angel leaned in. "Christ. Don't tell me you're after her."

"I am not." Temple stood, water sloshing over the edge of the bathtub to form great pools on the floor.

He wasn't.

He couldn't be.

Chase threw him a linen towel from nearby and tossed another into one of the puddles. "She robbed you of your life—metaphorically, then nearly literally. And now you're intrigued by the chit."

Temple dried haphazardly, unable to use his bad arm. "She remembers everything about that night. I remember nothing."

"What's to remember? She drugged you, fled, and left you holding the debt for a murder you did not commit."

There was more. The whys. The hows.

The repercussions. The boy with his hair and her eyes.

He wrapped the towel around his hips, and pushed past Chase, returning to his chamber. "She will tell me everything about that night, and she will prove my innocence to the rest of the world. That's why I'm—as you say—intrigued by her. That's why I worry that Asriel will lose her."

But that's not all of it.

He ignored the thought that should have sounded like Chase but instead sounded like himself. He was not intrigued by her. Not by her strength and her will and her fearlessness. Not by her long neck or her full lips, either. There were thousands of women in London more beautiful and more biddable.

He was not intrigued by Miss Mara Lowe.

Intrigued seemed a tame description of how he felt about her. Drawn. Tempted.

He was consumed by her.

Chase was silent for a long moment, watching as Temple dressed, sliding into trousers, then a white lawn shirt, and the sling that had been designed for his injured arm.

He did it all with one arm. Perhaps Chase wouldn't notice.

Chase noticed everything. "How does it feel?"

It doesn't.

"I could still fell you."

A golden brow rose. "Big words." Chase headed for the door, one hand on the handle before a thought occurred. "I nearly forgot. We've been watching the orphanage since Lowe attacked you."

Temple was not surprised—Lowe had no money and no allies now that he'd crossed the Angel. He could not show his face anywhere in London without threat. He only had his sister.

Anger threaded through Temple at the thought. "And?"

"He sent her a message. We intercepted it."

Idiot boy. "What did it say?"

Chase smirked. "What do you think? He needs money."

Memories flashed: Mara's second-in-command hinting that the orphanage could use a charitable donation; the threadbare skirts she wore when she did not expect him; her bare hands, red with cold.

"She doesn't have what he needs."

"She doesn't have anything at all."

"Did we take the note?"

"No. We read it and let it pass."

They had set her up to help her brother. To betray Temple. *Again.*

"I want to speak with her."

I want to see her.

I want her.

Chase was quiet for a long moment, then said, "Send her back to MacIntyre's, Temple. Asriel will have a half-dozen men watching the place 'round the clock."

Temple's gaze shot to Chase. "MacIntyre's."

Chase hesitated. Chase *never* hesitated.

Temple pounced. "MacIntyre's. You are not the type to care about the name of some half-house filled with aristocratic by-blows."

"Not typically, no, but are you surprised I know of it? Of course I know where our members send their bastards."

It was information Chase had to know. Information that kept the Angel in power. It was information Temple could not stop himself from wanting. Christ, did he want to shout the question from the rafters.

Is one of the boys mine?

Is one of them hers?

Ours?

He settled on: "Did you know she was there?"

"I did not."

Temple searched his friend's eyes for truth. Couldn't find it. "You lie."

Chase sighed and looked away. "Mrs. Margaret Mac-

Intyre. Born and raised on the Bristol docks, married to a soldier who died tragically at Nsamankow."

Anger turned to betrayal. *"You knew she was there and you didn't tell me."*

"What good was your finding her? She drugged and stabbed you."

And then to hot, undeniable fury. "Get out."

Chase sighed. "Temple—"

"Don't you dare attempt to placate me." Temple advanced, hand fisting, itching to wipe the smug expression from Chase's face. "You have played your games with us for too long."

Chase's eyes flashed. "I saved your ass from a dozen men out for blood."

Temple's gaze narrowed. "And you've lorded it over me for *years*. Bourne and Cross as well. Playing guardian and confessor and fucking *mother* to every one of us. And now you think to own my vengeance? You knew her. You knew my name rested on her existence."

A memory flashed. Chase in Temple's rooms at the Angel all those nights ago. *There's no proof you killed her.* Anger flared.

"You knew from the beginning. From the moment you picked me up on the street and brought me into the Angel."

Chase did not move.

"Goddammit. *You knew. And you never told me.*"

Chase raised both hands, attempting to calm. "Temple . . ."

But Temple did not want calm. He wanted a fight. Pain shot through his chest and sizzled down his arm as the muscles around the wound tensed. Sizzled into nothingness at the midpoint of his forearm.

The pain of the lack of feeling was not near as bad as his friend's betrayal. "Get out," he said, "before I do something you'll regret."

The words were so soft, so dangerous, that Chase knew

better than to stay, turning back at the door. "What would you have done if you'd known?"

The question landed like a blow. "I would have ended it."

Chase's blond brow rose. "You still can."

But Chase was wrong. There was no ending it. Not now. They were all too far down the road.

"Get out."

Chapter 14

She'd prepared for battle that morning. She'd been ready to fight her imprisonment, ready to negotiate her release.

She'd spent three days locked in The Fallen Angel, given the freedom to move about the myriad of hallways and secret rooms, though always with a companion. Sometimes Asriel, the solemn, quiet guard, sometimes with the Countess of Harlow, when she arrived to check on Temple's wound, and sometimes with beautiful Anna, who was at once filled with words and empty of them.

It was Anna who had been sent for her that afternoon, barely knocking before opening the door to Mara's room and stepping inside, shaking out her skirts. "Temple has asked for you," she said, simply.

Mara was shocked at the words. She hadn't seen him since the morning he woke, sputtering tea and mistrust all over them both. She'd thought he had forgotten her.

She'd wished she could have forgotten him—the way he'd lain still and pale in the hours before that moment when he'd regained consciousness and temper. The way she'd feared for him. The way she'd willed him well.

The way she'd realized that this moment . . . this whole situation . . . had spiraled utterly out of her control.

The way she missed him.

She'd sent word to the other men—Bourne, Cross, and the mysterious Chase—that she wished to leave. That she had a position to return to at MacIntyre's. That she had boys to care for.

A life to live.

No word had returned, until now. Until Anna arrived and stole her breath and set her heart racing with the simple words. *Temple has asked for you.*

She would see him again.

She would see him now.

Excitement warred with trepidation, and she nodded, standing and smoothing her skirts. Nervous. She steeled her spine. "Like Boleyn to the chopping block."

Anna smirked. "Queen of England, are we?"

Mara shrugged. "Something to aspire to."

They started down the long, curved hallway, walking in silence for several long moments before Anna said, "You know, he's not a bad man."

Mara did not hesitate. "I have never thought he was."

Truth.

"No one trusts him," Anna said. "No one who isn't very close to him. No one who doesn't know him well enough to know that he could not have . . ."

She trailed off, but Mara finished the sentence for her. "Killed me."

Anna cut her a look. "Just so."

"But you knew him well enough?"

The beautiful blonde looked down at her hands. "I do."

Mara heard the present tense. Hated it. This woman was Temple's mistress, Mara had no doubt. And why not? She was his perfect match. Blond where he was dark, flawless where he was scarred, and so beautiful. They would make beautiful, unbearable children.

But Temple had bigger plans than to marry his mistress.

It ends with the life I was bred for. He'd told her once. *With a wife. A child. A legacy.*

Proper ones. Perfect ones. The kind due a duke. No doubt a wife beautiful and young and able to make perfect children. Jealousy flared. She did not like the idea of such a woman bearing his children.

She did not like the idea of any woman bearing his children.

Except—

She ended the thought before it could finish. Kept the madness at bay. Protected herself.

"He is lucky to have such good friends," she said.

Anna looked to her. "And you?"

"Me?"

"Who are your friends?"

Mara laughed, the sound lacking humor. "I have been in hiding for twelve years. Friends are a luxury I cannot afford."

"What of your brother?"

Mara shook her head. Kit was family. Not friend. Now, he never would be. She released a long breath. "He nearly killed Temple. What kind of a friend is he?"

Anna turned away, setting her hand to a nearby door handle. Turning it. The door opened wide before she said, "You should make sure Temple understands."

Mara did not have time to ask for clarification. Instead, she stepped into Temple's rooms, the door closing on Anna's cryptic statement, her gaze settling on the open door she now understood led to the ring.

She headed in that direction.

He stood at the center of the empty room, at the center of the ring itself. Strong and silent and ever so handsome, even in shirtsleeves and a white linen sling that held his arm firm against his chest. Perhaps *because* of those things. His black trousers were perfectly pressed, and Mara's gaze followed their line to the sawdust-covered floor, where his bare feet peeped out from beneath the wool hem.

She was transfixed by those bare feet. By the strength

of them. The curves and valleys of muscle and bone. The straight, perfect toes. The clean white nails.

The man even had handsome feet.

Her gaze snapped to his at the ridiculous thought, and she registered the curious smile there, wondering if he'd somehow read her mind.

She would not put it past him.

Empty of spectators, the room was cold, and Mara wrapped her arms about herself as she approached him, a foot above her and somehow so much farther. He watched her, making her keenly aware of each step, of the way she looked to him. She itched to smooth her hair. Her skirts. Resisted the temptation.

She reached the ring and faced him, looking down at her, expression guarded, as though he wasn't sure what she would do. What came next.

She wasn't sure, either.

But she knew he would wait an eternity for her to speak, so she spoke. "I am sorry."

It was not the first time she had thought the words, but it was the first time she'd said them aloud. To him.

Dark brows lifted in surprise. "For?"

She reached out, taking one of the coarse ropes in her hand. "For all of it." She looked up at him, his black eyes seeing everything but revealing nothing. "For my brother's actions." She paused. Took a breath. Confessed her sins. "For mine."

He came to her then, reaching down and helping her through the ropes with one rough, callused hand, warm and strong against hers. Once she was inside the ring, he stepped back, and she mourned the loss of him.

"Do you regret it?" He'd asked her the same question a lifetime ago, on the night she'd approached him outside his town house.

"I regret that you were caught in the fray." Her answer was the same, and somehow different. Somehow more true.

She did not regret her escape. But she deeply regretted his part in her stupid, thoughtless play. "And I regret what my brother did more than you can ever know." She paused. He waited. "Yes," she told the truth. "I regret it. I regret your pain. I regret the way I took your life. Toyed with it. I would take it back if I could."

He leaned back against the ropes on the far side of the ring. "Then you did not know his plan?"

Her eyes went wide with the shock of the question. "No!" How could he think she would—

How couldn't he think it?

She shook her head. "I would not hurt you."

His lips tilted in a half smile at that. "I called you a whore. You were quite angry."

The words stung, even now. She did not look away. "I was, indeed. But I was handing the situation."

He chuckled at that, the sound warm and welcoming. "So you were."

He was quiet for a long moment, until she could not help but look at him again. He was watching her, those dark eyes somehow seeing everything. Perhaps it was because of those eyes that she said, "I am happy you are recovered, Your Grace."

The truth.

Or perhaps a terrible lie. Because *happy* did not begin to describe the flood of emotions that coursed through her as she watched him, restored to his power and might. To his strength and health.

Relief. Gratitude.

Elation.

She released a long breath, and he came off the ropes, approaching her, sending a thrill of anticipation through her. He reached for her, and she did not hesitate, leaning into the touch, to the stroke of his thumb high on her cheek. She lifted her hand, holding him there, skin against skin against skin, and whispered, "You are alive."

Something flashed in his gaze. "As are you."

For the first time in a dozen years, she felt so. This man made her feel it, somehow. This man, who should have been her enemy. Who likely remained her enemy. Who no doubt wanted her destroyed for all the things she'd done. All the sins she'd committed.

And who, somehow, saw her for all she was.

"I thought you would die."

He smiled. "You wouldn't have it. I did not dare disappoint."

She tried to match his smile. Failed. Instead, thinking of another patient. Another death.

He saw it on her face. Had to have. "Tell me."

And suddenly, she wanted him to know.

"I couldn't save her," she whispered.

He didn't move. "Who?"

"My mother."

His brow furrowed. "Your mother died when you were a child."

"I was twelve."

"A child," he repeated.

She looked down between him, at her silly silk slippers, peeping out from beneath her plain borrowed frock, toes nearly touching his bare ones.

So close.

"I was old enough to know that she was going to die."

"She contracted a fever," he said, and she heard the consolation in his words. *You couldn't have known. There was nothing to be done.* A dozen people had said the words to her. A hundred.

They'd all believed the same story.

Except she hadn't had a fever.

Or, rather, she had . . . but not the way her father told the story. It hadn't come with sickness. It had come with infection. With a wound that would not heal.

And she had been in terrible pain.

Temple's hand moved, lifting her chin, raising her gaze to his. All warmth and strength, huge and rough. And honest.

She looked up at him, into those eyes, dark as midnight and with its focus. "He killed her," she whispered.

"Who killed her?"

"My father." Even now, years later, it was hard to label him as such. Hard to think of him that way.

Temple shook his head, and she knew what he was thinking. It was impossible. A husband did not kill a wife.

"He did not like it when Kit and I went against his wishes, and she did all she could to protect us. That day . . ." she hesitated, not wanting to say more but unable to stop herself. Lost in the memory. "He'd purchased a new bust. From Greece or Rome or Persia—I cannot remember.

"Kit and I were running through the house, and I tripped on my skirts." She laughed without humor, lost in the memory. "I had just been allowed to wear long skirts. I was so proud of myself. So grown up. I tumbled into the statue, which was perched atop a table on the upper landing of the house," she said, and Temple inhaled sharply, as though he could see what was coming. What she had been unable to see as a child.

She shrugged. "It toppled over the banister. Fell two stories to the floor of the entryway."

She could see it now, the way it lay broken and unrecognizable what seemed like a mile below. "He was furious. Came charging up the stairs, met me on the landing."

"You didn't run?"

The words surprised her from the memory. "Running would have made it worse."

"The beating."

"I could have taken it. It was not the first time he punished us. Nor would it be the last." She hesitated. "But my mother decided she'd had enough."

"What did she do?"

"She went at him. With a knife."

He sucked in a long breath. "Christ."

Mara had played the scene over again and again, nearly every day since it happened. Her beautiful mother, an avenging queen, placing herself between her children and their father.

Refusing to let him at them.

"He laughed at her," Mara said, hating the softness in the words. Hating the way they made her sound like the child she had been. She swallowed. Met his gaze again. "He was too strong for her."

"He turned the knife on her."

Another wound, blossoming with blood. This time, unlucky. "The doctors came, but there was nothing to be done. She was dead the moment he struck the blow. It was only a matter of time."

"Christ," he said again, this time reaching for her, pulling her tight against his broad, strong chest. Speaking into her hair. "And you had to live with him."

Until he offered me to another man, and I had no choice but to run.

She kept those words to herself, in part because she did not wish to remind him that he disliked her. That she was the reason his life had taken such a turn. She liked the comfort and strength of him too well.

A lie of omission.

She pressed her face into the warm smoothness of him, inhaling the scent of him, thyme and clove, letting herself have this moment, however fleeting, before she was faced once more with the world. And she said the words she'd never uttered. "If I hadn't broken that statue . . ."

His hand came to her chin then, long blunt fingers lifting her face to the light. To his gaze. "Mara," he said, the name still foreign to her ears after a decade without it. "It is not your sin."

She knew it, even if she did not believe it. "I paid for it, nonetheless." One corner of his mouth twitched in the threat of a smile, and she read the irony there. "Paying debts that do not belong to you. You would know a great deal about that."

"Not as much as you would think," he said, his thumb sliding like hot silk across her cheek, back and forth, the stroke at once calming and unsettling.

He watched the movement, and she took the opportunity to study him, his broken nose, the scar beneath one eye, the other that had split his lower lip. For a long moment, she forgot their conversation, her thoughts lost in that steady promise of his touch.

When he spoke, she saw the words curving on his lips. "I thought it was my debt."

He did not meet her gaze, not even when she whispered his name—that name that he'd taken when he'd become a new man, forged from exile and doubt.

"I thought I killed you," he said, simply. As though he were discussing something thoroughly inconsequential. The morning paper. The weather. He cleared his throat, and his hand fell away from her cheek. "I did not, however."

The loss of his touch was immense.

I'm sorry, she wanted to say.

Instead, she lifted her own hand to his cheek, the shadow of his beard tickling her palm. Tempting it. He met her gaze then, and she saw the regret in his eyes, tinged with confusion and frustration and, yes . . . anger, so well concealed that she would have missed it if she weren't looking so closely.

"I never meant to hurt you." She paused, her gaze flickering over his shoulder to the mirror where the women had watched the fight. "It never occurred to me that you would suffer."

He didn't say anything. Didn't have to. The idea that her actions would have no consequences for him was pure idiocy. She kept talking, as if her words could keep the past at bay. "But, when I heard them . . . when they watched you . . ."

"Who?" he asked.

She nodded in the direction of the mirror. "The women. I hated the way they spoke of you," she said, her fingers sliding away from his chin, down his chest, tracing the hills and valleys of his muscles beneath the linen. "I hated the way they looked at you."

"Are you jealous?"

She was, but that wasn't what she meant. "I hate the way their eyes devour you—like you're an animal. A treat. Something to be consumed. Something less than . . . what you are."

He captured her hand and pulled it from him, and she hated the loss. "I don't need your pity."

Her eyes went wide. "Pity?" How could he possibly think that this emotion—this wicked, unsettling feeling that coursed through her and upended everything she thought she knew—was *pity*?

It was nothing so simple as that.

"I wish it were pity," she said, extracting her hand from his grip. Returning it to his torso, where the muscles of his abdomen stirred and stiffened, drawing her touch. "If it were pity, perhaps I could avoid it."

"What, then?" he said, so low and dark that it made her feel as though this enormous room were the smallest she'd ever been in. Quiet and secluded.

She shook her head, every inch of her aware of him. Every ounce of her desperate for his touch. For his forgiveness. For him. "I don't know. You make me feel—"

She stopped, unable to put the emotion into words.

His hand came to her neck, fingers sliding along the pulse there, brushing just barely, as though she might flee if he weren't careful. "What?"

Her fingers moved of their own volition, threading into his hair, glorying in the softness of it. He stopped the caress with his good hand, pushing her back to the ropes, fisting her fingers around one thick cord—first one hand, then the other. When he was finished, he tilted her face to his. "What do I make you feel, Mara?"

After their sparring in the ring, all of London thought her his mysterious mistress. Was it not the thinking that made it so? Did it matter that it was in name only? Did it matter that she wanted him in more than farce? That she wanted him in truth? Hands and lips and body and . . .

She hesitated over the completion of the sentence. Over its meaning.

Over the way it would ruin her more thoroughly than any punishment Temple himself could mete out.

But the match had started, and she knew it was futile to fight.

Especially as she wished him to win.

She clutched the ropes, her mooring in his tempest. "You make me feel . . ." She paused, and his lips found hers in the hesitation, his kiss more gentle than ever before, tongue stroking with delicate, devastating force.

He pulled away before she could have her fill. "Go on," he whispered, not touching her and somehow destroying her. Holding her over a wide abyss, with only the ropes of his ring to keep her sane.

"You make me hot and somehow cold."

He rewarded the words with a long, lovely, worshipping kiss at the base of her neck. "What do you feel now?"

"Hot," she answered, even as a shiver threaded through her. "Cold. I don't know."

He smiled against her skin, and she adored his lips curving against her. "What else?"

"When you look at me, you make me feel like I am the only woman in the world."

His gaze was on the edge of her borrowed dress, where the bodice seemed brutally tight. He slid a finger along the simple line of fabric, barely touching her skin, making her wish the whole thing was gone. And then he tugged on the little white ribbon that fastened at the front, slowly tugging at the crisscrossing tie down her bodice until he gave her what she wished, the fabric coming loose. Instinctively, she released the ropes, moved to catch it. To hold it to her.

But he was there, guiding one arm from the woolen dress, then the other.

And she let him. When he was finished, he said only, "Take the ropes."

She turned herself over to him, grasping the ropes once more.

The dress was caught on her breasts, threatening to fall. He watched the way it held there, tenuous, and she wondered if he might be able to remove it with her gaze.

He ran a finger beneath the wool, gently, perfectly, and it pooled at her feet. She gasped.

"Cold?" he asked.

"No." Hot as the sun.

He bent his head, taking the tip of one breast in his mouth, chemise and all, worrying it through the fabric, leaving it wet and aching for more. For him. He lifted his head, meeting her gaze.

"What else, Mara?" he asked. "What else do I make you feel?"

"You make me wish it was all different," she said.

He rewarded the confession by sending her chemise to the floor, leaving her in nothing but her woolen stockings and those silly silken slippers that had matched the gown she'd worn the night she'd arrived, but had no place here. Now. He watched her for a long moment, drinking her in, keeping her warm, even as he blew a stream of cool air across the tip of her breast.

She sighed her pleasure, and he lifted his head, finding her. Seeing her. Just as she saw him. The way he desired her. The way he craved her. And when he ran the back of his hand across his lips like a starving man, she went weak-kneed, grateful for the strength of the ropes behind her.

"You make me wish I were different," she confessed. *You make me wish I were more.*

He shook his head. "It's strange; I don't wish that at all."

The words brought a cacophony of thought, too tangled for understanding. All she wanted was to say the right thing—the thing that would bring him closer to her. That would give her what she wanted. What she ached for.

The thing that would make him hers.

"Everything," she whispered, finally. "You make me feel everything."

And there, in the ring that was his castle and kingdom, he sank to his knees before her, wrapped one strong arm about her waist, and pressed his lips to the soft swell of her stomach before responding, "Not everything. Not yet."

He trailed kisses from her navel to the core of her, to the wicked edge of the soft curls there, and he stilled. Lingered. "But I will," he promised her, his tongue sliding along the soft, unbearably sensitive skin there.

She sighed, one hand moving to his head, sliding into his curls.

He froze, snapped to attention at the touch, turning instantly to capture the flesh at the base of her thumb in his teeth. Nipping gently. "The ropes."

She stilled. "Why?"

He met her gaze, and she saw the wicked promise there. "The ropes," he repeated.

She did as she was told, grasping the rough cords behind her, and he rewarded her, his hand stroking from her ankle up the long line of her leg, around the curve of her knee, up the soft, untouched skin of her inner thigh, above her stocking. He lifted the leg from the pool of her skirts with one hand, hooking her knee over his good shoulder, as though it weighed nothing at all.

Her cheeks burned with embarrassment as the rest of her

burned with desire. She was horrified and desperate all at once. A contradiction, as ever it was with him.

"Watch."

As if she could do anything else. All she could do was watch him.

Watch him see her.

"In the mirror," he said, and her gaze shot to the enormous mirror across from them, she'd been so caught up in him that she'd forgotten it—forgotten that it could give her a view she'd never imagined. Never dreamed.

She was nude, bared to him and the ring and the mirror, her hands tangled in the ropes, and she looked an utter scandal, spread wide like a sacrifice at this strange altar. But it was he who was on his knees, shoulders wide between her bare thighs, one leg tossed over his shoulder in wild, wanton abandon.

Anyone could see them.

The knowledge of what was beyond that mirror should have devastated her. Should have frightened her. Should have scandalized her. But instead, it made her want it more.

What had he done to her?

"Temple," she said, softly, closing her eyes to the vision. To its power. Terrified of what he would do next.

Terrified of what he would not do next.

And then he did it, spreading her wide, looking at her, seeing her in a way no one ever had. A way no one ever should.

And she loved it.

That hand—that glorious, magical hand—moved again, one finger sliding along the most secret part of her, exploring folds and valleys and ridges, sending pleasure coursing through her. She closed her eyes at the sensation, leaning back, the ropes creaking beneath her, their rough threads scraping along her back, coarse where he was soft. Harsh where he was gentle.

"My God," he whispered, his words at once sacrilege and benediction as his finger swirled and stroked, stealing breath and thought from her. "I don't know how I thought I could ever resist you."

An echo of her own thoughts. This had been inevitable. From the moment she'd approached him on the street. From before.

And then his mouth was on her, and she could not think at all, his tongue stroking in long, slow licks, teasing and tempting and torturing even as it wrought pleasure she could not believe. "Temple," she cried, lifting, offering herself to him. Giving herself up to him.

Trusting him.

Trusting someone for the first time in what seemed like forever.

He rewarded her with his glorious mouth, wrapping his arm around her waist and pulling her tight to him, closing his lips tightly around some unbearable, unthinkable place and sucking more deeply, licking more firmly, scraping with a barely-there pressure that had her crying out for him.

"William." She sighed the name that she'd thought a hundred times in the dead of night. A thousand. Never once believing that he could unlock such glorious pleasure.

He stilled at the name on her lips, and she looked down at him, finding his black gaze across the expanse of her naked body, knowing that this was at once terribly wrong and ever so right.

He swirled his tongue against her in the most wonderful way, and her eyes slid closed, unable to bear the torture of the pleasure. He lifted his mouth then, just long enough to say, "Watch."

She shook her head, color rising on her face. "I can't."

"You can," he promised, turning his face to press a kiss to the high curve of her thigh. "Watch me give you all there is to give."

He set his mouth to her again, and she did watch, her gaze

sliding from their reflection to his beautiful face, knowing that it was immodest and scandalous, but unable to take her gaze from his. Unable to stop herself from letting go of the ropes and sliding her hand into that glorious dark hair of his, and holding him tight to her. Unable to stop herself from moving against him. Unable to ignore the flood of powerful pleasure that coursed through her when that movement made him groan against her.

Made him redouble his efforts, his tongue and lips and teeth moving in perfect concert, sending her high, higher still on a wave of unbearable pleasure, until she came apart against him, calling out his name, fisting her fingers in his hair, taking every last ounce of glorious feeling from him.

Never once looking away, not even as she rocked against him, the ropes behind her sighing with the movement.

He held her as she returned to him, as her feet found the floor once more and, unable to hold herself upright, she sank to her knees with him.

He pulled her into his lap, and they sat there, hearts pounding, breath coming hard and fast, for an eternity, neither speaking, but both knowing that everything had changed.

Forever.

She'd never felt anything like this. Not even that long-ago night, the one she lorded over him, when they'd lay in her bed and kissed and touched. When he'd whispered teasing words in her ear and played with her hair and made her promises he'd never intended to keep.

When she'd taken his world from him.

She could not hide from him any longer. She could not lie to him. She would find another way to save the orphanage. To keep the boys safe. There had to be a way.

A way that did not rely on using this man any longer.

She could give him that, at least.

Sadness coursed through her as she looked up at him,

meeting his inscrutable gaze. Wishing she could hear his thoughts. Wishing she could tell him everything. Wishing she could lay herself bare for him.

Wishing their future had not been so well cast in such strong stone.

"I promised I would tell you—" she began.

He shook his head, cutting her off. "Not now. Not because of this. Don't sully it. It's the first time it's felt real in . . ."

He trailed off, the words singing through her, bringing hope and promise with them—two things she could not accept. Two things she had learned long ago would destroy her if she gave them quarter.

She did not give them time to take root. "We never . . ." She moved from his lap, sliding to the floor. "It started, but did not get to here . . ." He closed his eyes at the words and took a deep breath, and as much as she wanted to stop, she soldiered on. "I should never have let you believe we did."

His gaze found her. "So it was another lie."

She nodded, wanting to tell him everything. Wanting to tell him that that night, long ago, when she'd done the thing she most regretted, was also the night she'd done the thing she least regretted.

He'd made her laugh and smile. He'd made her feel beautiful.

For the first time in her life.

For the only time in her life.

She opened her mouth to tell him just that, to try to explain, but he was already speaking. "Daniel."

The name confused her. "Daniel?"

"He is not mine."

Shock threaded through her at the words. At their meaning. She shook her head. "I don't understand . . ."

"You said he'd been with you forever."

Daniel, with his dark hair and blue eyes and his age—exactly correct if they had done this. If they had done more.

For a moment, she let the vision of it crash over her. Temple, strong and sure and handsome and hers. And a son, dark and serious and sweet.

And theirs.

It was the life he wanted. A wife. A son. A legacy.

But it was not real. She shook her head, finding his gaze, seeing the emotion there. Regret. Anger. Sadness.

She'd hurt him again. Without even trying. She shook her head, tears in her eyes. "Forever—since I founded the orphanage. He is not . . ." She trailed off, wishing the truth were different.

He laughed then, the sound harsh and humorless. "Of course he isn't. Of course we didn't."

The words cut through her.

He stood, in a single fluid movement, taking himself to the opposite side of the ring, all grace and economy even now, even with one arm in a sling. Even with a wound that would have killed a lesser man.

His back to her, he scraped his hand through his hair. "Just once, I wanted the truth from you." He looked over his shoulder at her. "Just once, I wanted you to give me a reason to believe you are more than what you seem. More than a woman out for blood and money." He laughed and turned away again. "And then you gave it to me."

She should tell him.

The whole story.

The money, the debt, the reason she'd run. She should lay herself at his feet and give him the chance to forgive her. To believe her. To believe in her.

Perhaps then, they could start again. Perhaps then, there might be more to this strange, unsettling, remarkable thing between them.

Dear God, she wanted that more than she wanted her next breath.

"I was not out for blood," she said, coming to her feet, her dress in her hand, shielding her nakedness from him. "And not for money, either." She took a step toward him. "Please. Let me explain—"

"No." He turned to her, hand slashing through the air.

She stopped.

"No," he repeated. "I am tired of it. Of your lies. Of your games. I am tired of wanting to believe them. No more."

She pulled her dress around her, knowing that she deserved this. Knowing that, for twelve years, her life had been heading for this. For the day when she faced this man and told him the truth, and suffered the repercussions.

But it had never occurred to her that the pain would come from losing him. From hurting him. That she might care for him.

Care for him.

What a silly, tepid phrase in comparison to the emotion that coursed through her now, as she watched this remarkable man battle his demons. Demons she had sent after him.

"I don't care what your reasons are, or how well you've fabricated them. I am done. How much was this worth? This afternoon?"

The words were a blow. He couldn't believe she would ask to be paid for— *Of course he could.* It was the arrangement they'd made.

She shook her head.

"And now you are too high for our agreement?"

She didn't want it now. She didn't want any of it. She only wanted him.

And, like that—like a sharp, wicked blow, she understood.

She loved him.

And if that was not bad enough, he would never believe it.

But still, she tried. "William. Please. If you'll just—"

"Don't." The word cut through the air, frigid and frightening. And she realized that now, here, she faced Temple, the greatest fighter London had ever seen. "Don't you ever call me that again. You don't have the right."

Of course she didn't. She'd stolen the name from him when she'd stolen his life. Tears threatened, and she swallowed them back, not wanting him to think them fabricated. Not wanting him to think *her* fabricated. She nodded. "Of course."

He was cold and unmoving, and she couldn't look at him any longer. She wrapped her arms about herself as he took his final shot. As he ended it. "Tomorrow, this is over. You show your face, you restore my name. I'll give you your money. And then you get the hell out of my world."

He left her there, at the center of his ring, in the heart of his club.

It was only once the door to his rooms was closed and the lock thrown that she dressed, and allowed the tears to come.

Chapter 15

*H*e'd left her naked in the ring.

At no point in his entire career as a bare-knuckle boxer had he ever left an opponent so stripped of honor.

He'd never had an opponent so keenly strip him of his dreams.

What rubbish. Temple leaned over the billiard table in one of the upper rooms of The Fallen Angel, sending the carom balls flying.

"Christ, Temple," Bourne said, watching two balls sink into the pockets at the far end of the field. "Should we leave and let you play on your own?" He tossed back the remainder of his scotch. "And with one arm."

The mention of his arm, still lacking feeling and weak from the fight, brought back his anger. Her brother had taken his strength. His power. But she'd done one worse. She'd taken his hope.

He'd let himself believe that things could be. That she might be that for which he ached. Wife. Family. *More.*

Love.

The word whispered through him, part shock, part frustration, part desire.

He ignored it and took another shot with furious precision. And a third.

Cross leaned back on his heels, one long arm dangling over the end of his cue. "All right, it's clear you're not interested in the game so much as the win," he said. "So what is it that is at you?"

"It's the woman," Bourne said as he headed across the room to pour himself a glass of scotch.

Of course it was the woman.

Temple ignored the thought and sank another ball.

Cross looked to Bourne. "You think so?"

Bourne passed a glass to Cross. "It's always the woman."

Cross nodded. "You are right."

"He's not right," Temple said.

Bourne raised a brow. "I'm right."

Of course he was right.

Temple scowled. "You can both go straight to Hell."

"You would miss us if we were gone," Cross said, finally getting a chance to take a shot. "Besides, I like the woman. It's fine with me if she's your problem."

Bourne cut Cross a look. "You *like* her?"

"Pippa likes her. Thinks she cares for Temple. I believe her."

Memory flared. Mara's eyes liquid with tears as she sat naked in the ring. As he treated her abominably. Temple gritted his teeth.

She had robbed him of his life, then lied to him. Again and again. She didn't care for him. It was impossible.

Cross was still speaking to Bourne. "And, she took a fist to your face."

"You needn't say it with such glee," Bourne retorted.

"There is glee. You were trounced. By a woman."

"You're a bastard," Bourne grumbled. "And besides, how was I to know she threw a punch like Temple?"

Memory flashed—Mara in the foyer of the MacIntyre Home for Boys, her hand flat against his chest, strong and warm. *I don't wish to hurt you.*

Another lie.

Cross interrupted his thoughts. "So, Temple. What have you done wrong?"

A vision flashed, Mara in the center of his ring, begging him to listen to her. What would she have said? What would she have told him?

He pushed the memory aside. When had she ever told him the truth?

Minutes prior.

"Nothing."

"Oh, that means you've definitely done something." Bourne collapsed into a nearby chair.

"When did the lot of you turn into chattering magpies?"

Cross leaned against the billiard table. "When did you lose your sense of humor?"

The question was not out of bounds. Had it been Bourne or Cross in such a foul temper, Temple would have been the first to ask questions.

Indeed, in the past year, Temple had had the great pleasure of watching both men flirt with insanity as they resisted, then courted their wives. He'd laughed at them more often than not, and been happy to add to their misery.

But while this might involve a woman, this was not about a wife.

This was about absolution. A much more important goal.

"I let her go," he said, simply.

"Where?" Bourne asked.

"Home."

"Ah," Cross said, as though the word explained everything. Which it didn't.

Temple scowled at the irritating ginger. "What the hell does that mean?"

"Only that when they leave, it's never as pleasant as you think it will be."

"Mmm," Bourne added. "You think you'll get peace, and instead . . . you can't stop thinking about them."

He looked from one of his friends to the other. "You've

both become women. I would easily stop thinking about her if she weren't . . ." He hesitated.

If she weren't so infuriating.

If she weren't so all-consuming.

If she hadn't been so damn beautiful as she stood tall and proud in his ring and took the blows he delivered like a champion. Like she'd deserved them.

Which she had.

But what if she hadn't?

"If she weren't . . . ?" Cross prodded.

Temple poured himself a glass of scotch. Drank deep. Hoped the burn of liquor would erase the burn of her memory. "If she weren't my link."

"To?"

To Lowe. To the past. To truth. To the life he'd so desperately wanted for so very long.

More than that. *She was his link to everything.*

He pushed the thought aside and leaned over to take another shot, ignoring the twinge of pain that sizzled down his arm, disappearing as though it had never been.

He missed. Bourne and Cross looked to each other in surprise. He gave them his best glare. "You try it with one arm."

A knock sounded on the door, and they turned as one, Temple grateful for the change of topic. "Enter," Bourne called.

Justin entered, followed by Duncan West, the owner of no fewer than eight newspapers and magazines in London, arguably the most influential man in Britain, and the man who was going to restore Temple to his rightful place in the peerage.

West surveyed the room. "Room for a fourth?"

Temple extended his cue toward the newcomer. "You may have mine." He moved to a sideboard and refilled his glass before pouring a second as West shucked his coat and tossed it to a nearby chair.

"Who is winning?"

"Temple," Bourne answered, taking his own shot and missing.

West gave Temple a look, accepting the proffered drink. "And you don't wish to continue the streak?"

Temple leaned against the back of a nearby chair and drank. "I'd rather speak unencumbered."

The newspaperman stilled. "Should I, too, be unencumbered?"

Temple waved the glass in the direction of the carom field. "You play until I say something worth listening to."

The suggestion seemed to work for West, he moved to survey the game. "Fair enough. How is the arm?"

"Attached," Temple answered.

West nodded, setting the glass on the edge of the table, leaning over and lining up his shot. As he pulled back on the cue, Temple announced, "Mara Lowe is alive."

West missed the shot, but he wasn't paying attention, already turning to face Temple, eyes wide. "You've said something worth listening to."

"I thought you might feel that way."

West set his cue down. "As I'm sure you can imagine, I've a dozen questions. More."

"And I'll answer every one of them. What I cannot, she will."

"You are able to speak for the woman?" West let out a low whistle. "This *is* a story. Where is she?"

"It is not important," Temple said, suddenly uninterested in sharing the private details of Mara's whereabouts. He drank again. *Liquid courage.* Where the hell had that thought come from? "Do you plan to attend the Leighton Christmas Masque?"

West knew a good story when he saw one, and he knew better than to refuse. "I assume Miss Lowe will be in attendance?"

"She will be."

"And you intend to introduce her to me?" Temple nodded.

West was intelligent, and able to put the pieces together. "That's not it, though."

"Is it ever?" Cross said from his place at the carom table.

"You want the girl ruined," West said.

Did he?

"I don't blame you." The newspaperman continued, "But I won't be your puppet in this. I came because Chase summoned me, and I owe him. I'll hear your story. Your side. But I'll hear hers, as well, and if I don't think she deserves the shaming, she won't get it from me."

"Since when are you so noble?" Bourne interjected. "The story will sell papers, will it not?"

A shadow crossed West's face, there then gone so quickly that Temple would have missed it if he hadn't been watching so closely. "Suffice to say, I've ruined enough people with my papers that I am no longer required to do the bidding of every aristocrat with a vendetta." He met Temple's eyes. "Does she deserve it?"

It was the question Temple had hoped he wouldn't be asked.

The question he'd hoped he'd never have to answer.

Because a week ago, he would have said yes, unequivocally. A week ago, he would have argued that the girl deserved everything that came her way—every ounce of justice he could mete out with his power and strength and influence.

But now, the unequivocal was becoming more complex. And he could not think of her simply. Suddenly, he thought of the way she teased him when she forgot that they were enemies. The way she faced him as his equal. The way she dealt nimbly with her students and with the men at his club. The way she gave herself up to his kiss. To his touch. The way she cradled that idiot pig in her arms as though she were the best companion for which a woman could ask.

The way insidious little thoughts inched into the back

of his mind, teasing him into wondering if he couldn't be something better than the damn pig.

He downed the rest of his scotch, turning back to get more.

Christ. He was comparing himself to a pig now.

So, did she deserve his vengeance? He didn't know any longer. But when he thought of his past—of the life he could have had, of the pleasure he'd taken in his title, in his role, in his potential—he couldn't stop the anger from threatening.

If not for her, he would be far less angry.

And much less hurt.

This bed had been made years ago. Far be it from him to resist lying in it.

She had lied to him. Again and again.

And when she'd finally told him the truth, she'd stolen his last ounce of hope. The last promise of the life he'd desired in the darkest parts of his soul. The beautiful wife. The strong, happy child. The family. The name.

The legacy.

She'd stolen it, as though it had never been his to begin with.

Anger flared, hot and welcome, and Temple met Duncan West's gaze. "She deserves it."

West turned back to the table, and took his shot. Sank the ball. Straightened and lifted his glass, toasting Temple. "If that is true, I shall happily assist you," he said. "I shall see you at Leighton's ball." He drank deep before he tossed Temple the cue and made his way to the door. Once there, he turned back. "What of Chase?"

Temple hadn't spoken to his partner since their falling out several evenings earlier. "What of him?"

"Where is he tonight?"

"Busy," Bourne said, the reply in no way welcoming further discussion.

West pretended not to notice the irritation in Bourne's tone. "No doubt. But when is he going to realize that I'm friend enough to keep his secrets?"

Cross raised a brow. "When your livelihood isn't dependent on the telling of them."

West grinned and downed his scotch before making for the door. "Fair enough. I'm for *vingt-et-un*." He nodded to Temple. "Tomorrow?"

Temple inclined his head in West's direction. "Tomorrow."

"And my questions will be answered?"

"That, and more," Temple promised.

West nodded and was gone within seconds, the tables on the floor of the casino an irresistible pull. His agreement should have enhanced Temple's excitement. Should have made him feel vindicated.

Instead, they left a knot of something not altogether pleasant in his gut. Something he was neither interested in nor capable of defining.

He turned back to his friends, each watching him carefully.

"Once he reveals her, her reputation is gone. And he puts the orphanage at risk," Bourne pointed out.

"No one likes the idea of an orphanage run by a scandal," Cross explained, as though Temple didn't understand.

He understood. And he did not like the unpleasant sensation that coursed through him at the words. At the suggestion that his plan was a danger to a houseful of innocent children.

At the way Bourne so easily dismissed Mara as a scandal.

He didn't like which of those things grated the most.

"If he has access to orphanage files, he'll discover within minutes who the boys are," Bourne said. "He'll out the fathers."

"The girl won't be able to survive it. She'll never be able to show her face in London again," Cross added. "If she's not run out by the men who've sent their boys there, she'll be destroyed by the women of the *ton*. And she'll blame you. Are you prepared for that? To lose her? Entirely?"

Temple narrowed his gaze on Bourne. "Why would I care about losing her? Good riddance."

The lie grated, even as he refused to acknowledge it as such. His friends knew better than to press the issue.

"West is a friend," Cross added. "But he is also a newspaperman. And a good one."

"I realize that," Temple said.

He wasn't a monster. Once she was ruined, he would protect the boys. He would build them a palace outside the city. He'd fill the damn thing with sweets and hounds.

And pigs.

He imagined her, holding that damn piglet, a smile on her pretty lips, and felt a pang of something close to guilt.

Damn.

He flexed the hand of his wounded arm, hating its stiffness.

"I'll keep West from the orphanage," he vowed. "He's a decent man. He won't do anything to harm two dozen children."

Cross's gaze fell to his hand, still opening and closing in careful rhythm. "How does it feel?"

"Eager to get me back in the ring, are you?" Temple joked, not feeling entirely humorous.

Cross did not smile. "Eager to get you back. Full stop."

Temple looked down at the forearm of his ruined side, turning it over, considering it. Wondering if he should tell them what he suspected in the dark hours of the night, when it twitched and tingled and burned.

What would they say if he told them that he could not feel part of his arm? What would he be to them if he was no longer the unbeatable Temple? What would he be to himself?

No longer the friend they'd made, the man with whom they'd gone into business. No longer Britain's legendary bare-knuckle boxer. No longer the man who spent his days in Mayfair and his nights in Temple Bar. Instead, he was something else. Some perversion of identity, born aristocrat and raised on the streets. The Duke of Lamont, who had not seen his land or his family in twelve long years.

No longer the Killer Duke.

Of course, he never had been.

A vision flashed, Mara in the ring, standing proud and unmoving. Stronger than any of his prior foes. Fiercer. Far more compelling.

Who would he be to her?

He ran his good hand over his face.

What had she done to him? What had he done to himself?

"You don't have to do it, you know," Bourne said quietly.

He looked in his friend's direction. "Now you defend her? Shall I get you a mirror to remind you of the purple ring about your eye?"

Bourne smirked. "She is not the first to deliver such a blow. And she will not be the last." That much was true. "All I am saying is that you can stop this. You can change it."

"What's put you in such a forgiving frame of mind?"

The marquess shrugged. "You care for the girl, obviously, or you wouldn't be so destroyed by her. I know what that is like. And I know what it is to give up revenge for it."

For a moment, he entertained the idea. He imagined what it would be like if he could change it. Imagined what life he would craft if given the opportunity. Imagined a little row of dark sons and auburn-haired daughters, each with strange, beautiful eyes and spines of steel.

Imagined their mother, leading their charge.

But imagination was all it was.

Reality was a different thing entirely.

$\mathcal{T}$he Duke and Duchess of Leighton had hosted their annual Christmas masque every December since their first year as man and wife, and the party had become so legendary that most of London made a point to return to the city despite the cold, dreary December weather to attend.

According to Lydia (who was much more of a gossip than Mara had ever realized), the Duchess of Leighton prided herself on filling out the guest list with dozens of impressive, if not aristocratic, London dignitaries. Lydia had actually used the phrase, "everyone who is anyone," in the excitement that followed Mara's receipt of Temple's invitation—if a single line of black scrawl stating a time and the dress he would prefer she wear could be called such a thing—which Mara assumed meant that it was not coincidence that this was the event at which she would be unmasked to London. Literally as well as figuratively.

Except yesterday, before everything had gone pear-shaped, it might have been different. Yesterday, before she'd reminded him of their past—of the dozen ways they were enemies—they might have been friends.

And he might have reconsidered this moment.

Dream.

She gave a little huff of laughter at the thought. It was a dream. For there was nothing that would erase their past. That would erase what she had done. No amount of forgiveness that would change how this scenario played out. How this night ended.

With her ruin.

In all honesty, Mara was rather happy that the evening was finally here. Once her ruination was at hand, she would no doubt have a chance to return to her ordinary life, and be forgotten by the rest of Britain.

Forgotten by him.

It would be best. A boon, perhaps.

At least, that's what she told herself.

She'd told herself that as she turned the orphanage over to Lydia that day, articulating the ins and outs of the place—pointing out the histories of all the boys, the files where she kept their work and the remnants of their past. The evidence of their birth.

She'd told herself that as she promised Lydia the funds

she'd earned from Temple, even as Mara ached at the idea of calling the debts due. She hadn't a choice. The boys needed coal, and Lydia needed funds if the orphanage was to be hers to run.

She'd told herself that as she'd packed her small traveling case and tucked away enough funds to get her to Yorkshire, to the place to which she'd fled twelve years earlier. To the place where she'd reinvented herself. Where she'd become Margaret MacIntyre.

She'd told herself that when the dress arrived in a beautiful white box, complete with a gold-embossed H and an elaborate golden mask in delicate filigree that she'd had to resist touching.

There'd been underclothes, too—silks and satins and lace—clocked stockings and perfectly embroidered chemises at once stunning and utterly unnecessary. It had been more than a decade since she'd worn such softness against her skin, and she'd luxuriated in the feel of the fabrics against her even as their purpose echoed in her thoughts.

They were underclothes designed to be seen. By men.

By Temple.

And the cloak—a stunning green shot through with golden threads to match the rest of the ensemble, lined with ermine, worth more than a year's worth of the orphanage's bills. Mara had been shocked to find it in the box, as it had not been discussed when she'd been at Madame Hebert's for her thoroughly embarrassing fitting.

Her cheeks went warm at the memory of his eyes on her in that dimly lit room. And when that memory gave way to one from later that evening, of his lips on hers, her cheeks burned.

And she told herself that she was happy to meet her executioner as she stood in the foyer of the MacIntyre Home for Boys, waiting, Lydia perched on the steps to the upstairs, Mara's case at her feet, Lavender on her lap.

Now, as she stood in the foyer of this place she'd built

with work and tears and passion, she realized that she was no longer Margaret MacIntyre, and no longer Mara Lowe. No longer headmistress, no longer sister, no longer caretaker, no longer friend.

She was blank again.

Her heart constricted. And somehow, none of it mattered but one, devastating truth: She was nothing to Temple, either.

She turned to Lydia. "If my brother comes, you'll tell him I've left? You'll give him my letter?"

Kit's message had been waiting for her when she'd returned from The Angel, requesting funds to leave the country. Promising that this was the last he'd ask of her.

Mara had written him a letter articulating the truth—that she had no funds to spare, and that they were both in a place where they had to flee. She'd thanked him for the years he'd kept her truths from the world, and she'd said good-bye.

Lydia pursed her lips. "I shall, though I don't like it. What if he comes after you?"

"If he does, so be it. I would rather he come after me than you. Than this place," Mara said, adding quietly. "Than Temple."

The words brought the echo of that night, her knife high in Temple's chest, Kit gone, disappeared into the crowd as Mara panicked. This was the solution. It would end it. It would free Temple.

Kit would never bother him again.

And after tonight, neither would she.

She sighed, desperate to resist the emotions that came more and more readily at the thought of him.

"And everything else—"

Lydia nodded and set Lavender down, coming to Mara, taking her hands. "And everything else." They stood like that for a long moment. Friends. "You don't have to do this, you know. We could fight it."

Tears threatened, and Mara blinked them back.

"But I do. For you. For the boys." She spread her hands down the smooth silk of her skirts, forcing herself to remember that tonight, he would make good on his promise. And she would make good on hers. Finally.

Tonight, it would end.

Lydia knew better than to argue. "It's a beautiful dress."

"It makes me look like I'm for sale," Mara said.

"It does not."

Lydia was right. Yes, the neckline was low, but Madame Hebert had somehow given in to Temple's request without making Mara appear indecent. But Mara did not wish to acknowledge the fact that the dress was stunning.

"It makes you look like a princess."

She pulled the cloak around her. It was her turn to say, "It does not."

Lydia grinned. "A duchess, then." Mara cut her a look, but she kept speaking, scooping Lavender up from where the piglet danced at their feet. "Cor. Imagine that. You, married to his father."

"I'd rather not," Mara said.

"The man's stepmother."

She closed her eyes. "Don't say it."

"Imagine that life—filled with impure thoughts about one's stepson."

"Lydia!" Mara protested, grateful for the distraction.

"Oh, tosh," Lydia said. "The man's older than you are."

"It doesn't mean—"

Lydia waved one hand. "Of course it does. Look at him. He's enormous. And handsome as sin. Are you honestly telling me you haven't had a single impure thought?"

"Yes."

"Liar."

Of course she was a liar. She'd had more than impure thoughts about him. She'd had impure deeds with him. And worse.

She loved him, somehow.

What an unfortunate turn of events that was.

And then the object of her thoughts appeared, saving her from having to think too much on the last.

Her heart was in her throat as she took him in, in his black trousers and waistcoat and coat, perfectly tailored despite his sling—also black. Dear Heaven, his shoulders were broad. The black was broken only by the stark white of his shirt and cravat, starched and tied as though by one of London's best valets.

She could not imagine him with a valet. He did not seem the kind of man who ever needed another's assist, let alone for something as frivolous as a perfectly tied cravat.

But perfectly tied it was, nonetheless.

"Your Grace," Lydia said with an enormous smile. "We were just speaking of you."

He tilted his head. "Were you? What were you saying?" He bowed low over Lydia's hand, missing the gleam in her eye as Mara glared at her over the wide expanse of his back, willing her not to say any more.

"We were discussing the fine puppetry of fate."

He stroked Lavender's little furry snout, and the piglet turned traitor, leaning into the touch with a snuffle before Temple gave his attention to Mara. "Fine puppetry indeed." His gaze swept over her, leaving her alternately hot and cold in its caress. Nervous, she clutched the ermine trim together at her neck, feeling as though he could see straight through the fabric. His attention fell to her hand, and he hesitated for a long moment before saying, "You are ready?"

"As I might ever be," she said quietly, but he was already moving to the door, no doubt eager to get her destruction under way. No doubt tired of her. No doubt tired of living his life without all the privilege into which he'd been born.

She followed him, knowing with each step tonight, her life would change. Tonight, she would no longer be able to escape her past. She would have to claim it. And with it, she would likely lose everything for which she'd worked.

Because of him.

At the door, Lydia stopped her, throwing her arms around her, and whispering in her ear, "Courage."

Mara nodded around the knot in her throat, and lifted Lavender into her arms for a long cuddle and a kiss on the head before relinquishing the pig to the new proprietress of the MacIntyre Home for Boys.

The coach was silent as a tomb, and Mara tried not to notice him.

She tried not to notice the way his chest rose and fell beneath the crisp linen of his shirt and the soft wool of his jacket. The way his breath came in long, slow inhales and exhales. The way his strong thighs engaged as the carriage rocked along the cobblestone streets. The scent of him— clove and thyme and Temple.

She tried not to notice him until he leaned forward in the darkness, across the unspoken line of demarcation between his side of the carriage and hers, and said, gruffly, "I brought you a gift."

It would be rude not to notice one with a gift, after all.

And sure enough, he punctuated his words by extending a long, slim box toward her. She recognized it immediately, the white with gold embossing, the mark of Madame Hebert, and she shook her head in confusion as she accepted the parcel. "I'm wearing everything you ordered. More."

The words were out before she could keep them back— before she could stop herself from reminding them both that she was wearing his clothes. Clothes he'd chosen as she stood half naked in front of him in a dark room.

He could have taken the moment to push her on the topic. To force her to admit each scrap of clothing was his before it was hers. But he didn't. Instead, he leaned back on the seat and said, "Not everything."

She opened the box, pulling back gossamer-thin paper to reveal a pair of beautiful satin gloves, perfectly matched to her dress with stunning embroidery and dozens of little buttons all along the inside of them. She lifted them gently from the box, as though they might fall apart in her hands.

"You never wear gloves," Temple said. "I thought you might require some."

These were not workaday gloves, however, these were gloves for one night, for one ensemble. *For one man.*

She pulled one glove on before realizing that she would not be able to fasten them one-handed. But before she could say anything, he was leaning forward again, extracting a button hook from his coat pocket, as though it were the most ordinary thing in the world for a man to carry. He crowded her in the small, dark space, reaching for her hand. He'd freed his arm and folded back the sleeve of her cloak, using his bad arm to hold her steady as he set to work on the task of buttoning the endless line of little green buttons.

She wanted to hate him for controlling even this, even her gloves.

But instead, she loved him all the more for it, her heart heavy in her chest, knowing this was their last evening. Perhaps the last time they would be alone together.

"Thank you," she said softly, uncertain of what else to do as she sat, her free hand worrying the paper from the box.

He was quiet, focused on his task, and she settled into watching the top of his dark head, unable to take a deep breath for his nearness, wishing he weren't so very close to her imperfect, scarred hands. Grateful for the fact that she had covered the years of history written on her palm before relinquishing the extremity to him.

Utterly unsettled by his gentle, deft touch.

She could feel the softness of his breath on the skin of her wrist as he hid it from view, the soft touch of his fingers along the inside of her arm the last thing chased away by silk.

No. Not chased away. Imprisoned by it.

Because it felt that way, as though the glove itself was protecting his touch from ever escaping.

He finished the first glove after an eternity and she released the long breath that she had not known she had been holding, realizing that he had clasped her other hand in his without any warning. She tugged on it, but his grip was steel. "Thank you, I can—"

"Let me," he said, lifting the second glove from her lap.

No, she wanted to say, *don't look at it*.

Heat washed across her cheeks, and she was thankful for the darkness of the carriage.

He saw it anyway. "You are embarrassed of them," he said, the pad of his thumb rubbing softly—maddeningly—across her palm.

She tugged on the hand again. Futilely.

"You needn't be, you know," he said, that slow, circling stroke an endless torture. "These hands helped you survive for twelve years. They worked for you. They won your funds and shelter and safety for more than a decade."

Her eyes flew to his, coal black in the dim light. "Women's hands aren't supposed to show their work."

He continued, his voice barely above a whisper. "But what I cannot understand, Mara, is why you required it of them?"

Fear. Fate.

Folly.

"I wish they were untried. Soft. The way ladies' hands should be."

The way you no doubt prefer them.

No. She did not care how he liked his hands. Her hands.

He slid the silk glove over her hand, working her fingers into the fabric channels, pressing his own fingers into the valleys between hers. Who could have imagined that the skin in those places was so sensitive?

"They are your hands," he said, lifting her hand, lowering his head, whispering to the bared skin at her palm. "They are perfect."

"Don't say that," she whispered.

Don't be nice to me.

Don't make me love you any more than I already do.

Don't hurt me any more than you already plan.

He pressed a kiss to the soft pad of muscle at the base of her thumb before he fastened the buttons and made his way to her wrist, where he pressed another soft kiss, and fastened more.

And so it went, on and on, up the inside of her arm with light, delicate kisses, each sending a shock of heat through her, each locked in by silk. By him. Each one a ruination of its own, as it made her want to crawl into his lap and do his bidding without question.

When he reached the final stretch of buttons, the one that would encase her elbow, he lingered on the bare skin there, pressing his warm lips to that sensitive place that she'd never before known, lingering when she gasped at the pleasure of the caress. Parting his lips. Stroking his tongue in a long, languorous circle of glorious heat.

She couldn't stop herself from sliding her free hand into his hair, holding him there, at that wicked, wonderful place.

Hating the damn glove that kept her from touching him.

Cursing it aloud.

She felt his lips curve against her skin, the smile chased away by a painless, unbearable scrape of his teeth before he finished his torture, and then his task.

In that moment, he could have had anything he asked.

She would have given it with deep, abiding pleasure. Which was what made this man more dangerous than anyone in London thought.

He could control her with a touch, and his control was more serious, more dangerous, than that of any of the men who had controlled her before.

And it was terrifying.

"Temple," she whispered in the dark, "I . . ."

She trailed off, a million things wishing to be said.

I'm sorry.

I wish it could be different.

I wish I could be the perfect woman you want. The one who will erase the past.

I love you.

He didn't give her a chance to say any of it. "It's time for you to put on your mask." He sat back against the carriage seat, looking utterly unmoved by the entire experience. "We've arrived."

Chapter 16

The gloves had been a mistake.

He realized that the second he started buttoning her into the damn things. Not that he hadn't imagined buttoning her into them the second they arrived at his home.

Not that he hadn't imagined unbuttoning everything else and leaving her in nothing but those long, silk gloves.

Except imagination paled in comparison to reality, at least when it came to Mara Lowe, and he hadn't been able to stop himself from touching her. From kissing her. From tasting her skin. From making himself impossibly distracted and unbearably hard in the process.

In his life, he'd never been so thrilled and so furious to arrive somewhere. Except, as he climbed down from the carriage, reaching back to help her descend, the silken glove sliding through his grasp, he realized that he'd made an enormous mistake. After all, he'd have to touch her all evening, and every stroke of silk against his skin would be a lick of flame.

A reminder of what he'd touched.

Of what he would never touch again.

He guided her up the extravagantly decorated steps to Leighton House and inside, where he watched as a footman removed the fur-lined cloak from around her shoulders, revealing an extraordinary expanse of smooth, pale skin.

A too-bare expanse.

Shit.

He never should have pushed Hebert to keep the line of the dress so low. What had he been thinking? Every man in attendance would be watching her.

Which had been his plan all along.

Except now, as she adjusted that stunning golden mask that only highlighted her strange, beautiful eyes, and faced him with a quiet smile, he did not like the plan at all.

But it was too late. He had handed over his invitation, and they were inside the ballroom in moments, part of the teeming mass of revelers, all of whom had made special return to the city to attend this event. Which was why he'd chosen this event for her unveiling.

For his own return.

His hand fell to the curve of her lower back, and he shepherded her through the throngs of people clustered around the door, resisting the urge to throttle the men nearby whose roving eyes lingered on the high swell of Mara's breasts.

He cast a sidelong gaze at the bosom in question, considering the perfect pink skin there, the three small freckles that stood sentry just above the edge of the jade green silk. His mouth went dry.

Then watered.

He cleared his throat, and she looked up at him, eyes wide and questioning behind the mask. "Well, Your Grace? You have me here now—what do you intend to do with me?"

What he wanted to do to her was to take her home and spread her bare in his bed and rectify the missing events of that evening, twelve years prior. But that was not the answer she was expecting. And so instead, he captured her gloved hand in his and led her into the crowd. "I intend to dance with you."

She wasn't in his arms for half a second when he realized

that the idea was nearly as bad as gifting the woman gloves. Now she was warm and smelling of softness and citrus, and she fit perfectly in his good arm as he fell into the steps he shouldn't remember. And there, in thinking of the steps, he hesitated over them.

He captured himself, but she noticed the misstep as she had his prior smoothness. She met his gaze, her eyes light inside gold filigree. "When was the last time you were somewhere like this?"

"You mean inside a legitimate aristocratic ballroom at a legitimate aristocratic event?" She inclined her head as he executed an elaborate turn to avoid another couple. "More than a decade."

She nodded. "Twelve years."

He did not like the exactness of the answer, but he could not say why. When Temple rubbed elbows with the elite of the *ton* it was most often on the floor of the casino after a fight, when he'd proven his worth with muscle and force. He was the strongest of them. The most powerful.

No longer.

His bad hand flexed in the sling, unfeeling and unsettling. And he hated it, in part because of the woman in his arms. Because he might never feel her skin with it. Her hair. And if she discovered his new failing, he might be less than a man for her.

But he should not care; after all, he would never see her again after tonight.

It was what he wanted.

Lie.

"Tell me about it," she said, and he wished she hadn't. He wished she was not interested in him. Wished she did not so easily draw his attention. His regard.

Wished she did not make him feel so goddamn out of control.

"Now is hardly the time for a conversation."

Her beautiful gaze turned wry and she looked around the

room at the couples dancing around them. "You have some-where to be?"

She was entirely at his whim. He could tell her to remove her mask that moment. He held all the cards, and she none of them. And still, she found room to tease him. Even now, minutes from her destruction, she stood her ground.

The woman was remarkable.

"I was forced to attend the coming-out party of a neigh-bor."

Pink lips curved beneath the mask, underscoring the pro-vocativeness of her costume. "You must have enjoyed that. Being forced into little mincing quadrille steps to even the ratio of males to females at the ball in question."

"My father had made it clear that I had no choice," he said. "It was as future dukes did."

"And so you went."

"I did."

"And did you hate it? All the young ladies throwing their handkerchiefs at your feet so you'd have to stop and retrieve them?"

He laughed. "Is that why they did it?"

"A very old trick, Your Grace."

"I thought they were simply clumsy."

Her white teeth flashed. "You hated it."

"I didn't, actually," he said, watching her grin fade to a curious smile. "It was tolerable."

It was a lie. He'd adored it.

He'd loved every second of being an aristocrat. He'd been thrilled at all the mincing and my lording and the sense of pleasure and honor that he'd had as all of London's youngest, prettiest women had chased after him for attention.

He'd been rich and intelligent and titled—all privilege and power.

What wasn't to love?

"And I am certain the ladies of the land were grateful that you did your duty."

Duty.

The word echoed through him, as faded as the memory, gone with his title when he'd woken in that blood-soaked bed. He met her eyes. "Why the blood?"

Confusion passed through her gaze, chased by understanding. She hesitated.

It was not the place for the conversation, in the home of one of London's most powerful men, surrounded by hundreds of revelers. But the conversation had come nonetheless. And he could not resist pressing her. "Why not simply run? Why fake your death?"

He wasn't sure she would answer. And then she did. "I never planned for you to be saddled with my death."

He'd expected a number of possible answers, but he hadn't expected her to lie. "Even now, you won't tell me the truth."

"I understand why you do not believe me, but it is the truth," she said quietly. "They weren't supposed to think me dead. They were supposed to think me ruined."

He couldn't help the bark of shocked laughter that escaped at that. "What kind of perverse acts were you expecting them to think I'd performed?"

"I'd heard there was blood involved," she said, clearly not amused.

His brows rose behind his domino. "Not that much blood."

"Yes, I rather gathered that once you were accused of murder," she grumbled.

"It must have been—" He thought back on the morning. "A pint."

He laughed in earnest then. "A pint of pig's blood."

She smiled then, small and unexpected. "I have made up for it by treating Lavender very well."

"So I was to have ruined you." He paused. "But I didn't."

She ignored the words. "I also never expected you to sleep so long. I drugged you to keep you in the room long enough for the maids to notice. I'd been careful to make sure we were seen by two of them." She met his eyes. "But I swear, I thought you would be up and escaped before anyone found you."

"You'd thought of everything."

"I overdid it." He heard the regret in the words as she paused as the orchestra stopped playing, instantly releasing his hands. Wondered if it was regret for her actions, for their repercussions, or for now—for the revenge he had promised her.

Wondered if it was for herself, or for him.

He did not have a chance to ask, as she stepped backward, colliding with another masked man, who took the moment to have a good look at her. "If it isn't the fighter from The Fallen Angel," he leered.

"Find someone else to admire," Temple said, darkly.

"Come now, Temple," the man lifted his mask, revealing himself to be Oliver Densmore, king of idiot fops, the man who had offered for Mara as she'd stood in the ring of the Angel. "Surely we can make an arrangement. You can't keep her forever." He turned to Mara. "I'll pay you double. Triple."

Temple's good hand fisted, but she spoke before he could strike. "You cannot afford me, sir."

Densmore cackled and returned his mask to his face. "You would be worth the trouble, I think." He tugged on one of Mara's auburn curls, and was gone into the crowd, leaving Temple seething with anger. She'd protected herself.

Because she could not trust him to protect her.

Because he had vowed to do just the opposite.

As though the run-in had never happened, Mara returned to the conversation. "I know you don't wish to hear this, but I think it's worth telling you nonetheless. I really am sorry."

"You are ignoring him."

She paused. "The man? It's best, don't you think?"

"No." He thought it was best for Densmore to lie facedown in a ditch somewhere. Right now he wanted to chase the man through the crowd and put him there.

She considered him, her beautiful eyes clear and honest through the mask. "He treated me like a lady of the evening."

"Precisely."

She tilted her head. "Is that not the point?"

Christ, he felt like an ass. He couldn't do this to her.

"At any rate," she continued, unaware of his riotous thoughts. "I am sorry."

And now she was apologizing to him, as though he hadn't given her a dozen reasons to hate him. A hundred of them.

"It's nowhere near a decent excuse," she pressed on, "but I was a child and I made mistakes, and had I known then . . ."

She trailed off. *I wouldn't have done it.*

No, he might not want to hear the apology, but he most definitely wished to hear that she would take it all back if she could. That she'd give him back his life. He couldn't help himself. "If you had known then . . . ?"

Her voice grew soft, and it was as though it were just the two of them in that ballroom, surrounded by half of London. "I would not have used you, but I still would have approached you that night. And I still would have run."

He should have been angry. Should have felt vindicated. Her words should have chased away all his doubts about his plans for the evening. But they didn't. "Why?"

She looked to the wall of doors, opening out onto the Leighton House gardens, several left slightly ajar to allow the stifling air in the ballroom out. "Why, which?"

He followed her, as if on a string. "Why approach me?"

She smiled, quiet and small. "You were handsome. And in the gardens, you were irreverent. And I liked you. And somehow, in all of this, I still rather do."

Like was the most innocuous, tepid of words. It did nothing to describe how she should feel for him. And it did absolutely nothing to describe how he felt for her.

He couldn't stop himself. "Why run?"

Tell me the truth, he willed. Trust me.

Not that she should.

"Because I was afraid your father was like mine."

The words came like a blow, quick and in his blind spot, the kind that made a man see wild stars. Bright and painful, like truth.

She'd been sixteen, and set to marry a man three times her age. A man whose last three wives had met unfortunate fates. A man who counted her bastard of a father among his closest friends.

A man whose son was an inveterate womanizer, even at eighteen.

"I would never have let him hurt you," he said. She turned at that, her eyes liquid.

He would have protected her from the moment he met her. He would have hated his father for having her.

"I didn't know that," she said softly, the words filled with regret.

She'd been terrified. But more than that, she'd been strong.

She'd chosen a life in the unknown over a life with a man who might well have been her father's second.

Temple had been collateral damage.

She was frozen, all long limbs and grace, poised at the edge of the ballroom, staring at the doors, leading into blackness, and the metaphor was not lost on him. It was another time. Another threat. Another moment that had revealed too much of Mara Lowe. And she was no longer afraid of the darkness beyond.

She had lived twelve years in the darkness.

Just as he had.

Christ. It did not matter how they had come to be here. How different their paths had been.

They were the same.

He reached for her, her name soft on his lips, not knowing what came next. Not knowing what he would say or do.

Knowing only that he wanted to touch her. His fingers slid over her silk-clad wrist even as she pulled away from him, already in smooth, graceful motion.

Already heading to the doors.

He let her go.

It was bitterly cold, and she wished she'd thought to fetch her cloak before escaping the stifling ballroom, but she couldn't very well head back inside.

She wrapped her arms tight across her chest, telling herself she'd been colder and worse off. It was true. She was comfortable with cold. She understood it. Was able to combat it.

What she could not combat was his warmth.

I would never have let him hurt you.

She took a deep breath and hurried down the steps from the stone colonnade to the dark gardens of Leighton House, disappearing into the landscape, thanking Heaven for the shadows. Leaning back against a large oak, she stared up at the stars, wondering how she had come to be here, in this place, in this dress, with this man.

A man against whom fate had pitted her.

With whom she was intertwined.

Forever.

Tears threatened as she heaved great, cloudy breaths in the fading light from the ballroom, as she wondered what would come next. She wished he would go ahead and unmask her and be done with it, so she could hate him and blame him and get on with her life.

So she could get on without him.

How had he become so very vital to her in so short a time? How had he changed so much? How had he come to say such things to her, to be so kind and gentle when they'd started their recent acquaintance with his vowing to destroy her? How had she come to trust him?

How did he remain the only person she would betray?

As if summoned by the traitorous thought, her brother stepped from the blackness. "This is fortuitous."

Mara took a step back, away from him. "How did you know I was here?"

"I followed you from the orphanage. I saw him fetch you," Kit said, eyes wild, face unshaven. "You make a handsome couple."

"We are no such thing."

He was quiet for a moment, then said, "What if you'd been betrothed to him instead? Then maybe we wouldn't be in this mess."

The question stung. What if.

If she had a shilling for every time the words had floated through her head, she'd be the richest woman in London.

The words didn't help. All they did was fill one's head with empty dreams.

But still, the words echoed. *What if.*

What if she'd married him, that handsome young marquess with the wicked smile, who kissed her as though she were the only woman in the world? What if they'd married, and built a life together, with children and pets and kisses trailed down her arm and silly private jests that proved they belonged to one another?

What if they'd loved?

Love.

She turned it around in her mind, considering its curves and angles.

Even now, she didn't understand it as others did. As she had dreamed of it when she was a child. As she'd mourned it during that wicked month leading up to her wedding, when she'd cried into her pillow and bemoaned the lack of love between her and her ancient fiancé.

But now . . . now, she loved. And it was hard. And it was painful.

And she wished it would go away.

She wished it would stop tempting her with ideas of a different life. Imagining another life was all danger—the fastest way to pain and anguish and disappointment. She lived in reality. Never in dreams.

And still, the thought of that boy twelve years ago . . . of the man now . . .

Of the life they might have had . . . if everything had been different.

"Did you receive my letter?"

She nodded, hot guilt spreading through her. Kit was here. Temple, mere feet away. Even speaking to her brother felt like betrayal of the man who had come to mean so much.

"You understand why I need your help," Kit said, coming closer, tone all kindness, devoid of the anger no doubt simmering. "I have to leave London. If those bastards find me . . ."

But they weren't bastards. They were the most loyal men she'd ever met. And Temple—he had the right to be so angry. She'd stolen his life all those years ago, and Kit had nearly taken it from him again.

"Mara," Kit said, an echo of her father. "I did it for you."

She hated him then, the younger brother whom she had loved so much. Hated him for his impulsiveness and his recklessness and his stupidity. Hated him for his anger. His coldness. The choices he'd made that impacted them both. That had made her life this elaborate, unbearable mess.

"Don't you see that he's done this to you?" Kit said, the words smooth as silk. "The Killer Duke. He's turned you into his whore, and he's turned you against me."

She might have accepted those words as fact at the beginning of all this, but now she knew better.

Somewhere, while he'd taught the boys of MacIntyre's that vengeance was not always the answer, and protected Lavender from certain death, and saved Mara from attackers, he'd made her love him.

And in that, he'd set her free.

"You think I don't see it? The way you think of him?" Kit came toward her, disgust in his words. "I see the way you look at him. The way he owns you, the way he manipulates you like a puppet on a string. You don't care that he took everything from me."

She didn't. She cared only that Temple was avenged. That he finally, finally had the life for which he was destined— that perfect wife, those perfect children, the perfect world he'd deserved from birth, and that she'd stolen from him.

The only thing she had to give him.

Tears stung. "Go away, Christopher." She chose the name purposefully, for he was no longer a child. And she would no longer be blamed by him. "If you are caught, they will punish you."

"And you won't stop them."

Not even if she could. "I won't."

He hated her; she could see it in his eyes. "I need money."

Always money. It was always paramount. She shook her head. "I don't have anything for you."

"That's a lie," he said, coming toward her. "You're hiding it from me."

She shook her head, telling him the truth. "I haven't anything for you." Everything she had was for the orphanage. And the rest . . . it was for Temple.

She had no room for this man.

"You owe me. For what I suffered. For what I still suffer."

She shook her head. "I don't. I've spent twelve years trying to convince myself that what I did was right. Thinking that I hurt you. That I made you." She shook her head. "But I didn't. Boys grow. Men make choices. And you should count yourself lucky that I do not scream until half of London comes running and finds you."

He stilled. "You wouldn't."

She thought of Temple, still and wounded on the table in his rooms at the Angel. Thought of the way her chest had ached and her heart had pounded and she'd been terrified that he would not wake.

A centimeter left or right, and Kit would have killed the man she loved.

"I would not hesitate."

His anger overflowed. "So you are his whore, after all."

If only it were that easy. She stood firm in her place, refusing to cower.

When he saw her strength, his voice became a high-pitched whine. "You also made mistakes, you know."

"And I pay for them every day."

"I see that. With your pretty silk dress and your coat lined in fur and your mask made of gold," he said. "What a hardship."

He seemed to have forgotten what was to come for her. How she would assume the mantle of punishment for his crimes. "I have paid for it every day since I left. And more since I returned. You are lucky I have taken the brunt of the punishment for our sins. And for yours alone."

"I don't require your protection."

"No," she snapped. "You require my money." He stiffened at the words. She knew that she had no choice but to drive the point home. "I should turn you over to him. You nearly killed him."

"I wish I had."

She shook her head. "Why? He never hurt us. He was innocent in all of this." He was the only one.

"Innocent?" Kit spat, "He ruined you."

"We ruined him!" she cried.

"He deserved it!" Kit's voice rose to a fevered pitch. "And the rest of them took every penny I owned!"

Twenty-six and still a child. "Every penny of mine, as well, brother." He stilled. "They did not force you to wager."

"They did not stop me, either. They deserve what they received."

"No. They don't. *He* didn't."

"He's turned you against me—me, who kept your secrets all these years. And now you choose him over me."

By God, she did. She chose Temple over all else.

But it didn't mean she could have him.

She was sorry for Kit in that moment, sorry that he'd lived the life he had—that they hadn't been able to protect each other. To support each other. And she mourned him, that laughing, loving boy he'd been, who'd found her a pint of pig's blood and sent the maids across the grounds of Whitefawn Abbey to ensure that she and Temple would be seen before she faked her own ruin.

Before she ruined a man who had never deserved it.

She shivered in the night, running her silk gloves over her arms, unable to keep the cold at bay, perhaps because it was coming from within. And there, wracked with sorrow, she reached into her reticule and extracted the only money she had. The last of her stash, designed to get her to Yorkshire. To start again.

She gave her brother the coins. "Here. Enough to get you out of Britain." He sneered at the paltry amount, and she hated him all the more. "You are welcome not to take it."

Kit was quiet for a long moment before he said, "So that's it then?"

She swallowed back her tears, tired of this life she lived, of the way she'd had to run and hide for so long. Of the way she'd lived in the shadow of her past.

There was a part of her that thought the money might buy her freedom. It might send Kit away and give her a chance at something else. Something more.

Temple.

"That's it."

He disappeared into the darkness, the way he'd come.

Guilt flared, but not for Kit. Not for his future. She'd given him money and a chance at a new life. And, in doing so, she'd stolen Temple's retribution.

Somehow, that was worse than all the rest.

She had betrayed him.

And it did feel like a betrayal, even as she stood outside the place where he planned to take his revenge. Even as she knew that she should loathe him and wish him ill for making his revenge somehow paramount, even as he treated her with kindness she'd never received from another.

If this was love, she wanted none of it.

Long after her brother left, Mara sat on a low wooden bench, feeling more alone than she ever had in her life. Tonight she would lose her brother, the orphanage, and this life she'd built for herself. Margaret MacIntyre would join Mara Lowe, exiled from Society. From the world she knew.

But none of that seemed to matter. Instead, all she could think was that tonight, she would lose Temple.

She would give him the life for which he'd been born—the highborn wife, the aristocratic children, the perfect legacy. She would give him the life that he had always wanted. Of which he'd dreamed.

But she would lose him.

And it would have to be enough.

She was beautiful.

Temple stood in the darkness, watching her as she sat straight and true on a low wooden bench carved from a single tree trunk, looking as though she'd lost her dearest friend.

And perhaps she had.

After all, in the moment she'd given Christopher Lowe the scraps from her reticule and sent him from England, she'd lost the brother she'd loved, and the only person who knew her story.

A story for which Temple would raze London.

He should loathe her. He should be furious that she'd helped Lowe escape. That she'd sent him running into the night instead of turning him over. The man had tried to kill him.

And yet, as he watched her, cold and alone in the Leighton gardens, he couldn't loathe her. Because somehow, in all of this madness, he understood her.

He could see it in the way she held herself, stiff and unmoving, lost in her thoughts and the past. In the way she owned every one of her actions. In the way that she had never once cowed from him since that dark night that had changed both their lives.

She thought she deserved the sadness. The loneliness. She thought she'd brought it upon herself.

Just as he had.

Christ. He didn't simply understand her.

He loved her. The words came like a blow, surprising and strong, and true. He loved her.

All of her, somehow—the girl who had ruined him and somehow, at the same time, set him free, and the woman who stood before him now, strong as steel and everything he'd ever wanted.

All those years, he'd imagined the life he might have had. The wife. The children. The legacy. All those years, he'd imagined being a part of the aristocracy, powerful and entitled and unquestioned.

And he'd never guessed that it would all pale in comparison to this woman and the life he might have had with her.

He would have saved her from his father. Would have loved her better. Harder. With more passion. He would have protected her. And he would have waited for her.

He knew it was wrong. And scandalous. But he would have waited until the day his father died, and then taken her for his own. And shown her the kind of life she deserved.

The one they both deserved.

She sighed in the darkness, and he heard the sorrow in the sound. The deep, enduring regret.

Was she sorry she hadn't left with her brother? That she hadn't taken the chance to run without ruin?

Ruin. Somehow, that goal had been lost in the darkness.

He'd waited too long. Come to know her. To understand her. To see her.

And now, all he wanted to do was to take her home and make love to her until they'd both forgotten the past. Until all they could think of was the future. Until she trusted him to share her thoughts and her smiles and her world.

Until she was his.

It was time to begin again.

He came out of the darkness. Into her light. "You must be frozen."

She gasped, her chin snapping up, her eyes finding his in the small clearing. She shot to her feet. "How long have you been there?"

"Long enough."

To see you betray me.

And, somehow, to realize I love you.

She nodded, her arms wrapped tightly about her. She was cold. He shrugged out of his coat, holding it out to her. She shook her head. "No. Thank you."

"Take it. I am tired of standing by as you shiver in the cold."

She shook her head.

He tossed it to the bench. "Then neither of us will use it."

For a long moment, he thought she might not take it. But she was cold, and not an idiot. She pulled it on, and he took the movement as an excuse to come closer, wrapping the enormous coat around her, loving the way she curled into the heat of it. The heat of him.

He wanted to wrap her in his heat forever.

They stood in silence for a long moment, the scent of lemons curling around him, all temptation.

"I wish you would get on with it," she said, breaking the quiet with anger and frustration.

He tilted his head. "With what?"

"With my unmasking. It is why I am here, is it not?"

It had been, of course. But now— "It is not yet midnight."

She gave a little laugh. "Surely you needn't stand on ceremony. If you unmask me early, then I can leave, and you can resume your position of valued duke. You've been waiting long enough for it."

"Twelve years," he said, watching her carefully, seeing the desperation in her eyes. "Another hour is nothing."

"And if I told you it was something to me?"

His eyes tracked her face. "I would ask why you are suddenly so eager to be revealed."

"I am tired of waiting. Tired of standing on tenterhooks, until you decide my fate. I am tired of being controlled."

He wanted to laugh at that. The idea of his having any control over her was utter madness. Indeed, it was she who consumed his thoughts. Who threatened his quiet, logical life. Who threw it into disarray. "Have I controlled you?"

"Of course you have. You've watched me. Purchased my clothes. Inserted yourself into my life. Into the life of my charges. And you've made me . . ." She trailed off.

"Made you . . ." he prompted.

For a moment, he thought she might say she loved him. And he found that he desperately wanted the words.

She stayed quiet. Of course. Because she didn't love him. He was a means to her end. As she was to him. Or, rather, as she had been in the beginning.

Anger flared. Frustration. How had he let this happen? How had he come to care for her even as she fought him? How had he forgotten the truth of their time together? What she'd done?

How did he no longer care?

The fighter in him pushed to the surface. "I know he was here, Mara," he said, seeing the shock on her face. After a moment, he said, "You are not going to deny it?"

"No."

"Good. At least there is that."

Tell me the truth, he willed. *For once in our cursed time together, tell me something I can believe.*

As if she'd heard him, she did. "The night I found you," she said, "I came to you because of Kit."

He looked to the sky, frustrated. "I know that," he said. "To restore his funds."

She shook her head firmly. "Not in the way you think. When I opened the orphanage, pretending to be Margaret MacIntyre seemed like the easiest solution. A soldier's widow was respectable. Would not tempt questions." She paused. "But no bank would allow me to manage my own funds, not without a husband."

"There are women who have access to banking facilities."

She smiled, small and wry. "Not women with false identities. I could not risk questions."

Understanding dawned. "Kit was your banker."

"He held all the funds. The initial donations, and the money that came from each aristocratic father who left his by-blows with us. All of it."

Temple exhaled his frustration. "And he gambled it away."

She nodded. "Every penny."

"And you were desperate to get it back."

She lifted one shoulder. "The boys needed it."

Why hadn't she told him? "You think I would have let them starve?"

"I did not know." She hesitated. "You were very angry."

He paced the little copse of trees, finally placing his hand flat on one trunk, his back to her. She was right, of course, but still, the words stung. "I'm not a goddamn monster!"

"I didn't know that!" she tried to explain, and he spun to face her.

"Even you thought I was the Killer Duke. Even then." Disappointment raged through him. She was supposed to know him. To understand him. Better than any. She was supposed to know he was no killer. She was supposed to see that it was all lies.

But she'd doubted him, too.

He wanted to roar his frustration.

She saw it. Raised a hand to stop him. "No. Temple."

More lies. But he couldn't stop himself from asking, "Then why?"

She spread her hands wide. "You told me that nothing I could say—"

The memory flashed, intertwined on the platform in Hebert's shop, at odds. He'd been furious with her. "Christ. I told you there was nothing you could say to make me forgive you."

She nodded once. "I believed you."

He released a long breath, a cloud in the cold air. "So did I."

"And there is a part of me that believed I deserved to pay for his sins. I turned him into that as much as I turned you into this," she said. "I left you both that night, and my father no doubt punished him brutally just as London punished you." She grew quiet. "My mistakes seem never to end."

He was quiet for a long time. "What utter nonsense."

Shock coursed through her. "I beg your pardon?"

"You didn't make him. You saved yourself. The boy made his own choices."

She shook her head. "My father—"

"Your father is the greatest bastard in creation, and if he weren't dead, I'd take great pleasure in killing him myself," he said. "But the man was not a god. He did not mold your brother from clay and breathe life into him. Your brother's sins are his and his alone." He paused, the words echoing in the darkness, and added, softly, "As are mine."

She shook her head, moved toward him. "Not so. If I hadn't drugged you. Left you. Failed to return . . ."

"You are not a god, either. You are just a woman. As I am just a man." He exhaled, harsh in the darkness. "You didn't make me. And we have made this mess together."

Her eyes were liquid in the darkness, and he wanted to

hold her. To touch her. To take her home and make her his.

But he didn't. Instead he said, "I only wish it were over."

She nodded. "It can be," she said. "It's time."

She meant the unmasking. And perhaps it was time. God knew he'd waited long enough to have this life back—the one he'd been promised. The one he'd loved and missed with a stunning, stinging ache.

But as he stared down at her, it was all gone, lost to this woman, who owned him in some remarkable, unbearable way. He lifted his hand to stroke her cheek in a long, slow caress. She leaned into the touch, and his thumb traced the curve of her lips, lingering.

Something had happened.

He whispered her name, and in the darkness it sounded like a prayer. "I can't."

Tears sprang to her eyes, betraying her confusion. Her frustration. "Why not?"

Because I love you.

He shook his head. "Because I find I no longer have a taste for vengeance. Not if it will hurt you."

She went still beneath his touch, and he saw the myriad of emotions race through her before she reached for his hand. He pulled away before she could catch it and reached into his jacket pocket.

He extracted the bank draft—the one he'd planned to give her after her unmasking this evening. The one he had to give her now. The one that would release them both from this strange, painful world. Handed it to her.

Her brow furrowed as she took the paper in hand, reading it. "What is this?"

"Your brother's debt. Free and clear."

She shook her head. "It's not what we negotiated."

"It's what I'm giving you, nonetheless."

She looked up at him then, sadness and something else in her gaze. Something he hadn't expected. Pride. She shook her head. "No."

"Take it, Mara," he urged. "It's yours."

She shook her head once more and repeated herself. "No." She folded the draft carefully and tore it in half, then in half again, then in half again.

What in hell was she doing? That money could save the orphanage a dozen times. A hundred of them. He watched as she continued her tearing, until she was left with little bits of paper, which she sprinkled on the snowy ground.

His heart pounded in his chest as he watched the little white squares dust the toes of his boots. "Why would you do that?"

She smiled, sad and small in the darkness. "Don't you see? I'm through taking from you."

His heart pounded at the words and he reached for her, wanting her in his arms. Wanting to love her as she deserved. As they both deserved.

She let him catch her, pressing her lips to his in one long, lush kiss that stole his breath and flooded him with desire. He wanted to lift her and carry her away, and he cursed his wounded arm for making it difficult to make good on that desire.

Instead, he held her close and reveled in the feel of her lips on his, in the smell of lemons that consumed him, in the soft promise of her fingers in his hair. He ravished her mouth until she sighed her pleasure and melted against him. Only then did he release her, loving the way her fingertips found her lips, as though she'd never been kissed quite that way before.

As though she did not know that he was going to kiss her that way forever.

He reached for her once more, her name already on his lips, wanting to tell her just what she could expect from his kisses in the future, but she stepped backward, out of reach. "No," she said.

He had waited for twelve years. He did not want to wait any longer.

"Come home with me," he said, reaching for her. Wanting her. "It's time we talk."

It was time they did more than talk. He'd had enough of talk.

She danced back from his touch, shaking her head. "No." He heard something firm in the word. Something unyielding.

Something he did not like.

"Mara," he said.

But she was already turning away. "No."

The word came on a whisper in the darkness as she disappeared for the second time that night.

Leaving him alone, and aching.

Chapter 17

"*Y*ou appear to have lost your coat."

Temple emptied his third glass of champagne, trading it for a full one from a passing footman's tray, and ignored his unwelcome companion. Instead, he watched the throngs of revelers spinning and swirling across the ballroom floor, their excitement having risen to a fever pitch as wine flowed and time marched.

"You also seem to have lost your companion," Chase added.

Temple drank again. "I know you are not here."

"I'm afraid I am not a hallucination."

"I told you to stay out of my affairs."

Chase's eyes went wide behind a black domino identical to Temple's. "I was invited."

"That's never stopped you from avoiding events like this before. What the hell are you doing here?"

"I couldn't very well miss your crowning moment."

Temple turned away, returning his gaze to the room at large. "If you're seen with me, people will ask questions."

Chase shrugged one shoulder. "We are masked. And aside from that, in mere minutes, you shan't be such a scandal. Tonight is the night, is it not? The return of the Duke of Lamont?"

It was supposed to have been. But somehow everything had gone sour, and he'd found himself in the gardens, staring down at the woman upon whom he'd placed twelve years of anger . . . no longer having the stomach for retribution.

If only that were all.

If only he hadn't stared down at that woman and seen someone else entirely. Someone he cared for far too much. So much that he didn't seem to mind that she'd sent her brother into the darkness, free.

All he minded was that she'd left as well.

Because he wanted her back.

He wanted her. Full stop.

Christ.

"I told you to leave me alone."

"How very dramatic," Chase said, the words dripping with sarcasm. "You cannot avoid me forever, you know."

"I can try."

"Would it help if I apologized?"

Surprise flared. Apologies from Chase were uncommon. "Do you plan to?"

"I'm not fond of the idea of it, I'll tell you."

"I don't particularly care."

Chase sighed. "All right. I apologize."

"For what, precisely?"

Chase's lips went flat. "Now you're being an ass."

"I find it is best to fight fire with fire."

"I should have told you she was in London."

"You're damn right you should have. If I'd known—" He stopped. If he'd known, he would have fetched her.

He would have found her. Earlier.

It might have been different.

How?

"If I'd known, this mess might have been avoided."

"If you'd known, this mess might have been worse."

He cut Chase a look. "I thought you were apologizing."

Chase grinned. "I am still learning the ins and outs of it." The smile faded. "What of the girl?"

He imagined Mara was halfway returned to the orphanage, desperate to claim her freedom. Worse, he imagined he'd not have a reason to see her again. Which should not grate nearly as much as it did. "I let her go."

There was no surprise in Chase's gaze. "I see. West will be sorry, no doubt."

Temple had forgotten the newspaperman. He'd forgotten everything once she'd looked up at him with her beautiful blue-green eyes and confessed the fear that had set this entire play in motion. "No one deserves the humiliation I had planned."

Especially not Mara.

Not at his hands.

"So. The Killer Duke remains."

He'd lived under the mantle of the name for twelve years. He'd proven himself stronger and more powerful than the rest of London. He'd built a fortune to rival that of the dukedom that he would not touch. And perhaps, now that he knew that she was alive, that he was not a killer, the name would sting less.

She was alive.

She should have come to him that night and told him the truth. He would have helped her. He would have kept her safe.

He would have taken her as his own.

The thought wracked him, along with the images that came with it. Mara in his arms, Mara in his bed, Mara at his table. A row of children with auburn hair and blue-green eyes. Hers.

Theirs.

Christ.

He thrust his good hand through his hair, trying to erase the wild thought. The *impossible* thought. He met Chase's eyes. "The Killer Duke remains."

With a barely-there nod, Chase's gaze flickered over Temple's shoulder, drawn by something across the ballroom. "Or does he?"

The words sent a thread of uncertainty through Temple, and he turned to follow his friend's gaze.

She hadn't left.

She stood at the far end of the ballroom, at the top of the stairs that led down into the revelers, his coat dangling from her fingers, tall and beautiful in that stunning concoction of a dress, several fat curls having escaped from her coif, now long and lovely against her pale skin. He wanted to lift those curls in his hand, run his lips across them.

But first—

He took a step toward her. "What in hell is she doing here?"

Chase stopped him with a hand on his arm. "Wait. She's magnificent."

She was that. She was more.

She was his.

Temple turned back. "What have you done?"

"I swear, this is not my doing. This is all the girl." Chase's attention returned to Mara, a surprised smile flashing. "I wish it were my doing, honestly. She's going to change everything."

"I don't want her changing anything."

"I don't think you can stop her."

The orchestra's music came to a close, and Temple's gaze flew to the enormous clock on one side of the ballroom. It was midnight. The Duchess of Leighton was making her way up the steps toward Mara, no doubt to lead the revelers in their raucous unmasking. Mara met her halfway, whispering in the duchess's ear, giving her pause.

The Duchess of Leighton pulled back in surprise, and asked a question. Mara replied, and the duchess asked another, all seriousness and shock. And all of London watched the exchange. Finally, the hostess nodded, satisfied, and turned to face the crowd, a smile on her lips.

And Temple knew it was happening.

"She might just be the strongest woman I've ever known," Chase said, all admiration.

"I told her I didn't want her doing it. I told her I wasn't going to do it," Temple said, angry. Amazed.

"It seems that she does not listen well."

Temple didn't reply. He was too busy pulling off his own mask, already pushing through the crowd, knowing he was too far from her.

Knowing he couldn't stop her.

"My lords and ladies!" The duchess was calling out to the world below as she took her husband's hand, and began the proceedings. "As you know, I am a great fan of scandal!"

The room laughed, thrilled by the mysterious events, and Temple kept moving, desperate to get to Mara. To stop her from doing something reckless.

"To that end," the duchess continued, "I've been assured there will be a truly scandalous announcement tonight! Before we unmask . . ." She paused, no doubt adoring the excitement, and waved a hand to Mara. "I present . . . a guest whose identity even I did not know!"

Temple attempted to increase his pace, but all of London seemed to be in the room with them, and no one wanted to give up a spot so close to promised scandal. He lifted a woman out of the way with his good arm, ignoring her squeak of surprise.

Her companion turned to him, all bluster, but Temple was already moving forward, whispers of *The Killer Duke* trailing behind him.

Good. Maybe people would get out of the goddamn way.

Mara came forward and spoke, her voice clear and strong. "For too long, I have hidden from you. For too long, I have allowed you to think that I was gone. For too long, I have allowed you to place blame on the innocent."

The clock began to chime midnight, and Temple began moving faster.

Don't do it, he willed her. *Don't do this to yourself.*

"For too long, I have allowed you to believe that William Harrow, the Duke of Lamont, was a killer."

He stopped at the words, at the sound of his name and title on her lips, at the gasps and shock rolling through the crowd as though they were thunder.

And still, the clock chimed.

She lifted her hands to the mask, untying the ribbons. Finishing her announcement. "But you see, he is no killer. For I am very much alive."

He couldn't reach her.

She removed the mask, and sank into a deep curtsy at the feet of the Duchess of Leighton. "My lady, forgive me for not introducing myself. I am Mara Lowe, daughter of Marcus Lowe. Sister to Christopher Lowe. Thought dead for twelve years."

Why would she do it?

She met his gaze through the crowd. Saw him.

Did she not always see him?

"Not dead. Never dead," she said, sadness in her gaze. "Indeed, the villain of the play."

The last bell of midnight echoed in the silence that followed the announcement, and then, as though they'd been set free, the crowd moved, exploding into excitement and scandal and madness.

She turned and ran, and he couldn't reach her.

Gossip and speculation exploded around him. He heard it in snippets and scraps.

"She ruined him—"

"—how dare she!"

"Using one of us!"

"Ruining one of us!"

This was it . . . what he'd thought he wanted for her. What he'd wished for in the dead of night on the street outside his home all those nights ago. Before he'd realized that her ruination was the last thing he wanted. Before he'd realized he wanted her. He loved her.

"That poor man—"

"I always said he was too aristocratic to have done any such thing—"

"Aye, and too handsome as well—"

"And the girl!"

"The devil herself."

"She'll never be able to show her face again."

She'd ruined herself. For him.

Only now, once he had it, once he heard the loathing in their voices, he hated it. And he hated them. And he had half a mind to battle the entire room.

He'd battle all of Britain for her if he had to.

A hand came down on his shoulder. "Your Grace—" He turned to face a man he did not know, all good breeding and aristocratic bearing. Hating the title on his lips. "I've always said you didn't do it. Join us for a game?" He indicated a group of men around him, and nodded toward the card rooms off the ballroom.

This was it . . . the goal for which he'd wished.

Acceptance.

Absolution.

As she'd promised.

As though none of it had ever happened.

Killer Duke no more.

But she wasn't there. And it was all wrong.

He turned away from his title. From his past. From the only thing he'd ever wanted.

And he went after the only thing he'd ever needed.

She should have left immediately.

He was trapped in the ballroom with all of London hoping to reconcile, and she could have outrun him. She had meant to. But she couldn't bear the thought of never seeing him again.

And so she stood in the shadows outside his town house in Temple Bar, blending into the darkness, promising herself that she would only look. That she wouldn't approach him.

That she'd leave him. Redeemed.

She'd given him everything she could.

She'd loved him.

And that, plus one short glimpse of him in the night, on gleaming cobblestones, would be enough.

Except it wasn't.

His carriage clattered down the street at breakneck speed, and he leapt from inside before it came to a stop, calling up instructions to the driver. "Get to the Angel. Tell them what's happened. And find her."

The carriage was off before he'd entered the house, and she held her breath in the darkness, promising herself that she wouldn't speak. Drinking him in—the height and breadth of him. The way his hair fell in disheveled waves on his brow. The way his whole body hovered on the edge of movement as he extracted his key and opened the door.

But he did not enter; instead, he stilled.

And turned to face her, peering into the shadows.

He couldn't see her. She knew it. And still, he seemed to know she was there. He stepped into the street. "Come out."

She could not deny him. Refused to. She stepped into the light.

He exhaled, her name a white whisper in the cold. "Mara."

She shook her head. "I didn't mean to come. I shouldn't have."

He came toward her again. "Why did you do it?"

To give you your life. Everything you wanted.

She hated the words even though they were the truth. She hated that they represented something she was not. Perfection.

So she settled on: "It was time."

He was in front of her then, tall and broad and beautiful. And she closed her eyes as he raised his good hand to her face and stroked his fingers across her cheek.

"Come inside," he whispered.

The invitation was too tempting to deny.

Once the door was closed behind them and she was at the foot of the staircase, he spoke again. "The last time you were here, you drugged me."

A lifetime ago. When she thought she could make a stupid arrangement with no repercussions. When she thought she could spend weeks with him without coming to know him. To care for him. "The last time I was here, you scared me."

He started up the stairs to the library where she'd left him unconscious. "Are you scared now?"

Yes.

"As I am without my laudanum, I don't think it's relevant."

He stopped. Turned back to look down at her. "It's relevant."

"Do you wish for me to be scared?"

"No."

The word was so firm, so honest, that she couldn't help herself. She followed him up the stairs, as if on a string. He did not stop at the library, instead climbing the next set of stairs, up into the darkness. She hesitated at their foot, struck by the keen sense that if she followed him, anything could happen.

And then struck by the keen realization that she didn't care.

Or, rather, that she might want it to happen.

How had this man consumed her so quickly? How had she gone from thinking of him as the enemy to thinking of him as something infinitely more terrifying in mere weeks?

How had she come to love him?

She could not stop herself. She followed him up to darkness. Up to the unknown. At the top of the stairs, he lit a candle and moved to a large mahogany door.

She really should speak.

"I think it best if I speak to your newspaperman," she started up again. "Tell him the entire story—as was our agreement—and then leave you in peace, your perceived sins absolved. In fact," she babbled, "I should really leave you now. I don't belong here."

He grasped the handle and turned to face her, the golden light of the candle flickering over his handsome face. "You're not going anywhere until we speak." He opened the door and let her enter before him.

She came up short just inside the room. "This is a bed-chamber."

He set the candle down. "Indeed it is."

And what a chamber it was, utterly masculine with its heavy oak and its dark wall coverings and books everywhere—piled on tabletops and in one of the chairs by the fireplace, and stacks around the posters of the bed—

The massive bed.

"This is *your* bedchamber." She stated the obvious.

"Yes."

Of course he had a massive bed. He needed to fit in it. But this one rivaled the Bed of Ware.

She couldn't take her eyes from it, from its great wooden posts and the web of slats that made up the utterly masculine headboard in beautifully wrought oak, and the lush coverlet that promised Heaven even as it was no doubt woven in Hell.

"We are to speak here?" The words came out on a squeak.

"We are."

She could do this. She'd been on her own for twelve years. She'd faced far more terrifying moments than this one. But she wasn't certain that she'd ever faced any moment more tempting.

She turned to him. "Why here?"

He was approaching, having left the candle on a nearby table, and his face was deep in shadow. Her heart began to race in her chest, and perhaps she should have been afraid. But she wasn't. There was no threat in the movement. Only promise.

"Because once we have spoken, I'm going to make love to you."

The frank, honest words tore the ground from beneath her, and her racing heart began to thunder, so loud in her ears that she was certain he could hear it. "You are?" she asked.

He nodded once. All seriousness. "I am."

Good Lord. How was a woman to think, knowing that?

He continued. "And then I am going to marry you."

Her hearing was failing her.

"You can't."

It wasn't possible. She was ruined. And he was a duke.

Dukes did not marry ruined scandals.

"I can."

She shook her head. "Why?"

"Because I wish to," he said, simply, moving to light the fire. "And because I think you wish to as well."

He was mad.

She watched him crouch low in the glow of the flames, silhouetted in orange light. Prometheus, stolen to Olympus to thieve fire from the gods. He was magnificent.

He stood and slipped his wounded arm from its sling before taking the large, empty chair by the fire, removing the black slash of fabric that kept his wounded arm in place before extending his good arm toward her. "Come here." The words should have sounded like a command, but were a request.

She could have refused.

But she found she did not wish to.

She approached, heading for the chair piled high with books, prepared to move them and make space for herself, but he caught her hand in his. "Not there. Here."

He meant for her to share his chair. To share his lap.

"I couldn't—" she said.

White teeth flashing in the firelight. "I shan't tell."

She desperately wanted to join him, but she knew better. She knew that if she were in his lap, touching him, she'd never resist him. She hesitated, desperate for clear thought. "I thought you were angry with me."

"I am. Quite. Very, even."

"Why? I did as you wished. I returned your name."

He watched her for a long moment, those black eyes seeing everything. "Mara," he said softly, turning her palm to him, running his fingers over the silk there, sending heat shooting through her as though she were wearing nothing at all. As though they were skin to skin. "What if we did not wear the mantle of our past? What if we weren't the Killer Duke and Mara Lowe?"

"Don't call yourself that," she snapped.

He tugged her closer. "I suppose I can't anymore. You've ruined my reputation."

She stilled. "I thought you wanted it ruined."

He tugged again, spreading his thighs, pulling her between them. Staring up at her with that serious black gaze that seemed to promise everything she'd ever wanted if only she'd give in to him. "I thought I did, too."

Confusion flared. "But you didn't?"

He captured her in his good arm, pulling her close, pressing his face into her skirts, his hands stroking down her legs, leaving heat and confusion in their wake. She could not stop herself from threading her fingers through his hair, hating that the gloves kept her from feeling its softness. From touching him.

He rocked his face against the soft swell of her, and whispered, "You gave up too much."

She shook her head. "I righted a wrong. You were innocent."

He laughed into the silk of her dress, the sound coming

on a warm breath that sent a shiver of pleasure through her. "I am not innocent. The things I've done . . ."

"The things you've done are because of what I did to you," she said, loving the feel of his hands on her, of his face against her. Of him.

"No," he said. "Enough of that lie. I've told it enough for both of us. The things I've done are mine to bear. They are who I am. Who I was." He looked up at her. "I was no prize to begin with."

It wasn't true, of course. "Nonsense. You were—"

"I was an entitled, arrogant ass. That night we met. The first time?"

She thought of him then, fresh-faced, with a quick smile. "Yes?"

"I followed you to your bedchamber. I assure you, it didn't occur to me that we might forge a love for the ages."

She smiled. "I assure you, Your Grace, I was not thinking such things, either."

"Was I rude to you?"

She shook her head. "No."

He did not meet her gaze, instead asking her torso, "Would you tell me if I were?"

Her hands slid down his cheeks, tilting his face up to hers. "It occurs to me that few men would concern themselves with such things," she said, unable to keep the surprise from her tone. "Few men would care, considering that the night in question left you unconscious and thought responsible for a murder you did not commit. A murder that did not occur."

He was quiet for a moment, thinking on what she'd said, and she resisted the urge to prompt him into speech. Finally, he said, "I am very happy that it did not occur."

He tugged her toward him again, and she toppled into his lap. Into his arms, and she should have protested, but they both seemed to have lost their minds, and she found she did not care.

His arms came around her, and she could not help but say, "I don't understand why you tossed out revenge."

One of his hands slid into her hair, working at the pins that held it together. She felt the wild mass protesting its moorings as he slowly removed them. "I don't understand why you gave it to me anyway."

The single hand worked gloriously through her hair, massaging her scalp, sending waves of pleasure through her as her hair came down around her shoulders.

Perhaps it was the luxurious caress that made her tell the truth. "You freed me, but it wasn't freedom."

His touch stilled as he considered the words, then began anew when he said, "What does that mean?"

She closed her eyes. Leaned into his caress. Told a half truth. "You left me bound by my actions. By the things I've done to you." She stopped, but his touch continued, drawing more words forth. "Not just twelve years ago. The night Kit met you in the ring. Tonight." She released a long breath, hating the guilt that consumed her over what she'd done that night. She captured the hand of his wounded arm, held it tight in hers. "Tonight, I betrayed you, and you freed me."

And I love you.

And I could give you the one thing you wanted.

She didn't say it. Couldn't.

Was afraid of what would come if she did.

Afraid he might laugh.

Afraid he wouldn't.

Her eyes opened, finding his, hot and focused on her. "You think too much of me."

"When was the last time someone thought of you, Mara?" he asked, his fingers sliding free of her scalp, tracing the rise of her cheekbones, the column of her neck, the ridge of her shoulders. "When was the last time someone cared for you? When have you ever allowed it to happen?"

He was mesmerizing. The barely-there touch on her skin, the soft skim of his breath as he spoke. She shook her head.

"When have you ever trusted someone?"

I would never have let him hurt you.

The words that had nearly destroyed her in the ballroom that evening whispered through her. The promise that even then, twelve years earlier, without knowing a thing about her, he would have protected her.

The thought devastated her with its temptation.

She shook her head. "I can't remember."

He sighed, pulling her close, setting his lips to her forehead and cheek, to the curve of her jaw and the line of her neck and the corner of her mouth. She turned to him, wanting to kiss him in earnest. Wanting to hide from the overwhelming thoughts he planted in her mind. Wanting to hide from him.

In him.

But he wouldn't allow it.

"You once asked me how I came by the name Temple."

She stilled, not certain she wanted the truth now. Not certain she could face it. "Yes."

"It's where I slept the night I arrived in London. After my exile."

Her brow furrowed. "I don't understand. You slept in a temple?"

He shook his head. "Under one. I slept under the Temple Bar."

She knew the monument, mere blocks away on the eastern edge of the city, marking the place where the unfortunates of London toiled and lived, and she thought of that bright-faced young man—the one who'd shown her kindness and pleasure—there, alone. Miserable. *Terrified.*

"Were you—" She tried to find the words to finish the question without insulting him.

His lips twisted in a humorless smile. "Whatever you are thinking . . . the answer is likely yes."

It was a miracle he could look at her.

It was a miracle he could be near her.

She did not deserve him.

"What happened after the first night?" She asked.

"There was a second, and a third," he said, working at the buttons of her glove with one skilled hand, doffing the garment with the same efficiency with which he'd donned it. "And then I learned to make my way."

He slid the silk from her fingers and she immediately placed the hand on his arm, feeling the muscles there bunch and ripple beneath the touch. "You learned to fight."

He turned his attention to the other glove. "I was big. And strong. All I had to do was forget the rules of boxing that I'd learned at school."

She nodded. She'd forgotten every rule she'd ever learned as a child in order to survive once she'd run. "They no longer applied."

He met her gaze as the second glove slid off. "It worked well for me. I was angry, and gentlemen's rules did little to assuage that. I fought on the streets for two years, taking any fight with money to pay." He paused, then smiled. "And any number of fights without money to pay."

"How did you come to the Angel?"

His brow furrowed. "Bourne and I had been friends at school. When he lost everything that was not entailed, he found himself down on his luck, and we decided to form an alliance. He ran dice games. I made sure the losers paid." She was surprised by the turn of events, and he saw it. "You see? Not so honorable after all."

"What then?" she prodded, desperate to know the story.

"One night, we went too far. Pushed too hard. And backed a group of men into an unpleasant corner."

She could imagine. "How many of them?"

He shrugged his good shoulder, his hand sliding down the side of her thigh, distracting her. "A dozen. Maybe more."

Her attention returned to him. "Against you?"

"And Bourne."

"Impossible."

He smiled. "So little faith in me."

Her brows shot up. "Am I incorrect?"

"No."

"Then what?"

"Then Chase."

The mysterious Chase. "He was there?"

"In a sense. We'd been fighting for what seemed like an age, and they kept coming—I really did think we were done for." He pointed to the scar at the corner of his eye. "I couldn't see out of my eye for the blood." She winced, and he instantly stopped. "I'm sorry. I shouldn't have—"

"No," she said, lifting her hand to the thin white line, tracing it with her fingers, wondering what he would do if she kissed it. "I just don't like the idea of you hurt."

He smiled, capturing her hand and bringing it to his lips, placing a kiss on the tips of her fingers. "But drugged?"

She met his smile with her own. "At my hands, it's a different matter."

"I see," he said, and she loved the laughter in his voice. "Well . . . suffice to say, I thought we were done for. And then a carriage pulled up and a group of men piled out—and then I thought we were definitely done for," he added. "But they fought on our side. And I didn't care who they worked for, as long as Bourne and I lived."

"They worked for Chase."

Temple inclined his head. "So they did."

"And then you worked for him."

He shook his head. "With. Never for. From the beginning, the offer was clear. Chase had an idea for a casino that would change the face of aristocratic gaming forever. But that idea required a fighter. And a gamer. And Bourne and I were precisely that combination."

She let out a long breath. "He saved you."

"Undoubtedly." He paused, lost in thought. "And never once believed me a killer."

"Because you weren't," she said, this time having no

choice but to lean in and press a kiss to his temple. She lingered on the caress, and he caught her close. When she pulled away from him, he moved to capture her lips.

They lingered there, tangled together for a long moment, before Mara pulled away. "I want the rest of the story. You became unbeatable."

His bad hand flexed against her hip. "I was always good at violence."

Her hands moved of their own volition, sliding across his wide, warm chest. He was magnificently made, she knew, the product of years of fighting. Not simply for sport, but for safety.

"It was my purpose."

She shook her head. "No," she said. "It wasn't."

He'd been clever and funny and kind. And ever so handsome. But he hadn't been violent.

He captured her chin in a firm grip. "Hear me, Mara. You didn't make me into that man. If I hadn't had the seed of violence in me—I never would have succeeded. The Angel never would have succeeded."

She refused to believe it. "When one is forced into a role, one assumes it. You were forced. Circumstances forced you." She paused. "*I* forced you."

"And who forced you?" he asked, threading his fingers into hers, holding her hand against his chest, where she could feel the heavy beat of his heart. "Who stole you away from the world?"

Their entire conversation had come to this. He'd recounted his story with precision and purpose, bringing her slowly around to this moment, when it was her turn. When she could tell him the truth, or tell him nothing at all.

One way, she was safe.

The other way, she was in terrible danger.

In danger of becoming his.

Temptation was a wicked, wonderful thing.

She focused on the knot of his perfect cravat. "Do you have a valet?"

"No."

She nodded. "I wouldn't have thought so."

He reached up and unknotted the neck cloth, unwrapping it until he revealed a perfect triangle of warm, brown skin, dusted with curling black hair.

He was beautiful.

It was a strange word to describe a man like him—broad and strong and perfectly made. Most would choose *handsome* or *striking*, something with heft that oozed masculinity.

But he was beautiful. All scars and sinew and, beneath it all, a softness that she couldn't help but be drawn to.

The words came easily. "I have always been afraid. Since I was a girl. Afraid of my father, then of yours. Then of being found. Then, once I heard of my mistake—of what I did to you when I left—of not being found." She did look at him then, meeting his beautiful black gaze. "I should have returned the moment I discovered you'd been accused of my murder. But the dice had been thrown, and I did not know how to call them back."

He shook his head. "I run a casino. I know better than anyone that the roll is final once the ivories leave one's hand."

"I didn't know what happened to you for months. I went to Yorkshire, and the news there was spotty at best. I didn't even know the Killer Duke was you until . . ."

He nodded. "It was too late."

"Don't you see? It wasn't too late. It was never too late. But I was terrified that if I returned . . ." She paused. Collected herself. "My father would have been furious. And I was still betrothed to yours. And I was afraid."

"You were young."

She met his understanding gaze. "I did not come back

when they died, either." It had occurred to her. She'd wanted to. She'd known that it was the right thing to do. But. "I was afraid then, too."

"You are the least fearful person I've ever known," he said.

She resisted the label. "You're wrong. My whole life, I've been terrified of being controlled. Of losing myself to another. My father. Yours. Kit. You."

His gaze caught hers. "I don't want to control you."

"I don't know why," she said.

"Because I know what it is to be controlled. And I do not wish it on you."

"Stop," she said softly. "Stop being so kind."

"You would prefer harshness? Haven't I given you enough of that?" He shifted beneath her, clasping her face in one hand. "Why did you do it, Mara? Why tonight?"

She didn't pretend to misunderstand. He was asking why she'd unmasked in front of all of London. Why she'd returned, when he'd made it clear that she needn't.

"Because I was afraid of who I would become if I didn't."

He nodded. "Why else?"

"Because I was afraid that if I stayed hidden, it would only be a matter of time before someone found me."

"Why else?" he asked again.

"Because I am tired of living in the shadows. Ruined or not, tonight, I live in the light."

He kissed her then, taking her lips in a long, lingering caress, his hands sliding down her sides, pulling her closer, leaving a trail of heat in their wake.

When he stopped the kiss, he pressed his forehead to hers and said, almost too softly to hear, "Why else?"

She closed her eyes, loving the feel of him so close to her, wishing she could live there, in his arms, forever. "Because you didn't deserve it."

He shook his head. "But that's not why."

She took a deep breath. "Because I did not wish to lose you."

He nodded. "And what else?"

He knew. He saw the truth, yawning beneath them, a great chasm. All he asked was for her to say it aloud. To leap.

And on this, their last night together—their *only* night together, she leapt, her gaze on his, her body entwined with his.

"Because, somehow, in all of this . . ."

She resisted the truth, barely, knowing that if they were said, they would change everything. Would make everything more difficult. " . . . you—your happiness—your wishes— they mean everything."

But what she said in her mind was: *I love you. I love you. I love you.*

And perhaps he heard it, for he stood, and in one fluid motion, lifted her in his arms and took her to his bed.

Chapter 18

She'd never felt so valued as she did at his bedside, draped in silk, still warm from his touch and the promise of what was to come. His fingers trailed over her cheek and jaw, down the column of her throat, and over her racing pulse.

He traced the line of her collarbone and then the curve of her breast, lingering when she drew in a heavy, ragged breath. His black eyes met hers. "Do you wish me to stop?"

"No," she said instantly. Wishing he would start again. Wishing he would keep going. Forever.

"I won't hurt you," he said.

She stilled at the words, at the way the promise came from deep inside him. She wondered how many times he'd had to make that same promise to other women. To calm them as they stood an arm's length—closer—to the Killer Duke.

"I know," she said, capturing his bad hand in one of hers, pressing his fingers against her skin, holding his touch to her. She reached her other hand up, threading her fingers through his hair, pulling his lips down to her. "You'll never hurt me," she whispered against his lips.

He groaned his desire, snaking his free arm around her waist and pulling her tight to him. He whispered her name and took her mouth in a powerful kiss, more devastating than any they'd shared before. Where the previous ones had been rivers of temptation, tickling at the seams of her, this was a wide sea filled with wicked promise. It was *wanton*.

It was wonderful.

His hand was everywhere—lush, stroking sin—and hers followed suit, sliding up the soft wool of his coat and into his hair, holding him close, matching his kiss with her own, not stopping until he groaned his pleasure and pulled away from her, leaving her gasping for air and desperate for more of him.

"No," he whispered, turning her away from him, to face the massive bed, at once ominous and irresistible. His hands came to the fastenings of the gown, working the buttons and ties.

"Faster," she sighed as he fumbled at the fabric. "Hurry."

The buttons were stubborn beneath his touch. Or perhaps it was his choice to move with such slowness. "I will not allow you to tempt me to speed," he whispered in her ear as he worked, the breath of the words sending shivers of antici-pation through her. "I want the whole night." He pressed a kiss to the curve of her shoulder, his tongue coming out to stroke along the skin there as the fabric of her bodice came loose and she caught it to her chest.

He lifted one of her hands, kissing her palm, then worry-ing the pad of her index finger with his teeth. Her dress fell to the floor, his gaze falling to her fine-spun chemise and beautifully boned corset, desire flaring hot and wonderful. "I want longer."

She sighed at the words. Of course, she knew they couldn't have longer. But they could have tonight, and he was enough to make her forget everything else.

Tomorrow, they would return to their lives—he, to the one he'd too long missed, and she to the one she'd too long deserved.

He guided her hands to the bedpost, leaving her there

as he worked at the ties of her corset, his fingers pulling at silken strings, loosening the piece until it dropped to her feet, and his strong touch sent her silk chemise after it.

She was naked in the clocked stockings he'd bought her, the ones she'd imagined him removing when she'd donned them—even as she'd desperately tried to ignore the thought.

And his hands, those strong, wonderful hands that she'd come to love for their gentleness as much as their force, slid over her bare skin as his lips settled on the curve of her shoulder.

Not hands. Hand.

Always one hand. Always the good hand.

She turned to him. "Wait."

He waited. Because she told him to. And she loved him all the more for it. She lifted his wounded hand to her lips, pressing a kiss to his knuckles, letting her tongue slide out to dip into the valleys between them. He watched, his eyes dark with passion, but something was missing. Something she might not have seen if she had not been looking.

He couldn't feel her.

She turned the hand over, pressing a kiss to his palm. Whispering there, "What have we done to you?"

He snatched his hand away, but she would not let him escape.

Instead, she lifted his other hand and repeated her ministrations until his breath caught in his throat and he shifted with desire and want and a dozen kinds of lust.

Shock rocketed through her. His hand. They'd stolen it from him.

"Temple," she said softly, reaching for it. Loving him more for it.

"No," he resisted, turning her once more, returning her hands to the bedpost. Kissing the spot behind her ear, the place where neck met jaw. Where shoulder met neck. Her spine.

Distracting her with pleasure and wickedness. "You are trembling."

And she was, too wrecked by his touch, by his nearness, to stop. To return the conversation to his hand. "I can't—" she started. "It is too much."

He growled, low and dark and promising at her ear. "It is not nearly enough."

He kissed his way down her spine, the tip of his tongue licking and swirling as he marked his path. As he marked her, as cleanly and clearly as if he'd done it with a needle and ink.

And when he reached the place where back met bottom, he worried the soft, untouched skin there until she was gasping her pleasure. Only then, once she'd given herself over to his touch, to his kiss, did he turn her to face him.

She should not have been surprised to find him there, on his knees staring up at her once more, but she was, a thread of panic and desperation coursing through her. A desperate desire to repeat the events of the previous morning in the ring. A desperate desire never to repeat them again.

"Temple," she whispered, reaching for him, letting him catch her hand in his, letting him press it to his cheek.

"William," he corrected her.

Her gaze flew to his. "But you—"

"You're the only one who thinks of me as such. The only one who has ever seen me."

The truth ached. Reminding her of all she'd done. Of all this night could be. Of all it couldn't be. "I'm so sorry," she whispered, tears in her eyes. "I never—"

He came to his feet with stunning grace, pulling her to him. "No. You mustn't regret it. Your seeing me has changed everything. It's changed my life. It's changed me." He kissed her, long and thorough, and added, "Christ, Mara, of course it's you. It's always been you. It always will be."

The words shattered her. "I cannot stand."

"Then don't. I have you."

She fell into his strength, and he laid her back on the bed, spreading her legs wide as he sank between them, draping them over his shoulders, leaving long, lush kisses along the soft skin of her inner thighs, coming closer and closer to delivering on their promise as she writhed on the silk bedcovers and wondered how it was that she had come to be here. Come to deserve him.

She hadn't.

She hadn't, and this would be her greatest sin—taking this night. Stealing it from someone who might deserve it. Who might be more for him. Who might be better for him.

Taking it, with no regret.

Taking it for the memory.

For her lifetime.

For his.

And then his mouth was on the heat of her, and her fingers were in his hair, and he was giving her everything she desired, and she couldn't stop herself from moving against him, from lifting to meet him, from begging him for—

He stopped, lifting his head. "What is it, love?"

The word was enough to send rivers of pleasure through her, if not for the slow slide of his fingers, the way they dipped and teased, the way they stroked, but not deep enough to give her everything she wanted. She raised her hips to him.

"My, that's a pretty sight," he said, and she couldn't stop herself from watching him, his eyes on her, his tongue sliding over his beautiful bottom lip, as though he couldn't wait to taste her again. "All pink and perfect." His gaze found hers. "Tell me, when I did this in the ring . . . did you see it? How hot you get? How pink? How wet?"

She closed her eyes at the wicked words. Nodded.

"And you liked it."

She nodded.

"One day, when I have more patience, we'll try it again, with a smaller mirror. Closer. More private. I'll let you tell me what to do. I'll let you watch yourself come."

The words sent a thrill through her, even as she resisted the idea of giving herself over to something so unexpected. So unclear. So strange and perfect.

He saw it—the hesitation—and raised one brow in a wicked challenge before he blew a long stream of cool air over her hot, desperate center. "You don't think you'd like that?"

She exhaled on a shaking sigh. "I—"

"You are so perfect—" He flicked his tongue over the heat of her, sending a shock of sensation through her, her body somehow not her own when he was involved. "So wet." She gasped as he licked and sucked, working her with unbearable pleasure, sending her spiraling tighter and tighter and higher and higher until his fingers joined his tongue in symphony, exploring and moving in glorious circles, teasing and touching. "I want you like this, open to me, aching for me, forever."

To punctuate that word *forever*, and all its temptation, he slid one finger deep, and she could not keep her moan from escaping.

"Now *that*," he said, his voice as dark as his gaze, "might be the most beautiful sound I've ever heard." That wicked digit retreated, and she bit her lip, face flamed with embarrassment even as she wanted to clasp him to her and demand he repeat the experience. She did not have to. "Let's see if we can make it happen again."

A second finger joined the first on a long, irresistible slide.

Dear God, he was ruining her.

He played her like a virtuoso, as though she were an instrument he had studied for a lifetime. She moaned again, louder and longer, and he rewarded the sound with his mouth, working her in that dark, secret place that was suddenly the center of her. She would never think of pleasure in the same way again.

It was forever entwined with him.

She came apart in his arms once more, lost to his kiss and his touch and the scent and sound of him. Lost to the knowledge that this man was everything she'd ever desired and dreamed and imagined. Lost to pleasure. Lost to him.

And somehow found.

She returned to earth in his arms, all strong, corded sinew, holding her to his chest, where her head rested on his good shoulder and she was easily lost in the heat and scent of him. His fingers stroked through her hair, spreading it long across his massive bed, and he pressed a kiss to her temple, whispering against her skin, worshipping it, "You are the most beautiful thing I have ever seen."

She shivered at the words and curled into his warm body, her hand spreading across the white of his shirt. She spoke to the wide expanse of linen there. "You scare me."

His touch stilled. "How?"

Her fingers worried at his shirt. "I never thought I would be so drawn to you. So connected. I never thought you would own me so well. That you would have such"—she hesitated over the word—"control over me."

He captured her hand in his, sliding out from beneath her to face her. To have a better look at her.

She sat up, trying to explain. "Even now . . . with you inches away . . . I can't help but mourn the loss of you."

He reached for her at the confession, his hand stopping short of touching her, as though he did not know how to proceed. "Mara," he said softly, as though he might scare her away. "I don't want you to ever think that I take pleasure from—"

Her fingers moved to his lips, stopping the flow of words. "No," she said, tears coming to her eyes. "You don't understand. I ache for you when you're not with me." His eyes went black with desire, and her breath caught at the vision of him. At his promise. "I am in your thrall," she said. "Of your touch and your kiss and your beautiful eyes. Quite desperately."

And it will make everything more difficult.

She did not say the last. Instead she said, "You control me."

He stared at her for a long moment, and she wished he would touch her. Instead, he left the bed, and she thought she might have ruined everything. But he was back within minutes, his shirt and boots gone, clad only in black wool trousers and the black bands of ink at his arms and the stark white of the bandage on his shoulder.

She drank him in, every inch bathed in golden candle-light, and she wondered at him. How had this glorious god of a man, built like a Greek statue or a Michelangelo, come from one of the finest aristocratic lines in all of England? There was nothing mincing or foppish about him. He was the most masculine thing she'd ever seen, all power and grace and strength.

Her gaze rested on his good hand, clutching the cravat he'd tossed away earlier, the long stretch of cloth at once promise and threat.

"You worry about control," he said.

Her heart began to pound. "Yes."

He extended the cravat toward her. After a long moment, she took it, and he lay down on the bed, extending his arms up until his hands met the slats of the headboard.

Her mouth went dry at the look of him, spread out before her, broad and beautiful. And he was beautiful. He was per-fect in every way.

And then he said, "Take it. Be in control," and desire coursed through her, hot and heavy and far too powerful to resist.

She ran the cravat through her fingers, eyes wide, and said, "Are you certain?"

He nodded once, his grip tightening on the headboard. "Trust me, Mara."

She inched up the bed, naked but for those silken stock-ings, watching his gaze on her, loving it. Kneeling beside him, she said, "You wish me to tie you to it?"

He smiled. "I wish you to do whatever you like to me."

He was turning himself over to her. To her pleasure. And all she could think was that her pleasure was somehow inexorably tied to his. The thought gave her courage, strength to do the unthinkable, to straddle his torso, the heat of her pressed against his naked skin. He groaned and closed his eyes, lifting his hips from the bed, pressing up against her, his body making promises she hoped desperately that it would keep. His eyes flashed. "But if you plan to blindfold me, love, do it now. Before you torture me with this view any longer."

Blindfold him. Good Lord. Did people do such things?

She wanted to. Desperately.

She couldn't help the smile that spread at the words, and she loved the way he laughed when it appeared. "You minx. You enjoy it."

"You want me."

"Want does not begin to describe the way I feel about you," his low voice promised. "Want is nothing compared with the level of desire I have. With the desperation I feel. With the way I long for you."

She leaned over, unable to resist pressing her lips to his, taking his mouth in a deep, thorough kiss that she'd learned from him—in long, lush strokes that left them both breathless.

When she lifted her head, it was to find her courage. She slid the cravat over his eyes, and when he lifted his head from the pillows, she reached behind him and tied it tightly, loving the way his body tensed beneath her, loving the sound of his exhale, low and harsh and perfect.

She leaned forward, pressing her breasts to his chest, being careful of his wound as she whispered in his ear, "You are mine."

He growled at the words. "Always."

Not always, though.

She couldn't have him always. It wasn't the life he

deserved—married to a scandal, to a woman no one would ever accept, to a woman London would never forget. As long as she was with him, he would be the Killer Duke.

And he deserved to be so much more.

But tonight, she could pretend.

She pressed long kisses to his warm skin, across one shoulder and up his good arm, where his tattooed muscles strained against his grip. She couldn't resist running her tongue along the edge of that inked spot, worrying the dips and curves until he growled his pleasure and she moved on, lower, along the outside of his chest and then across it, paying special attention to the scars dotting his chest and stomach. Kissing them. Tracing their raised surfaces with her tongue.

He hissed at the sensation, and she lifted her head. "Do they hurt?"

"No. It's just—" She waited for him to finish. "No one has ever wanted to touch them before. Not like this."

She wanted to touch them. She wanted to touch every inch of him, and the realization made her bold. She lifted herself up and slid down his body, working at the fall of his trousers, sliding buttons from their moorings—instinct and desire overtaking experience. He lifted his hips from the bed, allowing her to slide the trousers down, revealing him, long and hard and perfect.

And hers.

She sat back on her heels, taking him in, spread out upon his bed, his good hand locked at the headboard, knuckles white, straining to stay there. Eager to give himself up to her.

Turning himself over to her.

Giving up his control. For her.

She reached for him then, hand trembling, uncertain. She stilled, an inch from him. Closer.

He sensed it. "Mara," he said, teeth clenched, anguish and desire making the words thick and lovely.

She wanted to give him everything he wanted. But—"I don't know what to do," she confessed, the words somehow easier because he was blindfolded. "I've never—I want to do it correctly."

His breath came in a short, panting laugh. "You can't do it wrong, darling. I promise. I want you too much."

She leaned forward, taking her confession with him. "I've only ever dreamed it," she told him. "In the dark of night. I've wondered what this would be like."

He shook his head. "Don't tell me. I don't want to think of you dreaming of another."

Shock coursed through her. "It's never been another," she said. "It's always been you."

And it was her turn to touch, her hand settling on the length of him, feeling him leap and harden even more—if it were possible. He groaned his pleasure, long and loud, and she reveled in the pure, masculine sound. "You're so hard."

"I am. For you."

"And soft, too," she said. "Like velvet over steel."

One hand released from the headboard, coming toward her for a split second before he seemed to recall his promise. Before he forced it back to its position. "Not as soft as you."

"You seem to be having trouble," she said, her hands running up and down the hot length of him, loving the way his hips moved with her.

He tilted his head. "Are you teasing me?"

She grinned. "Perhaps."

He scowled. "Remember, Miss Lowe, turnabout is fair play."

A thrill shot through her. "What a pretty promise."

The growl again. He couldn't help himself, the glorious man. "Harder," he said.

"I thought I was in control," she said.

"Love, if you don't think you are in control, you are mad."

She smiled again, increasing the pressure of her touch. "How could I know I am in charge?"

"Because if I were in charge, we would not be playing silly games."

She laughed at that, and he said, "I love the sound of your laughter." She stopped. "It's so rare. And I want to hear it every day."

It was the most beautiful thing anyone had ever said to her.

She rewarded him with a long stroke, down and then up his shaft, until his breath was coming hard and fast. "Tell me . . ."

"Anything," he promised.

"Tell me how you like it."

He moaned at the words, long and low. "I like it however you wish to give it."

She leaned forward, kissing him on the lips, surprising him briefly before he reciprocated, the kiss wild and wanton and wonderful. She pulled away and whispered, "Would you like it if I used my mouth?"

He swore, harsh and dangerous, and she took the foul word as a yes, sliding back down the length of his body and considering the length of him . . . wondering what might feel best.

She hesitated too long, evidently, because he called out her name, the word an agonized plea. She pressed a kiss to the tip of him, loving the way he leapt in her hands, against her lips. "Tell me," she whispered to the most private part of him.

He did as he was told. "Suck it."

The instructions were scandalous, utterly improper.

And all she wanted.

She did as she was told, following his harsh, aching direction, experimenting and learning with tongue and lips and pressure until he prayed and swore and moaned her name, his head rocking back and forth, his hands desperately clinging to the bedposts as she gave him everything for which he asked.

As she worshipped him.

As she loved him.

Until she realized that it wasn't enough. That she wanted everything. And she stopped.

"No . . ." The words panted from him as she pressed a final kiss to the throbbing, crimson tip of him. "Why?"

She lifted herself over him then, spreading her legs wide over his hips. Holding him straight until the tip of him touched the curls that protected the most intimate part of her.

The part she would give him.

The part she would never give another.

He shook beneath her. Literally quaked. "Is that— Oh, God. Mara." She smiled, spreading herself wide, letting the tip of him slide through her secret folds. "Love, you're so wet." He swore, the words blasphemous and beautiful. "So hot. So beautiful."

She smiled, working herself over the head of him. "You can't see me, how would you know that?"

"I always see you," he said. "You're burned into me. I could be blind for the rest of my life, and I would still see you."

The words took her as much as his body did, as she slid down the hard length of him, and he fit inside her so perfectly that they both sighed, half prayer, half blasphemy. He stilled at the sound of her pleasure. "It doesn't hurt?"

She shook her head. "No." It was glorious. "Does it hurt you?"

He grinned. "Hell, no."

"I shall move, then, if that's all right with you."

He laughed. "You are in control, love."

She was in control, lifting and lowering herself on him, testing the pressure and speed, pausing every now and then to revel in a particular angle. A specific pleasure.

He let her guide the moment, whispering his encouragement, lifting his hips to meet her when she found a particular cadence or rhythm that he enjoyed. She memorized those, coming back to them over and over, loving the way they seemed to destroy him with desire and sensation.

It was glorious.

But there was something missing.

Him.

His touch. His gaze. The piece of him that she desperately wanted. She didn't want to control him. She did not wish to take this moment for her own.

She wanted to share it.

So she did, leaning up to remove his blindfold, pulling it over his head and flinging it across the room, not caring where it fell. His gaze was hot and heavy on her, and she nearly swooned when he instantly captured the tip of one of her breasts in his mouth, worrying it. Loving it.

And still, he kept his hands locked on the headboard. Until she released him with simple, honest words. "I am yours."

Free, his hands fell to her hips, his strong, gentle grip guiding her hips in perfect rhythm, changing the angle, giving her the chance to find the movement that brought her immense pleasure, and she was suddenly rocking hard and fast against him, crying out as his fingers found the heat of her, pressing and rolling in that secret place until she could not bear it any longer.

His gaze was on hers, his lids heavy with desire, and she placed her hands on the bed by his head and whispered, "Don't stop."

Don't stop looking at me.

Don't stop moving in me.

Don't stop loving me.

He heard it all. "Never," he promised.

She gave herself up to ecstasy. And to him.

And only once she had taken her pleasure did he take hers, rocking once, twice, three times against her, and crying out her name, releasing high inside her, holding her to him—still joined together—until their heartbeats calmed as one.

After long moments, she stirred, the chill from the room making her shiver in his arms, and he pulled one edge of the massive coverlet over her, refusing to let her out of his arms.

Instead, he buried his nose in her neck and said, "I can't get enough of you. Of that scent. You make me want to buy every lemon in London so no one can get a whiff of you. But it's not just lemons. It's something else. It's you."

The words warmed her. "You've noticed my scent?"

He smiled at the words he'd used with her a lifetime ago. Repeated her reply. "It's impossible to miss."

They lay there in silence, his good hand stroking over her skin, up and down her spine like a benediction. She wondered what he was thinking, and was about to ask when he broke the silence with "What if I cannot fight again?"

His arm. She turned to kiss the warm expanse of his chest. "You will."

He ignored her platitudes. "What if I never regain the feeling? Who am I then? Who will I be? What am I if not unbeatable? If not a fighter? If not the Killer Duke? What is my value then?"

Her heart ached at the questions. He would be everything she'd ever wanted. He would be all she'd ever dreamed.

She lifted her head. "You don't see it, do you?"

"What?"

"You are so much more."

He kissed the words from her lips, and she was desperate for him to believe her, so she put all her love, all her faith, into the caress. And when he ended it, she whispered. "Temple, you are everything."

"William," he corrected her. "Call me William."

"William," she whispered the name against his chest. "William."

William Harrow, the Duke of Lamont.

The man she'd destroyed. The one she could restore. She could give him back the life she had taken. She could return him to his former glory—to the world he'd loved, the women and the balls and the aristocracy. The world he could not have if he did a stupid, noble thing and married her.

No. This was the greatest gift she could give him, even if it would take the greatest sacrifice she had ever made.

The one where she gave up everything she wanted.

The only thing she wanted.

Him.

She wasn't his dream. She wasn't his goal. She couldn't be the wife, the mother, the legacy. "We cannot marry," she said, softly.

He kissed the top of her head. "Sleep with me tonight, and let me convince you tomorrow why it is the best of all my ideas."

She shouldn't. She should leave him now, while she had the strength. "I can't—"

He interrupted her with a long, lush kiss, one filled with something more than passion. With something she did not wish to identify, for if she identified it, she might never do what needed to be done.

"Stay."

Her heart broke at the word, dark and graveled on his lips. At the desire in it. At the promise in it. At the knowledge that if she did, he would do everything in his power to keep her. To protect her.

At the knowledge that if she did, he would never have the life he deserved. One free of scandal and ruin. One free of the memories of his past and his destruction.

He was too perfect. Too right. And she was all wrong.

She would only ruin him again. Only destroy everything he ever wanted. She had to leave him. She had to leave before she was too tempted to stay.

And so she told one final lie. The most important one she'd ever tell.

"I will."

He slept then, and once his breathing was deep and even, she told the truth.

"I love you."

Chapter 19

*H*e woke at peace, for the first time in twelve years, already reaching for Mara, eager to pull her into his arms and make love to her properly. Eager to show her all the ways it was right for them to marry. Eager to show her all the ways he would make her happy. All the ways he would love her.

And he would love her, as strange and ethereal as the word seemed, as much as he'd never thought it would have place in his life. He would love her.

He would start today.

Except she was not in the bed. He came up with a handful of empty sheets, too cool to have been left recently.

Dammit. She'd run.

He out of bed within seconds, already pulling on the trousers she'd stripped from him the night before, doing his best to block the memory from his mind. Not wanting his reason or judgment clouded by the things she made him feel. Passion. Pleasure. Sheer, unadulterated frustration.

He was dressed and down the stairs within seconds, out to the mews to saddle his horse and in front of No. 9 Cursitor Street within thirty minutes. He took the stairs to the orphanage three at a time and was inside before most people could knock. It was a good thing the door was unlocked, or he might have torn it down himself.

Lydia was crossing the foyer when he entered, stopping her mid-stride. He did not hesitate. There was no time for pleasantries. "Where is she?"

The woman had learned from a master. "I beg your pardon, Your Grace, where is who?"

He had gone more than thirty years without throttling a female, and he was not about to start now. But he was not above using his size to intimidate. "Miss Baker, I am in no mood for games."

Lydia took a deep breath. "She is not here."

At his core, he knew it was true, but he did not wish to believe it. So instead of continuing their useless conversation, he went to her office and opened the door, hoping to find her there, behind her desk, auburn hair pulled back in a tight knot.

But she was not.

The desk was pristine, as though it had been placed perfectly for the London stage, and not for any useful purpose.

He turned. Met Lydia's eyes, sad and full of truth. "Her chamber. Take me to it."

She considered refusing. He saw it in her. But something changed her mind, and instead, she turned to climb the stairs, up two flights and down a long hallway until she stopped in front of an oak door, firmly shut. He did not wait for her permission, opening it. Entering.

It smelled like lemons.

Lemons, and Mara.

The little room was neat and clean, just as he would have expected. There was a small wardrobe, too small to hold anything more than the bare necessities, and a little table on which sat a half-burned candle and a stack of books. He moved to look at them. Novels. Well-worn and well-loved.

And there was a tiny bed, one she no doubt hung off of when she slept, the only part of the room that was imperfect, because it was currently covered in emerald silk. The dress she'd worn the night before, when she'd revealed herself to the world, and next to it, the matching ermine cloak, and in a little, neat stack, the gloves he'd given her.

She was out in the world, and she did not have any gloves.

He lifted them from the bed, bringing them to his nose, hating the slide of silk, wishing it were her skin. Her heat.

He turned to face Lydia. "Where is she?"

There was sadness in her eyes. "Gone."

No.

He was losing his patience. "Where?"

She shook her head. "I don't know. She did not say."

"When will she be back?"

She looked to the floor and he heard the answer before she spoke it. "Never."

He wanted to scream. He wanted to rail against idiot women and cruel fate. But instead he said, "Why?"

Lydia returned her gaze to him. "For us."

What utter nonsense. The words were nearly spoken aloud when Lydia continued.

"Thinks we are all better off without her."

"The boys need her. You need her. This place needs her."

Lydia smiled, small and sad. "You misunderstand. She thinks you are better off without her as well."

"She's wrong." He was better with her. Infinitely so.

"I agree. But she believes no aristocrat will leave his children with someone with a past as dark as Mara's. No donors will give charitably to an orphanage run by a liar. And no duke will ever return to Society with a scandal like her hanging over him."

"Fuck Society."

The crass words should have shocked Lydia, but instead, she grinned. "Hear, hear."

"How did you meet her?" Temple asked, not knowing where the question came from, but desperate to know more about this woman whom he loved so much.

Christ. He should have told her he loved her. Maybe then she would have stayed.

Lydia smiled. "That's a bit of a story."

"Tell me."

"There is a house in the North Country. A place that is safe for women who are looking to change their fate. Daughters and sisters. Wives. Prostitutes. At this house, women get a second chance."

Temple nodded. It was not unheard of for such a place to exist. Women were not always as valued as they should be. He thought of Mara's mother, stabbed by her husband. Of her, beaten and forced into a marriage with a man three times her age.

He would have protected her.

Except, he wouldn't have been able to. Not once she was married. Not once he was returned to school.

And he'd have always hated his father for marrying the woman of his dreams.

Lydia was still speaking. "Mara was there for several years before she was offered the chance to return to London to open MacIntyre's. I had been there for a year. Maybe less. But she spoke of this place as something more than a simple home for boys. I think it meant more to her. I think it meant everything." She met Temple's gaze. "I think she was trying to make up for the punishment she'd given one aristocratic son by helping two dozen others."

Of course she had. The truth of the words threatened to destroy him.

And those boys were the most important thing in her life.

When he retrieved her, he'd buy them an estate in the country, with horses and toys and enormous grounds on which to run and grow. He'd give every one of them the chance at life she dreamed.

But first, he would give that chance to her. "I asked her to marry me."

Lydia's eyes went wide. "Well."

Indeed.

"I offered to make her my duchess, to give her everything she ever wanted. And she ran." He ran his fingers over the gloves. "She didn't even take the damn gloves."

"She didn't take anything."

He turned to face her. "What do you mean?"

"She said she couldn't take anything more from you. She left everything. She wouldn't take the clothes, or the cloak."

He stilled, remembering the way she tore up the note he'd offered her. The funds she'd earned during their idiot arrangement. "She has no money."

She shook her head. "A few shillings, but nothing substantial."

"I offered her enough to keep her for years. A fortune!"

Lydia shook her head. "She wouldn't have taken your money. She wouldn't have taken anything from you. Not now."

"Why not?"

"You don't understand women in love, do you?"

In love. "If she were in love, she wouldn't have left me in the first place."

"Don't you see, Your Grace," Lydia explained. "It's because she loves you that she left. Something about a legacy."

A wife. Children. A legacy. He'd told her that's what he wanted.

And she'd believed him.

"All I want is her."

Lydia smiled. "Well. That is something."

He couldn't think of her loving him. It would make him mad. He had to retain his sanity if he was going to find her. And then he would lock her in a room and never let her go, hang sanity. "She left here in the dead of winter with no gloves and no money."

"I'm not certain why the gloves matter so much—"

"They matter."

"Of course." Lydia knew better than to argue. "So you

can see why it is that I was rather hoping you would turn up. I was rather hoping you would find her."

"I will find her."

Lydia let out a long, relieved breath. "Good."

"And then I will marry her."

She smiled. "Excellent."

"Don't get too excited. I just might throttle her after that."

Lydia nodded, all seriousness. "Entirely reasonable."

He bowed, short and perfunctory, turned on his heel, and left the room, leaded down the stairs to the exit. Halfway down the final set of steps, a small voice came from the shadows, staying his movement.

"She left."

Temple turned to find a collection of small boys above him on the landing, each looking more worried than the last. Daniel was holding Lavender under one arm.

Temple nodded. "Yes."

Daniel scowled at him. "She was crying when she left."

Temple's chest tightened at the words. "You saw her?"

The boy nodded. "Mrs. MacIntyre does not cry."

Temple remembered the tears in her eyes that night that he'd left her naked in the boxing ring, and shame coursed through him.

"*You* made her cry."

The accusation was harsh and honest. Temple did not deny it. "I am going to fetch her. To make it right."

Henry spoke up, frustration and anger on his little face, as though he were prepared to avenge his lady. "What did you do to her?"

There were a thousand things he'd done.

I didn't believe her.

I didn't trust her.

I didn't show her how much I loved her.

I didn't protect her.

He settled on: "I made a mistake."

George nodded. "You should apologize."

The other boys seemed to agree with this course of action. "Girls like apologies," Henry added.

Temple nodded once. "I shall do that very thing. But first I must find her."

"She's very good at hiding," Henry said.

Another boy nodded. "The best of all of us."

Temple did not doubt that. "I, also, am good at hiding. And one good at hiding is excellent at seeking."

George looked skeptical. "As good as she is?"

He nodded once. "Better." He hoped it was true.

Daniel did not believe it. "She's left us. I don't think she is coming back."

The fear in the boy's eyes echoed that in Temple's chest, and he was reminded why he'd thought Daniel was his son.

The boy looked down at the pig in his arms. "She left Lavender."

She'd left them all. She'd left the boys, thinking it was best for them. She'd left Lydia, thinking it would be easier to run an orphanage without the weight of scandal over her head. And she'd left Lavender, because the post road to wherever it was she was going was no place for a pig.

Another one spoke up then, repeating the sentiment. "She forgot Lavender."

He came up the stairs, crouching low to face the collection of boys, finally reaching out to take Lavender in his arms.

She forgot Lavender.

He knew how the little pink piglet felt. The boys, as well. She'd also forgotten him.

"May I borrow her for the day?"

The boys considered the question, huddling together to come to a unanimous decision before Henry turned to face Temple. "Yes. But you have to bring her back."

Daniel stepped forward, extending the pig. "You have to bring both of them back."

Temple's heart thudded in his chest, and he nodded solemnly to the boys. "I shall do just that."

If he could.

"She is not here."

Temple paced Duncan West's office on Fleet Street, refusing to believe it. "She has to be here."

He had come to understand her. She would not leave London before she had honored their arrangement and cleared his name. He believed that with every ounce of his being. He had to. Because if he didn't, he had to allow for the possibility that she was already gone, and that it would take him time to find her.

He wasn't interested in giving up time to find her. He wanted her immediately. In his arms. In his bed. In his life.

He wanted to begin the life that they should have had a dozen years ago. The one that had been torn from both of them. He wanted them to have happiness. And pleasure. And love.

Christ, she could right now be with child.

With his child.

And damned if he didn't want that child—that beautiful little girl with strange eyes and auburn hair. Damned if he didn't want to be with them both for every possible minute.

She had to be here.

He turned on West, who was seated tall and straight behind a desk covered in papers, in notes and articles and God knew what else. "She would have come here. To speak to you. To give you your story."

West leaned back in his chair, hands spread wide. "Temple, I swear to you I would like nothing more than for that door to open and Mara Lowe to wander in off the street, full of a decade's worth of column inches." He paused, his golden gaze flickering to Temple's good arm. "But all I have is a duke with a pig."

Temple looked down at Lavender, asleep.

"Why do you have a pig?"

Temple scowled at the half smile on West's face. "It's not your concern."

The newspaperman tilted his head. "It's strange enough to make an interesting little side story."

"I shall make *you* an interesting little side story if you don't tell me the truth."

West seemed uninterested in the threat. "Are you planning some kind of meal?"

Temple clutched Lavender to him, disliking the implication that she might become dinner. "No. I'm—holding her for someone."

West tilted his head. "Holding her."

Temple shook his head. "Forget about the damn pig. You haven't seen Mara."

"I haven't."

"If you do—"

West raised his brows. "I assure you, all of London will know when I've had a chance to speak with the woman."

Temple scowled again. "You won't make a mockery of her."

"To be fair, she did destroy your life. She might deserve to have a mockery made of her. The illustrators are already working on the retelling of last night."

Temple leaned across the desk, fury coursing through him. "You. Will. Not. Make. A. Mockery. Of. Her."

West watched him for a long moment, then said, "I see."

Temple did not care for the words. "What do you see?"

"You care for the girl."

It was not every day Temple was laid bare. By a member of the media. "Of course I care for her. I'm going to marry her."

West waved one hand in the air. "No one gives a fig about marriage. Throw a stone in London and hit someone unhappily matched. The point is that you *care* for the girl."

Temple looked down at Lavender, sleeping in his arms. The only creature on earth who was not annoying him right now.

"Christ. Unfellable, unbeatable Temple. Felled. Beaten. By a woman."

He met the newspaperman's gaze, putting all of his darkness into the look. "If she comes here, you send for me. Immediately."

"Am I to keep the woman locked up until you arrive?"

"If that's what it takes."

She was alone with no resources on the streets of London. And he wanted her safe. He wanted her with him. And he would not rest until he found her. He turned on his heel to leave the room.

"I'll do it, on one condition."

He should have expected it, of course. Should have known that West would have his own half of the bargain. He turned back. Waited for it.

"Tell me why she is so important. After all, she's already restored your name. The world believes her alive. I found half a dozen women in that ballroom last night who recognized her. She's older, but still just as beautiful. And everyone remembers those eyes."

Irrational fury coursed through him at the mention of Mara's eyes. He didn't want people noticing them. He didn't want them thinking about them. They were not for all to look at. They were for him. He was the only one who had looked into them and seen more than their strange, mismatched color. He had looked into them and seen her.

West pressed on. "Why do you care if she stays or goes?"

He met West's gaze. "One day, the woman you love will slip through your fingers, and I shall ask you the same question."

He exited the room, leaving West to consider the implications of the statement.

The newspaperman waited long minutes, listening for the

exterior door to close, marking Temple's departure, before he turned to the window and watched as the Killer Duke mounted his horse and tore off to his next destination—in search of his love.

Only once the clatter of hooves faded away, he spoke to the empty room. "You may come out now."

A small closet door opened, and Mara stepped into the room, cheeks stained with tears. "He is gone?"

"He is searching for you."

She nodded, staring down at her feet, sadness like nothing she'd ever felt before coursing through her. Desire like nothing she'd felt before. *He loved her.* He'd said it. He'd come looking for her, and he'd confessed his love for her.

"He will find you."

She looked up at that. "Perhaps not."

Even as the words left her mouth, she heard the echo of Temple's promises. *If you run, I will find you.*

West shook his head. "He will find you, because he will not stop looking until he does."

"He might," she said, hoping it was true. Hoping he might decide she was not worth the trouble. Hoping he might find another life. Another woman. Someone worthy of him.

West smiled at that. "You think a man simply gives up searching for the woman he loves?"

The woman he loves. Tears came at the words, hot and stinging, and she couldn't hold them back. He loved her.

"Here is the part that I do not understand," West said, more to himself than to her, she thought. "You love him, as well."

She nodded at that. "Quite desperately."

"So what is the problem?"

She couldn't help it. She laughed. "What is the problem? It's all a problem. I ruined him. I destroyed everything that was supposed to be his. I stole his life. He deserves an aristocratic wife and perfect little children and a legacy that is not tarnished by me."

West tented his fingers beneath his chin. "He seems not to care a bit about all that."

Mara shook her head. "But I do! London does! He'll never return to his rightful place as Duke of Lamont if he's saddled with the woman who is responsible for all the black marks around the edges of his reputation."

"Reputation," West scoffed.

Her eyes went wide. "You make your living on it."

He grinned. "All that means is that I understand precisely how arbitrary it all is."

She shook her head. "You're wrong."

"I think you have been away from Society for too long," he said. "You forget that dukes—with or without scandalous wives—are forgiven everything as quickly as possible. They are, after all, the only people who can beget dukes. The aristocracy needs them, lest civilization crumble around us."

Perhaps he was right. Perhaps Temple could weather the storm of scandal that would no doubt come with her reveal to all of London.

But would he ever be able to forget what it was she had done to him?

She shook her head. "Do you have everything you require from me, Mr. West?"

Duncan West knew the end of a conversation when he reached one. "I do."

"And you shan't tell him I was here?"

"Not until after the story runs."

"Which will be?"

He consulted his calendar. "Three days."

Her chest constricted at the words. Three days to leave London. To get as far and fast and secret as she could. Three days to give him his freedom. And then, she would have to start forgetting him.

For both their sakes.

She left West's offices, careful to pull her cloak tightly around her and bring her hood low over her face before exiting to the street, where a cold, wet mist settled over London—the worst of English winter weather. She was instantly freezing, wishing for warmer boots. For a warmer cloak. For a warmer clime.

For Temple, who was always warm. Like a fireplace.

She longed for him. Ached for him.

She walked for a half mile, maybe more, before she realized that a carriage was following her, nearly at her shoulder, moving at her pace—fast when she sped up, slow when she slowed down. She stopped, turning to the great black conveyance, devoid of crests or any identifying marks.

It stopped, too.

The outrider leapt down from the back and opened the door, lowering the steps before he offered her a hand to help her inside. She shook her head. "I'm not going in there."

The young man looked confused, until a fall of violet silk peeped out at the doorway. "Do hurry, Miss Lowe," called a familiar female voice from inside, and Mara could not help but move closer. "The heat is all going out of the carriage."

Mara poked her head into the doorway.

Anna—the woman she'd befriended at the Angel—was inside. Mara's eyes went wide. "You!"

Anna smiled. "Me, indeed. I shan't hurt you, but I would prefer a warm conversation over a cool one."

Mara hesitated. "You are not here to return me to Temple."

The other woman shook her head. "Not unless you decide you would like to be returned to him."

"I shan't decide that."

"That's that, then." She wrapped her cloak about her and shivered, obviously. "Now please, come in and close the door."

She did, the warming bricks on the floor of the coach too welcome to ignore. Anna tapped the roof of the carriage, and the great black conveyance began to trundle down the street.

"How did you know where to find me?" Mara started with the most obvious question first.

The other woman's lips curved in a lovely smile. "I didn't. But Temple did."

"You followed him."

"He may know you better, but I know women better." She paused, "Also, I doubt any woman would pass up a chance to spend the morning with Duncan West."

Mara shook her head. "I don't understand."

Anna rolled her eyes to the ceiling. "Any woman who is not madly in love with Temple."

"I'm not—" she started, but stopped before the protest could fully form. She was, after all, madly in love with Temple.

"I know you are," Anna said. "Which is why I am here." Mara's brow furrowed, and Anna waved a hand broadly. "Someone has got to set you straight. We thought Temple would do it himself, but he seems too all-consumed to think intelligently."

Mara waited, quite desperate for whatever words might come out of this woman's mouth. She didn't know what she was expecting, honestly, but she did know that she was not expecting her to say, "You didn't ruin Temple's life."

She was growing tired of having a collection of strangers tell her that she was wrong. "I suppose you are an expert in the subject of ruin?"

Anna's lips twitched. "As a matter of fact, I am."

"You weren't there."

"I was not. Not when you blooded the bed and left him holding the responsibility for your death. Not when his father exiled him and the rest of the aristocracy shunned him.

"Nor was I there when he spent his first night under Temple Bar, or when he began leading with his fists or when he and Bourne concocted their idiot plan to run dice games among the worst of London."

Mara went cold at the words, hating that this woman

knew so much of Temple's past. But Anna seemed not to mind, instead pushing forward. "But I was there when they started the Angel. When he started the life he has now, as the winningest fighter Britain has ever seen. I was there when he won his first bout in the ring at the Angel. And I was there as his coffers and his standing and his respect throughout London grew."

"It isn't respect," Mara corrected, the words sharp on her tongue. "It's fear. And undeserved fear. They think him the Killer Duke, because I made him so."

Anna smiled. "I think it's charming that you think he's never done a damn thing in his life that earned that moniker."

Mara's brow furrowed. "Nothing like what he's thought to have done."

Ana lifted a shoulder in a little shrug. "Either way. It's respect. And fear. And one without t'other isn't worth the ink it takes to write either one alone." She paused, the carriage rocking beneath them, the cold drizzle turned to sleet on the window outside. "And either way, Temple likes it."

Perhaps it was true.

"He's money and friends and a club that any man would kill for. And he's got the half of London that matters—the one that judges a man on work and not blood—on his side. And he likes it all."

Was she right, this strange, mysterious woman? Did he enjoy this life he led? Or did he regret every moment that he did not have the life she'd stolen from him?

"The only thing it's missing is you." She stilled at the words, and Anna saw it. Pressed on. "Come back to the Angel. Ask him yourself." She leaned forward. "Come back, and let him show you how much he loves you."

The words ached, the offer so very tempting. She did not wish to run. "I owe it to him to leave. I owe it to him to give him back everything I took. To wipe the slate clean."

"Even if you are right, even if such a thing were possible," the other woman said, "don't you also owe him a chance at happiness?"

He'd called her the woman he loved.

And he was the man she loved.

Was that all that was required for happiness?

God in Heaven, if she thought she might be able to make him happy, she would race into his arms. She met Anna's gaze in the dim light. "Sometimes love is not enough."

Anna nodded. "God knows that is true. But in this case, you don't only have love, do you?"

It was hard to imagine they had even that. After a decade of hatred and lies and scandal. Longer. But they shared strength. And a past bigger than themselves.

Anna placed a gloved hand over Mara's, clasped together in her lap. "You once told me you did not have friends."

Mara shook her head. "I don't. Not really."

"You have him."

The words summoned tears once more. She knocked on the roof of the carriage as she had seen the woman do earlier. As if on strings, it slowed to a stop, and the footman came to open the door and lower the step. Mara stepped down, promising herself she would not turn back.

Even when Anna called out, "Do consider what I've said, Miss Lowe. You are welcome at the club any time."

Chapter 20

The floor of the Fallen Angel was packed with gamers. During Temple's recovery, in the absence of a fight on which to bet, club members were perfectly content to throw their money away on dice and cards. When wagering was involved, The Angel was more than happy to accommodate desire, and all of the staff—from footmen and croupiers to companions and cooks—was on hand to help do so.

Temple made his way through the owners' entrance of the club, Lavender at the crook of his arm, pushing his way onto the main floor of the hell, gaze sliding over the throngs of men clad in their perfectly tailored suits, all in danger of losing their fortunes to the casino, and all enjoying every second of it.

On any other night, he would have enjoyed the view. Would have found Cross and asked him about the evening's take. Would have played a round or two of *vingt-et-un* himself.

But tonight, he prowled the edge of the room, silent, frustrated.

Furious that now the rest of the aristocracy seemed to accept him, tipping heads and patting his shoulder in acknowledgment.

He was one of them, again, as though the last twelve years had never happened.

But it didn't matter. Nothing mattered as long as he couldn't find her.

He ached from a day on horseback in the rain, from his futile search for her, a beautiful needle in the filth-ridden haystack of London in December. He'd gone to the orphanage, and to West, and to the orphanage again. He'd checked the post, paid a fortune to the postmaster for information on his human cargo for the day, worried that she might have left the city already.

An eloping couple and two gentlemen had left on the North Road, headed for Scotland. But, even though apparently the female half of the elopers was quite attractive, the postmaster assured him that she was not auburn-haired, and her eyes were perfectly ordinary.

She was not Mara.

He should have been happy she was still here. But, instead, he was furious that she had so easily disappeared. There was no sign of her. It was as though she had vanished like smoke. If he didn't know better, he might think she'd never been there in the first place.

Except she'd left her gloves. And her pig.

And a hole in his chest. His lips twisted wryly as his wound throbbed at the thought. Two holes, he supposed—one healing, and one life-threatening.

He rolled his bad shoulder under his coat, the pain from the wound radiating down his arm and stopping at the elbow. He worked his fingers in his sling. Nothing. Exhaustion did little to help the damage to the feeling there, he knew, but he could not rest. Not before he found her.

If he was crippled when it was over, so be it.

At least he'd have her.

Frustration flared at the thought. Where in the hell was she?

He looked up to the ceiling, his gaze falling on the great

stained-glass window that marked the center of the main room of The Fallen Angel. Lucifer, falling from Heaven. In a stunning array of stained glass, the Prince of Darkness was depicted in free fall, halfway between paradise and inferno, a chain about his ankle, his scepter in one hand, and his wings wide and useless behind him as he tumbled into the pit of the casino.

Temple had never thought much about the window, except to appreciate its message to the members of the club—while the aristocracy might have banished him, Bourne, Cross, and Chase, the scoundrels who owned London's most legendary gaming hell, would reign more fearful, more powerful, than ever before because of it.

Chase had a flare for the dramatic.

But now, as he considered the great stained glass, as he watched Lucifer fall, he realized how massive he was. How strong. Somehow, the window maker had captured the rise and fall of muscle and sinew in the mottled panes of glass. And Lucifer's strength was useless in this moment. He could not catch himself. Could not stop himself from landing wherever it was that God had cast him.

And standing there with his weak arm and the utter sense of futility that washed over him as he realized that he could not find the woman he loved, Temple felt for the Prince of Darkness. All that beauty, all that power, all that strength. And still he landed himself in Hell.

Christ.

What had he done?

"You brought a pig into my casino."

Temple looked to Chase. "Has anyone seen her?"

Chase's gaze grew serious. "No."

Temple wanted to shout his fury at the truth in the words to the rafters. He wanted to tip over the nearest hazard table and rip the curtains from the walls.

Instead, he said, "She disappeared."

They stood, side by side, watching the floor of the casino.

"We still have men looking. Perhaps she will turn up on her own."

He cut the founder of The Fallen Angel a look, knowing that such a thing was virtually impossible. "Perhaps."

"We shall find her."

He nodded. "If it takes me the rest of my life."

Chase nodded and glanced away, no doubt uncomfortable with the emotion in his words. Not that Temple cared. "But you did find a pig."

He looked down at Lavender's sleeping face. "Her pig."

Chase's blond brows rose. "The lady owns a pig?"

"It's ridiculous." It was even more ridiculous that he had come to care for the little creature. His only link to her.

"I think it's charming. She's an intriguing woman, your Miss Lowe."

Except she wasn't his. Temple handed Lavender to his friend. "She needs to eat. Take her to the kitchens and see if Didier can find her something to eat." He was already turning back to the crowd, looking for someone who might know Mara. Perhaps she'd had a friend when she was a child—someone who might have offered her a bed.

But what if no one offered her a bed? What if she was on the streets even now, cold and without a place? He'd slept on the cold London streets once. The idea of her alone—freezing—

She didn't even have gloves.

His heart pounded with panic and he shook his head to clear it. She was no fool. She would find somewhere to sleep.

But with whom?

Panic flared once more.

Chase was still talking, and Temple listened if only to have something else to think on. "Didier is French. The pig might end up in a stew."

Temple looked back. "Don't you dare let her cook my pig."

"I thought it was Miss Lowe's pig?" Temple was tempted to clear the smug smile from his friend's face.

"As we are to be married, I prefer to think of her as *our* pig."

Chase grinned. "Excellent. I shall do my best to help."

"Don't help. I'm through with you meddling. Feed the pig. That's all."

"But—"

"Feed the pig."

For a moment, Temple thought Chase might ignore the instructions and meddle anyway, but the club's majordomo appeared at their shoulders. "We've a visitor."

For a moment, Temple thought it might be Mara. "Who?"

"Christopher Lowe. Here to fight Temple."

Chase's gaze narrowed. "Bring him to my offices. And fetch Asriel and Bruno. He'll get his fight. But it won't be with Temple. And it won't be fair."

"No." Temple said.

Chase looked to him. "Your arm isn't healed."

"Bring him to me," Temple said, ignoring his partner's words. "Now."

Within minutes, Lowe was on the floor of the club, flanked by Bruno and Asriel. "You made a mistake in coming here."

"You turned my sister into a whore."

Temple's good hand fisted, and he desperately wanted to destroy this boy. "Your sister is going to be my duchess."

"I don't care what she will be. I've no use for her." The words were slurred and angry. Lowe had been drinking, possibly since he'd left his sister the night before. "You ruined her. Probably did twelve years ago. Probably took all the valuable bits before you passed out."

Fury flared. "You should not be allowed to breathe the same air she breathes."

Lowe's gaze narrowed. "She sent me away, you know. With a few shillings. Barely enough to get me from the city."

"And you lost it."

Lowe did not have to admit it. Temple could see it in the boy's face before he whined, "What was I to do? Head off to make my fortune with three shillings? She wanted me to wager it. She wished me to lose." His eyes turned hateful. "Because of *you*. Because you turned her into your *whore*."

Temple's desire to destroy Lowe grew with every word. "Call her a whore again, and I shall make your poverty the least of your concerns."

Drink and desperation made Lowe stupid enough to smile at that. "Then you will fight me? I get my chance at my debt, you get your chance to protect my sister's honor?" He stilled. "Where is the bitch, anyway?"

Fury came hot and instant, and Temple grabbed Lowe's wilted cravat in his good hand, lifting him clear off the floor before saying, "You should have taken the chance she gave you. You should have run. I promise you, whatever you face out there is nothing compared to what I shall do to you in the ring."

Temple dropped the other man in a heap to the ground, ignoring the coughing and sputtering from below as he followed him down, crouching, taking Lowe's chin in hand and tilting him up to face him. "Get yourself a second. I'll meet you in the ring in a half an hour." If he couldn't have her, he could have his fight. Temple stood, adding, "You're lucky I don't lay you out here and now. It will teach you to speak ill of the woman I love."

"Cor! Listen to that! You love her," Lowe sneered. "What utter shite."

Temple did not look back, instead stalking away, heading for his rooms, already removing his cravat. The casino was silent as a grave, all the gamers having stopped their bets to watch Temple go mad.

Because of that, he heard it when Chase said quietly, "Well."

He did not turn back, instead calling over his shoulder, "Feed the damn pig."

*W*hen Mara arrived at The Fallen Angel, it was to a street virtually empty of people and noise, the opposite of how she imagined the exterior of one of London's most exclusive gaming hells would be.

She wondered, fleetingly, if she was too late. If Temple had closed the club and left. If he'd decided to end this underground life of his and return to the light. Return to his dukedom. Return to his right.

That's when panic set in.

Because in the damp, dark day, while she'd had nothing to do but walk and think, she'd realized that she loved this man beyond measure. And that she would do everything she could, for as long as she could, to make his life better than it ever would have been without her.

Of course, the moment she realized that, she realized that she was very very far away from the Angel.

But she was here now, and when she arrived, she knocked on the door, thrilled when a little slot opened in the steel. She stepped up to the space and said, "Hello. I am—"

The slot slid shut.

She hesitated, considering her next move. Knocked again. The slot opened. "I am here—"

The slot closed once more.

Honestly. Was every person having to do with this club obstinate? She knocked again. The slot opened. "Password."

She paused at that. "I don't—have one. But—"

The slot closed with a snap.

And that's when Mara became angry. She began to bang on the door. Loudly. After a long moment, the little slot opened, the black eyes inside narrowed with irritation.

"Now look here, you!" she announced in her very best governess voice, underscoring her words with banging on the door.

The eyes in the slot went wide with surprise.

"I have spent the entire day on the streets of London, in the bitter cold!"

She punctuated the last with *bang-bang-bang!*

"And I have finally decided that it is time for me to face my desires, my past, my future, and the man I love! So, you will let!" *Bang!* "Me!" *Bang!* "In!"

She completed her tirade with a clattering of hits on the steel door with both fists. And added in a kick for good measure. She had to admit it felt rather good.

The eyes disappeared, replaced by a lighter, more feminine set—Dear God. Were they *laughing* at her? "Miss Lowe?"

She raised a finger. "I would think very carefully about the expression you present to me when you finally open this door."

The locks on the door were finally thrown and she was allowed into the building to face a smiling Anna and a much more serious doorman. Indeed, he looked positively deferential when he said, "We've been searching for you."

Mara shook out the skirts of her damp cloak and accepted a mask from him, settling it on her face before saying, all decorum, "Well, you've found me." She turned to Anna. "Please take me to see Temple."

Anna did as he was told, a look of smug satisfaction on her beautiful face as she reached into a nearby drawer and extracted a mask. Once Mara was protected from view, they made their way through the private passageways of the club, silent for long minutes before Anna said, "I am happy that you decided to return."

"You didn't tell him you saw me?"

Anna shook her head. "I did not. I know what it is like to have no say in one's future. I would not bring it upon anyone."

Mara considered the words for a long moment. "I don't care about the future, as long as it is with him."

The other woman smiled. "May it be long and happy. Lord knows you both deserve it."

Warmth spread through Mara at the words, until Mara

remembered that it was Temple who needed to accept her—Temple who needed to forgive her. For running. And for so much more.

If only someone would deliver her to him, so she could repair all the things she had broken. But Anna did not take Mara to him. She took her to the long, mirrored ladies' side of the boxing ring, where it appeared all the people she had expected to see on the ground floor of the club had congregated.

She stepped into the dimly lit space, packed with women, her heart in her throat. She turned back to Anna. "There is to be a fight?"

"There is." The prostitute guided her to the front of the room, to a place where two chairs sat close to the window.

At another time, Mara might be curious enough to watch it—curious enough to show interest in the fighters, whoever they may be. But they would not be Temple, who was too injured for fighting, and that was all she cared to know. She shook her head. "No. I don't have time for this. I wish to see Temple," she whispered. "I've waited too long. I want him to know I've changed my mind. I want him to know—"

I love him.

I want to be with him.

I want to start again.

Fresh. Forever.

Anna nodded. "And you will see him. But first, you will see this."

The door to Temple's rooms opened on the far side of the ring, and Mara came to her feet to see him approach the center of the room, her hands instantly pressed against the window.

"No," she whispered.

He was naked from the waist up, devilishly handsome, and for a moment, all Mara could think of was how it had felt to slide against that skin, to touch him. To have him touch her. To want it again, the closeness. The pleasure.

The man.

And then her attention was on the bandage wrapped about his shoulder, protecting the wound he'd received in this very ring a week earlier. She turned to Anna. "No," she repeated.

Anna was not looking at her. She was watching Temple ease into the ring. She tutted her displeasure. "He is favoring his right side."

"Of course he is!" Mara said. "He is wounded! It shan't be a fair fight!"

She should tell someone the arm was hurt. Demand to see the Marquess of Bourne. The elusive Chase. She should force the fight to be ended.

The women around them were making raucous noise, shouting out their lewd comments. "Cor! You can't take the title from the man, but you certainly can take the man from the title."

"He doesn't look like any duke I've ever seen."

"My lord, he's a beauty."

"He might not be one, but he does look a killer if ever there was one."

"I'd happily turn myself over to him!"

"I don't believe she's really alive, you know," someone interjected. "I think he simply paid some painted whore to arrive and claim to be Mara Lowe."

"It's her. I came out the season she was due to marry the dead duke. Everyone talked about those eyes."

"Well, either way, I'm grateful to her. She's made the Duke of Lamont a marriageable match once more."

Mara burned with anger, wanting to take her fists to every one of these women.

Someone laughed. "You think you can land him yourself?"

"I heard that he loves her," Anna said, her eyes on Mara, her words deceptively lazy.

As she loves him. Quite desperately.

"Nonsense," one of the women replied. "Who could love someone who did such a thing? I'm sure he quite hates her."

He should. But somehow—by some miracle—he doesn't.

Mara began to fidget. She wanted this all done. She wanted him.

Immediately.

"And besides," the first said, "I'm a marchioness. And terribly young to be widowed."

As though all Temple should be considering for his future happiness was a title. Mara hated the thought.

"I imagine there is quite a queue lined up for the position of Duchess of Lamont," another said happily. "And not just the widows. My sister has a daughter nearly eighteen, and she would kill for a ducal son-in-law." The room laughed, and the speaker continued. "It is not a jest. I would not put honest murder past some of these mothers on the marriage mart."

Mara swallowed back the words that rose to her tongue, desperate to be spoken. He didn't need a title. He needed a woman who understood him. One who loved him. One who would spend the rest of her days making him happy.

One who would keep him safe from them.

From the ring beyond.

She turned to Anna. "You must stop it."

Anna shook her head. "The challenge was made. The bets have been laid."

"Bollocks the bets!" Mara said.

Anna's gaze filled with respect. "You sound like Temple."

"You're damn right I sound like him," Mara pushed, worry and irritation and frustration warring for dominant position in her emotions. "Take me to Chase. He shall listen to me."

Anna's eyes betrayed her surprise. "Trust me, Miss Lowe, Chase would change nothing about this night. There is a great deal of money on this fight."

"Then he's no kind of friend. Temple is not ready to fight

again. His wound is still unhealed. He could set himself back days. Weeks. Worse." She turned on Anna. "Was he forced to do this?"

The prostitute laughed. "Temple has never been forced to do anything in his life."

"Then why?" Mara's gaze moved to the ring, to where he stood half naked and proud and beautiful. She moved for the door, and the enormous security guard there blocked her from leaving. She turned back to Anna. "Why?"

She smiled at that, soft and sad. "For you."

"For me!" Insanity.

"He avenges you."

Even now. After all she'd done.

Her gaze fell on him, taking in the ripple of his muscles, the set of his jaw. The way his gaze tracked his opponent. But there was something different in this Temple. Something that she had not seen all the other nights.

Anger.

Desperation.

Frustration.

Sadness.

He loved her.

Just as she loved him. Mara closed her eyes. She might not deserve him, but she wanted him nonetheless.

She pressed her hands to the window. "He thinks I am gone."

"Yes," Anna said.

"Take me to him."

"Not yet."

That's when the second fighter entered the ring. Her brother. "What is he doing here?"

"Showing his idiocy," Anna said. "He came to the club and challenged Temple."

She'd given him money. A chance to leave. And still, he'd come here out of greed and insolence and childishness.

She shook her head.

"Your brother insulted you."

Mara had no doubt that Kit had done so with colorful aplomb. "Nevertheless, you must stop it."

Anna looked to her, eyes suddenly wary. "Why?"

"Why?" Was the woman mad? "Because he shall hurt himself!"

"Who? Your brother? Or Temple?"

Had everyone in the entire world gone mad?

Mara faced Anna. "You think I don't love him."

"I think he is a man who deserves more love than most. And I think you are the reason why. So yes, I worry that you don't love him enough. I worry that in this instance, you want the fight stopped for a different reason."

She wanted the fight stopped so she could be with him. So she could love him. So she could finally, finally put the past to rest.

But the fight began before she could say so, and this new, angry Temple led the bout, coming out hard and fast, striking first with several blows, a right hook. A right jab. A right cross.

Always the right.

Kit recovered, coming at him with one blow, a second of his own, sending Temple dancing back across the ring. Mara watched the bandage, saw the linen ties that kept it in place loosen. Turned to Anna. "Please. Take me to Chase. We must end this."

The prostitute shook her head. "This is his fight. For you."

"I don't want it."

"And yet, you receive it all the same."

Another right hook. A right jab.

That's when Kit saw the pattern.

Mara looked away. A child could see the pattern.

He was going to lose.

How many times had he told her he did not lose? How many times had she heard of him, the great Temple, the winningest bare-knuckle boxer in Britain. In all the world. Unbeatable. Undefeated. Unbreakable.

Kit might be drunk, but he was no fool. He knew that Temple was weak on the left side, so he went for it, landing blows inexpert enough to have marked his own demise ten days prior. But now, those blows were hard enough to inflict pain. Hard enough to set Temple back.

He was not unbeatable. Not tonight.

But Kit had insulted her, and he would take the loss for himself before he would take it for her.

"Christ, why doesn't he use the left? Why doesn't he block on it?" Someone asked, and Mara heard the frustration in the woman's voice.

"He can't," Mara whispered, her hand on the shaded window as she watched her love take another blow and another. For her. Again and again.

His arm wasn't working correctly.

He was going to lose.

Kit landed another blow, and Temple came to his knees, the crowd counting the seconds he spent on the floor of the ring, before he looked up at his opponent and spoke. Kit danced away, and Temple pushed himself up to stand once more, blood running down his cheek.

He would fight until he was destroyed.

He would not give up. Not when Mara's name was on the line.

He loved her.

His words from the prior night returned. *What am I if not unbeatable? If not a fighter? If not the Killer Duke? What is my value then?*

He would not stop. Not until her brother killed him.

Anna saw it then, the inevitable end. And when she looked to Mara, she said, "It will be over before we can stop it."

Mara wouldn't hear no.

The man she loved was ten feet away. Fewer. And he needed her.

Dammit, if she was the only one who would save him, she would.

She moved without thinking, lifting the chair in her hands before anyone in the room could predict her actions. Anna reached for it too late, calling out, "No!"

But Mara had one goal only.

Temple.

$\mathcal{H}$e was going to lose.

His left side was screaming in pain, the muscles protesting the bout—too soon after the stabbing. And that was without the nerves, sizzling in fits and starts down his arm, causing as much pain from the inside as Lowe was from the outside.

He was going to lose. He could not avenge her.

Not that it mattered; she had left him.

She'd run from him. Again.

Lowe landed two powerful blows to his left side, sending Temple to his knees. There, in the sawdust, he wondered when the last time was that he had been on his knees in the ring.

With Mara.

The afternoon they were alone here. The afternoon he'd driven her away the first time. The afternoon when he should have collected her in his arms and taken her to his bed and never released her.

He looked up at Lowe and said, "You may win today, but I will ruin you if you ever speak ill of her again."

Lowe danced back from him and taunted. "That's if I leave you alive."

Temple came to his feet for what he knew would be the final portion of the bout, assuming Lowe had the stomach for it. But before any further blows could land, the room exploded.

The mirror hiding the ladies' viewing room shattered in massive, ear-splitting perfection, every inch of it collapsing to the floor of the main room, like spun sugar. The sound was like nothing he'd ever heard, and he and Lowe—and the rest of the room—turned to watch as the window slid away, and the women inside went screeching and running for cover of darkness, not wanting to be seen or identified.

The men crowded around the fight stilled, hands in the air, clutching bets and markers, mouths frozen open in their perverse cheers, but Temple cared for none of that.

He cared only for the woman who had caused the devastation.

The woman standing alone at the center of that broken mirror, proud and tall and strong like a queen, the chair she'd used to shatter the window still in her hands.

Mara.

His love.

She was here. Finally.

She set the chair on the ground and used it to climb over the ledge and into the ring, caring not a bit about the men around her. Looking only at him.

He was moving toward her even as the last of the glass tinkled to the ground, caring only for her. Wanting to reach her. To hold her. To believe that she was there. She reached up and removed her mask, letting all of London see her for the second time in as many days.

A murmur of recognition moved like a wave through the room.

"I grew tired of waiting for you to come find me, Your Grace," she said, loud enough for those near to hear her. But the words were for him. Only him.

He smiled. "I would have found you."

"I'm not so certain," she replied. "You seemed somewhat occupied."

He looked over his shoulder. "What, him?"

Her gaze tracked his bleeding face, and he saw the worry in her eyes. Saw the way her hand lifted to touch. To soothe. "I thought I might help."

His brows rose as she climbed into the ring and faced her brother. "You, Christopher, are an ass, and still the child you were when I left you twelve years ago."

Kit's gaze grew dark and foreboding. "Well, this child would have destroyed your duke if you hadn't distracted us."

She ignored the words and the glee in them. "How unfortunate, then, that I did distract you." She looked around the room, taking in the hundreds of men who had come for the fight. Who had taken pleasure in watching Temple fall. "Let's make it easy, shall we?"

Kit smirked. "Please."

"One final blow. Whoever lands it wins."

Her brother's gaze flickered to Temple, battered and bloody. "I think that's fair. If I win, I go free. And I should have my money."

She turned to him, something warm and wonderful in her eyes, and he wanted this fight over more than anything he'd ever wanted. Because he wanted her. Now. Forever. "Temple?"

He no longer cared what happened to Lowe as long as Mara was his. He nodded. "I've always said you were an excellent negotiator."

She smiled at that. "Excellent."

And then damned if the woman he loved didn't turn back to her brother and lay him flat. With one punch.

She was an excellent student.

Kit dropped to his knees, wailing from the pain. "You broke my nose!"

"You deserved it." She stared down at him. "And you lose." Asriel and Bruno were already entering the ring to ensure that Lowe did not leave the club. "Now I name my terms. You will stand trial. For the attempted murder of a duke." She looked to Temple. "My duke."

Her duke.

He was that.

He was whatever she wished.

Temple covered his shock with feigned disinterest. "It was almost over, anyway."

She nodded, approaching him, not seeming to care that he was bruised and bloody. "I've no doubt you would have won. But I grew tired of waiting for that as well."

"You are impatient today."

"Twelve years is a long time to wait."

He stilled. "To wait for what?"

"For love."

Christ. She loved him. He came at her, caught her in his arms. "Say that again."

And she did, in his ring. In front of the entire membership of The Fallen Angel. "I love you, William Harrow, Duke of Lamont."

His unashamed, avenging queen. He stole her lips in a long, lush kiss, wanting her to understand now, and forever, just how much he loved her and she poured her love for him into the caress.

When he lifted his head, it was to press his forehead to hers. "Tell me again."

She did not misunderstand. "I love you." Her brow furrowed as she looked up at him, reaching up to touch the place where his eye swelled shut. "He hurt you terribly."

"It will heal." He captured her fingers, pressed a kiss to them. "All things heal. Tell me again."

She blushed. "I love you."

He rewarded the honesty with another deep, soul-stealing kiss. And when he pulled away, he said, "Good."

She put her hands to his chest, gently, her words matching the touch. "I couldn't leave you. I thought I could. I thought it was for the best, that it would give you the life you wanted. Your wife. Your children. Your—"

He stopped the words with his kiss. "No. You are my legacy."

She shook her head. "I thought that it would wipe the

slate clean. That you could once again be the Duke of Lamont, and I could fade away—and never bother you again. But I couldn't do it." She shook her head. "I wanted you too much."

His heart pounded at the thought of her fading away, and he tilted her face up to his. "Hear me, Mara Lowe. There is only one place for you. Here. In my arms. In my life. In my home. In my bed. If you were to leave, you would not give me the life I wanted. You would leave my life with an enormous, empty chasm at the center of it."

He kissed her again, and said, softly, "I love you. I think I've loved you from the moment you attacked me on a dark London street. I love your strength and your beauty and your way with children and piglets." She smiled, tears welling in her eyes. "You left your gloves at the home."

"My gloves?"

He lifted her hands in his, pressing kisses to each set of bare knuckles. "The fact that you don't wear them makes me at once mad with frustration and mad with desire."

She looked down at her hands. "My bare hands make you mad with desire?"

"Everything about you makes me mad with desire," he said. "Chase has Lavender, by the way."

Confusion flashed in her beautiful eyes. "Why does Chase have Lavender?"

"It's a bit of a tale, but the short version is that I couldn't bear to be without her. Without some part of you."

She laughed, and he realized he would carry that pig for the rest of his life if it would keep her laughing. "I love your laugh. I want to hear it every day. I want to be through all this darkness and devastation. I want happiness now. I want our due. I want what we've deserved from the beginning." He paused and stared deep into her eyes, willing her to understand how much he loved her. "I want you."

She nodded. "Yes."

He smiled. "Yes?"

"Yes! Yes to all of it. To happiness and life and love." She hesitated, and he saw the dark thought spread through her. Saw it in her eyes when she looked up at him. "I've done so much to ruin you. To hurt you."

"Enough." He kissed her quiet, lifting his lips from hers only when she was loose in his arms. "Don't hurt me again."

The tears welled over. "Never."

He wiped them away with his thumb. "Don't leave me ever again."

"Never." She sighed. "I wish we could start anew."

He shook his head. "I don't. Without the past, there would be no present. No future. I don't regret a moment of it. It all brought us here. To this place. To this moment. To this love."

They kissed again, and he wished they were anywhere but here, in front of all of London.

She broke the kiss and smiled at him, bold and beautiful. "I won."

He matched her smile. "You did. The first time anyone but me has won in this ring." He waved a hand in the direction of the oddsmaker. "Mark it in the book. The win goes to Miss Mara Lowe."

The crowd roared their disappointment, proclaiming foul play and bad bets. He didn't care. Chase would manage them, and the most bitter among them would no doubt be gaming before the hour was out.

"What do I win?" she whispered in his ear.

He grinned. "What would you like?"

"You." So simple. So perfect.

"I am yours," he said, kissing her. "As you are mine."

She laughed. "Always."

And it was the truth.

Epilogue

On the eve of her wedding, Miss Mara Lowe stood at the window high on the third story of the family wing of White-fawn Abbey, staring down into the dark gardens below. She pressed her hand to the cold glass, watching as the window fogged beneath her touch, then removing her hand to reveal the blackness beyond, dotted with reflections of the candles lit around the room behind her.

With a small smile, she traced a finger between the little starlike spots, connecting the dancing flames, distracted enough by the task not to hear her future husband's approach until he came into view, framed by her marks on the glass.

And then his arms were around her, his hands spreading wide across her body, pulling her back against him as he set his lips to the place where shoulder met neck in a long, lingering caress. "You smell like lemons."

She smiled and sighed, leaning into him, her own arms coming to capture him where he held her, fingers threading through his.

"What are you thinking about?" he asked when he finally raised his head.

She turned in his arms and told the truth, a lovely, freeing thing. "Another time here at Whitefawn. Another time here, in this room."

He did not pretend not to have noticed where they stood. Instead, he looked to the bed where she'd left him twelve years earlier and said, "Do you think anyone's slept in it since that morning?"

She laughed at the unexpected reply. "I don't, honestly."

He nodded, all seriousness. "It's a pity."

"It's to be expected, don't you think? After all, I was to have died there."

He pulled her close again, lifting her arms around his neck. "But you didn't," he said softly, and the sheer pleasure in the words sent a thread of excitement through her.

She met his gaze. "I did not."

"Neither did you marry that morning."

She shook her head. "I did not."

He brought her tight against him, their bodies aligned to each other without an inch of space, heat spreading through her as though they were discussing something altogether different than that day, twelve years earlier. "Lucky me," he said before stealing her lips in a long, lush kiss, his tongue stroking deep, a promise of pleasure to come.

Again and again.

From this day, forward.

She was so enthralled by the caress that she did not notice that he had walked her across the room until the backs of her knees were against the bed. She gasped in surprise as he toppled her to the bedsheets with virtually no effort, following her down. "You see what a shame it is?" He teased, dropping a line of soft, stunning kisses along her jaw. "This is a very comfortable bed."

Her hands moved of their own volition, coming to settle in his hair. Lifting his mouth from her. "Temple," she said, softly.

He looked up, dark eyes entirely focused on her.

There were a dozen things to say. A hundred.

He shook his head. "No. No more demons. No more memories."

Tears sprang to her eyes. "How could you say that? Here, of all places?"

He smiled, and his hand came up to caress her cheek. "Because the past is the past. I'm far more interested in the present."

He was a magnificent man.

"I love you," she said, wanting to make sure he knew it. Wanting to make sure he never doubted it.

He kissed her soundly, and there, in the caress, she found contentment.

When he broke the kiss, it was to reach his bad arm above her head and say, "Since we are speaking of presents . . ."

She marveled at the ease with which he moved, so soon after he'd been wounded. Feeling was returning to the arm, and while he might never be able to fight with his former precision, he was expected to mend.

Thank God.

Unaware of her thoughts, he produced a parcel that she hadn't noticed on the bed earlier. "Happy Christmas, my love."

She smiled. "Christmas is tomorrow."

He shook his head. "No, tomorrow, we marry. Christmas will have to come early." He grinned at her. "Open it."

She laughed. "You look like one of the boys."

The boys, all of whom had come to Whitefawn for the holiday—all of whom would likely stay on the enormous estate for years to come, no longer orphans, but wards of the Duke of Lamont.

He was their protector. Just as he was hers.

She put her hand to his warm, evening-rough cheek. "Thank you."

He raised a brow. "You don't know what it is, yet."

She smiled. "Not for the gift. Well, for the gift, but for all the others as well. For loving them. For loving me. For marrying me. For—"

He leaned down and stemmed the tide of words, distracting her with a long, lovely kiss. "Mara," he said softly when he finally lifted his lips from hers. "It's I who should thank you, love. For your strength. And your brilliance. And your boys. And for marrying me." He dropped a quick kiss on her lips. "Now open your present."

She did, pushing him off her to sit up and unwrap the package, spreading brown paper back to reveal a familiar white box, embossed with an elaborate golden H. She lifted the lid from the box and pushed back the festive red paper to reveal . . .

Gloves.

He'd bought her gloves. A dozen of them. More. In more colors and fabrics and lengths and textures than she could imagine. Yellow kidskin and lavender suede and black silk and green leather.

She lifted them from the box, laughing. Spreading them across both their laps and the bedcovers. "You're mad."

He lifted a long white velvet opera glove, sliding the fabric through his fingers. "I want you to have as many pairs as there are days in the year."

She smiled up at him. "Why?"

He lifted her hands to his lips. Kissing the rough hewn knuckles one at a time, punctuating his words. "Because, I never want you to be cold."

It was strange and frivolous and entirely beyond understanding. But it was the most beautiful thing anyone had ever said to her. And they were beautiful gloves.

She lifted a pair of short gloves in silver satin and moved to put them on.

He stayed her with a touch. "No."

She smiled up at him. "No?"

He shook his head. "When we're alone, I like you without them."

Her brow furrowed. "Temple, you're not making sense."

He smiled and pressed a kiss to her neck before lifting his

head and whispering, hot and wonderful at her ear, "When we're alone, I shall keep you warm in other ways."

And then he set about doing just that.

Which suited her quite well, indeed.

*N*early one week later, following tradition held sacrosanct by gentlemen across Britain, the founder of the Fallen Angel sat down to breakfast, and read the morning paper.

On this particular day, however, Chase broke with tradition, and began with the Society pages:

> *The Duke of Lamont and Miss Mara Lowe were married at Christmas in the chapel at Whitefawn Abbey, the place where they met for the first time, on a fated night, twelve years ago.*
>
> *The nuptials reportedly attracted a wide array of guests including several of London's most notorious scoundrels and their wives, two dozen boys aged three to eleven, a French chef, a governess, and a pig. No doubt when this caravan of oddities trundled up the long drive of Whitefawn Abbey, the servants in residence worried for their security. And their sanity.*
>
> *It should be mentioned, however, that the group, while lewd at times and raucous more often than not, is reported to have been tremendously well behaved for the ceremony itself, witnessing the rite with the happy solemnity that should be afforded such an occasion.*
>
> *All but the pig, we are told. Apparently, she slept through the whole thing.*

The News of Britain
December 30, 1831

With a satisfied smile, Chase closed the paper and finished breakfast before standing, smoothing her skirts, and leaving the house.

After all, she had a gaming hell to run.

Author's Note

$\mathcal{M}$edicine in the 1830s left a great deal to be desired. With virtually no understanding of germ theory, a man could die from far less than a knife wound, and a stabbing came with a very real threat of death, even if the blade missed all the major organs. Of course, when you're writing a book, none of this occurs to you—especially when you're writing a hero who is something of a magnet for violence.

Therefore, writers like me are very lucky to have dear friends who happen to be talented doctors. Many many thanks go to Dr. Daniel Medel, who put up with my crazy texts and late-night phone calls about stabbings and knife wounds and bloodletting and nerve damage, and never once told me Temple's survival was impossible, assuming the knife was somehow luckily and fastidiously clean. Which it was. I promise. It goes without saying that any medical errors in the book are entirely my own.

As with all my books, this one could not have been written without the always-right insight of my literary Sherpa, Carrie Feron, and the hard work of Tessa Woodward, Nicole

Fischer, Pam Spengler-Jaffee, Jessie Edwards, Caroline Perny, Shawn Nicholls, Tom Egner, Gail Dubov, Carla Parker, Brian Grogan, Eleanor Mikucki, and the rest of the unparalleled Avon Books team.

As ever, thank you to Sabrina Darby, Carrie Ryan, Sophie Jordan, Melissa Walker, Lily Everett, and Randi Silberman Klett for your help with Temple and Mara's story, and to Aprilynne Pike and Sarah Rees Brennan for emergency lunch that ended with both fresh ideas and Mara's heterochromia.

I've saved you for last! Thank you for taking this journey with my scoundrels, for loving them as much as I do, and for the endless encouragement online and by mail. I hope you'll join me for the Fourth Rule of Scoundrels—Chase's story—in 2014.

She is the most powerful woman in Britain,
A queen of the London Underworld . . .
But no one can ever know.

He is the only man smart enough
to uncover the truth,
Putting all she has at risk . . .
Including her heart.

*Never Judge a Lady
by Her Cover*
The Fourth Rule of Scoundrels

Chase's story, coming in 2014

At Avon Books, we know your passion for romance—once you finish one of our novels, you find yourself wanting more.

May we tempt you with . . .

- **Excerpts** from our upcoming releases.

- Entertaining **extras**, including authors' personal photo albums and book lists.

- Behind-the-scenes **scoop** on your favorite characters and series.

- **Sweepstakes** for the chance to win free books, romantic getaways, and other fun prizes.

- Writing **tips** from our authors and editors.

- **Blog** with our authors and find out why they love to write romance.

- **Exclusive content** that's not contained within the pages of our novels.

Join us at
www.avonbooks.com

AVON

An Imprint of HarperCollins*Publishers*
www.avonromance.com

Available wherever books are sold or please call 1-800-331-3761 to order.

FTH 1111